Penguin Books

WALK IN MY SHOES

Alwyn Evans is a freelance writer, editor and publisher, who began her working life as a teacher. She has written over 35 picture books, as well as teacher reference works and ghost-written autobiographies. Alwyn has edited countless books, and as founding Children's Book Editor for Fremantle Arts Centre Press she established their picture book and young adult lists.

Recently Alwyn and her partner, artist Owen Bell (Bela), created their own publishing imprint, Laughing Gravy, where they work on special projects. *Walk in My Shoes* is Alwyn's first novel.

WALK IN MY SHOES

ALWYN EVANS

Penguin Books

PENGUIN BOOKS

Published by the Penguin Group
Penguin Group (Australia)
250 Camberwell Road, Camberwell, Victoria 3124, Australia
(a division of Pearson Australia Group Pty Ltd)
Penguin Group (USA)
375 Hudson Street, New York, New York 10014, USA
Penguin Group (Canada)
10 Alcorn Avenue, Toronto, Ontario, Canada M4V 3B2
(a division of Pearson Canada Inc.)
Penguin Books Ltd
80 Strand, London WC2R 0RL, England
Penguin Ireland
25 St Stephen's Green, Dublin 2, Ireland
(a division of Penguin Books Ltd)
Penguin Group (India)
11, Community Centre, Panchsheel Park, New Delhi – 110 017, India
Penguin Group (NZ)
Cnr Airborne and Rosedale Roads, Albany, Auckland, New Zealand
(a division of Pearson New Zealand Ltd)
Penguin Group (South Africa) (Pty) Ltd
24 Sturdee Avenue, Rosebank, Johannesburg 2196, South Africa

Penguin Books Ltd, Registered Offices: 80 Strand, London, WC2R 0RL, England

First published by Penguin Group (Australia) Ltd, a division of
Pearson Australia Group Pty Ltd, 2004

3 5 7 9 10 8 6 4

Design by Marina Messiha © Penguin Group (Australia)
Cover photographs by Dirk Anschutz, Debra Schuler, Walt Seng/photolibrary.com
Dinkus taken from traditional Afghan embroidery
Typeset in 11/15.5 pt Berkeley Book by Post Pre-press Group, Brisbane, Queensland
Printed in Australia by McPherson's Printing Group,
Maryborough, Victoria

National Library of Australia
Cataloguing-in-Publication data:

Evans, Alwyn.
Walk in my shoes.

ISBN 0 14 300231 7.

1. Refugees – Australia – Fiction. I. Title.

A823.3

www.penguin.com.au

For my newly arrived and first grandchild, Evan.
May your generation move closer to
creating an enlightened and loving environment,
deserving of your perfection.

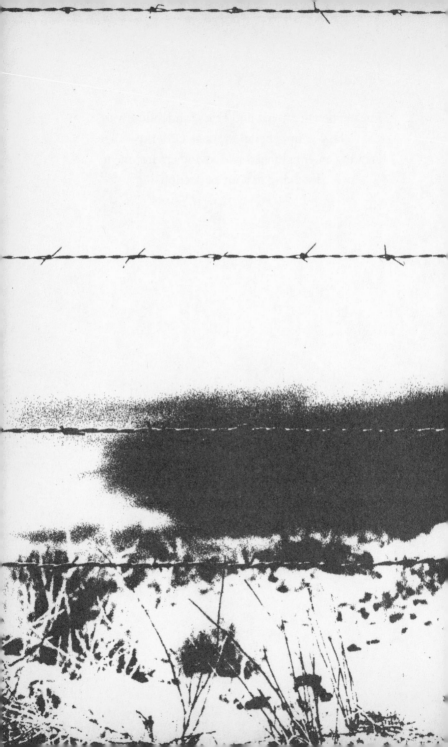

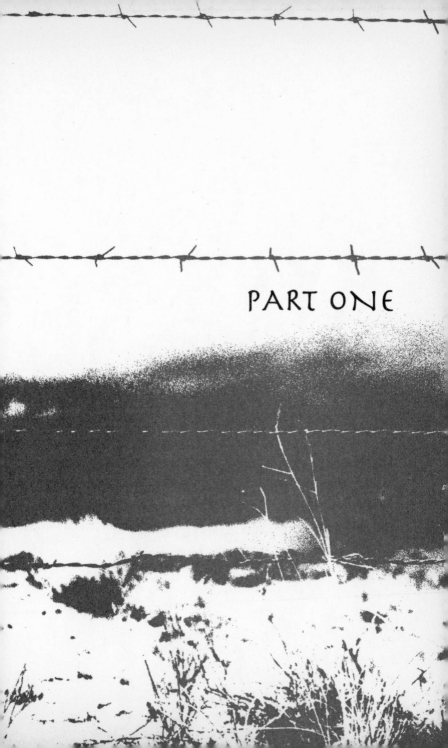

PART ONE

THE FIRST STEP

Perth: 29 May

I feel Australian now. I made this *big* decision as I was writing in my diary this morning. I came from another place and it's time to tell my story. It amazes me that although I've lived in Perth for over two years there's still so much I don't know about life here when I knew everything about the village we used to live in. I was more than four years younger then.

When we first arrived here I felt like anything but an Aussie. I was *so* self-conscious. I knew we looked different. Sounded different. And everything looked strange. I felt people staring all the time. I remember that clearly.

We couldn't speak much English either. Oh, we could count to twenty, and knew words like 'hello', 'yes', 'no', 'thank you', 'clean up', 'toilet', 'food' and some others we'd learned in the Camp. Nothing more. Try to have a conversation with those words. You don't get far.

Anyway, I was thinking all this and trying to remember back to before we came to Australia when it suddenly struck me: I can't see Dad's face clearly any more! I miss him so much but I can't picture his face like I used to in the daytime, when it was always in my mind's eye. I bet if he was here Mum wouldn't give me such a hard time. Nor Hassan, my seventeen-year-old brother. He is older than me by just a year but thinks himself so superior.

Of course I think of Dad often, but I only see him at night now if I have good dreams. And I'm worried I'll forget more, that even those dreams will fade. Bad dreams still come much more frequently than good ones.

No one had cameras where we used to live, so my words must be the pictures. I *must* capture the images in my head before they fade completely. Even the bad ones. They remind me of why I'm here, and why I can never go back there.

I'm not sure where to start. I know that when I write little things they trigger bigger memories, just like photos do. My English teacher says some of my school assignments are so real she feels she's there with me. Once I wrote about visiting my grandfather, Bahkhul Abdul, Mum's dad, just before he died. I was only eleven. My teacher said she cried and cried when she read it. She felt she was sitting next to his sleeping mat, holding his hand, even though she'd never been to Afghanistan or seen a sleeping mat or held a dying man's hand. My teacher had said to us, 'Visualise something precious to you and write about it.' I saw Bahkhul Abdul's brown hand lying on a rug my grandmother had made.

I've started a few times to tell my story like a diary, beginning when I was really young, but it doesn't work. I get bogged down with details. I've discovered that writing memories is a bit like going on the Internet – I 'enter' a few words and all this information comes up. And it's not only what happened before we came to Australia that starts me off. It's what happened here too. Especially in the Camp. Those memories are the most vivid, even though they're the hardest to write about. But I'm not going

4

to fight them any more. Instead I'll start with them. I'll start in the place I spent my first two years in this country, *before* I felt like an Australian. I don't care how long it takes. I want to always remember who I was then, and I want to remember what I went through on the way here.

I'll still keep my diary, of course, but separately. That'll be my real Australian story. Who knows who might want to pay me to write a book about it after I become a famous doctor? Yes, I think that's what I'm going to be, but a doctor who heals minds as well as bodies. That's the hardest part. I think if someone worked out how to heal our minds when they get so stressed they can't work properly and scary stuff takes over, then our bodies would get themselves better. So I'm going to be a psychiatrist and help people who suffer trauma. I already know a lot about trauma.

But I might be a writer instead. I know how that helps people too. I'm starting with my story not just for me, but also for my family and other people born in places where their lives are not their own. People whose only real choice is whether to stay where they are and accept a short violent life, or to risk escaping to find a safe place to build another life. Some people stay behind but choose to help family members get out. Mum accepted what our family in Afghanistan did for us. They told us it would make their lives worthwhile to know that they could make a difference, to know that we would be safe. But all the time we feel in our hearts how much those left behind have sacrificed for us.

Now, whatever I decide to do with my life, I know I want to make a difference, for them and for me, too. I haven't escaped death and survived hell to do nothing. So, for starters, I invite everyone to read my story and, for a little while, to take a walk in my shoes.

CHAPTER 1

That night we spent in the strange town by the sea shone in my memory like a lighthouse beam in the darkness. During our terrible journey, when days dragged one after another in a blur of fear, pain and despair, I didn't know it was possible to be so frightened yet still stay alive. Glimpses of that lighthouse night kept me going. Between gut-wrenching convulsions of sea-sickness and hanging onto ropes for dear life, as our fishing boat climbed one watery mountain after another and dropped into chasms dividing them, when the sea was calm and time seemed to stop, I let myself hope.

It was then I visited my treasures. Mum called them that. When I described how I saw our lighthouse night, and the most beautiful sunrise ever, her eyes brightened with tears, and she said, 'Treasure them in your heart, my daughter. Those treasures are sometimes all we have to remind us that life *is* beautiful.' Past weeks had given meaning to her words.

As I wriggled down on the big, comfortable seat of the bus, resting my forehead against the cool glass of the window, I tried not to notice the stale-sick smell, which seemed worse here than it had on the open sea. To block it out I tried to relive our lighthouse night and to feel the delight, the warmth, the love and the hope I'd felt then. I might just be approaching another lighthouse, I thought. And about time.

But I was too excited. I couldn't settle. There was little to see outside, just pools of light along the dark road and occasional ghostly buildings, glowing with lights. Soon, even those were behind us, leaving only thick blackness for the headlight beams to penetrate. This bus was much better than the one which, for a week, had been home to about forty of us in Indonesia. And that one had been better than the buses we rode to market on in Afghanistan.

If I craned my neck I could glimpse a starry road above us. As my eyes grew used to the dark I made out shapes on the ground which loomed suddenly as we passed, but disappeared before I could tell what they were.

'What can you see, Nessie?' Zahra, my three-year-old sister, cuddled between Mum and me, pulled at my sleeve.

'Nothing, baby. It's too dark.'

'Nessa! I'm big, now.' Zahra frowned at me.

'Of course you are, darling. "Baby" is a love-name.'

'I like "darling" best.'

'Go to sleep, you two. We'll be on the bus all night.'

Mum sounded exhausted. The waiting and quizzing by customs and immigration officers had lasted all day. Zahra's eyes, too, looked heavy. I winked at her. She tried to wink back but squeezed both eyes closed. They stayed shut.

More for comfort than warmth I pulled a rug up under my chin. The salt and sick had changed it from our familiar, soft, home-spun comforter to this foreign scratchy thing, so I pushed it away again and turned back to the window. Gazing into the darkness, I tried to picture what the landscape would look like in daylight. Would it be that amazing red dirt we'd stepped on for the first time, earlier that morning, in Broome?

I grinned, remembering how we walked off the ferry along the wide, sloping gangplank, and when my feet hit the firm wooden planks of the jetty I staggered, legs suddenly feeling like jelly, and almost fell over. My six-year-old brother, Zainullah, did sit down, and looked up in surprise at our big brother, Hassan, who was laughing his head off. When Hassan stepped onto the jetty his knees seemed to buckle, too. Mum, with Zahra in her arms, wobbled alarmingly. Abdul, our neighbour's son whose family had sent him with us to escape, although having difficulty, caught Mum's arm and held it until she could walk steadily.

Close behind, Asad, our friend we met on the boat, boomed, 'You've still got on your sea legs. Don't worry! You'll get your land legs back.' We did, but it took nearly all day. On the other hand, Zainullah and Zahra shook off their seasickness in remarkably short time. As soon as we stood on the shore, they skipped and jumped, then collapsed on the ground, giggling so hard they could hardly stand up again.

Mum said to me, 'I know how they feel. It's such a relief not to want to throw up all the time.'

Taking Mum's hand, I whispered, 'Are we really safe, here?'

A lit-up group of strange-looking buildings whizzing past the bus brought me back to the present. Trying to see more, I kneeled on my seat and, came eye to eye with Asad's wife. Uncomfortably, I smiled. A quick response lit her sad face. I slithered back into my seat and bent forward to look at Zahra's sleeping face, her thick black lashes brushing her pink cheeks, and her dark wavy hair spread over Mum's knee. Mum's scarf had slipped down her

8

forehead so it almost covered her closed eyes, and her face was peaceful at last. Across the aisle I could see Zainullah fast asleep between Abdul and Hassan. Hassan was thirteen back then. Abdul flashed me a funny sort of grin. I smiled back.

I thought how lucky we were to still have each other. Not like Asad's little family in the seat behind us where Sakina, who was around Zahra's age, slept between her parents. After a three-day storm at sea had battered our old fishing boat with its desperate human cargo, Asad had told us, 'Our baby son died last night. He had not even been with us for all the seasons of a year.'

I found myself praying as I became aware of Zahra's little foot kicking my thigh. Still sleeping, but obviously dreaming, too, her face was screwed up tightly and her legs pumped like pistons. 'Zahra, darling, I'm here,' Mum leaned over and, picking her up, rocked her gently. Zahra's eyes flew open, a panicky look on her face. I reached out and stroked her hair.

'Mummy, are they gone?'

'Who, darling?'

'The men with guns. I runded. Fast as I can.'

'There is no one with guns here, little one. We're on a bus. In Australia. Soon we'll have a new, safe home. No more being seasick on old boats. No more running away, either. And no more hiding.' Mum's voice quickly soothed Zahra's fear, but as she spoke she sighed deeply.

Knowing well the horror of nightmares, I squeezed Zahra's hand, adding, 'No more Terror. We're safe now, and you'll have sweet dreams.'

Zahra wriggled free. 'But they got Daddy!'

'That was a long way away. They can't follow us here.'

As Mum said this, I stretched my arm around her neck to hug her.

'Can Daddy find us?' Zahra persisted.

'I hope and pray he will, darling.'

'When?'

'Soon, I hope.'

'Oh.' Zahra always said that when she didn't know what else to say. 'I'm sleepy now.'

'Were you asleep?' I whispered to Mum.

'Just dozing. I was thinking of good times at home with Dad. And with your grandparents. During that terrible boat trip I didn't think, I just prayed. This is the first time I've thought of good things since before we got on the boat in Indonesia.' Mum's eyes smiled. 'Have you slept, Gulnessa?' Mum doesn't call me 'Nessa'. She says Gulnessa's a beautiful name and as 'gul' means 'flower' in our language she's not cutting that out.

'I can't.'

'Well, close your eyes and imagine the place you'd like them to take us to. My dream house has a warm kitchen with a good cooking fire. And water running from a tap like in the hostel in Indonesia.'

'My dream house has a toilet like the one on the plane. Inside. So we never have to go out in freezing dark again.'

'And I'd have shelves full of rice and flour and spices and dried fruits. And a vegetable garden growing all the fresh vegetables we can eat.'

'Mum, do you think the houses will be like ours at home? The ones we saw today in Broome weren't. I wish we could've gone inside them.'

'Well, we won't have much longer to wait and see.'

I leant back against the window, and shut my eyes. Drifting back to our lighthouse night in the hostel when we were so full of hope, I smiled to myself . . .

CHAPTER 2

The jolt of the bus pulling up woke me from the best sleep I'd had since that lighthouse night. My forehead was still jammed against the window. Next to me, Mum and Zahra stirred. It was daylight, the sun high in the sky. But what bright light! And the sky was the most intense blue I'd ever seen.

I squeezed my eyes shut, then opened them again, trying to make sense of what I saw. Alongside the bus a high wire fence with jostling crowds of people behind it blocked out everything else. The people looked like us. I saw their fingers, knuckles white, locked around the wire. Their faces pressed against it. They looked like they were shouting but I could hear nothing from inside the bus. Right in front of me a boy, Hassan's size, climbed the fence until a mess of wire at the top stopped him. I saw small blades glinting along the coiled strands.

My heart stopped beating. Was this war again? The sick feeling rushed through me. People waved hands, jumpers and other bits of clothing at us. Their faces screamed, Help! But we were the ones who needed help. What could *we* do for *them*?

Then the bus began to move again, through tall barred gates which closed behind us. I looked at Mum. She had this stunned

11

look on her face, just like I felt. I didn't say anything. The bus stopped and this time its door opened. Two strange pale men got onto the bus and stood behind the driver. I pushed the people behind the wire to the back of my mind.

One man spoke loudly in Dari, our language. 'Good morning. I'm an interpreter for the Immigration officer. As you arrived in Australia without permission, you have to stay in this Camp while officers check your names and where you're from. Then you'll be checked medically to see no one has any diseases. Follow us.' It was an order. No one questioned him, not even Asad. I'd no idea what many of the man's words meant, even in our own language.

No one mentioned the people behind the wire.

The men led us into an open area which had low, greyish-red buildings on three sides and a tall wire fence on the fourth – a fence also topped with coils of wire studded with those glinting blades. Everyone pressed together, following in silence. All the people who'd come with us on the fishing boat, carrying what was left of our few belongings after the rough trip. Mum and I had over our shoulders stiff, salt-encrusted bags containing warm clothes. Hassan and Abdul had rolls of our homemade blankets tucked under their arms. All that remained of our previous life.

A man and a woman in brown uniforms joined the men from the bus. The man spoke to the interpreter. 'The first thing to do is to give each one of you an ID,' he announced. 'Your identification number.'

Most people, although standing in family groups or with friends, moved closer together. I sidled up to Mum who gathered us all to her by tugging at our clothes. 'Stay close. Hold onto each other so no one gets separated,' she murmured. Twisting

Mum's skirt through the fingers of one hand, I held Zahra's hand firmly with the other. Zainullah grasped my top. I saw Abdul take hold of him and Hassan, who took Mum's arm. We formed a tight circle around her as she clutched the little ones in front. Looking down at the two Zs I could see only mops of dark hair and big eyes staring up at me. I smiled at them weakly. Abdul was like our big brother now. Ever since we'd left our village he'd looked out for us and we loved him for it.

When the shuffling stopped, and everyone stood looking at the interpreter, he went on, 'Because you arrived together, all your IDs start with AXZ. That's the code name for the boat you came on. Following that you each get a different number. In English.' I wondered why the strange language these pale people spoke was called English, not Australian. The man in the brown again spoke to the interpreter, who stepped aside.

Then the man in brown beckoned to Asad, who moved forward. Pointing in turn at Asad, his wife, Layla, then at little Sakina, he said, 'AXZ1. AXZ2. AXZ3.'

Asad's baby son would have been AXZ4 if he hadn't died, I thought, squeezing Zahra's hand. She looked up at me with her magic smile. Then the officers in brown moved around the room, giving numbers to each person.

Mum: AXZ21.

Hassan: AXZ22.

Me: AXZ23.

Zainullah: AXZ24.

Zahra: AXZ25.

Abdul: AXZ26.

When everyone was numbered, the woman spoke to the interpreter, who shouted, 'Now, the officers will take you to dongas where you'll sleep and keep your things.' After stopping to get more instructions, he went on, 'We understand you've been through traumatic experiences. We want to help. Customs saw you briefly in Broome but here Immigration has to process everyone. Check more details. You stay in this compound until Immigration officers have interviewed you.'

As I was about to ask Mum if she understood, I heard Asad's voice. 'Please, may I ask some questions on behalf of us all?'

'Yes. Go ahead.'

'Why do we have "identification numbers"?'

After murmuring with the officers, the interpreter said, 'You get a number so we know who you are.'

'But we have names.'

'They're hard to say. Numbers are better.'

'But people aren't numbers.'

No response. Asad continued, 'And this "process", what is it?'

'Checking each person. Finding out who you are. Where you come from . . . recording information. Seeing if you are *really* a refugee.'

'But why would we come here like this if we weren't?'

More murmurs. Heads shaking. Silence.

'What is a "donga"? And a "compound", please?'

'A donga is where you sleep.' The interpreter waved at the lines of low buildings. 'The Camp has compounds to separate people.'

'Are compounds prisons? Who are the people near the gate?' Alarm crept into Asad's voice.

'People who've been processed, waiting in another compound. *Not* a prison.' His voice was abrupt. 'It's to protect people. So you won't hurt people in Australia. And to be sure you've no diseases.'

'I understand about diseases. But why would we want to hurt people? And why after they have been processed are those people locked up?' Asad stroked his chin.

14

When consulted the officer spoke loudly, shaking his head. The interpreter said, 'They're waiting for Immigration decisions. Okay? No more questions. Follow.'

The man's words didn't make sense, but his tone was clear. I glanced at Abdul but his face was unchanged. How did he shut in his feelings so well? Hassan and Zainullah stood by him. Carbon copies. Without Dad, Hassan looked up to Abdul, and Zainullah was Hassan's shadow – when he was allowed to be.

We followed the interpreter and officers between two rows of long, low buildings. The walls were not made from mud bricks like at home, but from a grey material covered in dust from the fine, powdery, amazingly red sand which clung to everything.

Other than buildings and red ground, all I could see was brilliant blue sky overhead. The colours looked fantastic together. I'd like an outfit like that, I thought, looking down at my grimy dark top and pants, which I'd worn ever since our lighthouse night. Red dirt, blue sky. Brighter colours, brighter sunlight than I'd ever seen. Somehow, gazing at that intense blue calmed the anxiety growing inside me during the interpreter's speech. It was as if a weightless blanket enfolded and caressed me, like Arjay Aqila's rug had at home when I pulled it close as I snuggled down to sleep.

We stopped at a door with a large 'O' painted on it. The officer spoke to the interpreter, who announced, 'Six rooms in here. This donga's called "October". The ablution block for everyone's over there.' He pointed to another donga next to the fence, then looked at a sheet of paper the woman officer passed him, and called out some numbers. 'You lot, step forward. You're in room one.'

'Excuse me,' Asad interrupted, as a family of five stepped forward. 'What is this "ablution block"?'

'Where you wash, clean up, you know. Toilets, too, and laundry to wash clothes.'

'Thank you.'

'Now you can go in.' The officer nodded to the five. 'When you hear a siren,' he circled his head to include everyone and jerked his thumb in the direction we'd come from, 'come to the mess for dinner.' The woman officer opened the door and the family disappeared through it.

'Next in "O", room two, are AXZ21, 22, 23, 24, 25 and 26. Step forward . . .'

We followed the first family through the door into a room the width of the donga. In it were some chairs, a low table, but not much else I recognised in that first glimpse. The other family had vanished. Walking over to the only other doorway from the room, Mum pulled back its curtain. A passageway with three doors on each side ran to the end of the donga. Above each door was a symbol. Abdul, the only one who'd been to school, said, pointing, 'Here's two.' He led us to the second door on the left.

Inside the room were some of the weirdest contraptions I'd ever seen. We looked at each other, frowning. The Zs, who until now had been quiet, overwhelmed by the strangeness of everything, started to giggle.

'Play-house!' shouted Zainullah. 'We can make a play-house!'

'They're like those things we slept on in Indonesia. But these are balanced on top of one another,' I suggested.

'Yes. Of course. They're for us to sleep in.' Mum smiled, and nodded to me. 'Clever girl. But I'm not going to sleep up there.' She pointed at a top bed. 'If I rolled over I'd fall off!'

'Me neither,' the two Zs chorused. The thought alarmed me, too. Even Abdul screwed up his face.

'I'm going to test one out.' Hassan stepped onto the bottom bed, and catching hold of the top one, pulled himself up. The two Zs jumped around the room, clapping and laughing wildly. Hassan plonked his bottom in the middle of the mattress, bouncing up and down, arms flapping. His head hit the ceiling and he collapsed face down on the bed, making loud, fake groans.

After all of us except Mum had tried the top bunks, we agreed none of us would sleep there as the floor looked so far down.

'We'll work it out when it's bedtime,' Mum said. 'But now, we need to get clean. Gulnessa, you can help me.'

Abdul moved towards the door. 'I'm going to look around and find Asad's room,' he said. 'Back soon.'

'And I'll check out our dong-aa.' Hassan laughed self-consciously as he said the foreign word. Zainullah followed him out of the room. Since Dad vanished, Zainullah didn't let Hassan out of his sight in case he disappeared, too.

'Mu-u-um, can't we see where our friends are first?' I asked.

'Well, we should go and see this a-a-ab . . . place we wash. It's not in a river like at home.'

I took Zahra's warm little hand and followed Mum down the passage. We could hear Zainullah's excited voice through the walls.

As we got to the door leading outside, it opened. 'Hi,' Abdul greeted us. 'Asad's family is at the end of the compound, "D" for December. There's six dongas: October, November, December, January, February and March. Just like ours.'

Asad smiled. 'I wanted to see if you were all okay.'

'Thank you,' Mum nodded. 'We're going to look at where we wash. I don't remember the word.'

'"Ablution block",' Abdul put in. 'And "laundry".'

'That's really good.' I was impressed. No way had I remembered.

17

Asad nodded his approval. 'Shall we go together to see? I hope it's big. Everyone must share it. Nearly a hundred of us.'

By the time we'd got to the ablution block, Layla, Asad's wife, and some other women had stripped off their children's dirty clothes. The little ones stood nervously in hand basins lining one wall, with their mothers washing away the filth which covered everyone. Women and older girls waited outside three doors in the opposite wall. Noises of splashing and laughter came from behind the doors. After our time on the boat sharing food, sea-sickness and bodily functions, shyness hadn't yet returned.

As Mum, Zahra and I came out of the women's end of the grey, bare building, Mum said, 'One of my dreams has come true. Water comes out of a pipe. No more heavy buckets.'

'And half of my wish,' I added. 'The toilets are like the plane ones even though we still have to go out in the dark. But there's only three toilets . . .'

'Don't worry now. Let's go back and find the clothes Layla said would be in our . . . lo-or-ckers.' Mum screwed up her face as she tried out this new word.

Back in our room, I opened one of the small doors in the big, grey metal box standing against the wall. Pulling out a well-used towel and some faded greeny-coloured loose pants and top, I held them up. 'Look at these.' They were not ochre and blue, but they were clean.

Just then Hassan and Zainullah bounded in. Dry land, a night's sleep on the bus and room to move had restored their energy in triplicate. But ten days on that open, crowded, pitching deck crammed into a confined space had taken its toll on many older people – as well as Asad's baby.

'Hassan, I want you to take Zainullah to the men's wash room,' Mum said.

'Aw, Mum, can't he go with you?'

'Only boys under five can go with their mothers. You'll have to do it. Abdul'll help you.'

'I'm big now,' Zainullah puffed out his little chest. 'I go with the mens and wash myself.'

'Zainullah, you must let Hassan help you. Like Daddy did.' Mum stopped and swallowed.

'All right, Mum,' Zainullah said. Hassan nodded.

Soon, Mum, Zahra and I were with the crowd of women and girls in the ablution block. Listening to the splashing of water, something clicked. 'Mum, I think this is like the water pipe in Indonesia. The spout of water we played under.'

'Could be, Gulnessa. We'll find out soon. I can't wait to get out of these smelly clothes.'

'Me too.'

We waited for ages, watching others go in and out, before it was our turn. Behind the door we found a small room with a bench on one wall, and a plastic curtain screening off an even smaller room with taps and a pipe sticking out of the wall above them. On it was a squashed, bell-shaped thing with a flat circle of metal dotted with tiny holes covering the bottom. I turned on the tap for my first-ever shower. Brilliant!

We were still under it when the siren sounded. 'That's hodible.' Zahra clapped her hands over her ears, screwing up her face and eyes.

'It's nothing to worry about. It's telling us it's dinner time.' Mum smiled at her.

Zahra released her ears. 'I don't like it!'

When at last we returned to our room, squeaky clean and feeling great, we found mounds of damp, smelly clothes all over the floor. 'I see the boys have had their showers,' Mum said drily.

'Well, we can't wash their clothes now. Help me pile them in a corner and we'll go and find the others.'

Not for the first time I felt a pang of resentment that boys didn't have to do their own washing. 'I bet they've gone to dinner. They could've waited for us.' I was annoyed now. Boys *always* got to do things first.

When Mum, Zahra and I saw the boys in the mess my crankiness vanished. We all looked so different we burst out laughing. Really, I guess the clothes weren't *that* different – long, loose pants and floppy tops to wear over them, and Mum wore her headscarf like always. But what they were made from was strange, sort of much lighter than we were used to, and none of Mum's embroidery to decorate our tops. I caught Abdul looking at me in a way that Hassan had never looked at me, and I smiled quickly.

The mess was like a huge kitchen with long tables where everyone sat to eat. An officer pointed out where to go. It took a while to find out about getting trays, lining up, and serving food from steaming dishes.

At last I lifted my tray, carrying Zahra's and my full plates I turned around with Mum and Zainullah behind me. There were more, shorter lines of people. I tilted my head to see why they were waiting. Each line was in front of a giant, clear container, taller than Asad, filled with red, green, yellow or orange liquid. 'Zahra, which colour drink would you like?' I asked.

'Green please, Nessa.' When it was our turn Zahra pressed the tap eagerly. Nothing happened. 'Harder,' I encouraged. She looked at me questioningly, and pressed with all her might. Green liquid gushed into the mug and she smiled triumphantly.

I looked around. The nearby tables were all full, and then

I saw Zainullah waving from where he and Mum had found a space for us. Carrying the piled tray to the table was kids' stuff for me after many trips at home carrying dishes to and from the river, but sitting at tables was different. We gathered around in our family group as we'd always done, except at home we'd sit on the floor, eating with hands or spoons.

'Yum,' Hassan managed between mouthfuls. 'First good meal since you cooked for us, Mum.' It was rice and vegetables cooked together, with some kind of meat. It tasted all right.

'There's no chilli in this,' I put in.

'Well, it's still good.' Hassan was always determined to have the last word.

Mum put down her spoon and sighed, but she was smiling. 'I've no idea what will happen to us. But I know we're safe. We're not going to drown. No one will shoot us or whisk any of you away from me.'

'What about those people behind the fence?' I suddenly remembered their faces and the razor wire.

'I don't know. They must have done something wrong. People aren't locked up for nothing.'

'Oh.' I glanced at Zahra. Perhaps she'd caught that expression from me.

An insistent tapping noise silenced us. The officer was trying to get our attention. The interpreter spoke. 'While you're in the Camp you'll be looked after but there are rules. Firstly, everyone *must* come to the mess for meals, three times a day. Miss more than three meals and officers will investigate. If you're sick, report to the medical room. No food is to be taken out of the mess. No knives, forks, spoons, plates, mugs or anything. Is that clear?'

Yes, yes, yes. We were much more interested in food than instructions. The only other sounds in the room were clinks of

21

forks and spoons against plates. Finally the officer and interpreter left.

I heard a man's voice, low and slow at first, and then his song increased in strength and tempo, until it filled the room. A man at our table began singing, too. Then Abdul's and other voices joined the chorus, passionately, jubilantly, until the room rang with sounds of celebration. By the next song everyone had joined in, clapping or tapping if they didn't know the words. We pushed back tables and formed circles to dance. Ever since I could remember, celebrations and mourning meant music and dancing – though there'd been few celebrations at home for a long time. But this was an occasion for rejoicing. We'd been through hell and had reached a safe haven alive.

Our family circle danced and clapped and stamped as Mum, whirling her scarf around her head, led us through dances. Abdul drummed on the tabletop or danced frenetically, feet moving so fast even Hassan and I couldn't follow his steps. The two Zs danced 'til they dropped – literally. Then they sat, back to back in the middle of our circle, smiling tiredly, and clapping as one after another traditional songs swelled. *Makhta*, songs of mourning for those we'd lost, *Dobaiti* and *Chaharbaiti*, songs of home and loved ones, and newer political songs accompanied by intricate rhythms. Spoons ti-ta-ti-ta-ta-taed on table tops, hands tik-a-ta-tik-a-ta-tik-a-taed on tin-pot drums which took the place of the dayerahs, or tambourines, we played at home. We rocked to rhythms, clapping and stamping, or dancing riotously. Music to stir the soul.

Relief. Triumph. Uncertainty. Fear. Hope. Words didn't scratch the skin of our feelings, deep inside. Here there were no gunshots and explosions. No Terror to torture us, or to kidnap our loved ones.

22

Finally the singing faded. We'd said all we needed to, for now. I flopped to the floor next to the two Zs. Mum leant over us. 'Gulnessa, will you carry Zahra? I'll carry Zainullah.'

As I tried to scoop up the almost sleeping child, a hand pulled on my shoulder. 'I'll carry her, Nessa. You look as though you can only just manage yourself.' I looked up into Abdul's smiling, dark eyes. 'Here, I'll pull you up.' Abdul's hand stretched out to me and as we touched a tingle ran through my body.

We followed the crowd, many with arms around each other's shoulders or waists, wearily wandering back to our rooms, and sleep.

That night I felt safe in our warm room – for the first time I could remember. Zahra, who'd woken up, pulled out her grubby stick-doll, our grandmother, or Arjay, had made for her as a parting present. She hadn't let it out of her sight since we'd left home and it looked much the worse for wear. 'Gul's sleepy. I put her to bed. And sing to her.' Zahra busied herself at the top of the bed Mum was sitting on and, in her high little voice, sang our favourite lullaby, 'Lullaby baby my son'. She sang it over and over, even though Gul's a girl.

> *Lalay lalay, ate-aya*
> *Lalay lalay, babe-e aya*
> *Lalay lalay, dede-aya.*

Then, as we had on our lighthouse night, we dragged mattresses onto the floor, side by side, to sleep on. Soundly. Dreamlessly.

CHAPTER 3

It didn't take long to learn the routines of the Camp. Each day we got up and waited to take turns in the showers. If you didn't want to wait, you had to get up while it was still dark. I stayed in bed until breakfast and had my shower afterwards, when the lines weren't so long.

At 7.30 a.m. sharp the siren summoned us to a breakfast of cereal and toast. I'd never seen breakfast cereals before. I liked Cornflakes all right, but couldn't eat the others. And I couldn't eat toast. It was a million miles from the steaming, moist, flat loaves Mum used to make.

After breakfast we returned to our dongas to tidy and clean our rooms, wash clothes and wait. Wait to be called for medical checks. Wait for interviews. Wait to do jobs the officers gave us. There was nothing to do but wait.

There was a room in the compound where we could buy a few things like drinks, biscuits, sweets and toiletries. All these were new to us and we longed to try them. But of course we had no money, except if the Camp guards paid us to do their jobs. They'd only let us do things like clean toilets, or wash dishes, and they paid us just enough to buy a can of Coke. That's how

I found out Australian money wasn't afghanis, but dollars and cents.

We waited for the lunch siren, too, which was at 12.30 p.m. daily. The food we enjoyed when we were starving on the first day never changed. Meals other than breakfast were always rice cooked with vegetables, maybe with a bit of meat or chicken.

We had to stay inside mostly. Another bigger group of people arrived after the first few weeks and then we were only allowed outside for one hour each morning and one hour in the afternoon. Time passed slowly. Waiting. Even when we were outside we were supposed to stay in the exercise yard. There was nothing to do there, either.

In our first exercise period I realised there were many more men than women and lots of boys around my age or older. Most people looked like us or had darker skin. The kids, young like the two Zs, chased each other around the yard. The few girls I could see looked older than Hassan. No other girls were my age.

Mum walked with Layla, up and back between the fence and dongas. There were so many people crowded in the yard it was easy not to be noticed. I checked out every bit of the area, which Asad told me was about the size of a basketball court. This was a new game to me. High at each end was an old hoop. One was hanging down uselessly because, the rumour went, after losing a ball over the fence no one was allowed to get it back, so an angry man jumped up and dragged the hoop to where it now hung. We had no ball to shoot goals with anyway.

In the second exercise period I made up my mind to slip away. I trailed my hand along the fence as I walked from under the useless hoop towards the donga at the side of the yard. Unnoticed, I squeezed between the razor-topped wire which ran around the Camp and the back of the donga. I came to a corner

25

where there was just enough room to sit in the sun, hidden from view, and gaze out across the amazing flat, red land dotted with straggly, khaki bushes and tufts of plants. It stretched away forever until it met the cloudless blue sky.

In this hideout I could at last feel the space surrounding us. I'd missed that. Everything in the Camp was so crowded. Everyone was herded together. Families could never be by themselves. Except we were lucky in our room, as the officers hadn't squeezed in more beds when the new people arrived. Most families shared rooms with people they'd never met before.

This wide, flat land was so different from where I'd lived in our remote little village near the foothills of great mountains, and here there'd be no landmines if I was ever allowed out to explore. The sun's warmth and the shimmering heat haze over the landscape mesmerised me.

'Wa-a-a-a-a-a . . .' It took a few seconds to register where I was and realise that the nerve-jangling noise was the dinner siren. Hurrying back, I decided to keep my sanctuary secret for the time being.

Each day, the dinner siren sounded at 5.30 p.m. for a meal that was always the same as lunch. We couldn't work out which was left over from which. Mum and I soon learned to smuggle bread out of the mess so we had something to give the two Zs to eat during the long wait until breakfast the next day. Even bread and water was better than hunger pangs from tummies too small to fit in enough food to keep going for fourteen long hours.

After dinner we returned to our donga, where many people crowded into the common room. The men clustered around the table playing cards, and the women sat on the floor in groups, sewing and talking. Zahra and a new friend, Yasmine, with other young children, crawled giggling around the women. Yasmine shared the room next to ours with her parents, her brother, who was Zainullah's age, and two unrelated boys about Hassan's age who, like Abdul, had been sent to safety by their families.

Abdul, who often went to Asad's donga to play cards, sometimes stayed to play knucklebones with Hassan and me. Zainullah had improved so much that we let him join us. Hassan had collected these bones from sheep Mum had cooked for family feasts, sorting out the best ones and scrubbing off bits of gristle. Now their surfaces were smooth and they were the colour of the cream that we'd skimmed from cow's milk.

As we started our second game I heard Zahra's voice and glanced over my shoulder. Leaning on me, she was singing her lullaby to Gul. 'You'll have to play without me after this turn,' I told the boys. I usually got Zahra ready for bed. Mum followed a bit later with a protesting Zainullah. I couldn't remember a time when he'd gone willingly to bed.

We slept two in each of the bottom bunks as no one wanted to risk falling from the top ones. I loved feeling my little sister's warm body snuggling next to mine. Zainullah slept with Mum, and Hassan and Abdul topped and tailed in the third. The weather had been mild when we'd arrived, ages ago it seemed to me, though I knew it couldn't be more than a few weeks, and although the days were still warm, as soon as the sun neared the red earth the temperature dropped noticeably. I wondered how it could be winter again so soon, as the snow had not long melted before we left home. I didn't feel I could cope with a snowy winter here. There was no heating in the dongas. Nowhere to start a blazing fire to warm our spirits as well as our bodies.

The blankets on the bunks were thin and grey, so as soon as we'd washed our few belongings – for the first time in a washing machine – we made our room as cosy as we could by spreading our own blankets over our beds. We hung our coats and bags from the hooks on the wall and folded away our few clothes in the lockers. I longed for the colourful cushions and carpets we'd left behind. We had only our prayer mat. We took turns to pray in our room but we couldn't pray in the mess as we always prayed at home, before we ate. That felt strange, eating without first thanking Mohammed.

'Nessa,' Zahra's jet-black eyes shone at me above the thin blanket. 'Story? Ple-e-ease.'

'Okay, baby, what'll it be?' I settled myself on the bed next to her for our nightly ritual.

'Theermie! Theermie!' she squealed. Then she looked at me. 'I *not* a baby.'

'Sorry, darling. I forgot. Are you sure you want the Theerma story? We've had it *so* many times.'

'Ple-e-ease. I like it.'

'Okay,' I tucked her in again, 'but close your eyes and listen while I tell you.'

'But I mightn't hear.'

'You don't hear with your eyes, silly.'

'Oh.' She lay staring at me, eyes big, round and trusting.

This story was hard for me to tell. It's about Dad. I feel like someone kicks me in the stomach every time I think that we'll probably never see him again. That he'll never again come home as he used to, yelling, 'Come an' see what I've got you!' He always had something. A can of warm goat's milk, or a marbled rock from the mountains, or a spring flower . . .

Taking a deep breath, I started, 'One day when you were tiny, Dad came home when it was dark.' I concentrated and could hear his voice, and see him coming towards us as we sat around the fire out the back of the house. 'He was carrying his coat bundled up in his arms, like treasure that would break if he squeezed it too tight. Hassan and I pulled at him, swinging on his arms, and begging, "Show us, please show us . . ."

'But he kept saying, "Wait for the little ones. It's for them, too." Then, when we were all sitting in a circle on the ground, he ever so gently put down the bundle. I shivered so much I could hardly sit still. Carefully, Dad undid his coat's scratchy folds. We wriggled closer on our bottoms, craning our necks. He said, "Shhh. Be still. And calm. Or you'll frighten her." Then he dropped the coat open on the ground.

'"Oh-h-h . . ." We all breathed in together – we couldn't help it. She was so-o-o sweet. And so-o-o brave. Not more than a few hours old, the tiny, still, damp lamb struggled to stand. First she pushed on her back legs 'til they stood straight. Then one front leg unravelled and tried to straighten. But *blomp*, down she plopped. Again and again she tried until at last she was up on all four legs. She wobbled and staggered a step or two. *Blomp*. And we watched, spellbound. I reached out to help her but Dad caught my hand, shaking his head.

'"Let her be." At last he picked her up, saying, "Let's see if she's hungry. Milk will make her strong. Soon she'll be running faster than any of you." Looking at the grubby, wobbly, baby lamb, that was hard to believe.'

I glanced at Zahra. She was sound asleep, her 'blankie' wound around her neck and Gul clasped to her chest. The blanket was really a scarf made from Theerma's first fleece. Theerma means 'spring' in Dari, and it was early springtime when Dad had brought the lamb home. She was the first of lots of lambs we reared, and the best shepherd of all. And run? Not even Hassan could catch her.

I missed my grandparents so much, but when I touched the

29

blankets my grandmother had hand-spun and woven I felt Arjay Aqila was a little nearer. Mum must miss her terribly, but I didn't like to talk to her about them because once, when I'd said that Arjay Aqila would know how to do something, Mum didn't answer, she just looked away. Another time I watched her fight back tears when one of the Zs said miserably, at bedtime, 'I want Arjay to kiss me goodnight.'

I hated seeing my mother crying. It scared me. She was always so strong. I'd never seen her tears before that night the Terror took Dad. Now I didn't know what to say that wouldn't upset her, so I said nothing.

I crawled into bed beside Zahra. It was early but the night was cold. I tucked the blankets around us, stroking Arjay's blanket as I did.

CHAPTER 4

Shaking my head on the pillow, I tried to drive away a scene that haunted me. Awake, or distorted in my dreams, it tormented me. Squeezing my eyes tight I focussed on the lighthouse night. Where was that feeling of warmth and hope? It didn't work. I pushed my hands against my ears . . .

I hear stamping. The stamping grows louder and louder. I know who it is. I want them to go – anywhere. Away from our house. I've seen what they do. Then, hammering on our door. Bang! Bang! Bang!

Mum yells, 'All of you, go up to your beds!'

Bang! Bang! Bang!

We stumble up the steps holding on to each other.

Bang! Bang! Bang!

I push Zahra, to help her up into the room where we sleep.

Bang! Bang! Crash!

I glance down. The door swings open. Men in dark clothes lurch in. Lots. Guns point. Dad stands firm, facing them. Still. Strong.

Dark figures advance. Slow motion. Menacingly.

Mum drags at Dad, screaming, 'Ali . . . Ali . . .' He's a rock.

Closer, closer, the gunmen inch. Pitilessly.

Mum tears at Dad's sleeve. Frantically. Pleading. 'No! Please no! Leave him . . .'

A dark streak flies across the room. Smashes into the table leg. Drops to the floor. Lies there. Still, so still.

I half slip, half climb down the stairs.

Gunmen seize Dad's arms. They yank him out the door. He shouts, struggling to see us, 'I love you all. So much. Stay together. Look after each other 'til I get back. I lo-o-o-ove yo-o-ou . . .'

My head thumps. My gut retches. Mum. I must help Mum. I get to her as she stirs. Slithering down beside her, I lift her head onto my lap and sob, 'Mum, Mum, please be all right.'

Her eyes struggle open and she looks into mine. 'Shhh, darling.' Eyes close again. Then open. I see her swallow hard. She pushes herself up onto one elbow and whispers, 'I'll be fine. Shhh, we mustn't frighten the little ones. Try to act like everything's normal. What did they see?' Now I see a red lump on her temple. I can't turn away my eyes. I see it growing as I watch.

I force myself to answer her. 'I . . . I don't know. I was last up the steps. I saw everything. But I don't think the others . . . Mum, a giant egg's growing on your forehead. Will I get a wet rag to put on it?'

Mum reaches up to feel the lump, now the size of a pullet's egg – and still growing. 'Ouch!' She winces as her fingers touch the stretched skin. 'There's only a little water left in the jug and the little ones might want a drink in the night. Take a rag outside and scoop up some snow.'

Grabbing a cloth, I run towards the darkness behind the open door. At the front step I skid to a halt. Peering out of the candle-lit room I see only black. Straining harder to see any movement I hear a truck's engine in the distance. Gone. They must have gone. And taken my dad. At least he's not here with the red halo, lying in the snow. Like they left Abdul's dad. Cautiously, stepping down, one, two, three steps, I bend, scrape some snow into the rag in my hands, then bolt back

32

inside, pushing shut behind me what's left of the door.

By now the two Zs are clustered around Mum on the rug. No questions even. Eyes fixed on her egg. She's telling them, '. . . and I must have tripped on something and hit my head. Oh, thanks, Gulnessa.' Mum covers her forehead with my little bundle.

She looks at me. Something in her eyes makes me instantly forget the egg. 'Gulnessa, I want you to do . . . something . . . for . . . me.' She says the last bit slowly, moving her lips a lot, like she's teaching me to speak clearly. 'I have an important message for Bahkhul and Arjay. It's after bedtime for the two Zs so take them to bed. Tell them your stories until they're asleep, but . . . don't . . . leave . . . your . . . room. I'll join you soon.'

It's not the time to ask anything. I'll have to wait until she's seen my grandparents, Dad's parents. The two Zs eyes are still rivetted to her forehead.

'Now, go on. All of you.' She looks at me warningly as I open my mouth to speak. 'I . . . won't . . . be . . . long.'

Herding my young brother and sister up the steps, I can't get rid of a hollow, scared feeling. It often hovers there – but not like this. Think of something else, I tell myself. My mind races. I can only think of Dad. Where've they taken you?

❧ ❧ ❧

Mum met a nurse, Joanne, when she reported for her medical examination. She was shy because she had her period and didn't know how to explain that she didn't want to be examined then. When Mum returned to the donga I was sitting on the common-room floor playing knucklebones with Zainullah and Zahra. Hassan, Abdul and a couple more boys around their age were playing cards nearby. Others sat around turning the pages of old magazines that only a few Iraqi boys could read. Zahra had been at me to teach her knucklebones, so I gave her a couple of spare bones to practise with while Zainullah and I played a game. He was so good now that I had to concentrate or he'd beat me, and he always tried his best. For Zahra the hardest bit was to turn her little hand over quickly enough, then to hold it rigid so the bones didn't roll off the back of her hand.

'Gulnessa, come with me to our room,' Mum said, walking past. 'Zainullah, you play with Zahra for a few minutes.'

'Oh, Mum,' Zainullah complained, 'I was beating Nessa.' How like Hassan he was becoming.

'Stop arguing, Zainullah,' Mum's firm voice stopped me replying, 'and do as you're told.'

'But Zahra doesn't know how to play.' Arguments seemed to increase as the days dawdled past.

Inside our room Mum closed the door behind us and turned to me, pulling something from beneath her flowing tunic. Speaking softly she said, 'Gulnessa, I wanted to show you these.' In her hand she held a packet open at one end, showing soft, white rectangular shapes packed into it. She pulled one out and passed it to me. 'They're for women. To use with our period. You throw them away so you don't have to wash rags any more.'

'Wow!' I examined the sanitary pad. How I hated my bloody rags, and I cursed being a girl every time I washed them.

'The nurse was kind. She can't speak our language but understood why I didn't want to be examined right now. She said I could go back another time. She gave me these. I'll show you what to do with them in the bathroom.' There was no privacy in the dongas. No door had a lock. Even ordinary voices could be heard in neighbouring rooms. With thirty-four people sharing our donga, others had more in them, it was impossible to be alone, or to be really quiet, even at night. Someone always woke up after a nightmare or the clanging of the metal locker doors. Others played cards all night, or sat and talked, then slept when we got up. Lately the guards had taken to doing spot checks of us and could burst in at any time.

When Mum returned to the nurse the following week, the two Zs and I went, too. The nurse examined us first: eyes, nose, ears, throat, hair, fingernails, chest, temperature . . . everything that was easy to get at. It was so embarrassing but she was kind. When it was over I took the Zs to the morning exercise hour. We met Yasmine and her family there and the children raced off. I waited for the right moment to slip away for my few moments of quiet time.

It wasn't long before I was sitting cross-legged on the hard, red earth, gazing beyond the wire surrounding us, into freedom. How I missed the open country. I felt caged. We all did. The forever blue sky seemed a little paler today, but I couldn't be sure if it was my jaded spirits making it look that way, or the cooler weather. I had no idea what signs of changing seasons to watch for. Nothing looked different on the endless red plains, but a stiff breeze sending tufts of dry plants bowling into the distance made me shiver and tuck my hands up the sleeves of my thin top. When we arrived at the Camp the sun had been hot all day. Even when there was a breeze the air had only cooled after dark. Now the wind seemed to blow constantly and although almost lunchtime it was chilly.

Later in the mess, I caught Mum smiling as the guards were hustling the last few people inside so they could close the doors and begin their head count. Her smiles were rare now and I wondered what prompted it. Mum didn't worry about food, as there was a long queue. She came straight to join us and nursed Zahra. There weren't even enough chairs for everyone since the new group had more than doubled the number of people.

'I don't want it,' Zainullah pushed his plate away. 'I'm sick of it.'

'Eat up, Zainullah, or you'll be hungry.' Mum sighed. Every mealtime there was a variation of this conversation. Mum knew hunger would eventually drive him to eat but she couldn't let it go. He'd found that out, too, but it didn't stop him complaining. Zahra on the other hand said nothing and ate nothing unless we spooned it into her mouth.

'Come on, you two,' Mum coaxed, sharing their meal. She didn't eat much now, either. 'I've got something to show you.'

'Have not.' Zainullah said sullenly.

'I'm so tired of arguing with you, I can't do it any more.'

Back in our room, Mum said, 'Sit on the bed while I get out the surprise.' She opened her locker, then turned around. In her hands she held some sewing materials: a few different coloured cottons, needles, some tiny scissors and a length of white material – remnants of a worn-out sheet. 'Now I can make us things,' she said. 'Joanne gave me these. We must hide the scissors from the guards.'

'Is that *all*?' Zainullah was contemptuous. 'It's girl's stuff. I'm going to find Hassan.'

'Don't leave the donga,' Mum called. 'It's not exercise time yet.' Zainullah didn't answer as he stomped off. We turned our attention to the treasure trove.

After that, when we were allowed outside each morning, Mum went to the medical room to see Joanne, who taught Mum words in her language, starting with her name. Joanne often gave Mum things. Mostly for sewing, or wool, or sanitary pads. Sometimes it was soap which smelled like blossoms. Mum had made all our soap at home.

During the long, dragging hours of the endless days and weeks in the donga while we waited for the processing to finish, Mum remade Zahra's doll, and also new clothes for her with pieces of old sheet and needles and threads one of the nurses found for her. Zahra never tired of sitting and watching Mum sew if it was something for Gul. It was like her patience with animals. But there were no animals here. Except for mice. Dozens of them. And cockroaches and ants and spiders.

I sewed dolls' clothes, too, until my hand cramped and I had to stand up and walk around. Then I started teaching Zahra how to do tacking stitch. 'She's too little,' Mum warned. 'She'll prick her fingers with the needle and get blood stains on the material.' Zahra sat, tongue peeping out between her lips, concentrating as she slowly pushed the needle through the fabric on the line I'd drawn for her. Whenever Zahra asked me to show her something I would. If it was too hard for her after she'd *really* tried, she'd say, 'I'm tired now' and wander off. Left to Mum, Zahra would stay a baby forever. Anyway, what did a few blood stains matter? We'd washed them from clothes and out of Mum's and my rags all the time.

When Mum finished Zahra's doll's outfits from the first piece of sheet, she cut from the remnants a small square cloth like she'd often done at home, delicately hemmed it and embroidered in each corner, with her tiny, exquisite stitches, a traditional Hazara design. I went with Mum to give it to Joanne. I saw tears in her eyes as she hugged Mum tightly. After that Joanne brought Mum even more pieces of fabric, coloured cottons and wools to sew with, and braids and laces, too. Mum said she didn't know what she would have done without Joanne. Probably gone mad with nothing to do. I was getting near that point, too.

One day when Mum came in she sat down and took out her

sewing. After a bit she said, 'Gulnessa, I'd like your opinion on this.' I was so surprised that I turned around immediately. The fabric she held was white, but her fingernails were blood red.

One thought immediately filled my mind. Torture! The Terror chopped off people's hands and tore off fingernails. All kinds of tortures to find out what they wanted to know. It *couldn't* be like that here, could it? Jumping up, I reached Mum's side in one step. 'What happened?'

'Calm down, Gulnessa. It's nothing to worry about. Look.' Mum spread out her brown hands on the white cloth. Each of her blood-red fingernails was smooth and shiny, like jewels on her fingertips. I must have looked as I felt, totally baffled, because she went on, 'Joanne painted my nails and gave me this bottle of nail polish.'

'Wow!' was all I could manage.

'Would you like me to paint yours?'

'Yes, please,' I whispered.

It took ages to get it right, but we had all the time in the world. Zahra watched, fascinated. 'Me too, Mummy, please,' she begged.

'Can I do Zahra's, Mum?' I was itching to have a go. Women at home often wore silver and gold Hazara jewellery handed down in families, but nothing like this.

At dinner that night when our women friends saw our red nails they wanted to paint theirs, too. We spent the best evening painting each other's finger and toenails until we'd used up the rest of the bottle. But the next morning when we got up, Mum said, 'Girls, here's the remover. We must take off the nail polish before we pray.'

'That's not fair,' I protested. 'We've only just put it on.'

'We must pray like always for our safety and your father's return. It is disrespectful to wear nail polish when we pray.'

Nothing I could say would move her and we had our usual pink nails when we spread out our prayer mat for morning prayers.

A few weeks later when we went to visit Joanne, she wasn't there. Mum said proudly, in English, 'Joanne please.' A nurse who we hadn't seen before said something, shook her head and shrugged her shoulders. Mum tried to find out where Joanne was but the new nurse just kept shaking her head, shrugging. So Mum gave up.

When we were outside she, too, shook her head, and looking so sad said, 'Another friend vanished. And in our new country.'

To try to take her mind off it, I said, 'Mum, I haven't got a doll, so would you help me make one?'

'I've got Gul.' Zahra held out the spruced up homemade doll which rarely left her hands. 'Poor Nessa hasn't got a baby.'

I tousled her hair. 'Will you help?' She nodded seriously.

'All right, Gulnessa.' Mum's face looked strained. 'Let's look for a strong, forked stick.'

Shut inside for the rest of the day, we worked on the doll. Using double thread, Mum showed me how to bind fabric around the stick, building up a body and legs. Next, with more strips of fabric wound round and round the top of the single end of the stick, we formed a head. Then we made arms from cigarette-like fabric rolls. When they were ready, I stitched them firmly to the body, leaving a long neck below the head. Finally, using embroidery stitches I'd learned sitting with Mum and the other women in our village, I began to sew a face on the head.

'Make her eyes brown, Nessa,' Zahra instructed. 'Like yours.' I did as I was told using a dark brown thread. 'And black eyelashes. Like yours.' Zahra was very conscious of eyelashes since I started giving her 'butterfly kisses' to drive away her crankiness or tears.

Mum seemed more and more often to sit gazing out of the window, oblivious to us, so Zahra turned to me for help or comfort now. She'd always been like my human doll and I loved her dearly. I'd helped bathe her since she was a baby and fed her her first mouthfuls from a spoon. As I'd always helped care for her at first I didn't notice that now it was happening more frequently.

A few weeks earlier in the exercise yard Zahra had fallen over, scraping her hands and knees on the rock-hard dirt. She was sobbing, so I sat her on my lap. 'Never mind, baby. Try not to cry.' I rocked her back and forth. Just then I noticed a butterfly land next to us and said, 'Look what's come to make you better.' Zahra's sobs slowed. She wiped her eyes with the back of her grubby little hands.

'W-what?' she sniffed.

'Shhh,' I cautioned, 'there it is.'

'Oh-h-h, a buf-fly,' she breathed, her body shuddering as the tears dried up.

Then I'd remembered something Arjay used to do, so I improvised on it. 'Yes. The butterfly must have seen you fall over and hurt your knees, because it asked me to give you this to make them better.' I bent low to her cheek and blinking quickly brushed my eyelashes against it. She giggled as I lifted my head, and rubbed her cheek with the back of her hand.

'What was it?' she whispered. A soft touch always made her whisper.

'A butterfly kiss. Our secret,' I whispered back. From then on it never failed to bring a smile to her lips.

I sewed long black lashes on the doll's face and stitched her nose and ears in a pale tan that Zahra matched against my skin. Finally she chose bright red for the lips, like Joanne's lipstick, which fascinated Zahra.

'She's like you, Zahra,' Mum said when we showed her.

'No. Like Nessie,' Zahra corrected firmly.

For the final touch Mum showed me how to cover the back and sides of the head with black strands of wool hair, making it long enough to plait – just like mine. She was a 'real' creation, and ready to dress. Zahra and I planned to make many outfits for her from Mum's fabric. We draped piece after piece of material over her, wrapped her in others, and decorated our designs with laces and braids. Zahra wanted me to make one outfit the same as a pair of embroidered loose blue pants and matching top Mum had made for Gul. 'Then they'll be twins,' Zahra told me seriously.

'Yes, I'll try to, but first I want to make her an Afghan bride's dress.' Perhaps, I thought, I could use her as a model to design clothes for us to wear in our new country. I decided to wait until I 'knew' her better before naming her.

CHAPTER 5

A few evenings later, Hassan and Abdul went off to another donga, to play cards with some of the other men. Instead of sitting in the common room as we mostly did, Mum, the two Zs and I cleaned our teeth on the way back from the mess, and went straight to our room. Mum had another of her headaches and didn't want to be with a crowd. She was getting more and more headaches, and spending more time in our room rather than talking with Layla and the other women. She sat on her bed and I saw her fingering Arjay Aqila's blanket, sort of wistfully, so I said, 'Please, Mum, tell us the story about our blankets?' We'd heard it many times before but never tired of it.

'Yea! Story.' Zahra loved nothing better.

'Not until you two little ones are in bed.'

'Mu-um!' Zainullah said. 'Remember what you promised.'

'Sorry, I forgot.' Earlier, after yet another squabble between Zainullah and his friend Rashid, Yasmine's brother from the neighbouring room, Zainullah came in crying and told Mum how Rashid had punched him. She'd said, 'only babies tell tales'. Zainullah protested, so Mum promised she wouldn't call him little so long as he didn't behave like a baby.

Lying on the bunk next to Zainullah under the blanket, Mum began, a faraway look on her face. 'When I was a little girl, smaller than you, Zahra, I used to sit next to my mum's old spinning wheel. Just like you've done, too, many times, with Arjay Aqila. I'd play with dolls she'd made for me. I liked to make cosy beds for them out of pieces of wool Mum dropped to the floor as she spun yarn from fleeces the men had shorn from our family's sheep. When she'd spun enough balls of wool, I'd pile them into a basket and we'd take them outside. She'd sit with her friends and I'd play with the children. Our mums sewed clothes for us, or knitted wool into soft warm blankets, or coats for their families. The women often knitted their own hairs with the wool strands and their loved ones' hair, too, to be sure we were always wrapped up in love.

'Look, here . . .' Mum pointed to a dark hair, knitted into a row near the edge of the blanket on Zahra's and my bed. 'That's one of Arjay Aqila's hairs when she was a young woman. And those are mine when I was only a little girl.' She pointed further along to some finer, black hairs.

'And those are from my father's head. Arjay Aqila added them after Bahkhul Abdul died.' These last were white, and hard to see amongst the mainly creamy wool. Then, as always, we spent ages looking for more secrets knitted into the blankets. Whenever we found one, Mum told us a story about where it came from. As she told the familiar stories my mind wandered . . .

We're playing in Bahkhul Abdul's and Arjay Aqila's secret room – but we've promised not to tell anyone outside the family about it. We call it the 'hideout'. We're about to rescue a 'prisoner'. The two Zs are on watch to shout a warning if grown-ups come near.

'Stop!' I hiss to Hassan, who's trying to pull the rope over the

kid goat's head. 'Undo the rope from the pole, sheep-brain, not the kid's neck. I want to lead it to the hideout. You go ahead. Check with the Zs that it's safe.' Although he hates me bossing him, he makes no fuss as he's too impatient to be good with animals. I've put some milk into an old kettle which I hold just in front of the kid's nose as I lead it by the rope around its neck. It trots along, eyes rivetted on the kettle.

'Help Nessie? Help Nessie?' Zahra tugs at my arm. Even though she's only two she has some sort of magic with animals.

'Okay, pat it gently,' I instruct needlessly. 'Walk next to it with your hand on its back.' I show her what to do. 'Help me keep it quiet.'

Our little procession enters Arjay Aqila's living room. Hassan's already there, tugging at the trapdoor to the hideout. Behind me there's a shout. 'Hey, Nessa! Arjay Aqila's at our house. It's safe to go in.' Zainullah bursts into the room.

'Der . . .' I begin, but the kid jerks hard on the rope. Just keeping my grip I stop the animal from bolting. A handful of small black 'olives' rain over my feet, and over Arjay Aqila's floor.

Tiny Zahra, calm as can be, looks at Zainullah sternly. 'Zainullah, bad.' She strokes the kid's back until its shivering quietens. Then to Zainullah again, 'Shh. Clean.' Zainullah does, and we get the kid safely into the hideout.

Four times every day after that, Hassan or I carry our hidden kettle of warm milk down to the secret room, and feed our baby. We get away with it for three days but when I arrive early the next morning Arjay Aqila's waiting. 'Lovely morning, Nessa,' she greets me. 'I'm coming down today to check that awful smell.'

'Oh, don't you worry, Arjay Aqila,' I try to sound casual. 'I'll check what it is.' To tell the truth, although we carry out the poop wrapped in secret bundles, we notice the room smells. There are no windows. Only two grids high in the walls. Air gets in or out when the trapdoor's *open. Since we've had Awhal – we call him that because he's our first rescue and Awhal means 'first' in our language – we close the trapdoor as soon as we're inside.*

'I'll see for myself.' Arjay Aqila drags back the living room carpet and picks up the trapdoor's metal ring. Down the ladder she climbs, and as she steps off the last rung, I hear, 'Ha-huh!'

I find her on her knees feeling our baby's stomach and heartbeat. She looks up. Her face is stern – for about a second. Then it breaks into her customary smile. 'What a little beauty! Is it the one the old goat next door was looking for?'

I breathe out loudly. 'Yes, Arjay Aqila it is. P-le-e-a-se don't tell him. We couldn't bear its bleating all the time. It's so little. It was such a short bit of rope and it pulled so hard we thought it might strangle itself.'

We don't exactly get into trouble, but cleaning the hideout is almost as bad. We cart in buckets of dry sand to cover the floor, then we scrape up everything again and carry it away. We make brooms by tying small, leafy branches from the plum trees in the garden to a big stick. Then we sweep the hideout again and again until the floor's clean and Arjay Aqila is satisfied the smell's gone. Then she has one of her 'talks' with us. This time we have to promise not to take any live things down there again, without asking. She lends us old sacks for the floor, a wolf skin rug, bowls and mugs from her house so it's like a real hideout.

'But,' she warns, 'not a word to anyone outside the family about the hideout. It's a family secret and you never know when we might need to use it.'

Finally, when the Zs were asleep, I noticed Mum watching me, sort of anxiously. She said, 'It's nearly time for the guards to check the dongas. I hope the boys come back soon or we'll be out in the cold again. Do you know where they went, Gulnessa?'

'I think they're playing cards with RSW19. Want me to see?'

'Yes please, if you would, but be quick. I'm not up to standing outside tonight.'

Two nights earlier, at about three a.m., guards had stormed into our rooms, shining torches and shouting until we were all awake, not caring how frightened we were. Then they ordered us out of bed and outside into the compound. Heart pounding and clutching a blanket around me, with a sobbing Zahra in my arms, I trailed after Mum who carried Zainullah. Abdul and Hassan followed us, trying to reassure us, as armed guards jostled us into the crowd under the bright lights. A mean officer was in the middle yelling loudly, and prodding people.

'Guns!' I gasped. 'What's going on?' I trembled as much from fear as from cold. Why guns? Surely not a war?

Abdul gathered us together. 'Wait here. Don't move, anyone. I'll find out what's happening.' We stood together silently, people milling around us. Everyone had wide, scared eyes.

Just then a whistle shrilled and guards waved us back towards the dongas. Abdul reappeared following Asad, their faces stony.

Apparently during a spot check on one of the dongas the guards had found a bed empty so they herded everyone outside for a head count. It turned out that one of the men was playing cards in another donga. For that, everyone was scared for their lives. It took ages to get back to sleep.

Now although the evening was cold I was pleased to be out looking for Hassan and Abdul. I'd seen them less and less since we'd been in the Camp because they hung around with the men and Mum said it wasn't right for a young woman to be with men who weren't related. While I didn't mind not seeing my brother, I missed Abdul. His quiet presence since leaving home had helped and reassured me. And more and more I'd found I liked being near him.

As I banged on the common room door of RSW19's donga, I looked around to see if the guards' flashing torches were in sight. It was after people from the boat the guards labelled RSW came that we were only let outside for an hour each morning and afternoon. The guards always checked on us after exercise periods and around bedtime. It made me feel like an animal – or some sort of criminal. Especially one guard who Zainullah nick-named Dung-face. You could see he enjoyed upsetting people. I kept as far away from him as I could.

Banging on the door again, I almost hit Abdul as he suddenly opened it. 'Please get Hassan and come back. Mum's worried. She couldn't take another night assembly.'

'Your wish is my command,' Abdul said with twinkling eyes. 'Just a second. I'll be right back.'

Waiting out there in the dark, the hostility of the Camp bit into my soul.

A little later, snuggling with Zahra, but still feeling bad, I tried to focus on my treasures but they kept sliding away. Finally I must have drifted into a restless sleep . . .

The Terror storm into our house. They tear down cupboards, rip up carpets, smash plates. They shout, 'Come out! We know you're there. If you don't come out, we'll find you and shoot you.' They throw open doors, slash mattresses, tip over beds . . . Escaping through the bed-room windows we flee into darkness. The Terror destroys everything in the house, then bursts outside. The men poke and prod and throw aside anything in their way. Expose every hiding place. I watch help-lessly as they close in. We cling to the rough walls inside the town well. Silently, desperately, praying for a miracle. A twisted face appears above us. Breaks into a ghastly smile. I look into the barrel of a gun . . .

Terrified screams woke me. I saw blackness. Sweat dripped down my face. My body trembled as if possessed. Flooding my mind were pictures of the time I'd really seen the Terror tearing a village boy not much older than Hassan from the well and throwing him onto the back of their truck.

Then Mum was by my side, holding my hand, whispering, 'There, there, Gulnessa. You're safe. Really you are.' My eyes blazed my fear. 'It was only a dream, darling. It's all behind us now. Do you want to talk about it?' I managed to shake my head. What was the point? It would only bring it back again. And upset her. 'That's okay. Try to think of blue sky and warm red ground. And Joanne. Before she disappeared she said she'd try to help us get out of here.' She sat next to me, mopping my forehead, stroking my hair, until my trembling calmed.

'I'm okay now.'

'Are you sure you're okay?'

I nodded.

'Well, cuddle up to Zahra. I must go back to Zainullah. I can hear him whimpering.'

I lay listening to Mum whispering to Zainullah, and although I couldn't make out the words I knew what she'd be saying and it made me feel safer. Eventually her whispers were replaced by regular breathing but my eyes stayed open. I wondered who my screams had woken, and whether they'd gone back to sleep. Each night the same thing happened in our room or a nearby one. We'd grown used to hearing others' whispered words of comfort, and gaining comfort ourselves.

'You still awake, Ness?' Abdul's soft whisper made me smile.

'Yes,' I whispered back.

'Do you want to talk?'

'No. It's okay.'

I lay there for ages. Abdul's words warmed me. He cares, I thought. This time I caught our lighthouse night . . .

We're in a strange town by the sea. A smiling man who doesn't speak our language shows us to a clean, friendly room. In it is a table and chairs, a bit like those at home, and three other things I've never seen before. Each one has four legs holding up a thick, soft, rectangular top. Mum looks at the man standing by the door. She points to these things, then, turning her palms upwards, shrugs her shoulders and raises her eyebrows. The man smiles, puts his hands together, raises them to lie across one shoulder, and tips his head so his cheek lies on his hands. Mum nods, and smiles back – the first smile I've seen her give anyone in days. We too understand, and laugh. The man bows his head, and moves out of the room, closing the door behind him.

Dropping her bundle of blankets on the floor, Mum turns to us, holding out her arms. We throw our blankets and bundles onto hers, and run to her. Like bedtime at home we hug each other, relieved to see Mum's smile but still needing reassurance from physical contact. Abdul, too. I hear Mum whisper, 'Nothing's ever going to take any of you from me.'

So close are our bodies that we must look like a melting statue. But suddenly the statue starts to shake. I catch a glimpse of Mum's face smiling mischievously now. Slowly she raises her arms above her head, shaking her hips harder and harder. Recognising the familiar game, I let go and fall onto our pile of rugs, laughing until I'm smothered by wriggling, giggling bodies.

When we untangle ourselves, puffing and still giggling, I glance at Abdul, shyly. I like him here with us, but for a minute feel something strange. He looks at me and winks. We all jump up and explore. A second door leads to a courtyard. It isn't as big as our room, but has a hard, clean floor and leafy plants along the far wall. To the left of the

49

door, a toilet in the ground is screened off. To the right is a tap on the wall with a pipe sticking out high above it. Turning the tap makes a stream of water gush out of the pipe. In the warm evening air we play under it for hours, splashing each other, turning the tap on and off to trick someone, and filling mugs for water fights.

'Mum, come on . . .' one or other of us calls at intervals, spraying water as we wave to her.

'No.' She laughs, ducking watery missiles. 'That'd spoil my fun watching.' Finally Mum calls us inside to share an enormous wok full of delicious noodles.

'Where did it come from?' I ask.

'The man who showed us to the room brought it,' Mum tells me amidst slurping noises as we scoff this new, wondrous Indonesian food. Our meal, the first real one since leaving home – how many days ago was it, seven, eight? It seems a lifetime – is delicious. When we're all finished, Mum says, 'Bedtime. Who wants to try out the sleeping stands?' We have not yet learnt the word 'bed'.

We try to crowd onto one bed, but whoever's on the outside falls off. We try it different ways: six across, three heads at the top, three at the bottom – but Zahra's flailing foot kicks Abdul. 'Enough!' Mum sits up. 'Let's work this out before someone gets hurt.' No one wants to sleep on separate beds and it's clear we won't all fit on one. In the end we push the beds against a wall and pull the mattresses off, arranging them side by side and spreading our blankets over them.

Next morning, sitting around the table and eating strange, sweet, juicy fruit for breakfast, Mum tells us that after we fell asleep she had her own fun. She washed herself and our clothes under the stream of water. They're dry already in this hot climate, so different from home. Then we talk about what we think the day will bring. 'If we're going to live here, we have to learn how to sail a boat, and how to fish.' Hassan had made up his mind this was the safe haven we were looking for.

Suddenly I see Abdul putting his finger to his lips. Silence. Then we hear loud thumps on the door, and our agent's voice calls, 'Bus. All come to bus. Bus. Bring your things.'

Blinking in the darkness I found myself smiling but still wide awake. I forced my eyes closed. Where was my golden treasure?

I look to where light touches the sky. Most people sleep propped against one another or in huddled mounds on the crowded deck. Three insomniacs stand near the opposite railing looking out at a burnished sea. The boat rises and falls gently on a lazy swell as if the ocean is breathing. The only sound is the steady throbbing of engines, broken occasionally by squawks of birds circling high above the boat.

Beyond the three silhouettes, the sky glows with the most amazing colours I've ever seen. From the gentle, peachy-gold wash that tinges distant clouds and illuminates the heavens, fluorescent oranges deepen to an incandescent blood-orange, then fiery-red at a far point on the horizon. As I watch, a golden sliver appears at the heart of the deepest crimson. The sliver becomes a slice, which grows and grows until a glowing, golden peach balances on the rim of the world.

I close my watering eyes. The peach dances on a luminous background behind my lids. When finally it fades I open my eyes to feast them again on the real thing, only to discover it, too, has faded. A hint of the wonder remains in pink-tinged clouds which turn to grey as I watch. Again I close my eyes tightly to bring back my magic peach. Yes, there it is in my mind's eye. My symbol for our new life. Nothing can ever take it from me.

CHAPTER 6

One morning the wind seemed particularly cold as we walked back to our donga after breakfast and I pulled my only jacket around me, tighter. Although we'd each brought our warmest coats when we escaped, they'd taken a real battering on our journey, and had lost much of their padding.

'Cold, Nessa?' Abdul must have noticed my gesture. 'Want me to put an arm around you?'

I felt my cheeks flush, and looked around quickly. For once no one was near us.

'Don't fool around.' I giggled, knowing I sounded stupid but unable to think of what else to say. To cover my embarrassment, I asked, 'Abdul, do you think it ever snows here?'

'No,' he answered. 'This is as cold as it gets.' I could have kissed him. He didn't tease me like Hassan would have done. Abdul was about the only one I could ask things because Mum and the other women in the Camp knew no more than I did. So I made the most of this rare moment with him alone.

'How do you know? Winter had just finished when we left home. It should be mid-summer now.' I'd been puzzling about this for weeks as the weather had grown colder.

'It would be if we were still at home,' he replied. 'It's a bit hard to explain. We crossed the equator on the way here.' I screwed up my face. 'It's sort of an imaginary line dividing the world in half. Now we're on the opposite side. When it's summer in Afghanistan it's winter here. See?'

'I *think* so.' This was my first-ever geography lesson!

'Well, it's after mid-winter here, so it's after mid-summer there.'

'And this is as cold as it gets?'

'That's what RSW19 told me. He's got an uncle living in Australia and seems to know a lot about it.' We called people we met here by their IDs because we heard officers shout them so often. It started as a joke in our family, but as there were lots of people whose names we didn't know, the numbers stuck.

'Well, does he know how much longer we have to stay in this compound? The interviews are taking forever. Mum's had two. She thinks I'll have to go with her next time they call her up.'

'They're checking your mum's story.'

'What?'

'They check to see if the story is the same or if details change when another family member is there. RSW19 speaks English and he's got to know one of the guards, a good guy who told him how the Immigration officers try to prove you're lying.'

'But why would we lie?'

'He says some of them think that because Australia's a beautiful country everyone wants to come and live here.'

'But we still don't know what it's like. And we didn't know where the agents were taking us.'

'I know that. We all know that. But for some reason Australians don't. Perhaps their life is so good they can't imagine what the Terror is like. Or the abuses that force us to leave our countries. Or how bad it has to get to make us leave our families.'

'But if they don't want us, what'll happen to us?'

'RSW19's trying to find out what he can. He said the good guard told him interviews are taking a long time because there's so many of us and the Immigration Department won't send more officers. He's been trying to find out about the compound they'll move us to. From the closed compound.'

'Closed compound?'

'That's here. We're closed off from the rest of the Camp.'

'But I don't understand why. We've had medicals. The only sicknesses they found are headaches, and the runs. Everyone's had those.'

'Mmm. RSW19 said that wasn't the real reason we are separated. It's got something to do with not wanting us to know what happens afterwards. I can't make much sense of it.' We'd reached the donga now, and were standing not far from its door.

'I just wish they'd hurry. It's so boring . . .' I wasn't sure how to say this but I had to try before anyone else joined us. 'I can't say anything to Mum, Abdul, 'cos I don't want to worry her more than she already is. She hardly ever smiles now.' He looked at me so intently that I blurted out, 'I can't stop worrying about what's going to happen to us. No one knows anything. What's this country like? Why can't we see other people? Why do they keep us behind high wire fences like we're criminals?'

'Nessa, I'm so sorry. I know how you feel. I feel like it, too. I thought you'd talk to your mother so you were all right. You're nearly always with her.' He squeezed my shoulder, dropping his hand quickly to his side.

'That's because I haven't any friends. There are no girls my age. Anyway, Mum needs me to look after the two Zs. She's miles away half the time and doesn't even notice us.'

'Well, you can talk to me whenever you want to. It helps me

to talk to RSW19. He told me that a few years ago he tried to immigrate and join his cousins in Australia. They live in a big city. Melbourne. His uncle was an accountant in Iraq and has a good job and a good house for his family. But RSW19 couldn't get permission because he's a geologist and they said they had plenty of those in Australia. And he had no money to bring here. Anyway, things got so bad for him in Iraq that he *had* to get out before they killed him, like they killed his mother when soldiers broke into their home and arrested his brother. He ended up on a boat that brought him here. He says he hadn't a clue where the agent he paid was taking him. Just like us. He landed here, so he reckons that he must be meant to be here.'

'Mmm. I believe that stuff, too.'

'Ness, we'll find a way to talk.' Trying not to let him see his effect on me as he spoke, I stared at my feet, watching my toes curl and knead the red sand. 'But now I'd better get to RSW19's donga before the guards stop me. Men's business.' He winked. 'We're playing cards – again. Take care of yourself. See you at lunch. Try to think of somewhere we can talk that's okay for you.' He put his hand over his heart and *really* smiled at me. I smiled back, not daring to look into his eyes for long in case he saw how fast my heart was beating.

❧ ❧ ❧

During her interviews Mum had spent days with Immigration officers and a lawyer, explaining many, many times why we had to leave home, and how Dad was abducted. She said most officials and lawyers seemed to want to help but it was hard to understand each other, even though the lawyer brought an interpreter. They also asked about bad things we saw in our village and people we knew who were hurt or killed. They questioned Mum about recent events and those which happened long ago, even about her parents' early life and when she was a child. She told them how our people had been persecuted and abused for as long as they could remember because we are Hazaras, the group most oppressed by the dominant rulers. She tried to explain how it was even harder to live since the Terror ruled Afghanistan. Often when she couldn't get them to understand, Mum grew frustrated and upset.

I hated seeing her come back to our room like that. She'd sit on her bed and cry. Talking about horrors brought back vividly trauma, sadness and loneliness we'd been through. I didn't know how to comfort her when she cried that way – as if her heart would break. Then my fear swelled until I thought I'd explode. I felt empty and sick, hopeless and scared all at once. Pain stabbed like there was a real blade in my chest whenever I let myself think about Dad.

So I tried to block it all out.

After months interviewing adults and older boys who'd come without their families, like Abdul, the officials announced they were going to interview older children in the compound, like me and Hassan. So one evening, after we'd put the young ones to bed, Mum said she wanted to talk to us.

'It's about your interviews,' she started. 'I don't want you to be frightened. Just tell them everything that has happened to us, at home and since we left. There'll be an interpreter.'

'But you've already told them, haven't you?'

Mum looked so tired as she went on, 'They think I might be making up stories so we can stay in Australia.'

'What?' Hassan and I exploded together.

'What?' the two Zs sat up in bed.

Mum frowned at us as she said to them, 'Lie down, darlings. Hassan and Gulnessa didn't hear what I said. That's all.'

'Oh!' Zahra didn't want to hear any more. She closed down when anyone talked about bad things we'd been through. It's a good way of coping, I thought. I wished I could do it. Though I knew bad memories still attacked her, through dreams.

'Mum, I don't believe anyone could think *anyone* would make up stories like what's happened to us,' I whispered.

'How could you?' For once Hassan understood my thinking. 'No one could make up things like that. And who'd want to?'

'I don't *know* why they don't believe us,' Mum sounded defeated. Not at all like her old self. 'I don't understand. How could they think we'd leave our homes and Bahkhul and your Arjays unless it was impossible to stay? When I think how we *nearly* didn't get on the plane after Bahkhul sent us on that nightmare drive to the border, when I'd no idea we'd have to leave our country.' She sighed deeply. 'Now, I wonder if we made the right decision. I wouldn't have done it if I'd known people wouldn't believe us.'

'Mum, you don't really mean that. You saved our lives.'

I couldn't believe my ears. That brother of mine actually had a brain. It must have been Abdul's influence rubbing off.

Mum nodded. 'Still, every day I ask myself, "Did I do the right thing for my children?"' Pausing, she looked hard first at Hassan, then at me. 'I want to think only of good things about home, but when I *make* myself remember bad things, when I'm interviewed, I *know* I made the right decision. Each time I tell our story, it feels like it's happening all over again. Officials ask so many questions. Over and over and over. They want every detail. I don't want you to have to relive it, too.' She sighed so loudly I wriggled close and put my arms around her.

'It's all right, Mum,' Hassan's voice was soothing. 'You told the truth and we will, too. Nessa and I'll be okay. When we all say the same thing they *must* believe us.'

'Well, I want to go over some things that I told you for the first time in that dirty room at the border, when I was trying to decide whether to go on or turn back. If I can do it for officers, I can do it for my children. You need to know all about why our family and Abdul's family sold everything to send us somewhere safe.' We nodded, and she continued. 'I want you to ask if you don't understand anything.' We nodded again. 'As you know, the fighting in our country's been going on a long, long time. All your lives and a lot of mine. Like all parents, your father and I, and your grandparents, too, wanted to protect you children from the horrors. We tried never to talk in front of you about fighting, or killing, or bad men who destroyed our country.'

As she talked I tried to listen, but the picture in my head got in the way. I was back in our big, old mud-brick house where we lived with my uncle (Dad's brother), aunt and cousins and our other grandparents, Arjay and Bahkhul. They're Dad's mum and dad – or were; we don't know what's happened to them. Hazaras lived and worked in family groups, with the father's family.

When it was warm enough the women cooked at the back of our house, and we all sat around the open fire to eat. Afterwards we drank spicy tea, and played clapping games so the little ones could join in. Sometimes our faces got so black from smoke that at night we could only see each other's eyes and teeth glistening in the fire's glow.

When I was little, before the really, really bad times, Mum sometimes took us to the other side of the village to see her parents, Arjay Aqila and Bahkhul Abdul. On our spring visit we'd pull carrots from their garden – when they still had it – and chomp tender, young ones while we climbed sweet-smelling almond trees. Almonds were the first flowers to bloom after early spring sun melted winter snow, and skeleton trees grew soft cloaks of pink or green – almost overnight it seemed.

I tuned in again to Mum's voice, '. . . always fighting near us in the mountains and our villages. I can't remember a time when explosions and gun shots didn't frighten us, and we've always had to watch out for landmines.'

As she continued, I drifted back to a few days before we left Afghanistan . . .

We sit around the fire with our breakfast cups of steaming cardamom tea. Bahkhul joins us. He looks to where our vegetable garden used to be and spits, 'Those bartong, asinine stards . . .' We giggle. Even the little ones know what he means though he pretends not to swear in front of us. 'That useless-looking ground used to grow good food. Now look at it!' Our heads swivel to look at three tree stumps sticking out of the dry, uneven soil. Stony remains of a cubby-house lie beside the end one.

'Nessa, you and Zubidah, take little Zahra to wash our breakfast things in the river. She's old enough to learn, aren't you, Zahra?'

'Yes, Bahkhul. I growed up.'

'Good. And, Zainullah, go with them and look after your sisters and cousin.'

I see Zainullah swell with pride as he says, 'Yes, Bahkhul. I'm good as Hassan, aren't I?' Five days earlier Mum sent Hassan to Arjay Aqila's house at the other end of our village to hide in the secret room, so the Terror can't find him.

Mum nods to me. We collect the dirty dishes, piling them onto two large trays.

'Now, get behind me. I'm leader,' Zainullah orders, making the most of Hassan's absence. Zubidah and I each hoist a tray onto our heads and follow Zainullah, Zahra brings up the rear. We take a few steps and I hear the grown-ups' voices but I don't want to know what

they say. Zahra skips, singing to herself, 'I'm big now, I'm big now, I'm big now . . .'

When I was little older than Zahra is Mum showed me how to squat at the edge of the river and wash the dishes we eat from. Now, my oldest cousin Zubidah's and my first chore every day is washing up. Zahra often comes, too, and plays with Zainullah, or watches and plagues us with questions. This is the first time she's allowed to help. I must teach her how to clean off tea and gravy stains with fine sand, and rinse the cups and dishes until they sparkle.

As we cross the common land, slushy in patches from the last of the thawing snow, Zahra dances behind us. Suddenly Zainullah shouts, 'Freeze!' We do. Even Zahra dares not move.

I hiss, 'Stay where you are. I'll whistle.' A long, piercing note shrills out, then a short one, and another long, shrill whistle. Then silence. Immediately we hear an answering signal.

'Phew.' I sigh. 'Well spotted, Zainullah. Don't move. Just tell me. Where is it?'

'Over there. Look on that bare bit of ground. Next to the cow pat.' He points in front of him, a bit to the right. We see the tell-tale mound. Something's protruding from the mud at its top.

'I see it! I see it!' Zahra's triumphant shout betrays the fact she has no idea of the danger threatening us.

'Good girl. Now, be still and just watch it so you can point it out to Uncle when he gets here.' I try to calm her. This is the last thing we need when she's already hyper.

'I'm look-ing, I'm look-ing . . .' Zahra's chant tails off into a squeal as she overbalances and falls limply, giggling at my feet. Holding our breath, we silently count the seconds: one – two – three – four – five. Nothing. A simultaneous 'phew' signals our relief.

'Oh, Zahra.' I can't be cross. I'm so grateful we're still alive. 'Stay where you are so you can't fall again.'

'I stand up, Nessie?'

'No!' We all shout.

We're always told to look out for landmines. We're never allowed to go into the mountains without a grown-up. We have to be extra careful when we go near the grazing lands and where the men grow crops. They can't grow many now as no one knows what land is mined. But since a mine exploded near our homes all village children have learned to follow this drill whenever we see a mine. We treat each as if it is live. 'Live' seems to me a weird word for something that's built to kill. Even Zahra knows not to move until whoever comes to dismantle the mine says it's okay. But she doesn't understand why. None of us really understood – until we witnessed the explosion.

'We'll never see Hassan's friend again,' I had explained to Zahra. 'A landmine killed him.'

'Oh,' Zahra said thoughtfully. A bit later she asked, 'Him not like Hassan?'

I tried again, 'It's not that he doesn't like Hassan, Zahra. He's not here any more.'

'Where him go?'

'He's dead.'

'Why?'

'Because the mine killed him.'

'But he come back? Like Daddy. From mountains.'

'No, he won't!' Sometimes her questions drove me mad. 'He was blown into little pieces.' I was sorry I said it as soon as it came out of my mouth.

Zahra had just looked at me, wide-eyed. 'Oh.' She said nothing more then, but later I saw her sitting cross-legged by herself near the fire, elbows resting on her knees, hands clasped with her chin resting on them. Until then the only close family death Zahra had experienced was Bakhhul Abdul's, and who knew what she really made of it? Later, *when Arjay Aqila took her to his burial mound and talked about the grandfather she'd hardly known, she asked, 'Is Bahkhul Abdul there?'*

Arjay Aqila told her gently, 'Yes, what's left of his body.'

'Oh.'

Then, a few weeks after this conversation, Zahra was helping Hassan pull carrots from the soil for dinner. 'Remember when we planted seeds?' he asked her. She nodded. 'Well, they grew into these carrots.'

'Oh.' Zahra's brow furrowed and she seemed to be working out something. Finally, with perfect logic, she asked, 'Will Bahkhul Abdul grew into carrots?'

Now, looking at Zahra lying at my feet, I try to speak gently but firmly, like Mum. 'Zahra, you know how still you must be. Stay where you are. Close your eyes and see how far you can count.'

It seems we stand for hours, even after Uncle, wearing special clothes, arrives with his tools and dismantles the mine. We do nothing to disturb his concentration. It's the difference between life and death.

Motionless, Zubidah and I retell favourite stories to take our minds off how heavy the dishes have grown. Finally Uncle announces, 'Well done. It's safe to move now.'

Gratefully lowering our trays, we rest them on the ground and stretch our aching arms. I realise Zahra's unusually quiet. I turn to find her in the best position to wait out a mine scare – sound asleep.

'Gulnessa, are you listening? I'm talking to you as well as Hassan. It's important.' Mum's face reflected her annoyance.

'I am. I am.'

Mum continued. 'When the Terror started destroying our crops of wheat, and rice, and melons, and other food and animals, or stealing them, things got worse and worse. It became impossible to find enough food for us all. And even worse than that, what the Terror does to *people* makes life hopeless. Although we're all Muslims, because our ways of praying are different from theirs, they try to stop us doing what we've done for generations. They try to stop us praying on our mats to Mohammed. They try to make Hazara men grow beards to look like them. They say everything scientific is bad and want us to learn only their fundamentalist, religious habits and superstitious ways. They try to take *our* boys and force them to train as *their* soldiers. The Terror wants *everyone* to join them. If we refuse, they do *anything* to try to make us. Or get rid of us.

'Of course, that's why Abdul's with us. Since the Terror killed his dad, Abdul's family needs him more than ever, but they know if he'd stayed with them, he, like you, Hassan, would be killed because you won't go with the Terror.'

Mum's voice sounded so sad that I thought she was going to cry again. Instead, she closed her eyes for a few seconds, swallowed deeply and continued in the same tone. 'As for us women, the Terror wants us to be invisible, to stay out of the way. They want us only to have babies and to look after our homes. They try to make us wear burkahs, to cover everything but our eyes whenever we go outside. We can't decide anything ourselves. You know they won't let girls be educated. Or get jobs to help earn money for families to live on.

'And the only schools allowed for boys are the Terror's, where they teach boys *their* ways. They'll execute anyone found with books other than theirs. They search to find banned items, and torture people to get them to betray families and friends. They allow no social activities, no recorded music or pictures, no photographs of any living being. Anyone who disobeys can have their hands or feet cut off, or even be publicly executed.'

My head felt like it would burst, the drumming in my ears was so loud.

'The Terror tries to control everyone, by fear. Their gunmen raid houses with no warning, smash them up, and abduct or kill victims. Anyone they hear rumours about, or don't like. Just as they did to your dad. Day or night, no one's safe.'

I shut my eyes, but quickly opened them again, trying to wipe out the vivid image of that terrible night.

Mum's voice trembled as she went on, 'And you know they don't think twice before killing. Look how they made us watch what they did to Abdul's father. Even children.'

I tried to blink away the . . . creeping red halo.

'It happens for something as small as not handing over to them all the food you have. They torture and whip people to make them obey their rules. If they find anyone leaving the country, they kill them . . . The point is they take away our people's lives. One way or another. Either you do what they tell you and give your life to them, or they kill you.'

Mum stopped, closing her eyes. We watched her, stunned. When she spoke again her voice was so soft we had to lean in to hear her words. 'We can't live our own lives there. No future . . . The Terror has destroyed everything we value, but they *won't* destroy our spirit . . .' Mum's voice trailed away.

We'd lived in the middle of what Mum described but had tried not to see what was happening around us. I'd wanted to believe that everything would be all right. Mum's words made me realise what our parents must have known, and fought against, long before we escaped: the Terror made it impossible for them to protect and care for us at home. The horrors were real and present. Threatening our lives. I wanted to throw up.

'The Terror also started taking young girls from their families. They use them, brainwash them, and prevent them from *ever* going back to their villages.' The anger in Mum's voice startled me. I clenched my teeth, holding down the bile.

'They kill our boys if they don't fight with them. And our boys'll be killed if they do.'

I bolted for the plastic bucket–rubbish bin, which doubled as a potty for the Zs during the night – and threw up. Then, weak and trying to swallow away the horrible taste in my mouth, I crawled back next to Mum, trying to stop my body's trembling.

'Go on.' She put her arm around me.

'Well, only because you need to be clear about this. Your dad and I weren't going to let the Terror take any of you away, so he began to organise men who were prepared to fight the Terror. A resistance group. They came from our village and others nearby. Abdul's dad was one of them. The Terror had spies everywhere and they heard about it, so they began to hunt down and kill everyone they suspected of belonging to the resistance.'

Hassan and I scarcely breathed. So that was where he'd gone when he was away for days. Dad's face floated before my eyes, smiling gently, his dark, dancing eyes glowing with love. Pain stabbed my chest. I missed his hugs, the games we'd shared, his deep, gentle voice, and his strong, reassuring presence . . .

'After the Terror killed Abdul's father I asked Bahkhul when they'd stop killing Hazaras. Bahkhul couldn't answer. Finally he told me they wanted to get rid of us *all*. Even before the Terror took over, the people in power had said, "Hazaras only belong in the graveyard."' Mum put her face in her hands.

After a minute she looked up. 'I remember clearly his next words. He said them slowly as if he had to force out each one: "There is so much hate for our people that our families are no longer safe in this country. There is no future here for us."

'We cried together. We talked about your father. Then he told me I must take you children away but he'd stay, to be there if

65

Ali returned. He wanted Uncle's family to go, too, but Uncle said Ali was his brother and he wouldn't go until he'd done all he could to find him. The last thing Bahkhul said to me was, "I'll always love you. You are the most precious treasures in my heart. *No one* can take that away. Be strong. You *must* do this." My heart knows we did the right thing. Do you understand?' Her voice died away.

'I-I think so. Mostly,' I managed to get out, still struggling to take it all in. Hassan just nodded. I had to ask the question I'd tried not to think about ever since we left home. 'Mum, will we see Bahkhul again? Or our Arjays? Or our cousins and friends?'

'I don't know, Gulnessa.' Mum took a deep breath. 'Uncle and Bahkhul will try to raise money for Uncle's family to escape. They will sell the family house. Bahkhul and Arjay have given up *everything* to help us. Arjay Aqila, too. She sold everything to pay the agent for us. They say they've had their lives and want to give us ours.' Tears now ran down Mum's cheeks, but she sat straight and proud. 'My dearest hope is that they'll get enough money to help them all escape. Then they'll try to find us, but they don't even know which country the agent sent us to.

'If they come, I don't want them to be imprisoned here, like us. It would kill Arjay Aqila. She's so old and frail.' Then Mum's face brightened a bit. 'When we're moved to the other compound we might meet friends there who disappeared before we left home. Though for their sakes I hope they have freedom by now.' In spite of her effort to sound hopeful, I could tell she was as anxious as I felt.

Other things still puzzled me. 'Mum, why couldn't we say goodbye to anyone before we left? If they don't know where we are, how can they look for us?' Mum must've faced these fears the night we left. How could she have been so strong knowing it might be the last time she'd see her own mother?

'We couldn't tell *anyone*. If the Terror tried to get information from people at home, it would be easier for them *not* to know what happened to us than to try to *pretend* they didn't. Bahkhul and Uncle are the only ones who know. It was Uncle who sold the family's belongings and Bahkhul who found and paid the agent. All the others really know is that one day when they got up, we weren't there.' She paused, then shrugged. 'Who knows how they might find us? That's one of the reasons we pray.'

CHAPTER 7

In spite of boredom in the Camp and not knowing when we'd be released, we still had a sense of relief to be free of the fighting and abuse we'd always known. We wanted to believe there was hope for our future, in this land. We talked endlessly, about the medical checks and Immigration interviews, swapping descriptions and comparing experiences. We looked forward to finishing the business keeping us in this compound. And we talked about being free.

Looking out the common room window one day, I waited for exercise time and the chance to go to my sanctuary. A hand tugged at my sleeve. Zahra asked, 'Nessie, can I see, too?'

'There's nothing there, darling,' I replied.

At that moment the siren signalling exercise time blasted out. Zahra's face screwed up and her hands flew to cover her ears. I think that was when I first realised sirens were not simply a signal, but were designed to startle people, put them on edge. A way to control people.

There were other things which rang alarm bells, too. Once I overheard Asad telling Abdul and Mum that he'd managed to talk through the fence to men in the other compound's exercise

68

yard. He said it was hard as they had to keep walking because guards were watching them, too. But they managed to tell Asad that the real reason we were kept away was so people in their compound couldn't help with our interviews, or tell us what would happen afterwards.

Asad always seemed thoughtful, and calm. Strong. He never showed the sadness he must have felt after his baby's death. I thought of it often.

The day after the big storm Asad is standing on the roof of the boat's makeshift cabin. 'This is hard for me to say. You've all lost family. You know what it is to feel pain and to grieve. My family has just had another loss.' He pauses, dropping his head. We wait, watching silently until, looking up again, he continues, 'Our son was so young that he had not seen all the seasons of a year.' He stops, looking to the far-off horizon. Watching from below I see him fight back tears. Finally, he speaks once more. 'Our son died last night. He's been sick with fever, and the storm, the fear and the cold were too much. As we cannot bury his body in the soil, we must do it in the sea. It's a tradition of sailors. My family would be honoured if you'd all join us in prayer after I lower him to rest.' He turns, climbs down, and moves towards the front of the boat where his wife and small daughter wait, heads bowed, mourning. People on the crowded deck squash back to let him pass. Not a soul speaks. The engines seem to be drumming a chant: he-e's dead, he-e's dead, he-e's dead . . .

When he reaches his wife, our friend bends and lifts from her arms a cloth bundle not much bigger than a roll of blanket. Around it is tied a rope with one long end dangling. Carefully holding it in front of him in one hand, he holds out the other to his wife. As she reaches towards his outstretched hand I see glinting in the sun a metal shape tied to the end of the rope. As she puts this into her husband's hand the saddest sound I've ever heard spills from her lips. Ceaseless wailing that ebbs and flows as she bares her grief for our hearts to feel, and share.

Asad pauses for only a second before leaning over the deck rail and lowering his burden so far that it's hidden by the side of the boat. After a minute he straightens his back and I see his empty arms. Still facing the ocean, he sinks to his knees. We do the same, heads bowing low to the deck in prayer.

Some of the Camp officers were kind and wanted to help us, but others were cruel. That's what made us call them 'guards'. They hated that. The one Zainullah called Dung-face was an even bigger bully than the rest. He would pick out a victim, yelling abuse at them so the sound of his voice made you cringe. I couldn't understand the words, then.

One day I saw him shoving Hassan away as he tried to enter the toilet block. Dung-face shouted something and pushed Hassan so hard he went flying. Hassan picked himself up and raced towards our donga. As he came in the door I caught him, 'Why wouldn't he let you in?'

'Don't know.' Hassan, looking like he was about to cry, tried to shove me out of his way.

'You must have *some* idea?'

'Haven't.' Hassan growled. 'Leave it, will you? Get out of my way.' I knew my brother too well to push him further, but my anxiety antennae shot up.

'What's up?' Abdul had been watching us.

'Those guards are up to something,' Hassan muttered.

'Keep out of their way, mate. They're bad news,' RSW19 warned. 'If you see those jerks near the toilets, get outta there.'

'Listen to him, Hassan. He knows what he's talking about.'

Abdul looked meaningfully at Hassan as he said this. I made a mental note to ask as soon as I got a chance.

❧ ❧ ❧

A few days later an officer called Hassan's name at breakfast, announcing his interview. Zainullah insisted on going with Hassan to the interview room.

'They'll send him back,' Mum said, 'but I haven't the energy to argue.' I looked at her out of the corner of my eye. This wasn't the mother I knew who'd worked from sun-up to sun-down, never tiring. But she was right.

Zainullah came running back soon after and announced indignantly, '*She* said I was too little! What does she know? I could beat her up.' Since he hung out with Hassan and the men he'd become more macho and more argumentative.

Hassan was gone all day from nine until five fifteen. When he returned, his eyes looked like they had shrunk inside dark hollows. He said nothing, just flopped on his bed.

'Tell me about it?' I'd stayed in our room all day, waiting.

'I'm too tired.' There was no hint of his usual teasing.

'Are you okay?' I was worried to see him like this.

'I'm all right. Just tired. They didn't stop asking questions all day. The same things. Over and over.'

'What d'you mean?'

Slowly he sat up, swung his legs over the side of the bunk, staring straight ahead. 'Well, they asked things like, "Where's your father?" and, "What did the Taliban do?" and, "Why did you leave your country?" and they'd ask those questions over, and over, and over. If I added anything I'd just thought of, they'd say, "Why didn't you tell us that before?" I'd say, "I just remembered it." And they'd raise their eyebrows like they didn't believe me, and say, "Are you sure you aren't making it up?" Things like that. All day.' He put his head in his hands.

'Oh, I'm so sorry, Hassan.' I didn't know what to do to help my usually proud big brother.

He raised his head and looked at me, as serious as I'd ever seen him. 'I'm glad they're going to interview you with Mum there.' Without thinking I put my arm around his shoulders.

'And, it was only after the lunch siren went they let me go to pee and gave me a drink of water. Three and a half hours solid. Just questions. Then they started again as soon as I got back.'

'Did they give you lunch?'

'Nup. I know it's stupid, but on my way over there I remember thinking that one good thing about going was that I might get something different for lunch. Big joke. Unless you call "nothing" different.'

At that moment the dinner siren sounded.

'Come on. Dinner might taste all right when you're starving.'

'I'm too tired to eat.'

'But you *have* to come. Mum said she'd meet us at the mess. She's worried. You know we can't bring food back here.'

'Oh, all right.' Hassan pushed himself to his feet and slowly walked towards the door. I was so stunned to see him like this that I didn't know what to do but follow.

That night when I got into bed my head was still whirling with what Hassan had said, and what might happen in my interview – whenever it was. What if I said something different from Mum or Hassan? Would we be sent back? Or put in jail? Already the order of the terrible events in the weeks before we left was blurred in my mind, and I wasn't quite sure if some of the things had happened to us or our neighbours. My nightmares mixed up everything.

It had been the same all my life: gunmen robbing our village, setting houses on fire, crops too; gunfire all around us; and mine explosions; the Terror beating people, stealing food and animals; people disappearing; dead bodies thrown off trucks in the middle of the village to frighten us into obedience . . . And us always ready to run and hide. Like the time my parents and grandparents spirited us off one night to hide in a mountain cave for three days while the Terror looted our village and killed anyone who hadn't got away. When we returned we found our friends' bodies lying around just like we sometimes found lambs and sheep after a pack of wolves attacked. That was when things grew really bad . . .

How could I ever tell everything that had happened to us and around us? And exactly the same way my mother and brother told it? Sometimes we weren't together when things had happened. Would that mean the officials wouldn't believe us?

I tossed and turned, trying to shake off thoughts tormenting my brain. Every night something kept me awake. Sometimes a conversation during the day triggered memories. Often dreams lay in wait to ambush my sleep, and when they woke me I'd lie in the darkness trying to unscramble events in them, or struggling to get the real events out of my mind.

I must have disturbed Zahra, as she whimpered in her sleep. I cuddled her to me.

'Nessie, they were going to get me.'

'Darling, you were dreaming,' I whispered. It was better not to ask her about her dreams. That would wake her completely. 'It's only us here. You and me, snuggling in bed.'

'Not men with guns?' She peered over our blankets. A muffled bang from a nearby room made her jump.

'See. That's a locker door,' I said quickly. 'It's probably Yasmine's dad going to bed.' Soon her breathing became regular again. How

73

does she do it? I wondered, as I lay on my back gazing sightlessly at the bottom of the bunk above us. I closed my eyes, willing myself back to our lighthouse night. Tonight it was elusive.

The door of our room closed and I heard whispers as Abdul and Hassan got ready for bed. Not wanting to disturb Zahra again, I didn't speak, but carefully rolled onto my side, untwining myself from her clinging arms and legs, and willing sleep to rescue me. If only I could quiet my mind.

At the back of our house I help Mum pour water from pitchers she's filled at the well. Zainullah and I carry jugs and kettles of water into the kitchen. Zahra tries to help. Hassan arrives, arms full of firewood. Sudden yelling from in front of our group of houses makes us drop everything and race to see what's happening.

First to the corner, Hassan brakes sharply, throwing out his arms to stop us. Bearded men in dark clothes and turbans, guns slung over their backs, spill from an army truck. Their feet hit the ground running towards us, guns pointed, shouting over and over, 'Out, pig!' They want my father. Thank goodness he's in the mountains with the other men, I think.

Hassan, standing firm, calls, 'He's not here . . .'

Mum pushes past Hassan and stands in front of us. 'I've good food. Do you want it?' For months the Terror has demanded food. Sometimes they leave only grass for us to eat.

Ignoring my mother, a rough voice demands, 'Where is he? Where's your father?' Its owner's face a mask of hatred, with jet eyes glinting above a black thicket that obscures most of it, drilling into Hassan's brown eyes. The gunman pushes my mother aside with his weapon, poking it menacingly into Hassan's chest.

'I – I don't know.' Although Hassan tries to sound brave, I know how he feels. We all know fear . . .

'Well, if your father's not here, we'll take you. Soon. You're almost

big enough. We'll be back. When you fight for us you'll tell us where they are.' The gun flicks upwards, striking Hassan's chin with such force that his teeth crash together. The men march to our neighbour's door and beat on it. It opens. Arms reach inside. They drag out a man. Abdul's father. He works on the farm, with Dad. I can't watch.

The gunmen shout, 'Where are they? Where are they?'

Shaking violently, I clutch Mum and the two Zs. Hassan stands in front of us. Two fighters tear us apart, forcing our heads up. Others drag families in nearby houses into the open. And our neighbours Abdul, his mother and three sisters.

'Watch!' orders the man who threatened Hassan. 'If you don't do what you're told, this will happen to you. All of you. You're next.' He jerks his gun at Abdul.

Fighting to control my shaking, I peer through my fingers. Mum pushes the two Zs' faces into her skirt, her face an ashen mask. Hassan is an ice sculpture. I squeeze my eyes shut. Gun shots blast out. Not in the distance, next to us. My ears! Loud ringing – then nothing. Am I deaf? I force my eyes open. Silence. Terrible silence. I see steaming puddles melting the snow under my little brother's and sister's feet. They don't move. Heads buried in folds of Mum's dress. Mum and Hassan don't move either, their eyes frozen wide with fear. Mum's head swings round to me. I hear her voice, raspy, strange. 'Don't look. Keep your eyes on the ground.' Too late. I am looking.

There, not ten metres away, lies a still form wearing the familiar coat of our friend, Abdul's father. A spreading, red halo circles his head. Fear lurches from my belly. I throw up. An arm hugs me. I hear Hassan's voice, 'Don't look. Try not to think . . .' He, too, throws up. And my mother. We stand there, a shaking huddle of bodies, sobbing. A huddle repeated for each household.

An engine roars. No one looks up. No one speaks.

CHAPTER 8

The next morning I badly needed space but Mum said she wanted to rest instead of coming out for exercise hour. Luckily, the two Zs ran off to play 'Hidey' with Yasmine and Rashid, so I escaped to my sanctuary.

Sitting cross-legged in the sun, growing warmer again every day, a stray thought flicked through my mind. If that was winter, what's summer like here? I stared at the stunted khaki bushes dotting flat, red landscape reaching out until it met a dome of everlasting blue. The softening blue where sky met land fascinated me and I never tired of tracing the curve of the dome, absorbing the deepening colour until I drowned in its depth at the apex. Then, peace flooded through me.

After a few minutes sitting with my eyes closed concentrating on blocking out all sound I scanned the ground for a movement that might point to some kind of wildlife. I'd started to keep a mental list of ants, insects, spiders and lizards I'd seen. Watching these creatures gave me a small sense of freedom as I struggled with growing frustration and despair about our situation. A sun lizard darted from under the fence near my knee, pausing to look around before dashing across the uneven, cleared strip of ground outside, which doubled as a road for the few vehicles which made their way to this godforsaken place. The lizard disappeared over the ridge of red dirt at the far side of the road, and appeared again in the meagre shade of a wispy clump of long, slender leaves. It paused again. A set of strangely regular semi-circular patterns under the plant, etched in the dry sand, caught my attention. What made such curious marks? Studying the area nearby I made out other markings, and more scattered as far as I could see that amount of detail.

Quite suddenly I glimpsed a faint movement from the leaves and I watched intently as they swayed in a faint breeze. A stronger gust announced the wind's arrival and the leaves bowed gracefully towards the earth as if acknowledging a great presence. Wherever their tips touched the ground, as they moved back and forth, they drew in the fine, dry sand delicate semi-circles. Longer leaves seemed to guard shorter ones which swayed under their cover, etching parallel lines inside those of their guardians. Nature's artists at work!

'Hey, Nessa! What're you staring at?' Abdul's voice startled me. After our talk a few weeks ago, I'd thought about it hard before suggesting my sanctuary as a place we could meet to talk privately. He could join me during one exercise period each day but the other I'd have to myself. He was never to come without letting me know, and I'd made him promise not to tell anyone.

'You gave me a fright!' I pretended to be annoyed but couldn't keep it up. 'Look at this.' My discovery had, for the moment, driven everything else from my mind and I'd forgotten signalling him at breakfast. We'd decided it was easier to signal each other than to speak without someone hearing. If anyone in the family heard they'd want to come too, or at least know what was going on. So we hit upon a brilliant signal: cordials. Everyone drank them with meals so we wouldn't attract attention by doing anything unusual, and we simply used their colours as a code: green for a definite 'yes, I want to talk next exercise break, and yes, I can make it'; red for 'no, I can't next break'; and orange for 'I'm available but there's nothing special I want to talk to you about'.

Abdul squatted next to me, an arm draped casually over my shoulders. 'What am I supposed to be looking at?'

'Look, have you ever seen those swirls before?' I pointed. 'See . . .' I finished explaining and we watched in silence. The breeze was quite stiff now. The leaves blew rhythmically, etching their patterns clearly in the sand.

After a few minutes Abdul's arm tightened around my shoulders and he said, 'Nessa, you see so much that other people don't. I've never noticed those and I've sat for hours, looking out the windows through the fence and across the landscape, wishing . . . and wondering what's going to happen to us.'

'This is the first time I've noticed them,' I said quickly, not wanting Abdul to think I was weird. 'When your mind's on something, you don't notice other things going on around you.'

'I've never thought about why you might see things, or not see them. What you say makes sense. And you *are* observant. Most people wouldn't notice those marks, and even if they did they'd think nothing of it.'

I wriggled uncomfortably. I never knew how to accept a compliment – especially one from Abdul. I quickly changed tack. 'I was awake most of last night. I know that's nothing new, but what kept me awake was.' Abdul raised his eyebrows, looking at me seriously as he settled himself cross-legged facing me. I asked, 'Did Hassan talk to you about his interview yesterday?'

'Not really. I guess he thought I'd know what it was like. I've been through three so far. They don't get easier. He didn't join us for cards last night but he seems okay this morning.'

'Well, he didn't want to talk to me when he got back either, but I kept asking him things and he told me enough to make me worry all night.' I didn't want to mention my dream about Abdul's dad.

'What did he say? The officers make you feel awful, but they won't hurt you.'

'It's not that. I'm not *scared* of them. But what if they don't believe us?'

'The way I see it is, if you all tell about an event, even if it's in a different order, it shows you all know it happened.'

'Maybe, but what about when one of us wasn't there? Like when the Terror took away Dad. Hassan wasn't there – neither were you, Abdul, because after they . . .' I clapped my hand over my mouth. He must know I'd nearly said, 'killed your dad'.

'It's all right. We have to talk about it some time. Go on.'

'Well, after the Terror killed your dad, and your mum sent you to stay with your cousins, Mum sent Hassan to Arjay Aqila's hideout. So when Dad came back from the mountains neither of you was there. Dad wouldn't leave again as we had no men to protect us. Anyway, a spy must have told the Terror about Dad's return, because they came and got him a few days later, and only Mum and I saw them.'

'Yes, I understand all that.' Abdul's voice was gentle. He leaned towards me and took my hand. 'You must tell the officers just like that – and tell them the rest, too.'

'But they mightn't believe me if you and Hassan can't tell them, too.'

'Nessie, there's a perfectly good reason why we can't tell them and I think even they'll see that.'

'Mmm. There's something else I've been wanting to ask you,

Abdul. What did you mean last week about those guards near the toilets?'

'I was hoping you wouldn't ask that.'

'Why?'

'Because I don't know how to tell you.'

'Just say it.'

'Well, those two guards cornered some young guys who went into the toilets and hurt them. They watch out for someone young who's alone and then one of them stands outside while the other does his dirty work. They don't do it if there's more than one of us so we never go alone.'

I didn't need to know any more. 'That's as bad as at home.'

'It's bad, but at least they won't kill you.'

'I *hate* it in here! You can't get away from pigs like that.'

'I know. But it won't be for much longer – I hope.'

We sat in silence watching the wind making sand-swirls in the dust on the road. On the other side, stray, dry tufts of spiky grass tumbled over and over themselves in an endless row of somersaults blown into the distance until I could no longer see them. My gaze returned to the hateful fence imprisoning us from life. What if we dug under it? No one could see us if we started here . . .

Then I saw it! I grabbed Abdul's arm and pointed to a metre-long, dark greyish-green, smooth, pole-like body lying inside the wire, barely three metres from where we sat. Fascinated, we watched as it began to move and slowly glide along the fence away from us. Then, increasing speed, it turned, body constricting to fit through a hole in the fence, and rippled rhythmically across the road.

'Phew,' I gasped. 'Hassan told me there were snakes here but that's the first one I've seen. Wasn't that the most beautiful thing?

I mean, I'm scared of them because of the stories, but I didn't know snakes were beautiful. I'm glad you were here.'

'Me, too. Our talks mean a lot to me, Ness.'

'Me, too.' Why was it so hard to say what I felt? To tell Abdul that meeting him made me stronger to cope with our prison and its boredom. Helped me remain sane and keep my temper. Helped me look after the two Zs and watch out for Mum. All I could get out was, 'It's something to look forward to in this hole.'

'There's the lunch siren. We'd better go.' Standing up, Abdul took my hand, squeezed it and raised it to his lips. I tried to control the shaking that was a dead giveaway that I felt anything but calm inside.

CHAPTER 9

The following week when my name was called for an interview, Mum came with me to the small, almost bare room. Yasmine's mum had offered to look after the two Zs. In the room was a table, with the Immigration officer and lawyer sitting on one side and the interpreter at the end near the lawyer. *One* empty chair stood opposite. My stomach sank.

As we stood holding hands in the doorway, the interpreter rose and said,' Only AXZ23 can come in.'

'But they said we'd be interviewed together,' Mum replied.

'It must have been a mistake. Sorry, you must leave.'

'She's only a young girl. Twelve years. Can't I stay?' For once I was glad of Mum's protectiveness.

'No. I'm sorry, it's the rules. You must go. She'll be okay.' The interpreter looked genuinely sorry.

I turned to Mum. 'Don't worry, I'm okay.' I didn't feel okay. Mum bent and kissed my forehead. I squeezed her hand and tears filled her eyes. My strong mother.

The interpreter waved her out, shutting the door almost in her face as she stepped backwards. Then the woman guided me to the empty chair. 'We're here to help,' she said. I wanted to believe her but I couldn't. I can't describe the feeling that consumed me. It wasn't terror like when Dad was abducted. It wasn't fear like on the boat in the storm. It wasn't anxiety like I felt most of the time. It was more like a combination of all of them. I knew our family's future might depend on my answers.

The official's voice snapped me to attention. The interpreter spoke. 'AXZ23, where do you come from?'

'Afghanistan.'

'What part?'

'Qaryah Kandaloo in the Bamiyan province.' The name we called our group of houses, too small even for its own market-place, meant 'village at the foot of a mountain'. The families living there were all farmers.

As the interpreter spoke with the official and lawyer I sat tense, watching their faces.

She turned to me again, 'Why did you leave your village?'

'Because the Terror took away my father and they said they'd be back for my brother. They did lots of other terrible things, too.'

'Tell us how they took your father.'

I had been dreading this but I knew it'd come. I steeled myself, closed my eyes and swallowed. 'We were in our living room, Mum, Dad, the two Zs and me.'

The interpreter's voice stopped me. She translated, then asked 'Who are the two Zs?'

'My young brother and sister, Zahra and Zainullah.'

'Go on, please.'

I could picture it as clearly as if it were happening again. 'Suddenly there's loud stamping outside our door. The two Zs squeeze shut their eyes and put their fingers in their ears. We

83

know who it is. I want them to go – anywhere. I saw what they did to other families. Then, the hammering on our door starts. *Bang! Bang! Bang!*

'Mum yells, "All of you, go up to your beds!"

'They bang louder. *Bang! Bang! Bang!* I push Zainullah and Zahra up the steps. *Bang! Bang!* Then there's a crash! I'm on the top step and look down as the broken door swings open. Men in dark clothes lurch in. Lots of them, pointing guns. Dad faces them. Strong. They move forward. Slow motion.

'Mum drags at Dad, screaming, "Ali . . . Ali . . . " He's like a rock. Closer, closer, the gunmen inch. Mum tears at Dad's sleeve. Pleading. "No! Please no! . . . "

'Gunmen grab Dad's arms. A dark streak flies across the room. Smashes into the table leg. Drops to the floor. Lies there. Still, so still. It's my mother. I half slip, half climb down the stairs as they yank Dad out the door. He shouts, struggling to see us, "I love you all. Look after each other 'til I get back. I lo-o-ove yo-o-ou . . . " They're the last words I heard him say.'

My head was bent low as I opened my eyes and peered up at the interpreter. She was looking at me, a sort of stunned expression on her face. I hadn't even noticed her regular translations for the stony-faced officer and lawyer. I breathed in and out, trying to calm my racing heart. The lawyer spoke, the interpreter nodded, then the officer snapped something at her.

She turned to me. 'You have another brother?' I nodded. 'Where was he?'

'Hiding in my grandmother's secret room. A few days before, the Terror shot our neighbour, Abdul's father. They made us watch. They said they'd be back to get Hassan and Abdul so Mum took Hassan to Arjay Aqila's to hide him. Abdul's family went to hide in the next village. That wasn't safe either.' There was so much to explain. I didn't know how much I needed to tell them. The faces staring at me gave me no clue.

The interpreter was speaking to me again, 'You said you saw what the gunmen did to other families. What did you mean? Tell us about them.'

'Well, there was Abdul's dad. And lots of other times. They came to get food. If anyone had none to give them, the Terror pulled them outside and beat them with big sticks. Until they fell to the ground and then they'd kick them and yell at them to get more food before they came back. When I was small and the Terror came the first time, they made us stand outside and watch them take away a man from our village and his two sons. They beat them and held knives at their throats to make them get on the truck. A few days later we heard a truck's engine and hid. As it drove past our houses the Terror threw the sons' dead bodies off the truck. No one saw their father again. They burned houses near us . . .' I stopped, clenching my teeth. It was just as Mum and Hassan had said. Like you were living it again. I stared at my hands. They wrestled each other in my lap like they didn't belong to me. Through a roaring in my ears I could just hear the interpreter's voice.

'AXZ23. AXZ23!' I looked up with a start. Had I missed something? The interpreter asked. 'What did you see the gunmen do to Abdul's father?'

'Drag him from his house and shoot him.'

'Tell us exactly what you saw.'

I tried not to see it in my head as I talked through that terrible day, but it was impossible to shut out the feelings of horror and revulsion that flooded back. As I finished, '. . . and we held each other crying and shaking . . .', I felt tears flowing down my cheeks and held my hands tightly between my knees to cover up their shaking. When I could control them I wiped my eyes on my sleeve. It was all I had. Three blank faces watched me. They must've heard so many other stories like ours that they don't care, I thought. That's okay as long as they know I'm telling the truth.

The questions seemed endless. 'How did you escape?', 'Did you know where the agent was taking you?', 'What did you know?'

When I was asked to describe what happened the morning we left I took a deep breath and began: 'That night is a blur of dozing, waking, sobbing, watching Mum pacing the floor . . . Only the two Zs slept. Then, when it was still dark, I heard a door downstairs close, and footsteps. A sledge hammer pounded in my chest. Mum was up in a flash. "Come on, all of you. Bahkhul's here. No noise now. Shhh." Even Zainullah got up with no fuss and Zahra didn't try her games. Mum's face was grim, her eyes red and swollen. I kept swallowing, trying to hold myself together. Hassan looked like he was doing the same.

'We dressed in a double layer of clothes, and put on our warmest coats. Mum gave us each a bag to put over our shoulders. In them were extra clothes, blankets and food packages she'd prepared. Hassan also carried a pitcher of water.

'When we were loaded up, Bahkhul said, "It's time to leave."

'"I'm not going 'til my dad gets back." Zainullah sat down on the floor. Bahkhul picked him up and Mum picked up Zahra, pushing into her hand a doll Arjay Aqila had made for her.

'"Put your head on my shoulder," Mum coaxed.

'"When will we be coming home, Mum?" I had to ask.

'"I don't know, darling. It all depends . . . " I could see her biting her lip. She looked around, tears welling, but she blinked them back. Hassan and I looked at each other, silently making a pact not to upset her.

'"Pick up the bundles, follow me. Not a word from anyone."
Bahkhul moved towards the door. Mum looked around with a
lingering look. Hassan and I picked up extra blankets that Mum
had tied into tight bundles and stepped out into the half-light
of early dawn. Abdul's silent figure waited in front of the house.
We hadn't seen any of his family since the Terror shot his father.
We nodded to him, but no one spoke. Abdul, too, carried a bag
and large bundle.

'Bahkhul jerked his head and marched towards the outskirts
of the village. I remember wondering why Abdul was with us.

'When the houses were behind us and we were on the dirt
road that passed the village, Bahkhul spoke quietly. "You can put
down your bundles. We wait here."

'Just then a battered, old car rattled down the pot-holey road.
It stopped and a man got out. "You're the last ones for this trip,"
he said, "but I've already got seven passengers. Only ten and me
can fit in. Three of you have to wait for another car. It'll come
soon."

'"No!" Bahkhul looked madder than I'd ever seen him. "I paid
you to take my family. No one's waiting." Mum told me later
that Bahkhul had already paid the man in American dollars he'd
got from selling Dad's truck, our sheep and cows, furniture, and
most of his and Arjay's belongings. He also borrowed money.

'"But," the man started, "you see the problem . . . "

'"I can't see any problem," Bahkhul interrupted, holding out
a fistful of money.

'"Ahhh, I'm sure we can do something. Two of them are only
small, after all," he sleazed, pocketing Bahkhul's offering.

'The driver stuck his arm in the car and flipped open its boot.
Three men got out and climbed into the boot. The driver packed
bundles around them, wedged open the lid, then tied it with rope.

'We piled into the car, all six of us in the back. The other four passengers crowded into the front with the driver. As we moved off the driver said, "You must be silent. Any noise will put us in danger."'

I stopped, my throat dry. The interpreter was still translating. I swallowed hard to moisten my throat and wondered if the interpreter got it right. That worried me, too.

She turned and said to me, 'Tell us about your journey after that.'

'I can't remember much about the car journey . . . except it seemed to go on forever. We were so squashed we could hardly move, and everyone was quiet. Even when the driver ordered the little kids to get on the floor and the rest of us to cover ourselves with blankets. We could hear gunfire.

'Once or twice he stopped to let us pee, and to quickly eat our food. We could hardly see out of the car's darkened windows but I know we drove all day and long after dark. We dozed on and off until we stopped and tumbled out of the car to sleep a bit more, huddling together against its warm metal body to keep out the cold wind.

'It was still dark when a new driver arrived to take over. He brought more food but only enough for six people. It didn't matter. No one felt hungry.

'"Where are you taking us?" Abdul asked him.

'"To meet a man who is getting you out to safety."

'"Where?"

'"At the border. That's all they tell me. Now, everyone in the car. We have to be driving before daylight."

'We piled into our places and set off. Another day of the same. Dust, bumps, cramps – and worrying.'

The interpreter signalled me to stop. I wondered how much more they'd want to hear. Then the interpreter turned to me and said, 'Tell us about the next part. And when you knew you were coming to Australia.'

I began again. 'At dusk we rattled to a halt and the driver said, "Everyone out. Collect your things. Stay next to the car. I'll be back." Out we spilled. Uncrumpling ourselves, stretching our limbs and rubbing each other's backs. Then, picking up our belongings, we looked around.

'People milled as far as I could see. Every so often shouts pierced a continuous humming noise, which I realised was zillions of voices. In the half-light, the restless crowd and hovering dust cloud seemed to swallow us. I sidled closer to Mum, who gathered us all to her.

'"Stay close together."

'I've no idea how long we stood like that. Not speaking. Scarcely moving as the crowd jostled and murmured around us. My eyes examined one dusky figure after the other as I searched faces of strangers to see if by some miracle Dad was amongst them. That's how I kept from crying with fear.

'Suddenly a figure stopped next to Abdul and said something. Abdul nodded. Then the man looked at us, jerked his head and spoke louder. "Follow me. Obey everything I say. Immediately."

'"Hold on tightly." Mum's voice shook. We unwound into a silent line and the others from the car followed us closely. We snaked through the dusty crowd and past makeshift tents, hundreds of them. We walked like this for fifteen minutes or so before our guide paused at what looked like a sort of checkpoint. He showed papers to official-looking men sitting at crowded tables. They glanced up disinterestedly, and waved us on.

'I grew more anxious as we threaded through more crowds, tents and an occasional run-down building. My legs would hardly keep going they shook so much. At last the man stopped in front of one of the dirty, sprawling buildings. He turned to Abdul, gesturing towards a door. "This is your room. Don't talk to *anyone*. Don't come out. I'll be back."

'Abdul turned to Mum. "I'll check inside." He opened the door just enough to stick his head inside. Then, pulling back, he said, "It's okay. There are carpets and rugs." Mum nodded, and in we went.

'The room was dusty and practically bare. The carpets were threadbare. Dirty-looking blankets lay on them. In one corner was a large tin bucket and a cracked water pitcher. Mum kicked away the blankets and turned to us. "Hassan and Abdul, you and Gulnessa must help me shake the carpets." I expected Hassan to refuse, complaining that it was women's work, but he said nothing so I knew how scared he must be.

'We were still getting ready for the night when a loud pounding at the door made me jump. Mum gestured at us to remain where we were and moved to the door. Abdul grabbed her arm and opened the door slightly, peering out. Then he indicated to Mum she could go outside.

'Hassan put his arm around Zainullah's shoulders. I cuddled Zahra. Abdul stood beside the closed door, ready to jump to Mum's aid.

'We could hear a man's voice. "Here are papers you must keep until you arrive where you're going." It was the man who'd brought us to the room.

'"Where are you taking us? What sort of papers?" My mother couldn't read them as she'd never been to school.

'"These papers will get your family into another country."

'"We're not going to another country. We just want to live in peace." I heard Mum's voice quaver. "I only want to find my husband and take my children where it is safe. Not to another country."

'"You'll have to find your own way then. I can't take you." The voice was matter of fact.

'"Why not? You've been paid to."

'"Not to stay in Afghanistan. Nowhere here's safe for Hazaras. I've other families to escort, too. If you don't come with me, you're on your own."

'"*Where* are you taking us?"

'"Can't tell, yet. Have to see. I'll be back in the morning. You can tell me what you want to do then." We heard his footsteps fading.'

'Mum came in and we sat down to talk. She told us all she knew about why we had to leave home, and about our choices. Then I saw her shoulders set, and her strength seemed to return. "Afghanistan is our home, but if we're not safe, it can't be a real home. We must keep hoping that Ali, and your family, Abdul, *will* find us. And when they do, we'll be living in peace and safety. Yes, our only hope is to go. Do you all agree?" Abdul, Hassan and I nodded. The two Zs were asleep.

'Loud banging woke me the next morning. Mum was already up. As she opened the door and stepped outside, daylight flooded in and I caught a glimpse of the agent.

'"We're coming." Mum's voice was calm and strong.

'"I'll be back tonight. I'll tell you where we're going then. Don't leave this room until I come. Talk to *no one* outside. Here's food and water."

'Refreshed after our night's sleep, Mum, Abdul, Hassan and I shared some of the soft cheese and bread the agent had left for us. We put aside the two Zs' share until they woke. There was nothing to do in the room and we couldn't even leave to go to the toilet – the bucket had to do. Most of the time Mum prayed, and stared at the wall. Hassan, Abdul and I played knucklebones.

'At last the little ones woke and ate their food ravenously. It was early afternoon. That day dragged so much.

'When at last it was dark the agent banged on the door, ordering, "Come with me."

'"Just a minute," Mum said. "You said you'd tell us where we were going."

'"All I know is that I have to put you on an aeroplane which takes you to Indonesia. Come with me. Quickly."

'At the word "aeroplane" I felt a surge of excitement.'

I stopped until the interpreter turned to me and said, 'Did you go on the plane to Indonesia?'

'Yes.'

'And who met you when you arrived?'

'A different agent.'

'Did he tell you where he was going to take you?'

'No. We drove in a bus from the airport buildings, through more cars, vans, buses and trucks than I imagined possible. Lanes of traffic whizzed around us in all directions. I'd never seen anything like it. Gradually, the roads narrowed until there was only one lane of traffic each way. It was still heavy but there were fewer cars and more slow-moving vans and open trucks crowded with brown, smiling people like our agent.

'We drove through forests with leafy, green trees like none I'd ever seen. We passed villages of small houses, shelters, outdoor eating-places and food stalls. We passed fields where cows grazed and people worked amongst lush, green plants. It was so different from our country. Our first stop was in a village by a great expanse of water. It spread out as far as I could see.

'"You get out . . . five minutes." For the first time the agent spoke, haltingly but in our language. He pointed to a rough shelter nearby. "Toilets. Stay near bus. I bring food."

92

'Abdul called, "Where are we? Where are you taking us?"

'The agent shrugged as he walked down to where a group of men worked on huge fishing nets. Nearby on the water were fishing boats. I'd never seen boats before.

'Taking Zahra's hand we stepped off the bus for the first time in this strange land. Ever since we'd left home I'd felt I was living some weird dream. What was happening to us made as much sense as dreams did.

'For three more days and nights we drove from one village near the sea to another. The roads, no longer bitumen, often had deep pot-holes and bumps in them like the roads at home. We slept on the bus, getting off only when the agent let us for toilet stops and to eat. Mum seemed to be in her own world and I often saw her crying, silently.

'It was evening on the fourth day when the agent came back to the bus after talking to yet another group of fishermen. We sat in silence. There was nothing left to talk about. No energy left. No hope.

'"I find boat," the agent announced. "We stay here. Soon you get off bus. I take you somewhere to sleep."

'"Why do we need a boat?" Abdul asked him.

'"I tell tomorrow . . . " The noise as he started the engine drowned the agent's voice.

'This town was quite big. We passed lots of street stalls and a packed market square. The bus stopped in front of a long, low building. The driver turned to us. "Out now. You stay hostel. Don't leave rooms. Don't talk. We bring food. I come morning. Understand?" I call that night our lighthouse night.

'Next morning, when we were seated in the bus again, the agent announced, "We leave ten o'clock. I take you boat. Now, go markets. Get food and water for two-day boat trip. Meet bus.

93

Boat go Australia." He jumped off the bus and walked towards the markets. Everyone followed, talking.'

The interpreter stopped me, asking, 'That's the first time you knew you were going to Australia?'

'Yes. I'd never heard of Australia before.'

The interpreter turned to the lawyer and officer and as she finished talking the lunch siren sounded. Turning back to me, she said, 'There's a short break now. You can go to the toilet. Come straight back here, please.' When I returned, a glass of water sat on the table in front of my chair. Even though I'd had a drink at the basin in the toilet, I gulped this down, too.

The rest of the day was the same as the morning. Although it was bad going through our experiences again, the fact that no one showed any feelings about my answers was also hard to cope with. The lawyer and officer stared at me when they weren't writing until they seemed to look through my face right into my brain. I felt intimidated. It was as though they didn't believe a word I said.

The interpreter finally said to me, 'Thank you, AXZ23. You can go now. We'll look at your family's statements and give you our decision in a few weeks.' I pushed myself off my chair but sat down again, my legs unable to take my weight. I don't think the lawyer or officer noticed, they were so deep in discussion. The interpreter reached over and poured me a glass of water from a jug that had appeared after the lunch siren.

Walking across the exercise area back to the donga I felt like I'd dug trenches all day. My head and body ached. I felt sick. I wanted to lie down and sleep. As I stepped into the common room, Mum and the two Zs jumped up and ran to me, hugging me at different heights all at once. I burst into tears.

'Nessie, what's the matter?' Zahra's little voice piped up in unison with Zainullah's.

'It's over, darling,' Mum held me tight. 'It's all right. It's over.' And the dinner siren wailed.

'But, Mum, they said they'd tell us in a few weeks,' I got out through my tears. 'What if I didn't pass?'

'Darling, they say that to everyone. After my first interview I asked Layla about it. Asad found out that no one will know anything until we are released from this compound into the main Camp. Then those accepted as refugees have to wait for visas.' I wanted to ask when we'd go to the main Camp, and what visas were, but I had no strength. I sagged against Mum, face buried in the hollow of her shoulder, and said, 'Mum, I *have* to lie down.'

I heard Hassan's voice, 'Mum, you stay with Ness. Abdul and I'll take the two Zs to the mess.' Even in my state of exhaustion I registered how amazing this offer was from my macho brother.

'Come on, Zahra. Want a horsey-ride?' Abdul's voice was all I heard as Mum steered me to the bedroom.

'We'll join you in a bit,' she called.

Neither of us spoke as she lay me down . . .

Some time later I woke up with a start. 'How long have I been asleep?'

Mum was lying next to me holding my hand. 'I don't know,' she said. 'Your eyes closed the moment you lay down. Hassan and Abdul smuggled out some food for us. I'll check what they're doing.'

I nodded and tried to rub my eyes awake as I slowly sat up. The tribe burst in, Zahra racing over to me and climbing onto my lap. 'Here's Gul, and Aqila.' I'd called my doll Aqila after my much missed grandmother. 'I tell stories. They missed Nessie.'

'Thanks.' I squeezed her round the middle.

'That tickles,' she giggled, squirming.

'Look at what the boys brought us,' Mum said, as Abdul held out two plastic mugs of cordial, a green one for me and an orange one for Mum.

'Thanks,' I smiled at him, nodding my answer to our signal.

'My pleasure,' he replied, with a slight bow. 'The Good Guy was on duty tonight and RSW19 told him the drinks and sandwiches were for the two Zs to eat before bedtime. He said to hide them and to leave when he was checking someone else. He's got kids of his own and he hates to see us locked up here.'

'This is all we could manage under our shirts.' Hassan held out two sandwiches. 'At least it's curried mush tonight,' he added as we took them, gingerly. 'The Good Guy noticed you weren't there when they did the head count and told RSW19 that as long as you're at breakfast he won't say anything.'

'I hope you thanked him for me,' I said, taking the food.

CHAPTER 10

The next day I got to the sanctuary first. As I waited I wondered, as I often did, if ever we got out of this dot on the empty, wide, red land, where we would live. Is it all the same as this? How would we earn money to live on? The land looked so barren. So dry. But I wanted to leave the Camp so desperately. Venturing into the unknown was infinitely preferable to the boredom of this place, and to the uncertainty of our future – any future.

I focused on the far end of the straight road where it disappeared into tiny, shimmering shapes at a spot on the distant horizon. Abdul told me it was a town we passed through before I awoke in the bus. I knew the road led to the gate of this Camp, but I traced its route anyway, slowly, closer and closer to the fence my face pressed against, until I was studying the wheel-ruts that ran along the other side. There, something caught my eye. At first I thought it was no more than a lump of dirt but as I squinted in the bright sun, the lump moved. Only slightly, but I was *sure* it moved. I examined it as best I could through the fence. It had spikes and legs – and a tail. Fixing my eyes on it I willed Abdul to hurry.

It seemed like hours later that I felt the fence vibrating.

Allowing myself a quick glance to confirm it was Abdul, I hissed. 'Quick, look what's here!'

'A-a-amazing.' Abdul was as intrigued as I was. 'It's like a mini prehistoric creature. We've got to find out what it is. RSW19 will know. He knows about everything that crawls around here.'

'How?'

'His geology field trips.'

'Look at it hard so you can describe it to him.'

'It'd be better if he could see for himself. Ness, I know what I promised and I'll stick by it if you want me to, but if you let me bring him here I know he'd keep our secret.'

'Abdul!' I suddenly felt threatened. Our meetings were all that kept me sane.

'Did you hear what I said? It needn't change anything. You'd like him. He's okay.'

'Mum would go crazy if she found out.'

'Any more than if she found out *we* were meeting here?'

'I don't suppose so.' I was always careful how I behaved towards Abdul when everyone was around.

'Well, why not? I trust him completely.' Abdul sounded so keen that my resistance melted, so he went off to fetch RSW19.

Before I had time to work out how we'd all fit in, I felt the wire's vibrations. Abdul came first and stepped over me, before crouching and looking over my shoulder. RSW19 crouched in Abdul's usual spot.

'Hi,' I said, suddenly embarrassed. 'It's there.' I pointed to where it was as still as the ridges of dirt around it.

'I see. What a beauty!' RSW19 peered through the wire. 'It's like a small, rough, red cowpat with a tail sticking out the back.' I grinned, relaxing at the accurate description. 'It's a thorny devil. There are fascinating creatures in this country.'

'I can see how it got its name.' I smiled.

'It's one of a kind and only found in Australia, although his scientific name is after one of the ancient gods in our folktales.'

'Will it bite? Is it poisonous?' Abdul wanted to know.

'Actually, it's totally harmless. It only eats ants. Right now it's sitting in the sun to get warm. It changes colour to blend with its surroundings.'

'Wow!' I was hooked.

'If you get up early and come out here before anyone's around, you'll probably see lots of them. I'm in the end donga and it has a window looking out, across the desert. I've spent a lot of time documenting all the wildlife I see. Early in the morning their colour's quite different. During the night they lose heat and turn dark to help them absorb sun the next day. As they warm up they grow lighter, to reflect the heat. It also blends with the surroundings. Perfect camouflage. If the sun gets too hot they shelter under bushes – preferably across an ant trail. They can eat up to five thousand ants for one meal.'

'Phew, what an appetite!' I tried to visualise what five thousand ants would look like, and failed.

'What did you mean it was called after an ancient god?' Abdul was interested in histories of places and things.

'Its fearsome appearance gave it both its names. The scientific one is *Moloch horridus*. Moloch was a gruesome Middle Eastern god in traditional stories. People sacrificed their children to him.'

'If you see any other creatures, please show me?' I asked.

'Sure. I've seen a few unique things. The best was a frill-necked lizard. I made a mistake before I got to know the Good Guy, and asked another guard about it. Now he always tells me about how many dangerous snakes and lizards are out here.'

'He's joking, right?' I pulled a face. RSW19 shook his head. We watched the little devil intently, but before it moved the lunch siren summoned us.

❦ ❦ ❦

By now the weather had grown hot again during the day and the nights were warmer, too, pleasant. But the warmth had brought out insects in their trillions. Mosquitoes at night, flies by day, and ants and spiders all the time. The interview rate seemed to have increased, too. Mum, Hassan and I were called again, one day after the other, in one week. This time I didn't feel quite as bad as I knew what to expect. It followed exactly the same pattern except there was a different officer. But this woman had exactly the same manner as the last man – stony-faced and severe.

Abdul was called the day after my second interview for his fifth. I'd just returned to our bedroom with my towel after washing before dinner when he came in. He looked terrible. He flopped on his bed, his hand over his eyes.

'Abdul, can I do anything?' I felt stupid saying this, as I knew what his answer would be, but I didn't know how else to tell him I cared. He shook his head.

'Come to dinner. Food might help.'

'Please leave me alone.' His voice sounded like he was fighting back tears. I bent over him and quickly kissed his forehead before sliding out of the room.

As I walked in the throng of people heading for the mess I was back with Abdul in my head. I knew that at each interview he had to go over and over what had happened to his family. He was always down when he returned. He'd lie for hours on his back, staring at the ceiling. He must miss his family so much, but he never complained about it. In fact he'd hardly talked

100

about himself since we'd left the village. I could tell when he was sadder than usual. He wouldn't look at me, or anyone, and his head hung whether he sat or walked . . . Sometimes I'd try to cheer him up, like when I showed him my doll and told him how Zahra helped me, and I saw his eyes glistening with tears.

❧ ❧ ❧

It was in the early hours of the next morning when Zainullah woke us all, shrieking, 'Hold on. You'll drown. Hold on!'

'Wake up!' Mum urged him.

'Hold on, Mummy. Hold the pole tight,' Zainullah's scared, uncertain voice replied.

'It's okay. We're safe in bed,' Mum soothed. 'Really. See, you're dry and so am I. And here's Arjay's rug around you.'

I could hear sniffing, then his little voice said, 'I dreamed we were on the boat and this huge storm nearly drowned us.'

'That's all over. It won't happen again. Close your eyes and cuddle me.' As Mum rocked him back to sleep she crooned the lullaby she'd sung to us all when we were little. '*Lalay lalay, ate-aya . . .*'

I lay staring at the bunk above until I could hear steady breathing, then I whispered, 'Abdul, are you asleep?'

'No.'

I swung my legs over the side of the bed, taking care not to let the cool air in to wake Zahra, and tiptoed over to sit on the floor near Abdul's head. Hassan was fast asleep at the other end, face to the wall and snoring softly.

'What did they do to you today?'

'Same old, same old . . .'

'But you –'

'Something hit me, Ness. No, not someone,' he added as he

101

heard my quick intake of breath. 'The third time I had to repeat how Dad was shot, it hit me, what Dad asked me to do – and I couldn't . . .' He groaned as if in physical pain. 'What *have* I done? I shouldn't be here.' He continued talking, almost in a trance, as he relived his worst day . . .

We're in the kitchen at home. There's yelling out the front of our house. Dad shouts, 'Everyone, get out of sight, and stay there. If they come here, I'll go out. Abdul, you must look after the family if anything happens. Gham nadari, buz bekhar.'

We race to the front window and stand beside it, backs against the wall. Dad and I peer out, holding back the others. Bearded men in dark clothes and turbans, with guns spill from an army truck. Hassan races out between our houses. He brakes and throws out his arms to stop the rest of you. The gunmen run at you, guns pointed, yelling. They want your father. He's in the mountains with the Resistance. But my father's here. He steps towards the door. I drag on him. 'Dad, wait . . .'

He pushes my arms away. 'Stand back, Abdul. I stayed away to protect our people. I must do what I can.' Eyes fixed on the drama outside, he grabs his heavy stick and tenses his body. His other hand rests on the bolt of the door.

The gunman yells at Hassan, then signals to his followers. They run towards our house, guns raised.

Dad says, 'I love you all. Don't ever forget that. Take care of yourselves however you can. Gham nadari, buz bekhar.' With that he turns, raising his staff above his head, and throws open the door. Arms reach inside, roughly grabbing his coat and dragging him out. He crashes his weapon downwards but a gun knocks it from his hand.

'Where are they? Where are they? Talk! Or we'll shoot.'

My father says nothing. Before I realise it my mother pushes past me. I reach out to stop her. She stretches her arms across the doorway holding me back, and my sisters. I throw my arms around her waist so she can't run out. My sisters cling to me. We shake uncontrollably. Two gunmen march up and drag us outside. Others pull families in nearby houses out too.

'Watch!' orders the man who threatened Hassan. 'If you don't do what you're told, this will happen to you. All of you.' He swivels and points his gun at me. 'You're next.'

I squeeze shut my eyes. Gun shots explode. Not in the distance, next to us. My ears! Pain! Silence. Terrible silence. I force my eyes to open. There, not five metres in front of us, lies my father. Circle of blood around his head. Fear lurches from my belly. My mother's violently sick. I hug her and hear my voice, 'Try not to look. Try not to think . . .' then I, too, throw up. My sisters stand in pools of urine and sick. Frozen to the spot, we're a shaking huddle of bodies, sobbing . . .

'. . . *Gham nadari, buz bekhar* were the last words my father spoke. "Don't go looking for trouble." It was his favourite saying. But before that he told me to look after the family, and I'm here. I can't look after them. I should never have left.' Abdul fell silent.

'Abdul, if you'd stayed in our village, that would've been looking for trouble. They said you were *next*. We both heard them.' Abdul didn't answer, so I blundered on. 'The Terror attack *all* Hazaras. They want to get rid of us. But it's a bit safer for a woman and three little girls than for a man they suspect has connections with the Resistance.'

'I should be with them.'

I had to get Abdul out of this destructive mindset. I didn't dare to look at him. 'Abdul, they said they'd kill *you* next. Their informers are everywhere. They'll know that you've left the country. Do you think watching the Terror shoot you, like they shot your dad, would help your family? They might shoot your mum, too. You told me when RSW19's mum tried to stop soldiers taking his brothers, they shot her.' There was no sound but the regular breathing around us. I risked a glance at Abdul and saw tears rolling down his cheeks. I looked away towards Hassan's sleeping form and sat silently, waiting.

After a bit Abdul whispered, 'Okay. A dead man's no use to anyone. Nor a dead mum for my sisters.'

I breathed out soundlessly, and asked, 'Got your brain back again?' We were too near dangerous ground for me to show that I really felt so relieved I wanted to throw my arms around his neck and kiss him.

'You've made your point. Let it go, will you. But thanks. Not knowing gets to me. Not knowing if I should have come, not knowing what's happened to them, not knowing what's going to happen to me, to us . . .'

'Know what you mean.' I laughed weakly. 'I guess it's good I know something.' I struggled to my feet, stiff from sitting in one position for so long. 'Better both try to get some sleep.'

'G'night.'

And as I slipped into bed next to Zahra, I wondered, what did he mean 'to us'?

CHAPTER 11

A few days later at breakfast an Immigration officer and the interpreter appeared with a guard in the mess, and announced, 'We've finished interviewing all of you for the moment and you're to be moved from the reception compound.' For a second there was dead silence, then scattered cheering broke out.

'Thank you for your cooperation. Now, while we process your records, you'll stay in another compound. Camp officers will supervise the move after breakfast.' Process, process, process. That word came up so often but still I didn't understand it.

Asad, the mind-reader, stood up. 'Please tell us what you mean by "process" this time. You have already collected a lot of information about each of us.'

'ID,' barked the guard. It had to be Zainullah's Dung-face, today of all days.

'AXZ1.'

'AXZ1,' the interpreter said, 'yes we collected and recorded your information. The lawyer at your interview will try to help. But first, officers from the Department of Immigration have to take each person's information and check it with other records at their offices.'

'But you have no other records about us. We've just arrived. We've told you everything we can, many times over.'

'No, it's not information you have given, but records from other sources they check against your information. In the past people arrived here and told lies about their reasons for coming and their backgrounds. They also gave false names.'

'Why would people give false names?'

'Well, people try to get into this country when they could stay in their own, or who are criminal. Others want to harm Australia, and Australians. We want to keep them out.'

'Of course. But you can't believe one like that is amongst us?'

'Well, people who have been apprehended came in on tourist or business visas and outstayed them. But orders are to check everyone who enters the country without permission, and this is the way we're told to do it.'

'I see. How long will you take to process records this time? We've been here for five months now.'

'It depends. There's a backlog because we've so many to do.'

'I see. And in the next compound, will we be in the same kind of accommodation?' Asad continued.

'Yes.'

'So, will families occupy dongas together, as they do here?'

'No, that may not be possible. You'll be placed wherever there is space. If you've special reasons to be with someone, let the officers who are supervising know. Now, please return to your rooms, collect your belongings and stay there. The officers'll get you when it's time to move.'

It took the rest of the day to settle everyone into the new compound. Our donga was called 'A', for Antarctica. The others all had continents' names. No more imagination than in the last compound. Everything else about this compound seemed to be the same as the

106

one we'd left, just more people and more dongas. Eighteen, I found out, after Abdul, Hassan and I'd done the rounds. And there were three ablution blocks, six dongas to share each.

Four rooms in our donga were already filled, and Asad's family was to share one of the other rooms with Yasmine's – seven people all together – the six of us were put in the remaining room. It was the same as the one we'd just left except we had a window. There were lots more people sharing this donga, but I couldn't work out exactly how many lived here as the common room was crowded, and most faces I'd never seen before.

The outside of the donga impressed me enormously. Someone had painted it bright green with red window frames. Most of the others were the dreary, familiar reddish-grey. An even better discovery was the garden at one end, full of strange plants with bright red and pink flowers. I knew how Mum had missed our garden after the Terror destroyed it.

Excitedly, I burst into the common room to find Mum, Zahra and Zainullah talking with another family. Grabbing the door, I called, 'Mum, come and see what I found.'

'Oh, there you are, Gulnessa. You come here first, please, and meet Tara and Ali, and their parents.' I looked at Mum hard to see if saying Dad's name had upset her, but no, her eyes were smiling as well as her lips. First time for ages. My stomach had lurched but if Mum could be okay about it, so could I. My discovery would have to wait a bit.

'Hello,' I nodded and grinned as Mum introduced me to each. Tara had great dimples when she smiled back. I instantly liked her. She looked about my age. Fantastic – a friend at last! Ali was exactly the same height as Zainullah, so it looked as though there'd be someone as well as Rashid for him to play with in our donga. I hoped Ali could play knucklebones.

'Now, come with me.' I pulled Mum's hand and led the way outside. The whole troupe followed. As we turned the corner which revealed the garden bed I watched Mum smile. She turned to me. 'It's beautiful. D'you know whose it is?'

'I do.' Tara's father spoke slowly, and I realised that our language did not come naturally to him. He thought about each word before he said it. 'We've been here long time, Fatimeh. We try to make things good. We paint. We make garden. My wife, Shakeela, she likes flowers. I try to grow vegetable.'

'It's good,' Mum told him. 'We only had vegetables and fruit at home. May I help grow vegetables, please?'

'Yes. I work in kitchen I bring ends of carrots, tomato seeds, red pepper and melon seeds. What I can. Some grow, some not. We carry water in bucket from laundry.'

Mum turned to me, laughing. 'That'll be easy for us, Gulnessa?' Nodding, I thought, this looks as if it's helped Mum already. Then, turning back to our new friends, she said, 'But now we must put away our things and sort out our room. Please excuse us, Yousef? Shakeela?'

'Yes, of course. We go dinner together?' Ali's dad smiled questioningly, and placed his right hand over his heart. His wife did the same and Mum returned the gesture.

Back in our room, Mum explained, 'That family comes from Iraq. The parents learned our language at school in their country, and some English. The children had just started learning these languages before they escaped. The parents are teaching them more. They are good.' From what I'd seen, I agreed totally.

CHAPTER 12

The daily routine in this compound was much like the last one, minus the interviews – to begin with. The food was exactly the same. But there was one surprise. Television! The first time I'd seen it was on the plane to Indonesia. Although some of the people in the first compound had talked about it, I'd never seen a TV in a house. In this compound each donga and the common room had one.

To begin with, all us 'new' kids watched TV whenever we could even though we couldn't understand most of the programs. We loved animated movies and cartoons and could often follow the story from the pictures. Zahra loved *Rug Rats* and she sat an arm's length from the screen every time it was on. The first animated movie I saw was *Antz*, and I was hooked. It was like back at home when Mum or my arjays told us stories – but with real pictures, not just those I made in my head.

By the end of the week, Tara and I were best friends and although we couldn't talk easily at first, we managed to understand each other, by miming and signing. I introduced Tara to Aqila, and tried to explain how she was named after one of my grandmothers. By now Aqila wore the wedding outfit I'd made.

Her long top I'd trimmed with lace, and the full-length pants under it I'd embroidered with cross-stitch. Mum had helped me make a real-looking veil which had a short, white, see-through part over the face connected to a long, embroidered green part flowing down her back. Tara examined her carefully, turning her over in her hands. She looked up, beaming. Then she repeatedly made signs, until I realised she was telling me she'd never seen a homemade doll before, and wanted me to help her make her own. I nodded my promise.

Tara took me around the Camp – not that there was much to see – and introduced me to a couple of dolls, the first I'd ever seen that weren't homemade. These were much the worse for wear. One had only one leg, while the other had no clothes. The battered dolls were kept in an extra donga where no one lived. It was different from the others as it was divided into three big rooms leading from one into the next. One end was the playroom, where the few toys were kept. Everything I could see there, except for the soccer ball, seemed to be broken. And the ball was flat.

When Zainullah saw his first toy truck he raced over to it, eyes the size of full moons, and put his hand on its battered cab roof, pushing it gently. It moved a bit, so he pushed harder. Suddenly it dipped forward, grinding to a stop. Zainullah crawled around to inspect it, and held up a wheel. His face crumpled. He turned it upside down to inspect it and the rest of the wheels fell off! I thought he would burst into tears, so I said quickly, 'Let's go and see if Hassan and Abdul can fix it.' They couldn't, of course, but still Zainullah hugged the wheel-less truck to him whenever I took him to the playroom. He wanted to take it back to the donga but we were banned from taking anything away. I don't know why. The toys were old and broken and hardly anyone bothered with them.

The room at the other end of the donga was a sort of meeting room where women could gather to sew and talk. There was even an old sewing machine. Here Tara and I found a box with scraps of fabrics and chose some to make clothes for our dolls.

The first time I visited this donga with Tara, we peered under the curtain screening off the middle room. It was full of chairs smaller than I'd ever seen, arranged around little, rectangular tables pushed together. In one corner was a normal-sized table and chair. Lining all the walls were low cupboards and shelves in which I could see papers and things to write with, and books. On top of the cupboards was a clutter of all kinds of things: scissors, pots with coloured stuff in them, pots with brushes in them, piles of papers and many books. Near the big table was a white rectangular board, and pictures were stuck on the walls, with sticky tape. I looked at Tara questioningly and she held up two fingers, pointed to the room, and made motions of writing and some other actions. Then she took my hand and led me back to our donga, into her family's room where our mothers were sitting, and talking.

Tara spoke to her mother, who nodded. Then Shakeela turned to Mum and me and said, slowly in our language, 'Tara says she show Gulnessa Camp school.' Mum and I looked at each other. This was news to us. We'd no idea the Camp had a school.

Mum replied slowly so Tara's mum understood. 'Do Tara and Ali go to school?'

'Yes. Each day, two hours. When you come they stop. But go back soon.'

'Can Hassan, Gulnessa and Zainullah go, too?'

'Yes, I take you tomorrow, Monday.'

❧ ❧ ❧

The following morning as we walked across the exercise yard I asked, 'Mum, will the teacher expect me to know much?' Ever since our conversation with Tara's mum the day before, this had worried me.

'No, li'l sis,' Abdul answered for her. 'It's only to teach you to speak English. I told you that at breakfast. You'll get in trouble if you don't listen, though,' he teased.

I made a lunge for him but Mum intercepted. 'That's enough. We've got to get you to the schoolroom.'

'Yeah! School!' Zainullah raced around us cheering, followed by Zahra.

'Settle down,' Mum said automatically. 'Zahra, hold my hand. You're staying with me.' Zahra's face fell but brightened as Mum added, 'We'll go and find Yasmine and Sakina to play with.'

'I'll be in the donga playing cards with RSW19 and MTK79 and some others,' Abdul said with a wave. 'Good luck.'

A few minutes later, with Tara, Ali, their mum and a group of kids from the Camp waiting in the playroom outside the school-room, I gripped my hands behind my back to stop them shaking. This school *was* to learn to speak English, wasn't it? They didn't expect me to know how to write, did they? Unwanted memories of another attempt to start school flooded my mind.

Years ago, Mum arranged for me to go to a sort of undercover school in a neighbouring village, like the one Abdul went to before the Terror discovered it. But after she'd left me on my first day the teacher found out I couldn't read or write so she beat the bottoms of my feet with a stick. I'll never forget how much that hurt. Mum never made me go back.

Suddenly a hand appeared, sweeping aside the curtain screening off the schoolroom. A nervous-looking young man stepped forward. His light-brown hair, pushed behind his ears, hung in greasy strands down his back, and his skin was pale, the colour of Mum's bread dough, and spotty. His eyes darted about and when he spoke a few words we didn't understand, his voice quavered. Then, hesitatingly, he held out his right hand towards Mum. In his other hand he clutched a book and a pencil with its end chewed. Mum looked at his hand, then at Shakeela, who quickly leant forward to shake the teacher's hand.

'New teacher,' she said to Mum. 'Change often.' Then Shakeela greeted the teacher our way, placing her right hand over her heart. To us she explained, 'Shake hand means "hello" for Australians.' Looking back to the teacher, she gestured to Tara, who said, 'BTY16,' then to Ali, who said, 'BTY17.'

The teacher looked at his book and made two marks, then looked at Mum. She pointed to Hassan and said, 'AXZ22.' Quickly I said, 'AXZ23,' but the teacher scowled at me. Mum repeated, 'AXZ23,' and, pointing to Zainullah, 'AXZ24.' The teacher checked his book. Finally he looked up, shaking his head, pointed at Hassan and spoke in English. He pointed again to Hassan and to the outside door. Clearly Hassan wasn't welcome.

Tara's mum spoke to the teacher in English, and turned to Mum. 'He says Hassan's too old to come here.' Gesturing to the rest of us to go in, the teacher moved on to check the IDs of other waiting students. Hassan rolled his eyes, and Mum waved as we disappeared behind the curtain.

The small tables and chairs were now organised in rows facing the big table and whiteboard. Tara beckoned to me to sit with her, the two boys sat behind us. When the other kids were sitting, the teacher, whose name I never could say (and *he* didn't have a number), made us stick labels with our numbers onto our chests.

When at last we all sat, arms folded, looking at him, the

teacher picked up a small gadget. A red dot of light shone on the big table. 'Ta-ble,' said the teacher, waving his free arm towards us in an upwards motion. I stared, fascinated.

The kids who'd been to school before, chanted, 'Tai-ble.'

He flashed the light onto his chair and said, 'Chair.' I tried to see what made the light. He conducted the chorus again, and everyone said, 'Tsair.' I tried too but what came out was nothing like he'd said. So it went on.

The words he said sounded weird and I couldn't get them right. When we tried together I didn't feel too bad, but when the teacher made us say words by ourselves. It was so embarrassing.

'Sit!' said the teacher, drawing an air circle, so we sat in a circle on the floor. Fine by me. We'd done that all the time at home, but *he* sat on a chair looking down on us. Then he said a word and pointed at Tara, who stood, walked over to face his chair, and repeated the word. How does she do it? I marvelled. He sort of smiled and nodded. Moving clockwise around the circle he pointed to us in turn and sighed loudly whenever someone couldn't get a word right. After I tried he squeezed his eyes shut, wrinkled up his face and sighed.

Then he started around the circle again, repeating each word. My stomach's gymnastics increased with each try but still I couldn't get the words right. By the third round when my attempt at 'chair' once again sounded nothing like his, he cringed, shook his head *and* sighed. I could hear the difference when he said it but I'd no idea how to make it sound like he did. He didn't help, just made me feel dumb and stupid – and sick.

So, before it was my next turn, I slid backwards out of my place in the circle, 'walked' on my bottom behind the kids who'd had a go, then wormed my way back. The others sniggered, but said nothing, and Tara grinned whenever *he* wasn't looking. It worked for three rounds, then, I found myself eye to knee with the teacher's legs. I froze, stomach at boiling point.

'AXZ23,' he thundered, and gestured upwards, sharply. I jumped to my feet. 'Out!' His face looked as angry as his voice sounded. 'Out!' he thundered again.

I flinched, stood my ground and repeated, 'Out. Out.'

His dough-coloured face turned purple. Pointing, he roared something at me, 'out' amongst it, so I headed for the curtain. I could say that exactly as he did, but still he was annoyed. Running from the schoolroom I headed back to our donga.

Mum was with Asad, Hassan and Abdul in the telly room when I barged in. They looked up in surprise. Their familiar faces brought tears to my eyes, but I blinked them back. 'Whatever is it?' Mum's arm slid around me.

'Are *all* teachers mean?' I blurted out.

'No, Nessa. Why?' Asad stepped up. 'What happened?'

'Well, the first one I knew was, and this one is.'

'What did he do?' Mum's voice was gentle so I swallowed hard and began a blow by blow account of everything that had happened. When I got to the bit about banging into the teacher's legs, Hassan couldn't contain himself.

'What an idiot!'

I lashed out, swinging my arm in his direction as hard as I could. The back of my hand caught him across the bridge of his nose and he yelled, hands flying to his face. I saw blood trickling from beneath his hands and I turned and fled. Out of the donga, and as far as I could to the other end of the compound. Crashing into the fence, I slumped to the ground, sobbing as if all the sadness in the world was leaking out from inside me.

Suddenly strong hands lifted me. Arms circled my heaving body. 'Shhh, shhh.' Gradually my tears subsided but my knees buckled and my head flopped, and I let them. At last I gathered enough strength to look up – into the coal, velvety eyes of Abdul. My face must have registered shock because he whispered, 'It's okay. Let it out. It's good to let go.'

I sniffed loudly, wiped my face on my sleeve, and took my weight on my own legs. 'I'm really okay. Thanks. I don't know why I snapped.'

'I do.' He grinned, nodding and dropping his arms. 'I do.' Then he added, 'And don't worry about the teacher. I'll tell you about some run-ins I had when I went to school. Tara's mum already told us the new teacher seemed uncomfortable and she thought he wouldn't stay long. Don't go back 'til a new one comes. You don't have to. Another thing, remember I warned you about getting into trouble if you didn't listen?' The twinkle in his eye told me he was teasing now. I punched his arm.

'What about Hassan?' I suddenly remembered what had triggered my flight.

'It's only a blood nose. He deserved what he got. He doesn't know when to keep his mouth shut. Hey! There's the siren for lunch. I'm hungry. Beat you to the mess.'

'Not now. But thanks.' I grinned at him. 'I'm going to wash my face first.' I gave him what must have been a watery smile, but it was the best I could manage.

CHAPTER 13

Although we'd felt more and more anxious, frustrated and impatient as time wore on in the first compound we'd lived in, the atmosphere here was much worse. To begin with I couldn't put my finger on what was different. I saw people with empty eyes and miserable faces all around us. They walked slowly, heads bowed, and I often heard angry voices.

The weather was now hot every day and the only change from endless blue skies was when wind whipped up red sand into a haze. The only time I felt reasonably cool was after dark when the temperature dropped. The compond was so crowded we had to have two sittings for meals, and sometimes there wasn't enough food for everyone. We had to wait in line longer for everything: meals, showers, toilets, washing machines and even to get a decent telly-viewing space on the floor of the common room. Some women got up at four a.m. to have a shower without queuing and to be sure they'd get hot water. The exercise area was only about the size of the one in the closed compound so the guards rostered dongas for exercise periods. Ours was the hour before lunch and the hour before dinner, like before.

During the day, when we'd finished our cleaning chores,

and didn't have to stand in long lines waiting to use a washing machine, Mum began going to Yasmine's family's room where Zahra, Yasmine and Sakina played with their dolls while the three mothers talked. It was usually about where they'd lived, what they'd escaped from and who they'd had to leave, or what happened in the Camp and in interviews, and worries about how long we were being kept here. Nothing to cheer them up, nothing even to smile about. Occasionally they sewed – mending our well-worn clothes over and over again. There was little fabric to be had in this compound, and no Joanne to bring more.

Tara and Ali, Zainullah and I watched TV or went to the playroom when school was closed, until we could go outside for our exercise time. There was nowhere else to go. After I stopped going to school, the others decided that since they didn't like Dough-face, as we called the teacher, they wouldn't go back to school either, until he left. These close friends were the only ones we knew by name. Everyone else called each other by number.

Although Mum had seemed brighter when we first moved compounds, it didn't last long. Soon she dropped back into rarely smiling. When one of the other women came to see her, or ask if she wanted to sit with them, Mum would often say she was too tired because she woke so much during the night and needed to rest. She mostly sat or lay on the bed in our room and asked me to look after the two Zs.

One morning Shakeela came in with Tara and Ali to find Mum lying on her bunk, and she suggested Mum see the nurse. Here the medical staff had a permanent base in a separate fenced-off area with a gate into the main Camp area.

'Fatimeh, I take you?' Shakeela offered. 'Sometimes guard doesn't give permission to pass through gate. I speak with him.'

'I don't want to be any trouble,' Mum sounded unsure.

118

'No trouble,' Shakeela assured her. 'Tara and Gulnessa can look out for little ones.'

I agreed quickly, hoping this might bring back our strong, cheerful mother instead of the quiet, withdrawn woman she'd become. 'And, Mum, ask about these.' I took from my locker the empty wrapper I'd saved from the last of the sanitary pads. She shoved it up her sleeve and nodded.

'What's that?' Zainullah shouted. Lately he seemed to talk only at maximum volume.

'Nothing,' I said.

'Don't tell lies,' Zainullah pulled at Mum's sleeve, jumping at it as she tiredly stretched her arm high so he couldn't reach it. She shook her head as if to say, I haven't energy for this, and turned away from the bouncing little boy.

'Zainullah,' I tried to sound like Mum used to, indignant that he'd even try to do such a thing. It didn't work. He kept jumping, grabbing her arm, trying to force her to lower it. Mum staggered a couple of steps towards the door, dragging Zainullah.

I tried the mysterious approach. 'It's women's business.'

Zainullah stamped angrily, swinging his fists at me. He'd gradually changed from an energetic, cheeky, hot-headed scamp to a niggly, contrary, aggressive child. I changed tactics again. Turning to Zahra, I asked, 'Let's go to the playroom?'

Zainullah yelled, 'No way! School's in. Dough-face'll get us.'

'What about TV?' Tara put in quietly. Her Dari was improving daily. She moved towards the door, Ali and Zainullah followed.

The usual morning programs were on television and Zahra watched, spellbound, sitting close to the screen with other littlies who were there when we arrived. Their mothers sat on chairs in the room, talking and we sat on the floor. At first, Tara and I watched the pre-schoolers watching *Playschool*, fascinated at the way they sang the songs in a good imitation of English, without a clue what they meant. Then Ali and Zainullah started to poke one another, giggling loudly. I sighed and said to the boys, 'Bet we can beat you two at knucklebones.'

Zainullah accepted my challenge with relish, wriggling on his bottom to a space behind the TV set and fishing out 'the bones'. A mini Hassan, I thought – competitive, impatient, but still with a good heart in spite of the Camp's effects on him. Ali on the other hand seemed always easygoing without a competitive bone in his body. The tension around us had opposite effects on Ali and Zainullah. The longer I knew Ali, the more withdrawn he grew, the way Zahra withdrew from anything that upset her. Tara's relationship with Ali was like Zahra's and mine.

We'd finished our sixth game and were about to go out in the exercise yard when Mum and Shakeela returned. The boys waved and raced outside, Zainullah stuffing into his pocket the precious bones Hassan had lent him now he felt too grown-up to play. He had impressed on Zainullah that they were from home and threatened him with death if he lost one.

I took Zahra's hand and with Tara we followed our mothers to our room. 'What did the nurse say?' I asked.

'She gave me pills, to help me sleep,' Mum answered.

'Is that all?'

'Well, she say drink plenty water. We all must drink many mugs water,' Shakeela laughed.

'Mum, did you ask about the pads?'

Mum nodded as she sank onto her bunk. 'Yes, but there's none. If we want some we have to buy them.'

'But we've no money.' I knew I was stating the obvious.

CHAPTER 14

The only difference in the days that crawled past was who was sick or who was fighting. We'd given up asking if anyone had heard about visas. I noticed people doing strange things. One evening, as I returned to our room from the toilet block, I saw a man standing behind a donga banging his head against the wall. Hard. Over and over again as if he was trying to knock a hole in the wall. I stopped, staring in disbelief. Then I bolted. Back to our donga, straight to our room. Mum was telling the two Zs a bedtime story, an old folktale about a wolf nipping a boy's bare bottom in the moonlight when he went outside to pee. We had no inspiration for new stories here.

For a change Abdul was there, stretched out on his bunk staring into space. I hadn't seen nearly as much of him in this compound, as we had no sanctuary here – and I had Tara. Abdul spent most of his time with RSW19 and other young men, and Hassan usually went, too. Over half of the people in the Camp were young men. Now, for the first time in ages, I could talk to Abdul with no one else listening.

Sinking to the floor, I whispered what I'd seen, finishing, 'Why would he do that?'

'There are people in this compound, Nessa,' Abdul said softly, 'who've been here so long they've almost given up hope of leaving. They feel their life has been taken from them. They can't find out why they're still held here. One man showed Hassan and me scars shaped like the prongs of a fork all over his legs. The Terror had come into his home and asked him questions he wouldn't answer, so they heated a cooking fork on coals and burned him with it. Another man has lost one foot in a landmine. Many men have scars from torture. They don't understand why the officials don't believe them. They're frustrated and depressed, so they do things to hurt themselves.'

'But why? How could that help?'

'They're desperate. They have to do something or they'll explode. MTK79 shares the room at the end of our donga. It might have been him you saw. None of those men or boys have families here.'

I shook my head.

'MTK79 was a teacher in Kabul, where the Terror hit first. His family was so worried they'd kill him that they sold their house to get him out. MTK79 escaped soon after the Terror got into power.'

'But that was ages ago. Half of my life.'

'Yes, that's the point. The Terror tried to get him to join them and teach in their schools. He refused. They made him watch while they shot another teacher, his friend, who refused. Sound familiar?' I nodded, sick in my stomach. 'Eventually he got to Australia. He's been in here ever since. More than three years.'

'That's forever.'

'It must seem like it. And he's got no family here. I try to imagine what that's like. To be shut away from everyone you love for years.' A strange look flicked across Abdul's face, but he went

122

on. 'He's tried many times to find out when he'll be let out. Officials keep telling him they don't know.'

'But there has to be a reason.'

'For a long time he couldn't find out anything. Then, a few months ago, an officer told him his application had been rejected. He said she was nice, and cried for him when she had to tell him the news. At least he felt someone cared, a bit.'

'Did she say why?'

'She didn't know. She told him he could appeal and arranged for him to see a lawyer. His interviews started all over again. Afterwards the lawyer told MTK79 that he believed his story and would do all in his power to help him get justice and have the authorities release him, as a refugee.'

'That must have made him feel better?'

'It did, but what the lawyer said next made him feel worse.'

'Whatever was it?'

'The lawyer said it was difficult to get a just decision for asylum seekers because hearings were not in a court of law. The process was set up by the government to support its policy to keep asylum seekers out of Australia and to treat harshly those who arrive, to put off others coming.'

'Oh my god! So we're in prison here because the government doesn't want us, not because they don't believe us.' A million things revved in my mind. You'll never get out. How can ordinary people beat a government? Look what you left behind. Look what you've come to. But a persistent whisper in my head insisted, You were born for more than prison. Don't give up. Keep believing.

I looked up to see Abdul watching me. 'We have to be tough, Ness. It hasn't been easy for anyone here.'

'I'm not sure how tough I can be if everyone hates us.'

'No, not everyone. MTK79's lawyer said people like him are

trying to help us, to see we're treated like we should be under international agreements about human rights. He says organisations like the United Nations and Amnesty International criticise government policy. A major problem is that the government is trying to control what the Australian people are told. They try to make us look as bad as possible so no one wants us.'

'But we're locked up without doing anything. Doesn't that make them look bad?'

'You'd think so, but few people know what's really happening. Reporters are banned from visiting Camps unless they have official permission and this is hardly ever given. People don't know that Camps are like prisons, or how long we are kept here. Lies get splashed all over the television and newspapers. What chance do we have?'

'Abdul!' For a minute I couldn't speak, then I managed, 'How could anyone believe that?' I sat, face in my hands. The bottom fell out of my well of hope. Why did we come here? But what else could we have done? I'd never felt so wretched.

Abdul's voice continued. 'The lawyer explained that asylum seekers in Camps – and there are more – have no right to go to a law court, but appeals can be heard by a Refugee Review Tribunal. He will prepare MTK79's appeal. But we can't be represented by lawyers at hearings.'

'That's as clear as mud,' My head was exploding. Abdul went on in the same toneless voice.

'MTK79 says only one person from the tribunal hears the appeal. Although they don't have to be lawyers they are fairminded, but the government puts pressure on them to obey rules. Once, the tribunal approved appeals the government opposed, basing decisions on similar cases in Canada and the United States.'

'Were the people freed?'

'I'm not sure, but the minister was quoted as saying he'd be unlikely to renew those members' appointments to the Tribunal.'

'But that's like the Terror. Everyone who didn't do what *they* wanted was removed.' Had we landed in a situation like the one we'd just escaped from? I felt I should say something but I was still trying to absorb what Abdul had told me. 'I'd be crazy by now if I was MTK79.'

'A couple of weeks ago he was so depressed but also angry and desperate, so he starting head-banging. He was trying to drive out hurt inside him. It didn't work. He got bruises all right, but inside he felt as bad as ever. To make matters worse, it was Dung-face who found him. That *Khar-e Barkash*.'

At any other time I would have laughed at the insult, 'load-carrying donkey', often thrown at Hazaras at home. But I didn't have a laugh left in me.

'He said not to damage the walls and said that next time MTK79 felt like bashing his head he should let him know and he'd do it for him. Dung-face should go back where he came from – the *arsehole* of a *Khar-e Barkash*.' Abdul glanced at me apologetically, and added, 'Well, at least to jail – guarding crims, like himself. He really did that. He doesn't know how to treat people like human beings, let alone help someone.'

'That's *awful*.' I saw a vision of Dad's face. Where are you? What's happened to you? My mind froze.

'Nessa,' Abdul's voice gently prodded me, 'do you want to know more so you *really* understand what can happen?'

I nodded, not *wanting* to hear more, but unable to say no.

'Well, after that, MTK79 felt so bad. He couldn't see how things would ever change. So he tried to slash his wrists.'

I gasped.

Abdul continued, 'He told me that he didn't care if he died, but felt bad that his family had given up so much to help him live. If he died like this their sacrifice would be wasted. He wanted someone to find him before he died, and to realise how hopeless he felt, and help him.'

'Oh my god. Did he . . .'

'His friend MTK58 found him and took him to the medical centre. After the nurses checked him and bandaged his wrists they put him in an observation room. He said it was like being in solitary confinement. He was only allowed out to wash or shower, supervised all the time. No one could visit him except a medical officer and nurse. The room only had a bed and a toilet in it. An officer brought him food. Sometimes he saw an eye watching him through a peep-hole in the door. He was there for about a week, until yesterday. The nurse told him his case was ready to go before the RRT. He doesn't really believe it'll be successful but says he'll give it a go. If it's knocked back . . .' Abdul's voice trailed away. He lay on his back, face expressionless, staring into space.

I struggled to imagine being in MTK79's shoes. I felt rotten enough walking in my own and we'd not been here for all the seasons yet, not on the way to four times through them like MTK79. I knew what it was like when fear, anxiety and pain fought each other inside me, and when nightmares tricked me into believing I was part of them. And I knew what it was like to have my freedom stolen. Now, I could glimpse what it might be like to have lost even more – and worst of all, hope.

Then it dawned on me, Abdul had no *real* family here either. I *had* to help, somehow. So he'd never feel like MTK79. I jumped up and, sitting on the side of his bunk, threw my arms around Abdul's neck, hugging him as hard as I could, whispering. 'You *are* our family, and our mum is your mum, too. Abdul, you must remember that.' Lifting my head I saw tears in his eyes, but he was smiling and his arms tightened around me.

'I won't forget. I promise. I'm not that bad.'

I sat up and, making a fist of my left hand, spat on the back of it. Holding it out towards Abdul, I said, 'Now, you spit on my hand too, and promise again.'

Solemnly Abdul spat on my spit and said, 'I promise never to forget your family is my family. And you're my . . . Gulnessa.'

'Now, do what I do,' I ordered, dipping my right index finger in the wet patch on my hand, then holding my right hand over his heart. He did the same, holding his hand over my heart. We both bowed our heads. Looking up, I said, 'That seals the promise forever. It can never be broken.'

He grinned, and whispered almost mischievously, 'Never?'

'Never.'

'Then, we both agree that you're mine . . . Gulnessa?' His eyes added so much to his words.

I was relieved to see a flash of his humour return so I responded in kind, jumping off the bed. 'Forget it! I belong to me. And for that, take this!' I ducked towards him, wiping my wet hand on his cheek and leaping backwards out of reach. Abdul swung onto his feet.

Hassan, just coming into our room with Mum, who I hadn't noticed leave, called, 'What are you two doing?' He was at Abdul's side in a bound, afraid he was missing something.

'Keep your voice down,' hissed Mum, with questions on her face. 'The two Zs are asleep. And I want to talk to you all.' We shuffled into our favourite talking place, cross-legged in a circle on the floor. Then Mum went on softly, 'The weather's so hot and as our clothes are for cold weather. I asked the women where they got their light clothes. They said you can buy a few in the shop.'

The 'shop' was a room like the one in the closed compound, with things to buy, mainly basics: biscuits, toiletries, cool drinks, and clothes like T-shirts and shorts. We'd already checked it out. There were so many more people in this compound that it was hard to get the usual jobs. People even queued to be allowed to wash toilets.

Mum whispered, 'Abdul, do your friends know how we can get clothes?'

Glancing at me, Abdul replied softly, 'I'll ask MTK79 tomorrow. If anyone knows, he will. Hassan and I can see if there's any way to get jobs in the kitchen.' I knew Hassan would do anything to be included with the men but I could see by his face that he hadn't bargained on this. Still, he said nothing. The old Hassan *was* changing. 'I've got contacts. I'll check it out tomorrow.'

'With the men.' Hassan nodded conspiratorially. I rolled my eyes.

'Okay. Now let's try to get some sleep,' said Mum.

Climbing into bed next to Zahra, I tried to get comfortable without waking her. My body felt leaden, drained. Sleep came quickly, but not restfully . . .

Mum and I walk across the grazing land at home, calling, 'Theerma, Theerma.' I hear a shout, stop and turn around. Zahra's running after us, waving. I wait. Holding hands, we turn back. Mum's about fifty metres ahead, striding towards the river. A plane stands near it. Like the one we flew on to Indonesia. Then I see it. Why doesn't Mum see it, too? I open my mouth to yell a warning. Nothing comes out. No matter how hard I strain I cannot make a sound. Mum marches on, closer to the landmine, and closer. Only three more steps. Two steps. 'Mum!'

I'm desperate, but can only mime, mouth wide, jumping up and down, waving wildly. 'Mum, stop! Look on the ground!' I'm frantic. Face purple with effort. One step. I panic and, lurching ahead, throw Theerma, who's now in my arms, behind me. 'Mu-u-um!' A rasping noise comes out as – Mum steps . . . BOOM! Dirt flies, and legs! I can see two disembodied legs, and two arms, flying. In slow motion. I hit the ground and my face explodes. But I sob. Heaving sobs.

Gasping for breath I was suddenly conscious of small arms around my neck, cutting off my air supply. My hand reached up and unclasped them. Drenched in sweat, I lay face down, clutching my pillow between my teeth. Zahra's little face burrowed into my neck to find mine.

'Nessie, don't cry. You're in night-scares. Please, Nessie.'

With a huge effort I rolled towards her. Hugging her warm little body calmed my stiff, shuddering one. Trying to shake away the nightmare which had woken me many times before, I managed, 'Thank you, darling.' I struggled on. 'Now I'm awake I'm okay.'

'I sing you "Lalay", shall I?'

'I'd love that.'

And her true little voice, no longer her raspy whisper, sang out, comforting all who could hear it: *Lalay lalay, ate-aya . . .*

CHAPTER 15

The hot weeks had dawdled into hot dawdling months. Hope drained away. Laughter was rare. Tempers were frayed. Dreams still haunted us. Everyone we knew was *still* in the Camp. We felt like the forgotten people. The way we were treated when trying to get 'new' second-hand clothes was how we were treated generally. Batches of used clothes that charities collected for us sometimes arrived. Anyone who wanted them had to queue in the hot sun, sometimes for hours, only to be told that all the clothes had gone. This happened to us three times. We took it in turns to wait. Once Hassan made it to the top of the queue just as the last item was taken. The guard laughed at his distress.

Occasionally we heard of people being granted visas but they'd be whisked away so quickly we couldn't talk to them. Now *we* were the faces at the fence, staring at anyone who came or left. We watched enviously as people who were released walked straight again, clutching their temporary visas as they climbed onto the bus that would take them away.

'Don't forget us,' someone inside would call.

Then another voice would shout, 'Send someone to help.'

'Tell the people.' Cries followed as the lucky ones nodded

and waved through the windows of the departing bus.

I'd heard the word 'temporary' and it worried me, but I didn't want to think about it. I couldn't take any more bad news. Mum was even worse. She didn't want to talk to anyone outside the family and even talking to us was an effort.

Still the same routines. Everyone was bored. Everyone was miserable. I was miserable. No news about anything. Nothing to do. Nothing changed – except nurses and teachers. There was a lot of sickness. The mosquitoes made us look like there was a chickenpox epidemic. We caught colds whenever the weather changed. When one person got sick we all did. Germs passed quickly in the crowded dongas. And in the hot weather many people suffered dehydration. The dongas were so hot, and the only shade outside was shade from the buildings. There seemed to be three things the nurses could give us to cure everything: sleeping tablets, pain killers like Panadol, and 'the water treatment'. If anything was wrong with us, we were told to 'drink more water'. If a nurse took an interest and became friends with us, they'd vanish, like Joanne had.

Dough-face had left at last but no one had replaced him. There was no school. Tara said it was because there was this holiday called 'Christmas' that Australians celebrated, and that school would start again soon. We thought Christmas must be a bit like Eid, which follows our Ramadan. It was hard for any-one in the Camp to follow Ramadan fasting rules, as no food was allowed outside the mess to eat before sun-up or after sun-down. The guards wouldn't let us change meal times. Still, many adults tried. We all smuggled out bread for Mum and Abdul. But no one felt like celebrating anything here and there was no way to prepare our traditional Eid feast.

The only interesting, new things in the Camp were insects

and spiders we found, and an occasional lizard. Sometimes RSW19 could tell what they were, and if he didn't know he'd ask the Good Guy, who explained lots about Australia and its wildlife.

When school started again the weather was at its hottest. Tara, Ali, Zainullah and I went back, because we wanted to learn English. I felt nervous as we waited outside on the first day but this teacher was okay, and the schoolroom was bliss – cool, my first experience of airconditioning. The unit made a loud engine noise and we could hardly hear the teacher, but it was better sitting in the cool for the two hours at school than it was anywhere else in the heat. School was just as boring as the rest of the Camp. We did the same things over and over again so often that once the weather cooled down, Tara and I didn't bother to go. No one cared.

Then another new teacher arrived and we decided to check her out. As soon as I saw her somehow I knew it'd be better. She didn't make us wait outside while she checked our numbers, but stood at the door gesturing for us to go in, smiling and saying, 'Good morning,' to us all. She reminded me of my mother. It certainly wasn't her appearance – she had short, spiky fair hair and wore big dangly earrings, and although her skin was much paler than ours she looked healthy. She sort of glowed. She looked at us and listened – like Mum used to before we were shut in this Camp.

Inside the schoolroom, the teacher had arranged the desks in groups with chairs around them. It looked different – friendlier. On each desk was a little picture, still in its plastic wrapping. All showed wonders of nature, like flowers, trees, animals, birds or even stars . . . We milled around examining them until the teacher said in English, 'Choose one you like, and sit in that chair.' She only spoke in English.

Eventually we all found one we liked and sat down. I chose a flower the same as those in the garden at the end of our donga and Tara chose a beautiful green bird. We moved the pictures so we could sit together. When I saw that Zainullah had chosen a thorny devil like the one I'd seen on the road I really wanted that, but he wouldn't swap. Later, I was glad.

The teacher picked up from her desk a picture of a tree and held it so we could see clearly as she took off its wrapping. Then, as if she were peeling a peach, she peeled a transparent skin from the back, holding up the picture before pressing it firmly onto her orange shirt. When she took away her hand it stayed there.

When we all wore stickers the teacher said slowly, 'I don't like calling you numbers.' I didn't understand but some kids cheered. Tara smiled and translated. 'We'll call each other the name of our picture.' The teacher pointed to the picture and herself as she spoke. Tara explained in Dari.

'Gum tree.' The teacher pointed to her sticker. 'Gum tree,' she repeated, pointing to herself. We had to say it until she was satisfied with our pronunciation and then she gave us a thumbs up. Three other kids had their turn to learn their 'names' by watching her lips as she said the word and trying it until they got it. Then they turned to the class and said their 'name'. We repeated it. When it was my turn I could hear my heart beating as I stood facing 'Gum Tree'. 'Ger-a-ni-um,' she said slowly, nodding to me encouragingly.

Then she watched my lips carefully. 'Ger-u-umm,' I tried to make my mouth like hers but the sounds came out wrong.

Slowly she repeated, 'Ger-a-ni-um.'

'Ger-u-umm,' I knew the first sound I said was like in 'gum', not soft as she said it.

She smiled at me, took my hand and held my fingertips close

to her lips and as she said, 'Ger . . .' I felt a small explosion of air.

'A-a-ah.' That was how you did it. 'Ger . . .' This time I said it holding my hand in front of my lips, and got it right. She smiled as I repeated it – no hands. Then she showed me how to make each sound separately, and put them together to make 'Geranium'. It was hard, but Gum Tree made no grimaces, no head shakes, and no sighs.

After we'd all practised our names we spent the rest of our two hours trying to teach our names to each other. Tara's bird's name was 'Twenty-eight' and we laughed, but she said she didn't mind *that* number because it didn't make her think of the leaky boat her family had arrived on. And when Zainullah found out his picture was a 'Thorny Devil' he wanted to swap names with me. I told him it suited him better. I couldn't believe it when Gum Tree said, 'It's time to go. See you tomorrow.'

All the time Gum Tree was there we kept our picture names, and through learning each others' I could say more English words than I'd learnt all the rest of the time in Camp. If anyone misbehaved in class, Gum Tree didn't get mad, she just said, 'Please don't come back until you're ready to behave like the rest of us. I won't let you spoil it for the others.' There was one warning, then out. Lessons were trouble-free. The two hours we were allowed to spend at school with her went quicker than any others. We wished we could stay longer and hoped she'd stay at the school forever.

But it only lasted a few weeks. One morning when we arrived at the schoolroom there was another teacher waiting. Where was Gum Tree? Why hadn't she said goodbye to us? After checking out this new teacher and finding him okay, Tara dared to ask, 'Where's Gum Tree?' The new teacher frowned, puzzled. I guess it did sound strange. 'Our last teacher,' Tara added.

'Ah. She was transferred – sent away.'

'Why? Why didn't she say goodbye to us?'

'She didn't know. She wanted to stay. She didn't know until last night. She was put on a bus to the airport.'

That teacher was okay, but nothing like Gum Tree. None of the others were. I tried to imagine school away from the Camp. And the teachers.

CHAPTER 16

After school was exercise hour, then lunch. Tara and I sat in a corner by the side of a donga and the fence. At least we could see a bit of the open land surrounding us. We didn't speak, both feeling sadder than usual. Unconsciously I began to doodle.

'Is that a plane?' Tara asked, watching my finger tracing a shape in the dirt.

'Guess so,' I answered. 'I was wondering if Gum Tree's plane was like the one which took us to Indonesia.'

'We didn't escape from Iraq the usual way, on a plane. After we'd stayed in the first refugee camp for ages, we went to lots of places I didn't know. Dad said we'd never get out if we didn't help ourselves. So we went on long, long car journeys, and buses. We stayed with strangers who tried to help us, until in the end we were put on the fishing boat that brought us here. What was it like on a plane?'

I was surprised Tara didn't know. She seemed to have done so many other things I hadn't. 'Amazing.' I started to feel better, remembering the thrill when I'd first set eyes on the silver monster.

'Tell me about it, Ness. Everything.' We had a kind of competition to see who described things best.

'I can remember everything. We'd been shut in this room all day, and all the night before, and it was dark again when the agent banged on the door. We had no idea where we were going. Mum asked. She was great. Our leader.' I felt defensive about my mother and wanted Tara to know she hadn't always been like she was now.

'When the agent said "aeroplane" Zainullah spread his arms and took off around the room revving his "engine" loudly. The only planes we'd seen were the ones high above our village.'

'Me too,' Tara nodded.

'When we got to the airport, the noise, the crowds and buildings took my breath away. We held on to each other and stayed in a tight line following the agent through huge doors, which opened by themselves.'

'Were there more people than in Camp?' Tara listened closely.

'Seemed about the same – millions. We gawked at the strange flashing coloured lights, loud voices and music, and more different sorts of people than I ever dreamed of. At last the agent took us out onto a bus. The noise was deafening, so we couldn't talk. We were packed in so tightly I could see nothing but the back of a jacket rubbing my face. Only Zahra's hand clutching mine helped me not to panic.

'We stepped from the bus, in front of this metallic monster. It was bathed in bright light like an enormous messenger from the heavens. I couldn't believe the tiny planes we'd seen in the sky at home would look this big on the ground. It towered over the building we'd just left. Its wings alone were longer and higher than the bus.'

'Phew!' Tara whistled. 'How did it ever fly?'

'That's what we all wanted to know. We approached a ladder leading into the plane and I remember feeling both excited and scared. And climbing the steps I wasn't sure whether it was me trembling or the ladder was moving. Inside the plane looked like a gigantic cave lined with hundreds of seats, and small windows.

'The agent led us between seats I could only just see over. He stopped at a row near the back, and pointed to our seats. He showed us how to put on the seatbelts and where the toilets were. I'd worried about how we were going to pee. We waited to take off. I gripped the arms of my seat and held my breath. The engines' roar grew so loud I felt the plane vibrating. It was scary, and exciting. Then an invisible power forced me against the back of my seat. I shut my eyes and imagined flying, sort of this wafty, gentle feeling, a bit like floating in water in the river at home – but softer, touching nothing. I stayed quite still, only taking a breath when I couldn't hold it any more. And I waited . . . and waited . . . and waited . . . Zainullah's voice made me open my eyes. "Come and look out the window. We're above the clouds!"

'It was stupid but I was sure he'd made a mistake, and I said, "We can't be flying yet. It feels like we're going along the ground. Feel the bumps? Air wouldn't have bumps."

'Zainullah shook his head, "No. I can't see the wings flapping. But, Nessie, we *are* over the clouds." I undid my seatbelt, squeezed past Zainullah and kneeled by Hassan, whose face was pressed against the window.

'"Look, down there." Hassan sucked in his breath as he spoke, making his voice rise shrilly. Hundreds of pinpricks of light shone below us. Occasionally they blinked as clouds passed between the plane and the ground. My head knew we must be flying, but it didn't feel like it.

'At last the dusting of lights disappeared and all we could see was a light blinking on the plane's wing, so I returned to my seat.

For some reason I felt good to think of that huge, solid wing and the one on the other side, too, carrying us through the air. I looked across the aisle to tell Mum but her head was resting on Zahra's, their eyes closed. Zahra had Theerma's scarf wound around her neck. Hassan came back from the toilet laughing. "Wow! I nearly got sucked in!" he told me.

'I put off going as long as I could. When I did go the little toilet rooms intrigued me with their metal seat, and even a hand-basin with a tap. Before then I'd never even seen water running from a tap, let alone at the press of a lever. The only toilets we'd used were in a rough shelter with a deep hole and a foothold on either side.

'Anyway, when I sat gingerly on the toilet seat, I thought what a waste of water it was to let it run down there. I knew how heavy water was to carry and I imagined there must have been a sort of well built into the plane. So many people had to use the toilets I was worried that might leave us without enough water to drink.'

'How long were you on the plane?' Tara asked.

'I'm not really sure, because after we'd eaten, I slept until we were almost landing and that was the next day. When I left the tiny room to go back to my seat, I couldn't see the others. The tops of heads all looked the same. Slowly I walked down the aisle until I spotted Hassan and Zainullah and slid into my seat. I whispered, "Do you think pee and water from the toilet flies out a hole in the bottom of the plane while we're in the air?" Zainullah's eyes popped.

'"Probably," Hassan answered, nodding.

'I explored the pocket on the back of the seat in front of me and found a headset. Our village had no electricity, so I'd never seen any electrical appliances, or even lights, until we'd arrived at the airport. Abdul had his headphones on, so I copied how he

139

wore them. A flight attendant helped me. Music blasted in my ears! Then she passed us each a red can. It was icy cold. "Coke," she said clearly. I looked in the hole at the top and saw a dark liquid with tiny bubbles jumping out of it. She passed Zainullah a straw. He looked at her and screwed up his nose, so she bent down, placed the straw in the hole, and mimed sucking it.

'I can't describe my first taste of Coke. I remember clearly how it tickled my mouth as I swallowed.'

'I know.' Tara, too, loved it, but like us had no money to buy it.

'Before I'd finished my drink the smell of hot food made my mouth water. We'd only eaten dried fruit, bread and cheese since we left home three days before. A tray appeared in front of me. It was full of little packages. The food was all strange. Noodles, I think. I liked it all – except the tasteless bread.'

'Okay, leave out the food description. It makes me hungry.'

'Sorry. Me too. Anyway, Mum and Zahra woke up when the food arrived. Mum wouldn't eat. I took Zahra to look out from a window at the back, near the toilets. She saw the blinking light on the wingtip, and said, "Can I get it, Nessie?"

'"Get what?"

'"The light. To make Mummy happy," she explained. I realised the wet patch on Zahra's hair was Mum's tears.

'"Zahra, that's a lovely idea. But you can't go out there." I stroked her hair. I could see she was tired and as near to grumpy as she ever got. Tears weren't far away. I tried to explain. She couldn't even listen. I carried her back to her seat and she was asleep before I'd done up her seatbelt.

'Mum had tears running down her face. I tried to comfort her, but she said, "Leave me be. I'll try to sleep. I'll be all right. It's just that we've left so much behind. I can't help my tears." I felt awful not being able to help, but went back to my seat . . .'

'I know what it's like, Nessa. Mum didn't stop crying for days after we escaped. Dad just kept saying, "Shakeela, we have to do this. They killed my father and two brothers." I didn't know what to do, so I kept quiet, and prayed. So did Ali. What it was like when you landed?'

'I must have fallen asleep because I remember nothing more until I felt a hand shaking my shoulder. I opened my eyes to see the flight attendant smiling at me. She held out a tray of what looked like little yellow eggs wrapped in clear paper. I reached out to touch one but pulled my hand back in surprise. The paper crackled. The attendant pointed. "Barley sugar," she said and dropped three sweets in my lap. I sucked them to take my mind off worrying about how we'd get down, as well as to unblock my ears. Then the plane jolted, throwing me forward. My mouth flew open and my barley sugar flew out. I yelled, "Hassan, what happened?"

"It's okay, sis. We're down. That bump was the wheels hitting the ground. Now they've put on the brakes."

'I felt the plane shuddering and the roar was deafening. It wasn't until a voice announced, three times, in different languages, "We've landed safely at an International Airport in Indonesia . . . " that I believed it. Suddenly I remembered my barley sugar and scrabbled after it.'

'I hope I can fly one day,' Tara said. 'It sounds amazing.' The lunch siren sounded.

'I'm hungry,' I said, 'but lunch won't be amazing.'

CHAPTER 17

I'm on a slippery boat deck. A storm is raging. A huge wave rears over the boat. I watch it, petrified, cowering, trying to protect my head with my hands. The wave breaks. Vomit pours down on me. Amongst it is Asad's dead baby. I try to catch the naked body. Each time I do, it slips from my grasp, sliding on the putrid deck, washed by the breaking waves. I make an almighty effort and lunge to grab it . . .

Thump. Shaking my head, I found myself lying on the floor next to my bunk. There was a whimpering noise above me. I sat up.

'Are you all right, Gulnessa?' Mum whispered loudly.

'Yes.' I gulped back my fear and crawled back into bed, then I pulled Arjay's blanket up to my chin, stroking it and trying to see my grandmother's dear face behind my closed lids. I imagined I was sitting on the floor next to her spinning wheel playing with my dolls. I reached under my pillow to where my Aqila doll lay. Holding her close to my chest, I tossed and turned. I must have fallen asleep at last, as the dreams returned . . .

I'm in the ocean. An endless, flat, warm ocean. By myself. Nothing's in sight. I'm clinging desperately to a plank of wood, drifting, straining to get somewhere, I've no idea where – anywhere. Something touches my arm. It's the dead baby! Bobbing against me, nudging me. Its eyes aren't there but something moves ceaselessly where the eyes should be. Maggots! They seethe in its eye sockets. The stench is putrid. I retch and push it from me. The body bobs back. I push it again, desperately. Back it bobs. I heave, vomiting all over it. A circle of sick cradles the baby and floats it away. My arm clutching the plank feels so weak I have to concentrate to keep my fingers from slipping. Something touches my foot. Looking down through crystal-clear water I see the most ginormous shark. I realise it's circling me. Again it closes. This time it nudges my bottom with its blunt snout. I squirm away. Next time it's my thigh. Like it's deciding the juiciest bit to attack. Slowly it opens its cavernous jaws, revealing lines of jagged blades instead of teeth. It moves towards me. I kick out with all my might . . .

'Owwwww!' I saw Zahra sitting up, looking at me indignantly.

'Oh, darling, I'm sorry,' I breathed, realising what I must have done. 'It's that mean old shark coming to get me . . .'

'In your night-scares?' She looked so worried I felt the terror slipping away. 'Poor Nessie. You didn't hurt me.' Around my neck went the strong little arms and we cuddled each other back to sleep.

❦ ❦ ❦

My nightmares were increasing and getting even more vivid. Sometimes I'd be woken three or four times a night, by them or by visions of the Terror killing Abdul's father, or abducting Dad. On those nights, when nothing worked and neither the lighthouse night nor the golden peach would drive away the demons, I'd sneak into Mum's bed and cuddle into her warm back to reassure myself she was here, and we were safe. On her other side was Zainullah, whose bad dreams were increasing, too. The aggressive little boy of daylight hours turned into a clinging, tearful baby when it grew dark, and he even wet the bed sometimes. Every night Mum soothed Zainullah to sleep with stories and songs long after his eyes closed. Zahra, lying in our bunk cuddling her Theermie and waiting for me, seemed to fall asleep more easily, but I knew all about Zahra's 'night-scares' and there was hardly a night that passed without one.

Mum must have suffered, too, but she didn't say anything and I couldn't ask her because I knew I couldn't help. Coping with my own and Zahra's nightmares, the two Zs scrapping every day, not to mention my own problems, was all I could manage. I was really scared that any more and my head would burst – and then what would happen to us all? Even though Hassan and Abdul tried not to talk about their dreams I'd often hear them pacing the room at night, or sneaking out to play cards or watch television. There was always a group of insomniacs in the telly room at nights. They would try to sleep in the daytime, and this caused other problems.

Mum took me to the medical centre and we tried to tell the nurse about my dreams. There was never an interpreter to help us. After a bit the nurse said, 'Wait here,' and returned a few minutes later with another nurse. Together they tried to understand, but it seemed hopeless. Finally they got that I couldn't sleep. Anyway, they gave me some tablets to take before bed. 'Sleeping tablets,' the nurse called them. I took a pill that night and although I didn't dream, the next day I felt so disgusting: sick, headachy and out of it. I didn't know which was worse, the nightmares or the pill, so I refused any more.

As Mum got more and more miserable and disinterested I tried not to worry her with anything. I'd get the two Zs ready in the morning because Mum took so long to get up and dress herself, if she got up at all. Then I'd take her hand and lead them all to breakfast. Afterwards, on the mornings I tried to go to school, I'd take Zahra to play in the room next to the schoolroom. We'd leave Mum in our room as she didn't want to see anyone or move from there. But most often I didn't go to school, as I had to wash our few clothes, sheets and towels, clean our room and generally take care of us all. I'd get Zahra to help me, pretending I was teaching her 'women's things'. 'Oh,' she'd say seriously as we pushed our clothes into the washing machine, and 'Oh, yes', as we'd sweep up dirt from the floor. Like a grown woman herself.

I wondered how Tara's mum coped without getting sick like Mum, but I figured it might be because Yousef was such a kind man. He always asked if he could do things for Mum and us kids, but there was so little for us to do that we usually said, 'No, thank you.' For a short time Yousef had brought tops of carrots and potato skins with 'eyes' for Mum to plant in the garden, but when the weather grew hot and the guards rationed our water, forbidding any to be used on the garden, the young plants shrivelled and died. It was then I first noticed Mum's spirits start to droop again.

One day I told Shakeela how worried I was about Mum, so she came to our room to visit her. Mum could have won an Oscar for that performance. She sat up, saying she'd just been having a nap, smiled, though I could see it was only with her mouth, and asked after Shakeela's family.

Tara's mum answered her and then asked, 'And you? How are *you*, Fatimeh?'

'Fine, thank you.' Mum glanced in my direction.

'Gulnessa tell me she worry about you.'

'She worries too much. I'm just tired because most nights

I get up to comfort the children.' I don't think Tara's mum knew what to believe.

When Shakeela left our room, Mum said, 'Gulnessa, it exhausts me *so much* to face people and talk like that. Please don't talk about me to others. They've got their own problems. I'll be all right once we're out of here.' I knew the first part of what she said was right, and I hoped she'd be right about the last bit.

❦ ❦ ❦

Hassan, Abdul and RSW19 had got jobs in the kitchen through RSW19's contact with the Good Guy, so they hardly noticed what was going on. They worked long hours, getting up way before us so breakfast would be ready on time, and not finishing at night until all the dinner dishes were clean and the mess ready for the next day. They were paid one dollar each, for every day they worked, and they worked as much as they could because there was nothing else to do. An added bonus was the uniform they had to wear – white tops and black and white cook's pants – a thousand per cent better than their other old worn-out clothes. They'd give us money to buy things we needed, like soap and toothpaste, and even an occasional bottle of Coke to share. We still couldn't get sanitary pads. The rest of the money Abdul kept in a roll of cloth he wore around his waist. 'We'll need it when we get out,' he said. 'When we get out' had become one of the most used sayings in the Camp.

'You know, Ness, I've been thinking about what I want to study when we get out,' Abdul said on the way back to the donga after one lunchtime when he wasn't working. We'd been served half-frozen food and everyone seemed cranky.

Returning to the donga after meals was the only time we

managed to get a few words together other than late at night. Still, I watched out for every chance and Abdul did, too.

'I can't make up my mind, but kitchen work'll do to help look after us, while I study something I really want to do,' he said.

Us? I wanted to ask, What do you mean "us"? The whole family, or you and me? But I didn't.

'Have you thought of being a professional gambler?' I asked instead. 'You've played cards so much you could *teach* that instead of having to study.' Teasing was easier than risking revealing my feelings. Abdul was the one thing that made me feel good in this poisonous place.

'Yes, you're right,' he said seriously. 'It's a year since we arrived so I could consider it a year's study. Perhaps I could work in a casino and learn on the job.'

I looked at him in alarm. 'Abdu-ul, I was only –'

He burst out laughing.

'Why should I care what you want to do, anyway?'

'Well, you do, don't you?'

I wasn't about to go there so I changed tack completely, 'Did you say it was a year since we arrived?'

'Yes, a bit over now. That's why we were able to get jobs.'

'Why do we hear nothing?' I suddenly felt flat in spite of Abdul's nearness. A whole year we'd never get back. Wasted. Would we ever get out of this prison?

A sudden rush of people towards the fence along the outside of the exercise yard made me look up. Everyone surged in that direction. What was it this time? More visitors to inspect us? We hadn't had a recent flurry of cleaning up, fixing blocked drains and water heaters – the one in our ablution block hadn't worked for ages and now the weather was cold, showers weren't fun – so it couldn't be anyone important. We followed the crowd to see what was going on.

I saw three young boys climbing the fence, trying to attract attention and begging for help, just like when we'd arrived. The boys stopped just under the razor wire coils, clinging like monkeys with one hand and waving the other, yelling, 'Help! Free us! Help! Free us!' I squinted in the bright sun to see them more clearly. One of them was Zainullah! The others looked bigger.

I began to run, screaming, 'Zainullah, get down. Please. You might fall.' But my words were lost in the din around me.

'Help us. Free us!' The crowd's chant was interspersed with individuals' shouts.

'Tell them what's happening.'

'We only want to be free!'

'Women and children are locked up. Let the people know.'

'We're prisoners here. We only want help.'

Dung-face had recently shaved his head and his huge bulk in the guard's uniform looked as threatening as any member of the Terror. He pushed through the crowd, throwing people aside and hitting others with his baton. 'Get the bloody hell outta my way.' When he reached the wire he shook it hard. 'Get down here, youse little bastards. Wait 'til I get my hands on youse.'

Other guards came running. They tried talking to the people at the fence but most kept on shouting. Abdul and I managed to worm our way to the front where we could see a bus with its door open. Four detainees in manacles with guards on both sides were marched out to the bus. One of them was RSW19! They all got on, the door closed and the bus roared off.

Craning my neck to look at the wire above my head, I shouted, 'Come down, Zainullah. Now. Ple-e-ease.' He looked at me between his feet and started to slither downwards. I breathed loudly and reached up to catch him. Just as he dropped into my arms a hard blow crashed into my shoulders, then another and another. Clutching Zainullah in front of me, I fell forwards to the ground so my back took the beating.

I could hear Dung-face's voice, yelling, 'Get the bloody hell away from the fence. All of you . . .' Then it stopped and so did the blows. I looked up to see Abdul hanging onto the guard's back, and Dung-face trying to shake him off.

Grabbing Zainullah's hand, I yelled, 'Come on! Run for it.' We scrambled to our feet and ran with other fleeing figures to the dongas. Peering out the window, I saw the guard beating Abdul, who was trying to get to his feet. Two other guards pulled Dung-face away from him, and once his feet hit the ground Abdul kept running.

'Stay here,' I screamed at Zainullah. Racing back up the passage, I arrived in the telly room at the same time as Abdul. Unaware of anyone else, I threw my arms around his neck. 'Are you okay? Thank you, thank you. Are you okay?' I felt his arms around me, holding tight, then slacken. We both took a step back, looking into each other's eyes as we did, just for a second. At that moment I knew we both felt the same way.

The room was full of people talking about the scuffle. It was nothing unusual. That sort of thing happened at least three times a week, but it was the first time any of us had been directly caught in the action.

'Nessa, are you hurt?' Abdul's hands held mine and his voice was gentle.

'I'm all right,' I said, rolling my shoulders to see if that was true. 'Ouch.' A stab of pain made me add, 'My back's a bit sore but it's nothing to what it would have been if you hadn't pulled him off. Thank you, Abdul. You're not just a pretty face.' I smiled weakly and, suddenly I had to sit down.

'That dung-encrusted arsehole! I could kill him.' Abdul exploded as Hassan rushed through the door and, pushing his way through the talking people, reached us, out of breath. Abdul held out his hand and pulled me to my feet. We moved towards our room.

'What happened? Someone said Dung-face belted you, Ness. Are you okay?' Hassan hadn't seen the drama.

'A bit sore, but Abdul got him off me,' I replied, turning to Abdul as we reached the door. 'Abdul, he hit you pretty hard. Are you all right?'

'Yes. Takes more than that *Khar-e-Barkash* to hurt me.'

'What happened?' Hassan rather awkwardly put his hand on my shoulder in a show of brotherly concern, which touched me, but also hurt my bruises. I made no sound but must have winced as he quickly dropped his hand, adding, 'Sorry, Ness.' That's another first. Apologies from my big brother.

Gingerly I sat down as Abdul told Hassan the story, then I asked, 'Abdul, did you know RWS19 was going away.'

'Yes. The Immigration Department wanted him to give evidence in a trial in Perth. He'll be gone a few days. The fishermen whose boat he came on are being tried for people smuggling. Like Asad was taken to give evidence about the fisherman who brought us here.'

'But why did they put handcuffs on him. Did they do that to Asad, too?'

'Yes. Asad said he'd never felt so humiliated in his life. They made him wear them all the time, even at the trial, as though he was being tried. They do it to everyone they take out of the Camp if they don't have a visa. Even that man who was badly

150

injured in the riot last week in the other compound was put in handcuffs to go to hospital – and he was unconscious.' I couldn't think of anything to say that I hadn't said a hundred times before about this Camp. I felt like crying.

As Abdul finished talking I looked over to Mum and Zainullah's bunk and in the dim light made out Mum lying on the side nearest me, her back to the room, and Zainullah's wide eyes peering over her still form. Zahra must be with Yasmine and her mum, I thought, and made a mental note to check. Since Mum's withdrawal, Zahra often went with them in the afternoon.

I crooked my index finger and beckoned Zainullah over. He pretended not to see me, sliding down behind Mum and out of sight. I went over to their bed and tapped Zainullah on the shoulder, hissing, 'Come out of there. I want to talk to you.' For a change he did what I asked, climbing over Mum. Any problem that arose was too much for Mum now. Mostly she just lay on the bunk, eyes closed, trying to block everything out.

When I was back sitting on my bunk, with Abdul and Hassan flanking me and Zainullah standing in front of us, I asked in the sternest voice I could manage, 'What did you think you were doing climbing the fence, Zainullah?'

'Trying to help us get free,' Zainullah whispered defiantly. 'But I didn't mean for him to hit you, Nessie.' His face crumpled as he burst into tears, looking so tragic that I couldn't be cross with him. I put my arm around his shoulders and his sobs quietened enough for him to go on. 'I hate . . . this Camp.' Sniff. 'I want us to get out . . . so Mummy can come back.' Sniff, sniff. Pulling him closer, he rested his head on my shoulder and his small body shuddered as his warm tears soaked my thin top.

The realisation of how much Mum's decline had affected my little brother hit me like a truck. I had believed that he hadn't felt her slipping away, because he cuddled her at night and she comforted him. He's on the edge, like all of us, I thought, just showing it in his different ways.

'Okay. I know you were trying to help, but you mustn't do that again. You might get hurt.'

'Well, if I hurt myself . . . we might get out. I heard some big boys say so.' Sniff, sniff.

'No, bro,' Hassan cut in. 'That's not right. They don't know what they're saying. They're so tired of waiting for their visas that they say mad stuff.'

'I'm tired, too.'

'We all are, but hurting yourself won't help. *Promise* you'll talk to me first if you think of doing something like that again?'

Zainullah nodded, tiredly.

'Or you can talk to me.' I must talk to him more, I decided, and not leave him to play with the little kids, thinking he's not noticing bad stuff. I gave him a big hug and he hugged me back. 'Oww.' I tried not to squeal but my back really hurt now.

'Nessie, can I see?' Zainullah asked, his face so dramatic that I felt my own face screw up in a mixture of pain and amusement.

'Yes, c'mon, Ness,' Hassan said. 'Let's see the damage.'

Worried at how much it hurt, I slowly turned around, lifting the back of my top as far as I could, but even then thinking that if Mum was herself she'd be horrified that I'd do such a thing in front of Abdul. I heard sharp intakes of breath.

'Poor Nessie!' Zainullah sounded really impressed.

'That *bartong, assinine stard*!' I'd never heard Hassan use Bahkhul's favourite curse before. 'Ness, there's great red welts and he's even broken the skin.'

'He won't get away with this if it's the last thing I do here.' Abdul sounded angrier than I'd ever heard him. 'Ness, you lie down,' he continued, his voice now as soft as falling snow on a windless night. 'I'll get a wet towel to put on your back. That'll help the swelling and pain. You *must* lie down. Hassan, would you go to the nurse and tell her you've got a headache? She'll give you some Panadol. Unless you'd rather go and see her yourself, Ness?'

'Not now,' I replied, wriggling down to lie on my tummy. 'You never know who's on duty. Anyway, I don't feel I could walk that far. What about your back, Abdul?'

'I'm okay. I was moving – and I had this jacket on. Anyway on my tough hide there might be a few bruises, that's all.' With that he disappeared through the door.

'Are you okay if I go to get the tablets, Ness?' Hassan asked.

'Sure.' My head and back were really throbbing now. 'And when you find out who's on, if they're okay, I might go to see the nurse later if the pain's still bad. But please, Hassan, before you go, will you take Zainullah to stay with Ali? And see if Zahra's still with Yasmine and her mum? I need to sleep. I can hardly keep my eyes open.'

'Sure.'

I buried my face in my pillow.

'I want to stay with Nessie,' I heard Zainullah say to Hassan, but I thought they could sort it out for once . . .

I think I half woke when the coldness of the wet towel on my back startled me, but I fell asleep again immediately. Shock, Tara interpreted when she took me to see the nurse later. The nurse said she'd report the guard, but I didn't hope too much that anything would happen. I knew he'd been reported at least three times before.

CHAPTER 18

For me, the worst of all the Camp's effects was having to watch what was happening to Mum, because I could do nothing that seemed to help her. Now she hardly talked at all. She still hugged us a lot and when we had nightmares she'd rock us back to sleep, but without the soothing words we were used to. I knew she was *really* sick when she started to cry a lot and sit by herself in our room, only coming out for meals when I made her, and she ate almost nothing. It was then she stopped talking, even to us unless we pressed her urgently. Zahra couldn't understand what was happening. She didn't want to leave Mum for a second, even to go and play. I think she was frightened Mum would disappear completely like Dad had. I'd have to coax Zahra out to the telly room with promises to stay with her while she watched *Playschool*, and even then she had to sit on my lap on the floor and insisted we nursed our dolls.

Whenever I went back to our room, I'd find Mum crying. Her pillow was always wet. It was almost impossible to make her come to the mess. When I talked to Tara about it she suggested I talk to her mum. I tried to describe what Mum had been like at home and how different she was now, and although I tried to do everything, nothing seemed to help her.

'Nessa,' Shakeela said to me, 'I talk to your mother before. I try see her each day, only quick. She doesn't want me. I tell you what I tell her. Many people in Camp have this illness. Depression. People get sick when bad things happen. Your mum think she weak. I try explain, depression make many sick, but not all people. Each body is different. Not weak, not strong. Different.'

'I know what you mean. Zainullah's angry now. Zahra's withdrawn. She used to be so bright and bubbly. But I think it's making Hassan get some sense. Everyone gets nightmares.'

Shakeela and Tara nodded. 'I don't know anyone in the Camp who doesn't get them,' Tara put in.

Shakeela said, 'Sometimes same things make people behave different. Might make some people . . .' Here she paused and talked rapidly in their language with Tara, then continued, 'change inside body.'

'I don't know what you mean.'

'Well, bad things, terror, change people inside. Change . . . chemistry inside. Sick like your mum. Depression. You understand?'

'I think so.' I wasn't at all sure but I'd think about it later.

She went on. 'People get better from depression but it hard in bad place. In Camp no doctor. Nurses try but they not doctor. They give people . . .' another discussion with Tara, '. . . tablets. Sometimes tablets not good. Make people more sick. I talk your mother before. She want get better no tablets.'

'Could she get some now?'

'Yes, but must see nurse each day. Make her swallow tablets there.'

Tara interrupted, frowning. 'The nurse told Mum that people have been trying to kill themselves by taking overdoses they saved up, so they made this rule.'

155

I knew Mum wouldn't go. She only went to meals because she was afraid of the guards. She'd grown so thin. But, at least Shakeela helped me understand Mum's illness better.

❧ ❧ ❧

One cold, grey, windy day when Hassan and Abdul had taken the two Zs to lunch, I went to get Mum. She was in bed, curled up in a ball under the blankets, facing the wall. She wouldn't move. I already felt as bleak as the weather after a morning washing clothes by hand in cold water, because the old washing machines had broken down again. There'd been no hot water for months. Finding Mum like this unsettled me totally. I knew I *had* to do something drastic. I was scared that one day I'd find her dead.

Although Mum didn't care about herself, she'd make an effort to listen if I said something was wrong with me. So I sat on the bunk and said to her back, 'Mum *please* stop crying. I need to talk to you about something important. Ple-e-e-ease.' Silence, then sobs. 'I'm *so* worried. I don't know what to do. My head feels like it's going to burst.' I was telling the truth. Mum's back stopped shaking. 'I could ask the nurse for some sleeping tablets. I'd save them up. Only pretend to swallow –'

'No!' The croaky sound stopped me. Slowly Mum turned to lie on her back. Her enormous eyes stared from dark sockets contrasting starkly with her pale, tear-stained face. 'No, Nessa. Never that. No matter what. I'm sorry I'm a burden but I can't help it.' I could see the effort she was making. I'd usually tell her that of course she wasn't a burden. But today I said nothing. She *was* a huge burden and I didn't know how much longer either of us could take this. If only she'd talk to me and I could see her getting better. But she seemed to be getting worse and I didn't know what to do.

She started again in her funny croaky voice, 'We must help each other.'

'I want to, Mum. Really I do. But I don't know how to help you any more. You'll have to tell me what to do.' I was surprised at how together I sounded. I'd never been able to talk to her firmly like this. Like I was *her* mother. 'Tell me what will help you and I'll do it. D'you feel sick? Do you hurt somewhere?'

'Gulnessa, you have been so strong. My super-woman.' I smiled at the name she used to call me at home when Dad was away and I helped her with heavy jobs on the farm. This was better. 'I wouldn't be alive if you hadn't looked after us all.' She gathered her strength. 'Please help me a little longer.'

'I wasn't sure you noticed, Mum, or if you wanted me to do it. I even got to thinking that if I left everything for you, you might get better 'cos you'd see we needed you,' the new, braver me said. 'But now I know it's helping you, of course I'll do it.'

'Well, it does help me so much. I don't know why I'm sick. Sometimes when no one's in the room I try to get up. I tell myself that I should be able to. But I can't. That's why I was so bad when you came in. I'd tried to give you a surprise and be up.' As she talked, tears ran down her face and her voice was wobbly, but she was talking! 'You mightn't believe me, but thinking that shows me I'm a bit better. I wouldn't have thought of it a little while ago, I felt so wretched.' I hugged her, tears now running down my face, too.

'That's great, Mum!' Just hearing that she *wasn't* giving up on us made me want to dance.

'Darling, if you'll just stay strong and help me through this while we're in here, I *know* I'll be all right when we get out.' And I believed her. Everyone wanted to leave all the bad stuff behind and start a new life. But here, locked up for goodness knows

157

how long and not sure of any future, no one could recover. I knew I *had* to find a way of getting us out of there.

'Of course I'll help, Mum. Just help me and talk to me, please.' Phew, I thought. Now I can go on. 'It's lunchtime. Please come and eat?'

'I'm not hungry.' She sounded tired after her effort.

'But you didn't go to the mess this morning. The officers might come looking for you. Mum, did you hear me?'

'Yes. But I'm so tired. I can't face anyone.'

'We-ell, if I bring back some food, promise you'll eat it?'

'Yes.' She was just saying it so I'd leave her alone.

When I got to the mess I piled a plate high with rice and veg and joined the others at our usual table. There were no chairs left so I nursed Zahra, and ate a bit from my plate. Then I whispered my plan to Abdul and Hassan, and asked Tara if the two Zs could walk back with their family. Tara gave me a thumbs up. Since Gum Tree had shown it to us it was our favourite signal, and the Good Guy greeted us with it each time he saw us.

Carefully carrying Mum's plate of food under my loose top I walked to the door, hoping to be long gone before the officer started his checks. Rats! He was waiting, but it was Good Guy. I tried to be cool as he signalled me. I had to return it or he'd know something was up, so I grinned, heart hammering, pulled my hand out and gave the thumbs up. I felt something warm dribbling down my stomach.

'Hi, AXZ23! You're leaving early,' the Good Guy greeted me. The warmth trickled further, down my leg. Although I couldn't understand his words, I guessed he'd asked where I was going.

'Toilet,' I said innocently.

'You – come – back?' he said each word slowly. I nodded, and moved off quickly. I'd just got around the corner when I heard footsteps. A hand grasped my shoulder. I froze.

'What's this?' The hand tapped my arm holding the plate. I looked up, and slowly drew out the dripping plate of food. The Good Guy raised his eyebrows. 'Why?'

'Mum sick.' I tried to look unconcerned.

'See nurse?' he asked. I shook my head. 'Well, I'll get the nurse to see her. You come back to the mess with me.' I didn't know all he said, but he steered me back around the corner. There along the path was a wet trail sprinkled with tell-tale grains of rice.

The Good Guy said, shaking his head, 'Next – time – don't – spill.' Whatever his words, I smiled sheepishly.

When the two Zs and I got back to our room, Mum wasn't there. Tara put her head in and, taking in the situation, reached for my hand and led us to her family's room. Her mum said she'd check at the medical centre and the rest of us joined Tara's dad and the other men and boys playing cards. *Rug Rats* was on TV.

Before the movie had finished Mum returned with Shakeela, arms around each other's waists. Jumping up, I followed them to our room. Mum smiled weakly as she climbed into bed. Shakeela explained, 'She take sleeping tablets. And drink water. Tomorrow she see nurse again.' I went over and kissed Mum's forehead, pulling the blanket up to her chin.

'Thank you, so much.' I turned. Shakeela had left the room.

❧ ❧ ❧

The next morning I went with Mum to the medical centre.

'AXZ23, wait here.' The nurse showed me to a chair near the door. Meanwhile another nurse took Mum's arm and guided her into a small room and closed the door. I pretended to look at the pictures in some magazines but really watched from the corner of my eye as people came into the centre, took their medicines and left. Occasionally the nurse would keep someone longer, and put a little glass stick into their mouth, or wrap a thick belt-thing around their arm, then pump a rubber ball on a tube while she watched a dial. It intrigued me.

Now and again a mother would bring in her baby, and the nurse would take off the baby's clothes and feel it all over. Then she put it into a metal kind-of-dish thing on a stand with a dial under it. Sometimes the nurse patted the mother on the back and saw her to the door, and other times she gave the mother a package before seeing her out.

A commotion outside the door made me jump and open it. Two Kurdish boys we knew who were around Hassan's age and had been in the Camp a long time were trying to get away from Dung-face. He was yelling, 'Get the bloody hell back to the compound, you two.'

Breaking free, they burst through the door. One boy held up a sharp rock, calling in English, 'Look, nurse.' He began sawing at his wrist and blood started to trickle from the cuts he made.

The other boy jumped around the nurse, saying, 'Cutting good, Miss. We get visa. Yes?' The nurse looked horrified.

Following the boys inside, the guard shouted, 'Get the bloody hell outta here, you two. Wait'll I get my hands on you . . .' He grabbed the boy with the rock and chased the other around the room, hauling the first boy behind him.

'Leave them alone!' the nurse shouted. 'I'll handle this.'

I watched the nurse as she examined the boy with the rock. The cuts on his wrists weren't deep and had stopped bleeding. As she cleaned his wounds she talked but I couldn't hear what she said. After a while all three walked back to the door, 'Thank you, Miss. You kind,' one boy said.

The nurse smiled at him. 'It's my job. But I *will* try to help more when I leave tomorrow. And I *will* report that guard.'

The other boy looked hard at her, and asked, 'Are you just kind person? Or can you *really* help us?'

'I'll *really* try to help you,' she said. I could tell she meant it.

Just then Mum reappeared and walked towards me holding out her hand, but before she took mine she turned to the nurse she'd been with, and put her other hand over her heart. The nurse returned the courtesy.

Mum and I didn't speak until we were back in our room, then she said, 'She's a good woman. She tried to understand. She'll help. She gave me tablets with a glass of water. She said to drink plenty. I have to go each day. I will try these tablets.' I threw my arms around Mum's neck and gave her my best hug. This was a breakthrough.

CHAPTER 19

Days and weeks dragged on. The only way I could tell how much time passed was the weather. Here there seemed to be only two long seasons. Cool days, sometimes cold, with cold nights; and boiling hot days with hot nights. Between these two seasons the days changed quickly from cool to warm to hot, with the nights going from cold to cool to hot. Now, we'd finished our second cool season here. One and a half years gone.

Nothing changed. Boredom nearly drove me mad. I asked each new nurse who came to the Camp to help us get out. And every time I saw people arriving I'd rush to get in front at the fence and call out for help. But nothing happened. I'd given up on school. So had Tara, but the two little boys went sometimes.

There'd been no rain since we arrived except one or two thunderstorms. Now I understood why there were so few plants on the endless, flat, red earth. It amazed me that anything at all grew or lived out there. I often thought of RSW19's description after he returned from giving evidence at the trial in Perth. 'Perth was like paradise and coming back here was like returning to hell.'

I spent a lot of time wondering what 'paradise' was really

like. Although I learned some things about Australia from TV, we only saw programs in English and I'd no idea where most of those places were. What sorts of trees and plants grew in Perth? What sort of people lived there? What kinds of houses did they have? Where would we live? Would we have another donga? Perhaps we'd have to build our own house to live in as people did at home. Most of our village houses were mud-brick family homes shared by parents, married sons or daughters and their children. If new people arrived, not that there were many, they had to build their own mud-brick houses.

I hoped everyone in Australia didn't live in dongas. They were noisy at night, and anyone could come in at any time, so we were never alone with just our family. I missed that. We all did. Everyone was grumpy or sad most of the time, but I tried to hang on to the belief that we'd soon be released. When I felt really down I'd shut my eyes, block out everything around me, and concentrate hard until I was back in my lighthouse night. There I'd feel how it was to be happy and believe we'd find happiness again.

But I kept hearing sad stories and seeing terrible things people tried to do to themselves – just trying to get help. One man tried to burn himself, he was so desperate. He didn't get a visa. Just terribly burnt, and he was taken to a hospital until he was well enough to come back. And guards kept telling us that no one wanted us in Australia. They went on and on about the snakes and spiders and sharks that would get us, *if* we were ever released.

There were attempted suicides too. MTK79 tried again, and Abdul told me about another man. We felt so bad. All we could do was pray for them. Mum slept a little better now she was taking the pills and she tried to tell me how she felt each day. I never

163

talked to her about bad things but I talked more to Abdul. I lay awake waiting until he came back from the kitchen, or playing cards at night. When Hassan came back with him he sometimes joined us, but most often he was so tired he just crashed. He didn't want to hear about worries. I tried to explain about Mum, but I don't think either of them really understood. They hadn't seen the full extent of her helplessness or her sadness.

One night Abdul told me about a man from another compound who'd tried to kill himself. He'd felt so bad about bringing his family to this place where they were all so unhappy that he couldn't stand to see them like that any longer, and he could do nothing to help them. He was so depressed he tried to take his own life by climbing the fence and cutting his wrists on the razors in the wire coils at the top. He wanted the guards and officials to see how desperate he was. They saw him, pulled him down, took him to have his wounds dressed by the nurse and then put him in an observation room where they kept him for a month. Nothing changed.

Another time when Abdul was really down he talked to me about MTK79. He'd grown desperate, as he'd heard nothing from the lawyer. He'd been waiting months for the hearing but now believed he'd been totally forgotten. On the night MTK79 tried to kill himself the second time, Abdul was returning from work when he saw MTK79 outside our donga smoking, and stopped to chat.

'How goes it?' Abdul greeted the squatting figure. No answer, so he tried again. 'Anything the matter?' Still silence. Abdul reached down and touched MTK79's shoulder.

'Huh?' The man started, shook his head and looked up, eyes wide with alarm as if he'd been woken from a deep sleep. But Abdul knew MTK79 hadn't been asleep. He'd seen a red glow as he dragged on his cigarette.

'I said, how goes it?' Abdul repeated. MTK79 swore angrily, bitterly. Abdul wouldn't tell me the words.

'Hey, want to talk about it?' Abdul asked, crouching next to him.

'Why would I? No one cares.'

'Don't talk rot. What about your family at home?'

'Still don't know anything. They're probably dead. If they weren't, they'd try to contact me, wouldn't they?'

'They probably can't.'

'Well, I can't contact them either. Anything that goes into Afghanistan would be stopped. I can do nothing. I feel useless. Hopeless.'

'G'day.' The Good Guy's voice made them straighten.

'G'day.' Abdul had learned some conversational English.

'Wassa matter? Y'faces are as long as a wet week.'

'Huh?' Abdul grunted and MTK79 looked at his feet.

'Y'look sad,' the Good Guy translated.

'Friend sad,' Abdul replied. 'No family. Here lo-o-ong time.'

'Aw, sorry, mate. I dunno why they won't let y'out. Can't see why m'self. Seeya tomorra.' He strode off.

'He sounded like he wanted to help,' Abdul said.

'They all say that, but no one *does* anything.'

'Why don't you come inside and watch TV? Take your mind off things.'

'No. Anyway, I've got to go . . .' He jerked his thumb in the direction of the toilets. 'Good night.'

That was when he tried to hang himself, Abdul told me. On the fence behind the ablution block. He looked away, 'Ness, he's been in the observation room for weeks now and I know how he hated it before. I could've stopped him if I'd been with him.'

'He mightn't have done it that night, but he would've the

next, or the one after. The only thing that'll stop him doing it again until he succeeds is if he leaves the Camp.'

'You're probably right. Where did you get so wise?' Abdul stroked my hair, and I loved the feel of his hand. My scalp tingled, and although I didn't know what he meant about being wise, I knew I'd made him feel better – and I did, too.

❦ ❦ ❦

Another night as I lay awake, waiting for Abdul to return, I seriously considered trying what the Kurdish boys had done at the medical centre, to see if it would help get a visa. When Abdul arrived I didn't tell him that. Instead I told him about something that happened earlier in the day as I waited for Mum at the medical centre.

'This man came crashing in, carrying a woman, and yelling, "Save her, save her ple-e-e-ease. Don't let her die!"' I explained. 'It turned out that his wife had somehow been secretly saving up her sleeping tablets for weeks and took them all at once. Her husband found her unconscious in bed with their new baby screaming next to her, trying to reach her breast.' I glanced at Abdul, who was watching me closely. I felt my cheeks grow hot, so I went on quickly. 'They pumped out the woman's stomach and put her and her baby in an observation room.'

'What can I say?' He shrugged helplessly. 'You can't let it get to you. We've got a future.'

I had to do it. Find out if he meant what I hoped he did. The new brave me asked, 'We've got a future?' Then the old scared me saved me from hearing his answer, adding, 'Of course we're all going to get out of here and make a new home in Perth.'

'How do you know it'll be in Perth?' he asked, also avoiding the personal thing. 'They might put us on a bus to Melbourne.

We can't tell them we want to go to Perth instead. That's what they did to Asad and his family when their visa came last month.'

We'd hardly had time to say goodbye to our friend. After breakfast one day, Asad had been called to the interview room and told to go and get his family as their temporary visas had come through. A bus was waiting at the gate. The family came to tell us and we all cried and went to watch through the fence and wave goodbye.

Abdul went on, 'I got a phone call from him last night. He'd asked if they could be sent to Sydney to stay with his cousin's family there, but the guards said, "You go where you're sent." They ended up in Adelaide. He contacted his cousins in Sydney and they managed to raise money to pay for bus fares so Asad's family could join them. Asad said people they'd met there were kind and tried to help them get a house of their own, but it's difficult because their visas are only temporary. Many landlords say, "If you're temporary, how can you pay the rent?" Anyway, he said even though there are problems it's much better than the Camp.'

'That'd be easy. But it's good you've heard.' It made me feel better about our chances now that a few families we'd arrived with had got visas – even if they were temporary.

'What else did Asad say?'

'Not much. He's going to phone again when they've found a house. He also sent this card when they arrived in Sydney. It must have been held up.' The card had a beautiful pink flower on the front, and it read: *Dear Abdul and all the family, How good it is to see the sun and moon and stars outside the razor wire. You will join us soon. I pray for you every day. I will phone when we have a house in this beautiful city. Layla and Sakina join me in sending our loving thoughts.*

Asad.

CHAPTER 20

Mum kept her promise, continuing to see the nurse daily and take her medication, but she still wasn't like her old self. She tried to talk to us, and to Shakeela, but no one else. She said it exhausted her and gave her splitting headaches. But instead of lying in bed crying, she tried to do things like mending and learning a few English words. She said she'd never manage to speak English fluently but I told her to stop being negative – a Tara-word I'd learned.

I tried not to worry Mum, and every day I tried to work out a way to get us out of there. I pushed down my heart pain which often flared in the night when missing Dad and my grandparents hurt most. And I kept out of people's way. Except for our family, Abdul – of *course* – and Tara. She was a real friend. We hung out together, talking, sitting . . .

We agreed that the daily outbursts of violence, verbal and physical, we saw in the Camp, which were triggered by the slightest remark, look, or even thought, were because everyone tried to keep the lid on their hurts and worries. Our strategy was to keep to ourselves. There was nothing to do. Ages ago we'd used up the last fabric for making clothes for our dolls. They were all we had and we often made Zahra and Yasmine laugh, pretending to talk to the dolls like they were our babies. We did it so that they would copy us when they played by themselves. They were so cute.

During the long, hot summer months we sat for long, hot hours in the shade of the dongas, shifting with the sun, keeping out of the way of the hot tempers and misery inside, and out of sight of the guards. We talked about everything. We shared stories of our homes, our families and our plans for the future, but one thing I couldn't tell even Tara was how I felt about Abdul – even if I knew how to explain it. And I didn't. We sat in silence when we had nothing to say. In those boiling months Mum took to lying down again but at least she didn't cry. The dongas were like ovens but there was nowhere else to go and Mum said the heat was easier to bear lying down.

One week, thankfully as the days were getting cooler, the toilets clogged up and the men in the Camp had to dig up septic tanks, and empty them. The smell was so putrid as we sat in our scrap of shade that I exclaimed to Tara, 'Phew! This reminds me of the dung hole on the fishing boat that brought us here.'

'You haven't told me about that.'

'It was so gross I thought you probably didn't want to know.'

We made our storytelling graphic, trying to outdo each other for the best effects. Tara nodded encouragingly, so I continued. 'Well, we'd just finished eating our first meal on the fishing boat. It was the yummy food we bought at the Indonesian markets. I was sitting on the deck trying not to think about my need to pee, when Zahra announced, "Mummy, I have to pee."

'Mum replied, "Okay, darling. Gulnessa and I will take you. We should all go before we try to sleep." Saved, I thought in relief. Now at least I wouldn't have to experience the embarrassment of going by myself and climbing over the strangers, who'd all know where I was heading.

'We picked our way through the crowd, which covered every tiny bit of deck. As we climbed over bodies and squeezed between others, apologising and excusing ourselves, I heard groans. I saw one woman moaning loudly and she looked as green as the clothes my mother was wearing.

'Finally we got to the hatch and the fisherman pulled it open. I leaned over to see what was below and a putrid stink forced me to straighten, quickly. Mum did the same. The fisherman gestured to us to climb down the ladder. Mum took a deep breath and nodded at me to do the same. We descended into a dark, smelly cabin crammed with all sorts of things, from nets and lanterns to rubber boots and boxes, piled high. At the opposite end was a closed door, and in front of this a line of about six people squeezed between the clutter. I held my nose.

'While we waited, to keep our minds off the smell, Mum started to talk to the woman in front of her. It turned out she'd lived not far away from our village. We told her about our boys waiting on the deck, and where we were camped so that she and her family could come and see us later.

'At last we stood in front of the door. The stink made me retch. As the door opened I clenched my teeth. Our new friend came out carrying her child and her face scrunched up as she said, "It's bad in there."

'"We have to go." Mum gave me a tiny push towards the open door. My stomach heaved. "You next, Gulnessa." I swallowed, keeping my teeth clenched, and stepped inside the tiny space.

'In the centre of the floor was a hole with a wide pipe. As there was no bucket of water to flush with, disgusting masses had collected on the bend. There was a place at each side of the hole for feet, but these were so mucky I balanced my sandalled feet as far away from the hole as I could, and remained standing.

Almost before I'd finished I pushed open the door and bolted through it, retching and vowing never to come again. When I reached the ladder I stood holding its sides, stretching towards the open hatch, and gulped in what now smelled like fresh air. Another girl holding her scarf tightly across her nose climbed down the ladder. I swung back against the wall to let her pass, looking away to hide the expression on my face.

'At last I saw Mum piggybacking Zahra, struggling to get around a large man standing in line. I stepped forward, reaching for a white-faced Zahra and picked her from Mum's back so Mum could get past. Mum then took Zahra again, saying softly, "Are you all right now, baby?" Zahra nodded dumbly. "She threw up," Mum told me as she climbed the rungs.

'At last we sank into our places on deck. Hassan asked, "What's the matter? You all look green. Seasick?"

'"No. It's not very nice down there.' Mum, as always, made the best of things.

'Suddenly something in me snapped. "Don't go down there! It's gross, like nothing you could imagine! You boys can pee overboard with your spouts." I never dreamed I'd say anything like this out loud but I felt so stirred up. "And *I'm* going to pee over the side next time I need to. I'll *die* if I have to go there again."'

I glanced at Tara. She was almost exploding in the effort not to laugh!

'I didn't dare to look at Mum. I meant every word I said. No one spoke.

'"Gulnessa," Mum's voice was dead calm. "You're a young woman. We're in a difficult situation where we must do things we don't like."

'"Don't *like*!" I screamed at her. "Try hate! Loathe! I *can't* go there again. I'd rather die." Huge sobs wracked my body. It was as if the repulsive stench from that scummy, squalid dung-hole had penetrated the wall which held back all my fear, anguish and anxiety of the past weeks. Now, it flooded over me, whooshing out like water from a burst dam.

'Amidst the torrent I felt arms around me and smelled my mother's nearness. Gradually my sobs quietened and I sat in her arms, eyes closed, tears still pouring, silently now, down my face. My head dropped onto her chest and I felt her lips on my hair. A small head pushed onto my lap, and a little hand curled around my wet finger. When my tears dried I opened my eyes and saw Zahra's worried face, staring up at me.

'"I love you, Nessie," she whispered, and with her hand wiped my tears from my dear face.'

'What a story, Ness! I felt I was with you,' Tara said from her heart.

'Thanks.' I grinned. We sat silent, wrapped in our own thoughts.

❧ ❧ ❧

As I lay in bed that night the smell of the toilets was still nauseating. I couldn't get to sleep, and I couldn't get the fishing boat out of my mind. Nor Asad's baby's death. Memories are so weird the way some won't come back when you want them to, and others hit you without warning and won't leave you alone. The storm when the baby died was so vivid I wasn't sure whether I was reliving it consciously, or dreaming . . .

It's late in the afternoon and the ocean's almost dead-calm. The captain shouts, 'Sit down. Tie ropes tight. Hold on. Weather bad. Big waves.'

A storm seems unlikely. It's too quiet, but low clouds cover the sky. The windless air is heavy. It's hot, too. Sweat trickles down our faces. Asad's coming towards us, picking his way through the people on deck, stopping occasionally to talk. When he reaches Mum he says, 'There's no big boat to meet us after all and I think we're in for rough weather. This boat will toss around like a cork. You must tie the children tightly to poles on deck with this.'

He passes a piece of rope to each of us and helps us tie knots that won't come undone. Checking our ropes are securely fastened to poles near the deck rails, Asad asks Mum, 'Do you have something that we could use to tie you and Abdul to the poles, too? It would be much safer.' His voice has so much authority even Abdul doesn't complain. Mum takes Theerma's scarf and a small rug from her bag. 'Will these do?'

Deftly he knots the scarf above Zahra's and my ropes. Then he helps Abdul secure his rug above Hassan's and Zainullah's ropes tied to the pole next to ours.

'Theermie hold Mummy,' sings Zahra. 'Theermie hold Mummy.' Asad smiles and waves, then makes his way back to his own family. I notice a stiff breeze has sprung up, and the air's chilly.

We pack everything back into our bags, tie them to the posts and sit close together, wrapped in blankets. Riding the waves, the boat thumps and jolts as we push into the strengthening wind. Scudding, dark clouds look so low I think if birds are still circling above us we wouldn't know. They'd be flying right through them. Talk is almost impossible. Labouring engines and our boat banging on the waves drown out all other sounds.

Spray tears at my face. I can't tell if it's the waves we've ploughed through, or if it's rain pelting its stinging needles. Ballooning nausea pushes out the giant fish in my stomach as I hear Zainullah yelling, 'Mum, I feel sick. I'm going to be sick.'

I hear retching and moaning and my stomach heaves as I breathe the sickly smell of vomit. Turning my head towards the railing just in time, a gut-wrenching convulsion shakes my body and my stomach

173

throws up the food I've just eaten. The sight of the nauseating puke makes me heave again and again.

My body strains against the rope fastening me to the pole. Each time we rise on a giant wave I freeze. As we fall I spew. Groans, moans and the sound of puking surround me. Water smashes onto the deck. The boat shudders violently. Surely it'll break? I'll die. We'll all drown. It's not possible to be this frightened and to stay alive.

My mother moans, retches, and sobs, 'I feel so terrible. I want to die.' My heart stops beating. I can't go on without her.

'Mum, no!' I lunge out, releasing my hold on the pole. The boat rears, hurling me backwards. My rope jerks me to the deck before I smash into the railing. I feel a hand close around my ankle. It drags me. Like a bullet I slide across the glassy deck and slam into Mum. 'You mustn't die,' I shout.

'I don't want to.' She gathers me and Zahra in her arms. Her body convulses. I grab the pole. The smell of vomit clogs my nose. It's everywhere.

'Pray with me for our safety.' She kisses my puke-covered face and I kiss hers. We cling to each other and Zahra and the pole. Past Mum's shoulder I see Abdul, Hassan and Zainullah huddling together around their pole, struggling to hold a blanket around themselves. A disgusting mess sloshes around their feet. And I pray.

Relentless rain is bucketing down, soaking us to the skin. Or is it the huge, black waves towering again and again, washing over us? The boat climbs one mountainous, watery surface after another, and drops into the chasm dividing them. Endlessly it hurls us against ropes, poles and each other. How I pray the knots hold. Everyone on board pukes until there's nothing to bring up. Then we retch, grimly crouching, clinging to poles with one hand and whoever's nearest with the other.

Time drags in a blur of fear, pain and despair. No one sleeps.

174

Mothers and fathers cradle tiny children in sopping blankets. Little hands cling to parents. Fear silences their cries. Some time during the second night the winds and waves subside. We sink into the sleep of the dead. Wet clothes stink of vomit.

I wake. The sun's warmth seeps into my bones. I struggle to sit up. My top side's dry but my clothes are stiff with salt and sick. Parts I lie on are still soaking. All around are steaming heaps as the sun dries clothes and blankets.

'Mu-um, Nessa's awake.' Zainullah's voice. I look around. Mum stands with the three boys at the deck rail. The sea's quiet but the boat rises and falls on the swell, like it's still puffing after its rage. Two fishermen furl ropes and untangle nets, returning them to their places on deck. People try to clean themselves and their belongings. Only Zahra still sleeps.

'Stand up, Gulnessa.' Mum takes my hand and pulls me to my feet. 'Let's see if we can get some of that muck off you. Here, wrap your-self in this rug – it's nearly dry – and give me your clothes. You boys, turn around.'

I hear Zainullah suggest, 'Let's look for fish.'

I do as Mum says, handing her my stiff, reeking clothes. Then, clutching the scratchy rug under my chin, I squat.

Zahra's pulling at my blanket. 'Can I dress up, too?'

'You'll have to wait your turn. Gulnessa has the only dryish rug,' Mum answers for me, turning to shake my things over the railing and trail them in the water.

'You can get under with me,' I offer, feeling sorry for my little sister in her sick-covered clothes, although she doesn't seem to notice. She leaves her clothes in a pile on the deck, and crawls under the rug. It feels good to be warm and dry again, so close to my chubby sister, and my spirits lift, too. Popping my head under the rug, I whisper, 'Let's trick Zainullah. I'll stick my head out and call him. You hide under here until I say, "Theerma". That will be our signal for you to pop up.'

'Goody!' She jiggles around excitedly.

'But you'll have to sit still or you'll spoil it,' I warn.

'Little mouse.' Zahra curls up in a ball between my crossed legs.

'Zainullah,' I call, 'have you seen Zahra?' I feel her body shaking with giggles.

'She's still asleep,' Zainullah answers.

'Where? I can't see her.' Four faces swing around sharply.

'She's there.' Zainullah points to the small space on the deck from which I'd just whisked her clothes.

Out of the corner of my eye I see Mum watching me intently, frowning slightly, so I turn to her to warn her to keep quiet. She knows Zahra's awake.

'You'd better look for her. She might fall overboard –' I say.

'Enough!' Mum orders. 'After what we've just been through I won't have games like that.'

The boys look at her questioningly, and I shout, 'Theerma!'

Zahra, throwing back the blanket, yells, 'Surprise!' She springs up quickly and her head catches me under the chin, clashing my teeth together. She doesn't notice. I drop the blanket and rub my jaw.

Mum steps forward and, covering our naked bodies, murmurs to me, 'Perhaps that serves you right for trying to frighten the boys like that.'

'It was only a trick,' I protest.

'But a stupid one. We've enough to worry about. How would you feel if Zahra really disappeared?'

I murmur, 'Sorry, I didn't think of that.' The boys look at each other and shrug. Hassan pulls a face, and they turn back to spot fish.

CHAPTER 21

With the cooler weather came a major surprise. Without warning after lunch one day, Mum was called to see the Immigration officials.

'It's probably another interview. I'll take the two Zs back to the donga for a lie down and a story,' I told Mum as we left the mess. All morning they'd been grizzly, teasing each other and complaining they were bored.

'I don't know how you find stories to tell them in this place,' RSW19 remarked. He'd sat at our table for lunch as usual but as Hassan and Abdul were both working in the kitchen he walked back with us. 'This place's bad enough for men but when I see women and children here, especially mothers with young children, my heart cries. Children should grow up in good places or how can they be good men and women?'

'It is hard for us all,' I agreed. 'I usually tell the two Zs stories about home, and about Dad and our Bahkhuls and Arjays.'

'Yes, it's good they hear those stories. Not about things from here.' He stopped for a minute, looking like he was in a faraway place, then he went on. 'This morning a mother in our donga couldn't stop her little boy crying. She told me he had toothache and she didn't know what to do. She'd taken him to see the nurse but because he's a child the nurse wouldn't give him Panadol and said to drink water, water and more water. The nurse said the dentist wouldn't visit for a month. In here they say drink water for toothache, drink water for eye problems, drink water for stomach problems. If you say I drink ten glasses of water each day now, they say drink twelve. It doesn't matter how sick people are, they just say drink water.'

'I know. Like when Mum was covered in those insect bites. She was so itchy and looked like she had chickenpox. Then we all got the 'flu. What did they tell us?' I grinned at him.

'Well, this little boy was in such pain I told his mum about a traditional cure my grandmother used,' RSW19 went on. 'Squeeze juice from an onion and put it on the bad tooth.'

'Yuk!' I pulled a face. 'You couldn't get a small child to eat onion juice.'

'No, not eat it. I went to the kitchen and Abdul got me half an onion and I took it back to the donga and squeezed the juice onto a tissue. The boy's mum held the tissue on his bad tooth. Although he screwed up his face like you did, after a bit he stopped crying so it must have helped. It won't last long, though.' We were at the door to our donga.

'I'll remember that. You never know when it might be handy.'

The two Zs were lying quietly for the first time that day and I was telling them about the hideout at Arjay Aqila's house – again. Even though they were there when we saved our first prisoner, the Zs always loved me telling them about it. 'And when I arrived at their house, Arjay Aqila was waiting for me . . .' I stopped, sensing someone else in the room. Glancing up, I gasped. Mum was standing just inside the room with a trance-like expression on her face.

'Mu-u-um? Are you all right?' The little ones looked to where I was staring and then Zahra pulled at my sleeve.

'Mum,' I repeated, louder this time, 'what's the matter?'

Mum blinked a couple of times and her eyes came back into focus. She looked at me, and, speaking very slowly, announced, 'We're – leaving – tomorrow. They didn't give a reason – just said our temporary visas have come. At last they believe we're refugees. Gulnessa, they believe us! In the morning they'll put us on a bus. I asked where it would take us, and they said either to Perth or Melbourne. They don't know yet. But,' she paused, pain in her soft, brown eyes, 'and there is a big "but" . . .'

'What do you mean?' I was ecstatic. Our last night here! We'd have our lives back. *Nothing* could spoil that.

At least, not until Mum said, 'Abdul's not coming. They won't release him. His visa didn't come.'

'What?' I heard my voice scream as I jumped to my feet. 'They can't do that. He's part of our family now.' Panic flipped my switch to spin. Leaving Abdul? It can't happen. I couldn't go without him. 'Mum, we *can't* leave him here alone. He might die.'

'I explained all that, Gulnessa, but it made no difference.' Mum looked defeated.

'*I'm* going to see them.' I'd never felt so mad in my life.

'Gulnessa, come back here. It won't do any good.'

I hardly heard her. Racing out the door, I took off down the passage, through the telly room, tore open the door and covered the hundred or so metres to the Immigration inter-view room in world-record time. My fists hammering on the door kept time with my hammering heart. I gulped air into my starved lungs.

The door swung open. I nose-dived onto the carpet inside.

179

Scrambling to my feet and scanning the room, I shouted in English, 'AXZ23. I want talk. AXZ26.'

I jumped as a voice behind me said, 'Wait here, please.' The officer's hand was still on the door handle.

Jumping around to face him, I screamed, '*Now*.'

'Yes. I'll get someone.' Calmly the officer grabbed my flailing arms and lowered me into a chair. I jumped up as if it burned me, nearly tipping him backwards. A uniformed woman entered the other side of the room and spoke sharply to the officer, who let go of my arms, nodded, and left.

Looking at me like I smelled, the woman beckoned me, saying, 'Come inside.' Walking stiffly, she led me into the next room and sat herself in a padded chair with arms, pulling it up to a large table and indicating I should sit opposite her on a straight-backed, hard, armless chair. Then with deliberate, slow movements she opened a large book in front of her, smoothed out its pages, took a pen in her hand, and finally looked towards me, raising an eyebrow.

Looking up into her disdainful eyes I swallowed hard and, pointing to my chest, stuttered in my best English, 'AXZ23. M-Mum said . . .'

'Wait!' She snapped the order at me. I felt like a puppy begging. And I waited. My resolve almost faltered and I wanted to slink out of sight of this haughty woman. But then an image of Abdul's dear face blocked out hers. I heard him saying gently, 'I understand, Nessa . . .' Determination flooded back and, although trembling, I sat tight. No dragon can scare me off, I told myself angrily. I repeated this over and over, and each time I said it I felt stronger.

A soft knock made me look around. 'Come in!' the imperious voice ordered. A man entered the room. I recognised him as the interpreter who'd been at the Camp when we first arrived.

He pulled a straight-backed chair up to the end of the table, sat down, and talked in English with the dragon. Then, looking at me, he asked in Dari, 'Why did you come here?'

As clearly as I could I outlined the situation covering Mum's news, what it meant to us, and Abdul's place in our family, finishing with '. . . and we *can't* leave him behind. He might try to kill himself like MTK79.'

The interpreter turned towards Dragon-features and began to talk. Intently I watched her face to see if I could tell what she thought. Not a muscle moved. It was like a stone mask had replaced flesh and blood. When the officer stopped talking, Dragon-features began turning the pages of the book in front of her, checking each one. Then she picked up a phone, talked into it for a while, put it down and talked for a long time to the interpreter. He only asked a question once or twice – I could tell they were questions by the way he raised his voice at the end.

At last he turned to me. 'We've asked about the visa application for AXZ26, and have been told it's being processed but it isn't through yet.' His voice was kind, but his words froze my heart. 'It shouldn't be long, though.' I somehow knew that was just to make me feel better.

'Processed? They've been processing us ever since we arrived!' I made a spur-of-the-moment decision. Taking a deep breath before speaking, I thought, yes, I know it's the right thing to do. The others would agree, even Mum. So I said, 'Well then, we'll wait for him. We won't leave until he can come, too. We can put up with a few more nights in the Camp for Abdul.'

The interpreter's voice softened even more as he said, 'I'm afraid it's not as easy as that. We don't know how long it will take. It may be a few weeks, it may be a few months, but it'll be more than a few nights.'

My head hurt. No, this couldn't be right. Not after everything that had happened. 'Why?'

'I don't know. They don't give reasons. They only tell us the application is being processed.'

How I *hated* that word. 'But we *can't* go without him,' I shrieked. 'Don't you understand? He won't have anyone. He might end up like MTK79. I'd die, too, if he did, and it'd be *all – your – fault!*' I stood, glaring at Dragon-features as I shouted the last three words. Not a muscle in her stone face even twitched. She looked up from her writing, glancing at me eyebrows raised, and spoke to the interpreter. He said something back. She shook her head, shrugged and continued writing.

'I'm sorry,' he began, 'there's nothing we can do. It's in the hands of the Immigration Department.'

I bit my lips, gritting my teeth and fighting back tears that burned my eyelids.

'Listen to me,' the interpreter's voice was as soft as lamb's wool. 'Nothing will happen to AXZ26. I'll talk to him and explain everything I know. I'll follow up his visa application, too, and see if I can help get it through as quickly as possible. AXZ26 will understand that, I'm sure.'

I stared at him, drained, empty and helpless. I said in a flat voice, 'You can't make me leave Abdul. I had to leave my dad in Afghanistan. The Terror took him. If you make us leave Abdul, he might kill himself. The Terror made him watch them shoot his dad. Dead. Right outside their home. They made us watch, too. It was so bad. After that we had to escape to be safe, to try to make another life, *together.*' I took a deep breath. 'Why won't you let us do that? Why don't you see that?'

I could see distress on the officer's face as he said, 'I'm sorry. I can't help it. But I'll try to do *something*. I promise. *Please* go on the bus tomorrow. You are now classified as refugees. Your family has temporary visas to stay in Australia for three years. Then if you want to you can apply to stay permanently. When you find a house to live in, AXZ26 will have a home to come to when he gets his visa. Don't you think that will help him? And you can phone and tell him what you're doing and find out how he is.'

It sounded believable. I thought hard. I had to be clear about everything. It was Abdul's life – or death. And mine. Finally I asked, 'How can I phone? We haven't got a phone, nor has he.'

'You can get a house and phone and call the Camp. AXZ26 can talk to you.'

'Oh.' Even though this was much less than I wanted, I knew it was better than poor MTK79 had had. Abdul *would* know that we were waiting for him and that his visa was on its way. And if I could talk to him, it would help keep his spirits up – and mine. 'All right,' I said flatly, pushing myself from the table. I felt I'd lost one of the most important battles of my life.

❁ ❁ ❁

That night in bed, I lay awake waiting for Abdul to return, anxious and fearful. In my head I went over and over different ways to tell him our news. We'd told Yasmine's family and Tara's. Tara was happy for me, but she couldn't hide her disappointment, too. After all, they'd arrived before us and we were leaving first. But we exchanged dolls, promising to look after each other's until we were able to return them in person, when we lived nearby – in Perth.

Our friends were happy for us and promised to look out for Abdul but even this couldn't raise my spirits. I knew how everyone got absorbed in their own problems, and though they might try to include Abdul it wouldn't be the same as being with us. Especially me.

I was deep in thought and didn't hear Hassan come in. Mum had seen him in the mess and whispered our news. She'd asked him not to say anything to Abdul until he came back to our room after work so I could tell him and explain what the officer had promised, to try to give him hope.

Hassan said he stood beside the bed for minutes before I saw him. Then, sitting down, he said, 'Just after dinner an officer called Abdul out and he hadn't returned when I left.'

'What? I'm going to look for him,' I said.

'No, I'm sure he'll be here soon. He probably needed time to himself. He'll come back when he's ready. It won't be easy.'

Hassan realising that? I was impressed.

Hassan was asleep by the time Abdul came in. He headed straight over to where I was lying wide-eyed, and sat next to me. 'Thank you, Ness,' he said and smiled, sadly I thought. 'Thank you for what you did. The interpreter told me. I'll always remember it. Even if they separate us for a while. Don't think I'd ever forget you're all my family.' He took my hand, threading his fingers through mine.

'You know about it, then?' I whispered.

'Yes. I talked with the interpreter for ages. He told me the whole story, and lots more. There are good lawyers and other people – even some politicians – trying to help us. They know what's happening and that it's against all human rights agreements to lock people up indefinitely if they arrive in a country seeking asylum. Organisations like Amnesty International are taking up our cause, too. He's going to keep on their case in Canberra where they make the visa decisions. I believe him.'

'So do I.' I *had* to trust this man to do as he'd promised so I'd be strong enough to go through being separated from Abdul. I couldn't imagine the faceless people he said were helping. As soon as I'm out I'll try to do *something*. I promised myself. *I'm never giving up*.

Abdul was talking again, 'The interpreter hadn't known about what happened to us in Afghanistan until you told him. He doesn't know why Immigration didn't believe it straight-away. He said politicians don't care about sacrificing people like us to stay in power. He can't imagine how we could ever get over something like what we've been through, and he thinks we deserve all the help we can get. He couldn't believe how much guts you have. And, Ness, he talked to me about things that have happened in Australia that we don't know about. While it's true there are people who don't want us here, there are others who welcome us, and are happy to share their country with us. He said he's sure that if people knew what we'd been through, everyone would try to help. And people like us who have taken such risks to get their families to safety have the kind of courage Australia needs. Groups to support refugees have started, and they have started protesting against the Camps. He said not to worry, Aussies always help the underdog.' I must have frowned, as he added, 'That's someone not as well off as other people.'

He squeezed my hand, continuing, 'And, Ness, *you're* the one who gives me hope, makes me strong, able to put up with any-thing I need to until we can be together . . .' Did he really say, 'be together'? My heart sang. 'While I feel like hell because I can't come with you, it makes me feel better knowing you're not locked up any more. Watching you suffering, trying to keep the family together with your mum so sick and not being able to do anything about it, has made me feel a thousand times worse. You must real-ise that *I'm* not alone like MTK79. I have you all waiting for me. That's a huge difference. Especially you. I know you'll help me any way you can.' He sat perfectly still, head in his hands.

I didn't trust myself to speak. No one had ever spoken to me like this, sharing their soul.

For most of the night, we talked, remembering things from home, or from the past two years locked up in here, and the people we'd met. And we made plans for our new life . . .

I felt a hand shaking my shoulder. It was Abdul. 'Come on, Ness. Brekkie time.'

'But you're not at work?' I was instantly awake.

'Late start. I'll go after your bus leaves. You don't think I'd let you go without a goodbye kiss, do you?' I laughed at Abdul's words but my heart thumped madly.

The next hour was so terrible and so sweet and so hard. I felt excited and devastated all at once. When at last Mum, Hassan and the two Zs were at the door of the bus to climb on board, I stood facing the closed gate. With Abdul on the inside. We locked fingers through the bars, trying to say goodbye.

'Ness, remember everything that you do and phone me to tell me as soon as you can.' Abdul kept up the cheerful front and I was glad he did otherwise I couldn't have held back my tears.

'Of course we will! Will you phone us, too?'

'You'll need a number first, and a phone,' he teased.

'You're so clever.' I didn't want our last minutes wasted like this but I didn't know how to say what I really wanted to. There was a huge ache in my heart. I was going to miss him terribly.

He pressed his face between the bars and, hardly knowing what I was doing, I stood on tiptoes and kissed him. I registered cold, hard metal biting into my cheeks but then an amazing sensation swept through my body, spinning me out. After what seemed like a century and a second wrapped into one, I pulled

186

back. Our eyes locked, his searching mine as he extricated his fingers and pushed his hand deep into his pocket.

He pressed something cold into my hand, saying, 'Take this, Nessa. Its interwoven strands symbolise my feelings for you and my dream for our lives. Will you keep it for me until we're together again?'

I nodded. He smiled. I opened my hand and my eyes widened. 'But, Abdul, this is your family ring that your mother gave you. Don't you want to keep it near you?'

'Picturing you wearing it will give me strength to put up with anything, until I'm released. You give me hope and the best reason to live. If you have it, it will be right in my heart.' His dark eyes so soft, yet so strong and deep, underlined his words.

'C'mon, Ness.' Hassan's voice made me jump around. He was standing on the step of the bus and I could see the others sliding into seats inside.

'I'll keep it with me all the time,' I said, squeezing Abdul's hand before running to the bus. The door began to close as I leapt up the steps. Glancing back, I saw Abdul smiling at me, hand resting on his heart.

I stumbled to a seat, slid across to the window and waved as the bus pulled away, trying desperately to calm the hammering in my chest. I watched Abdul waving until he was swallowed by the dust. Then the pain that surged through me felt like it replaced all the blood in my veins. Head resting against the glass, I pictured him returning to the empty room we'd shared and stretching out on the bed as he used to, staring upwards with unseeing eyes, tears streaming down his face. Empty. Desolate. And tears streamed down mine.

PART TWO

CHAPTER 22

I've only a hazy memory of changing buses, from the small one which brought us from the Camp to a large one an officer put us on in the nearest town, outside those mirage-like buildings I'd so often seen on the horizon. I felt stunned, out of it, like I was running on auto-pilot. I must have followed my family and climbed aboard the huge vehicle, where we slipped into comfy seats cocooning us from staring eyes. We were all sad at leaving Abdul and apprehensive about what was in front of us, so we were all quiet and preoccupied.

For most of the first day I think we drove through the same sort of country that surrounded the Camp and I wondered again if all of Australia was like that. The same fine, red dust tinged everything we passed, and there were occasional buildings, cars, trucks and wrecks by the straight, dark road. But most of the time I sat, forehead pressed to the tinted window, seeing little of the flying landscape. In my head, feelings and thoughts wrestled to be first in line for me to process.

Taking the ring out of my pocket, I examined it. Secretly. I wasn't ready to show the others yet. Holding it in one hand near my heart, I closed my eyes. I could hear Abdul's voice telling me about the ring one night when everyone else was asleep. Nearly every one of the few possessions we owned had a special story.

'When Dad and Mum were married, he placed this ring on her finger as part of the ceremony. It was the only jewellery my family didn't sell to buy my safety. Mum said that the small amount of dollars the silver ring would bring in could never be as valuable as the tradition and memories the ring holds for us.

'The story goes that my great, great, great, great – I don't know how many greats – grandfather won this Arabian puzzle ring in a battle to the death between him and a war-lord who was trying to drive my ancestors' people from their land. Ever since then the ring, and the story of his courage against apparently insurmountable odds, has been passed from generation to generation, from parents to eldest son, as a kind of talisman. And when the eldest son marries, he places this ring on his wife's finger, until their eldest son's ready for marriage, when they pass on the ring to him, and so on . . .'

Opening my eyes, I turned the ring over and over in my hand, trying to figure out how the entwined strands fitted together. Then I closed my eyes and heard Abdul's voice again. 'Its interwoven strands symbolise my feelings for you, and my dream for our lives. Will you keep it for me until we're together again? Picturing you wearing it will give me strength to put up with anything, until I'm released. You give me hope and the best reason to live.' Phew! I thought. There's that rush again I felt when we kissed. I wish I could bottle this feeling.

Abdul had shown me how the ring came apart into eight separate strands but these strands were so cleverly entwined they could never be separated from each other. He told me how he'd sat with his father, who'd break the ring apart for Abdul to practise putting it back together. It took many, many times before finally he mastered the secret.

Although we'd never talked about it, I wondered if, when his mother gave him the ring, she thought he was ready for marriage. Or did she think she might not see him again? His family memories were entwined in this ring, so why did he give it to me now? Did he mean what I hoped he did by 'my dream for our lives'? As I tried to work out answers I reran in my head our parting scene, over and over. Each time I got to 'my dream for our lives' and 'if you have it, it will be right in my heart', the amazing feeling flooded back and my heart hammered twice as fast as usual.

Abdul was in *my* heart, too. So was my dad and my Arjays, and Bahkhuls. But even though I missed them terribly, with Abdul it was different. Thinking of him brought these surges of unfamiliar emotion, excitement and unspoken promises, as well as a racing heart. And I felt so optimistic – about everything. It was like a golden glow that wrapped itself around me, my ring, and my image of Abdul, and I wanted the feelings to last forever. While I felt like this, I didn't have to face tough questions about our future, and the pain of leaving Abdul.

❧ ❧ ❧

During that day the bus made one or two petrol stops when we could go to the toilet and buy food. Abdul had given Mum the money he and Hassan had saved from their kitchen job, saying it was his contribution to setting up a home for him to come to. Two hundred and eighty-nine dollars saved after nearly a year's work. We had no idea of its value or how much we'd be able to buy with it. Abdul said he'd earn more until he joined us.

When I woke the next morning, stiff from sleeping in a sitting position, our surroundings had changed completely. Green grass and scattered trees, rather like Gum Tree's picture at the Camp school, were all I could see. Grazing sheep and cattle flashed past and sandy side roads and small watercourses, too. Houses with nearby sheds and machinery were dotted around the wide, green spaces. Sometimes horses grazed alongside sheep or cattle, and sometimes fences separated them all. Fences, I thought. If we'd had them at home it would have stopped the sheep straying too far into the mountains. And always there was this smooth black road, so different from the dusty pot-holey ones we'd been used to.

We stopped at a service station on the outskirts of what looked like a big town. The buildings here were different from any I'd seen. And there wasn't a donga in sight.

A kind old couple seemed worried about our family travelling alone in a strange place. If we'd been able to say more than an odd word to them, I'd have put their fears to rest. Although we certainly felt nervous, we knew our lives weren't in danger. It was nothing compared to what we'd already been through. As it was, the old couple did all they could to help by guiding us around and showing us the toilets and where to buy stuff. They even bought food to share.

Most passengers, though, stared at us. So did people whenever we got off the bus, and I felt uncomfortable. I guess our worn, loose tops and pants were different from their clothes, and Mum wore a scarf over her head like most Muslim women. She looked pale and was quiet the whole way. I could tell she was silently praying. We kept to ourselves, which suited me. It gave me the chance to go over those last minutes with Abdul.

It was late afternoon when the scenery started to change again.

There were more houses, fewer animals and smaller areas of lots of different kinds of trees and plants growing close together, and in rows stretching as far as I could see. Some were fruit trees and vegetables I recognised. Soon we'd passed these, and the number of houses and buildings increased until they lined the sides of the road. The roads became wider and full of traffic of all kinds, a bit like those near the airport in Indonesia, but not as wide. The buildings were tall and packed close together.

We sat glued to the bus windows, entranced by what still seemed no more real than a television program. Weird things flitted through my mind. Where were the open markets? Would we have to return to the stalls I'd seen by the road near where the fruit and vegetables were growing, to buy our food? There weren't many people walking along these roads. Did everyone have a car? We didn't. Could we get one with the money from Abdul? But most important of all, though alert for signs of them, I saw no tanks or guns, anywhere.

Finally, the bus stopped in a busy street. Traffic and people everywhere. Most of the passengers got out. The bus driver nodded to Mum and pointed to the street, crowded with hurrying people. The strangeness of it all set my insides churning, pushing out the optimism that had filled me during the trip. Our family group stood close together on the edge of the footpath, holding our bags, and each other.

'The officer told me someone would meet us,' Mum said, looking around worriedly. 'We'll wait here.' Almost as she finished speaking a smiling man appeared out of the crowd and said in our language, 'Hello. Please come with me. You must be tired after your long trip?'

We all nodded, mumbling, 'Yes.'

'I'll take you to a backpackers' hostel where you can stay tonight.' We followed him a short way into a long, low building.

There were lots of people in the hostel lobby and the man spoke in English to one of the women. Then he said to us, 'I have to go now. In a minute Marnie will show you where you can sleep tonight. We'll collect you tomorrow morning. Good luck.'

Many people all talking in English surrounded us. The hub-bub made me feel panicky. I couldn't make out a word. But suddenly, Hassan's confused frown changed to a wide smile and he said, 'How goes it, KAZ81?'

The man coming towards us looked familiar, and greeted us warmly. 'Great to see you! But, no numbers, please.' He smiled. 'It's Mohammed.'

'Yeah, and I'm Hassan. This is my mother, Fatimeh, my sisters, Gulnessa and Zahra, and my brother, Zainullah.' Zahra peered out from behind Mum's top, which she'd half wrapped herself in, trying to hide from the staring people. I knew how she felt. Hassan explained, 'We worked together in the kitchen at the Camp. Mohammed's visa came through a couple of weeks ago.'

'Where's your friend?' Mohammed enquired. 'I don't know his name and I'm not going to use numbers.'

'Abdul. He's still *there*. His visa didn't come through.' Hassan's face reflected my feelings.

'Oh.' A shadow flitted over Mohammed's face but he said nothing more. Instead, he signalled to Marnie and took us to a big dormitory-like room, showing us the bathroom down the passage on the way.

'When you've put down your things and washed, come to the front lobby,' he said. 'I'll wait for you there with Zia. Remember him from the Camp?'

Hassan nodded. 'Sure do.'

'He's here, too. We're leaving for a town in the country tomorrow.

We think we can get jobs there. Tonight we'll take you to where we can get halal food.'

Before long, and feeling a bit more confident with Mohammed and Zia to guide us, we were walking down a busy street. Eating places lined the footpath and often we had to walk through tables and chairs outside them. Zainullah had regained his curiosity, darting backwards and forwards to examine shopfronts and restaurants and reporting loudly to us about what he found.

Soon we came to what Mohammed called a food market. Wow! Food markets at home were never like this. Stalls displaying an incredible array of foods already prepared and cooked surrounded an open space packed with tables and chairs where people sat eating and drinking. Delicious smells made me realise I was starving. Here we could get something other than rice and veg. My stomach growled embarrassingly.

Each stall had its selection of dishes behind glass windows, but there was such a huge choice. We walked around and around, feasting our eyes and teasing our tummies. We had no idea what all the different dishes were and didn't know how to ask.

Eventually Zia said, 'Would you like me to order?' We nodded gratefully. Mohammed led us to an empty table.

'Hassan, come with me and help Zia with the food. The others can wait here,' Mohammed suggested.

'Me too,' Zainullah butted in before Hassan could answer. The three of them threaded their way back towards the stall where Zia waited. I slid into a chair which gave me a good view of the food hall. Mum and Zahra sat opposite.

'Mummy, can I have a banana, please?' It was the first time I'd heard Zahra's little voice since we'd left the hostel. Her strange request reminded me that she'd fallen in love with bananas when she tasted them for the first time in Indonesia.

'I'll ask Zia when he comes back where I can get you one, if you eat some of what he brings us first,' Mum bargained. Zahra didn't answer. She rarely grizzled. Zainullah did enough for both Zs. Zahra also rarely did anything she didn't want to.

As we waited I looked at the people around us. What a variety! Mostly pale but some dark-skinned, too. All strange-looking to me – we were the only ones who looked like Hazaras. At a table near ours was a young woman with short, purple hair and small hoop earrings lining both ears. She was dressed in tight, black leather clothes. Sitting next to her was a young man, I think. He wore black leather, too, and both sides of his head were shaven, with what looked like a thick line of green grass down the middle. It had to be hair, but how did he get it like that? The shaven sides were covered in detailed, black line drawings, and his ears were lined with silver rings.

The purple-haired girl suddenly looked over, directly at me. She smiled and waved. I realised I must have been staring at her. That's a great strategy, I decided, waving instead of feeling uncomfortable – if only I could make myself do it.

As soon as the food arrived we devoured our steaming piles of noodles and delicious, spiced-meat sauce in a sort of slurping silence. Whatever it was, it was excellent, and I noticed Mum ate more than she had since she got sick. Even Zahra ate some noodles. 'Yum!' she said – high praise from her.

As he finished his last mouthful, Zia said, 'In Australia there are not nearly as many Muslims as in Afghanistan, so most meat isn't halal. But there are special butchers and eating places here in Perth, where we can buy halal food.'

'What's halal, Mum?' Zainullah asked what I wanted to know. I knew the word meant 'permitted', or 'allowed', but I didn't know why Muslims were not allowed some foods.

It had never been an issue at home where we all ate the same things.

'Muslims have strict laws which say some things are *haram*, forbidden to us. But people who aren't Muslims can eat them. Like meat from pigs.'

'Yuk!' Zainullah spat. 'Pigs're dirty, and they stink.'

Mum smiled, 'Perhaps that's why they're *haram*. Most other meats are fine if they are killed in the halal way.' This is great, I thought, Mum's talking again. Perhaps she *will* get better quickly now we're out.

With so much new stuff to gawp at, nothing held Zainullah's attention for long. Now he'd noticed a small boy playing nearby. 'Hey, look at that truck. It's like a mini-sized one of those *hu-u-uge* trucks we passed on the way down, and it's got extra loads to hook on and take off. Can I have one, Mum? *Ple-e-ease.*'

'We'll have to wait and see,' Mum answered. 'But now it's time to go back and get ready for bed. We have to be up when the man comes to pick us up tomorrow.'

'Please can I have my banana?' Zahra piped up.

'I thought you might be full,' Mum tried to put her off.

'You promised,' Zahra was on to her.

'Oh, all right, I'll ask Zia.' He led us to a stall where a woman was putting big pieces of fruit into a jug and whizzing them up in a machine. I could have watched it for ages. Zia proudly came away with a whole banana which he gave Zahra. And he bought what I now know is a huge banana smoothie for us all to share. Yum.

'Thank you, Zia,' Zahra said solemnly. He'd won a heart there. She jerked away as Mum reached down to start peeling it for her, handing it to Zia with the instruction, 'Zia can.'

'Come on,' Mum ordered, grabbing Zainullah's hand. Zahra,

munching on her prize, took Zia's hand. I have to say he looked quite pleased.

As soon as Zahra was asleep snuggling up next to me, I took Abdul's ring from my pocket and put it on my ring finger. It was too loose so I moved it to my thumb and clenched my fist to hold it on. Shutting my eyes, I saw Abdul's face smiling at me behind my lids, and that amazing feeling bubbled through me. During the day on the bus I'd mostly kept my hand in my pocket so I could hold the ring, enjoying the secret I wasn't ready to share with anyone, yet.

CHAPTER 23

The next morning after a hurried breakfast of flatbread we'd saved from our dinner the night before, we found our way to the hostel lobby. It wasn't a man who was waiting for us when we finally got there, but a woman with short, red hair and a wide smile. People bustled about everywhere so I stood close to Mum, holding Zahra's hand tightly. My other hand stayed in my pocket, ring on my thumb. I felt closer to Abdul that way and thinking of what he'd said brought back a rush that helped push out the anxiety that was trying to take over me. Mohammed and Zia stood near the door ready to leave, and we said our goodbyes, Hassan promising to keep in touch. How will he do that? I wondered. There are so many people here and we're so far away.

The red-haired woman pointed to herself, 'An-nie.'

'Hello, An-nie,' I said, then, pointing to myself, 'Nessa.' I'd jumped in to show Mum what to do.

The last thing Shakeela had said to me when we were leaving the Camp was, 'Your mum, she take time to get better. She try quick to do things. But hard for her. Nessa, you care for her. Help her. Show her things. If too hard – she get more sick.'

'Hello, Nessa.' Annie held out her hand. A vision of Dough-face doing that to Mum on our first day of school in the Camp flashed into my mind. I left my ring in my pocket and stretched out my hand to meet hers. We shook hands. I felt good about that.

Then Mum, one hand on her chest and holding out the other, said, 'Fatimeh. Hel-lo, An-nie.' Hassan and Zainullah introduced themselves, too, but I had to say Zahra's name, as she'd only peep shyly around me. Annie practised our names a couple of times and beckoned us to follow her.

She led us to a van, and smiled a lot as she helped us get settled. Then she picked up a belt thing attached to the wall of the van and nodded at me. My face must have shown her I hadn't a clue what she meant. She fastened it and said clearly, 'Seatbelt.'

We drove through busy streets lined with high buildings. How can you ever learn to find your way around a place like this? I wondered. All the streets looked the same. After a while we stopped at a low building where we all got out and went inside. Annie introduced a man from Iran, Rashid, who spoke Dari and who'd been in Australia for about three years. He spoke good English.

'Rashid's my friend,' piped up Zainullah. 'Yasmine's brother.'

'Do you know another Rashid?' the man asked Zainullah. He nodded. 'Must be a good guy.' Zainullah nodded again.

Annie spoke to Rashid, then left the room. He explained, 'This is the office of an organisation called CARAD which helps refugees. Annie has helped many of us. She's going to take you to a house which belongs to the organisation. It was set up by volunteers to help people like us who have nothing of our own when we arrive. You'll be able to stay there while Annie helps you find a house to rent.'

'What's rent?' I asked.

'It's where you pay someone to live in their house.'

'Oh.' I couldn't get my head around the idea of people being wealthy enough to own more houses than they could live in. Then something else struck me. 'We have no money. How will we pay rent?'

'Annie will take you to apply for money from a government agency. That's one reason we need visas. I got mine before they brought in temporary ones.'

'That's good they help us,' Mum sounded surprised. 'The guards told us that Australian people don't want us here. We've been so worried about what would happen to us.' Mum must have taken in what was happening in the Camp, even though she didn't seem to.

'Well, some people don't want us here, and let us know it. But there are lots who want to help, too. They understand that we arrived here suffering trauma, with nothing of our own. Annie's great. She'll help you settle in and show you around.'

At that moment Annie returned and spoke to Rashid, who said, 'Annie's going to take you to the house now. When she's finished helping you with official things, I'll come with her to take you shopping. That's a huge experience.' He smiled, hand over his heart. We returned the gesture.

'Goodbye. Good luck.' Voices called from the doorway through which Annie had returned. Looking over I saw two friendly, pale-faced, grey-haired women, smiling and waving.

'Thank you. Goodbye,' I said.

'Thank you. Goodbye,' everyone chorused.

Driving to the house seemed to take forever. We'd been in a bus for the last two days and were tired of sitting still, and we couldn't ask questions. As we drove along the busy roads there was so much we saw that I wanted to know about. Like, what was the wide expanse of water we passed? I didn't think it could be the sea, as I could see buildings on the far shore. A massive bridge crossed a narrow part of the water and as we drove over it I tried to work out how men could build something this size. We passed houses stretching as far as I could see, and sometimes high buildings. There were all sorts of other things, too, that were totally new. I couldn't take in everything. But I did take in the fact that there was no sign of dongas. Or guns.

This van was so different from the jeeps we sometimes rode in at home. My thoughts began to drift . . .

Dad borrows a jeep and eleven of us squash in to drive to the next village. It takes about half an hour, and much, much longer if you ride a donkey, or walk.

'Hold on tight, Hassan! You too, Jawad!' Dad yells as we take off with a jerk. My brother and cousin outside cling to the window frames. Each time we go over a bump, and there are millions of them, they yell. Dad just grins. We're all too busy hanging on to notice – that is until . . .

'Stop! Stop! Uncle, Hassan's gone! Please. Stop!'

We do. In a thick cloud of dust. Dad sticks out his head, and asks, 'Where?'

'At a big pot-hole. Back there. He bounced so high that when he came down he missed the jeep.' I see Jawad's dusty forehead creased with worry.

'We weren't going fast enough for him to be hurt,' Dad yells. 'When the dust clears, I'll back up.'

We crane our necks. In the swirling, brownish clouds I make out a darker shape, rapidly growing bigger. It looks like it's moulded from dust, then an arm waves. As the noise of the jeep's engine splutters and dies, I hear, 'Wait! Wait for me!' Hassan's voice. We all laugh.

204

'You okay?' Dad shouts, restarting the engine. Puffing up, Hassan manages to nod. 'Well, jump on, son. And hold tighter this time.'

As we pulled off the main road on to a tiny one I grabbed my seatbelt to stop tipping out of my seat. We were in front of what seemed to me an enormous, low house with huge glass windows along its front. These amazed me, as glass windows in the Camp were small, and we'd had none at home. I wondered how the wind didn't smash them.

Annie took us on a tour of the house, pointing to lots of things and saying their names. We recognised some of them, like beds and chairs and other furniture we'd 'met' in the donga, but this house had heaps more. Mum was so excited when she found taps in the kitchen as well as the bathroom – an inside one, with a bath (our first) *and* a shower. 'This really is paradise!' she exclaimed. The toilet was inside, too, another first for us, though I did wonder whether it'd smell. The Camp ones in the ablution block had at times, even with water to flush them out.

The kitchen was another world. We examined everything in it. Cupboards hid glasses, cups, plates, dishes, saucepans and much more. In drawers were all kinds of knives, forks and spoons and other gadgets. Annie had bought us milk, yoghurt and chicken, which she put in a really cold cupboard. 'Fridge,' she called it, and we repeated the name. Then she put a tub of icecream in an even colder part of the fridge. 'Freezer,' she said. We repeated that, too. We'd been introduced to icecream at the Camp one Christmas, and were instantly hooked. The only frozen food we'd had at home was in winter when something had been left outside by mistake.

Zahra danced around, saying over and over, 'Fridge, freezer, frish, frisher . . .' until Mum picked her up and cuddled her to try to shut her up, but she was too excited.

Finally, Annie said slowly, 'I'll go home now. Zahra's hungry.' *She'd* already learned our names – those Camp guards must have been so dumb.

'Thank you, An-nie,' Mum replied, smiling broadly, not because she was glad Annie was going but because of what she'd done for us. We'd quickly learned to say 'yes' or 'thank you' when someone spoke to us to cover up the fact that we'd no idea what they said – it was better than shrugging. But I felt so proud. This time I understood what Annie said, as did Hassan. We translated for Mum, who asked me to invite Annie to have dinner with us.

I tried. 'Annie eat us?'

She looked at me, the weirdest expression on her face.

Hassan almost rolled on the floor laughing, but finally managed to get out, 'Annie, you eat *with* us?' His conversational English from the Camp kitchen was more use than what I'd learned in the schoolroom.

Annie smiled and shaking her head said, 'No, thank you. Not today. But I'll come back tomorrow.'

CHAPTER 24

After Annie left we went from room to room checking it all out again. It was a bit like Gum Tree's English class. One of us would remember a name (or think we did) and shout it out. Everyone else repeated it. Goodness knows how many we got wrong. Some were easy, like carpet, because we knew what it was, although our rugs at home weren't fitted like these. Table, chairs, beds and TV we'd learned in the Camp, and towels, sheets, blankets, and pillows, too. But the thick, soft bedcovers, the big, comfortable seats in the lounge room, and things like electric appliances, kitchen utensils and most of the foods, we had no idea about.

Annie had bought us onions, carrots, potatoes, rice, flour, oil, sugar and tea, all of which we knew, and she'd shown us how to use the gas jets so we could cook our own meal. Mum organised Zahra and me and we laughed more than we had since the lighthouse night. It was so long ago that we'd cooked anything, and never this way. The best part was finding out how to use all the new things, and watching the life in Mum's face again. I even peeled onions without complaining! The worst things were the small pots. We couldn't find anything the size we used at home. How could we fit everything for a meal for five in one of these?

Australians must cook for one person at a time, we decided, and anyone who used the smallest saucepan must have a tiny appetite. Still, with a little creative thinking, we managed to prepare a meal to remember.

After a riotous bath time, washing our hair over and over to get rid of the last of the red dust, we were ready for bed. No one even had the energy to watch TV – in spite of not having to share it in a crowded room. Sitting on the big bed in the biggest bedroom, Mum looked happier than I'd seen her since that night of traditional singing when we first arrived.

'We're safe, really safe,' she said. 'This is real Australia. Now that we're here I've something for you all. From Bahkhul.' We crowded around as she unwrapped a small cloth bundle on her lap. 'He asked me to wait until we were safe, and then to give you these to remind you of home. They belonged to him and Arjay.'

She passed cloth caps like Bahkhul wore to Hassan and Zainullah, a small silver bracelet to Zahra, and a wider, etched one to me. Then she put on a pair of intricately designed silver earrings. I wanted to say something, but I couldn't speak. A lump got in the way. No one spoke. We looked at each other, eyes bright with unshed tears. Then we put on our treasures, smiling with soft eyes.

Mum said, 'Let's all sleep together.'

'Yippee!' cheered Zainullah, galloping around the room.

'Y'pee! Y'pee,' echoed Zahra. We pulled mattresses off beds, dragging them into the big bedroom and placing them side by side until there was enough room for us all. Snuggling under checked blankets from the house, with Arjay Aqila's blankets over the top, I thought sleepily how it would be perfect – well, almost – if Abdul was here, too.

Although my limbs felt heavy with tiredness and I fell asleep almost immediately, it didn't last for long. I don't know whether it was because our surroundings were so quiet after the noise of a donga, or whether I was too excited to be able to rest, but whatever it was, I dozed fitfully for most of the night. This time it wasn't nightmares that kept me awake but an overactive mind, thinking about what lay ahead . . . And Abdul.

❦ ❦ ❦

Next morning, sitting outside the back of the house on the grass in the sun for breakfast, we tried to eat the yoghurt Annie had bought for us. It was sweetish and there was something in it we decided was fruit. Not at all like Mum's homemade yoghurt.

'Yuk!' Zainullah screwed up his face, and flicked the bit of fruit on his spoon towards the fence. It stuck on the rippled, grey surface. Hassan and I tried it, too, and soon we were fishing out all the pieces we could find in our little pots, sending them on their way, and laughing hysterically.

'I'm getting low on bits,' I said, scraping the spoon around, 'but I think there is more inside.' As I stood up, Hassan and Zainullah fired a volley each, Zainullah jumping up and down like crazy.

At that moment Mum and Zahra appeared at the back door. 'What on earth are you doing?' The tone of Mum's voice stopped us immediately. 'If that's what I think it is, you're in trouble.' She marched over to the fence, hands moving to her hips as she turned to face us. Uh-oh. Her voice started out quietly, but firmly. 'Don't you know Annie was kind enough to give us that to eat, *not* to play with? Think of what you've been eating in the Camp.' She turned up the volume. 'I don't know how you could do such a thing! Food is so precious. Don't you remember how little we had before we left home? Annie mustn't see what you did with her gift. She'll think how ungrateful we are. Gulnessa, get water from the kitchen, and cloths. All of you can scrub every bit off the fence. And when you've finished, you'll eat the rest.'

Without speaking I moved towards the door. Even though she was mad at us I couldn't help thinking this was more like our mum, and I felt good about that. But hot-headed Zainullah, who didn't recognise this was no time to argue, said, 'Mu-u-um, that yoghurt's revolting. I'll be sick . . .' He emphasised his words with a loud, pretend retch.

'Enough! Do as you're told. Now.' Zainullah's eyes popped at the unfamiliar sharpness of Mum's voice, and this time he shut his mouth.

We were hard at work, scrubbing away the evidence, when we heard voices. Through the window, I saw Mum trying to steer Annie away. But Annie was talking and didn't seem to notice. She pushed open the door and when she saw us standing in line, backs to the wet fence, dripping cloths in our hands, she stopped, frowning in a puzzled sort of way. Our heads dropped, and I bit my lip. How could we get out of this one? I felt awful.

Taking a deep breath, I tried, 'Thank you, Annie.' Always a good start. 'Mum yoghurt . . .' I searched for the word 'different' but failed to find anything suitable in my meagre vocabulary.

Hassan took over, 'We don't know . . .' He picked up a yoghurt pot and held it high. 'We can't eat.'

Annie's face suddenly lit up and she said, 'That's okay. You don't have to eat it. We have different things in Australia.' Then she shook her head. 'But we don't wash fences. That's taking cleanliness to extremes.' She started to laugh.

We'd no idea what she said and I don't think she meant us to, but Hassan seemed to understand a bit and said to me in Dari, 'She doesn't mind if we don't eat the yoghurt. But I don't think she guessed we were washing it off the fence.'

Mum, who heard this, gestured for us all go to inside. Saved. We left the final traces of evidence and I carried the dish into the kitchen, washed it and put it away.

When at last we were ready, Annie packed us into her van and off we drove – somewhere, everywhere. Over the next few days we visited so many different offices and buildings that I lost count. Annie filled out endless forms and talked to official-looking people for us, arranging money for us to live on from something called Centrelink Special Benefit, help we might need, and other official things she said had to be done. We'd never seen multi-storey buildings before, let alone gone into them. Office blocks, government buildings, banks, Medicare offices, and so on. We rode on moving stairs, went in rooms which took us up and down to different floors, and visited food malls.

It was so weird hearing all around us a language I couldn't understand, and being able to talk only between each other. People everywhere looked so pale. There were darker faces amongst them, but not many. The clothes knocked me out. I was used to people dressing in a similar way and the variety of styles and colours here hypnotised me. I couldn't believe girls wore such brief skirts, shorts and tops. I couldn't look at them to begin with. I felt so embarrassed to think they'd go out showing so much of their bodies.

Annie took us to an old shop where we got cast-off clothes that were much better than our worn-out Camp gear but still in the style we were used to – long, loose tops and pants. Mum always wore a scarf, too, when she went outside. The boys got trackie pants and tops.

I can't begin to describe how everything we saw and did amazed and confused us. The electrical appliances that did every-thing from sweeping floors and cooking food to entertaining us with pictures and music left me speechless. I felt I was in fantasy land, one I'd never understand, or master. And all the time I wished Abdul was here to share it with us.

Then one afternoon as she left us, Annie tapped her watch and said, 'Tomorrow is shopping day. Be ready, ten o'clock.'

❧ ❧ ❧

When Annie arrived at ten o'clock sharp, we were just finishing the breakfast washing up. Even this chore was fun and different. No water to fetch, no dishes to carry to the river, no sand to scrub them. As I picked up the last pile of plates and reached out to open the cupboard door, Mum caught my hand, looking at Abdul's ring and my face in turn. 'You can tell me about this later,' she said, giving me a piercing look.

I was now so used to having it on my thumb to sleep that I didn't want to take it off at all. That morning when I'd got out of bed something inside me had kept saying, 'keep it on', so I did. I'd kept my secret until now, trying to work out how I was going to explain the ring, but I still didn't have a clue what I'd say.

Soon we were driving along in Annie's van. After a bit, we pulled off the main road on to one of the tiny roads which ran into each house. Annie stopped and tooted. The man from the first office we visited, Rashid, came out and jumped in the back with us kids. After speaking to Annie in English, and greeting Mum in Dari, he said to us, 'How do you like the house?'

'Fabulous!'

'Great!'

'Excellent . . .'

When he could get a word in again, he asked, 'What do you like best?'

Before anyone else could answer, Mum said, 'Taps.'

'TV.' Hassan didn't hesitate.

'Toilet inside!' Zainullah was scared of the dark, and still thought of the wolf story. Zahra just sat looking out of the window, clutching Theermie. I'd noticed that although she'd get excited when we did something together, she sat quietly in a kind of daze at other times. She needed to be drawn into joining us, never starting a game herself. She was better than in the Camp but far from my bubbly little sister.

Rashid laughed. 'Well. Just wait 'til you see the supermarket we're taking you to now. It might top even those things.'

'What's a supermarket?' I asked.

'Well, it's where we buy food, only it has *much* more in it than any market you've seen – that's why it's called "super"!'

He didn't exaggerate. Walking into this Aladdin's cave we were blown away. Here was *so* much and we'd known so little in Afghanistan. The fruit and vegetable display had piles of things we knew, but many more we'd never seen. And we'd never seen such massive quantities of food. My mother stood still, staring. Then tears started trickling down her cheeks.

'What's the matter, Mum?' I whispered.

'There's so much here. I can't help thinking of Arjay Aqila, Arjay, Bahkhul and all the others at home. And Abdul, too. They have so little to live on. The food at the whole market there would fit into one row of these shelves. And no one here will snatch food away from us, or tell us we have to pay twice as much if we want something. It doesn't seem fair.'

Rashid joined us. 'Don't worry, Fatimeh. We all feel just like you do whenever we come here. But seeing it the first time is the biggest shock. Now come with me and I'll help you find what you need.'

Shopping took a long time, as we had so much to learn.

So many things were strange. Often we asked Rashid what they were. We'd never seen things in packets, bottles, jars and cans. Or pre-prepared or refrigerated or frozen foods. Other than dried fruits, tea, nuts, seeds and grains, we'd known mainly fresh produce, and the variety and quantity had been tiny compared to what we saw spread out in this supermarket.

Handling Australian money at the checkout – another new concept – was the trickiest bit but the girl there was patient. She just grinned and giggled at Hassan. I guess sisters see the worst side of brothers.

At last, bags and bags of everything from toilet paper and toothpaste to a monstrous watermelon were piled in the back of the van. I thought Annie looked exhausted, but she said something to Rashid, who announced, 'Annie says she's starving and now she's going to take us for a picnic.'

'Picnic?' Hassan got in first this time.

'Just wait and see.'

The drive-through fast-food shop was eye-opening. As we drove away, the tantalising smell of roast chicken wafted from the bags. We were all drooling. Down the road we pulled into a place where lots of cars were parked, and piled out of the van. Rashid passed out bags and rugs for us to carry and we set off across a park, over a railway line, whatever that was, past big buildings and lots of people, until we saw the sea. I stopped with a jolt, our experiences on the boat flooding back. Backing off, I watched as Mum and Zainullah followed Annie and Rashid onto the whitish sand, where the water lapped gently and white birds flew. All was calm and peaceful. Looking around, I found Hassan had stopped nearby, and Zahra stood holding my top. Hassan nodded to me, I nodded back and we walked on to where the others waited.

Annie and Mum spread out rugs to sit on, setting the food in the middle – one box each of scrumptious chicken and chips, with Coke to wash it down. Although the food was new, this was how we felt most comfortable sitting and eating. 'Welcome to your first Oz beach picnic,' Rashid announced.

No one spoke until we'd cleaned out our boxes and picked the bones. Then Rashid said, 'Come on. Race you to the water.'

Standing on the wet sand I watched Hassan tease Zainullah, pretending to splash him. 'Go on. See if you can splash Hassan, like this,' I coaxed Zahra, crouching down to scoop the clear water in my cupped hands. Zahra tried it and some of the shining drops blew back in her face. Instead of squealing as I expected, she laughed and did it again, throwing the water straight up in the air so it landed on her head.

Then, giggling excitedly, Zahra danced around Hassan and Zainullah, calling, 'You can't get me . . .' Soon she was wet through, but so delighted by it all that no one cared. The sun shone warmly, and a gentle breeze feathered my cheeks. As I fingered the no-longer-secret ring and thought of Abdul, I felt pleasantly sleepy, and content.

Boom! Out of nowhere. Artillery fire! My heart leapt to my mouth. Body to Annie's arms. No! Not here. Please. It can't be. Squeezing shut my eyes, pulling my head to my chest, I curled into a ball. Then, through roaring ears and pounding head, I heard, as if from a distance, 'It's all right, Gulnessa. Nothing will hurt you here.' Involuntary trembling shook my body, as a giant hand inside me pummelled faster and faster. But through this I sensed movement. Annie lowered herself to the ground. Mum's voice said, 'Gulnessa, we're safe. Please look at me.' I felt her hand brushing my hair. Yes. It was hers. *She* wouldn't lie.

Cautiously I opened my eyes. Mum and Annie watched me

anxiously. No, I couldn't see blood. It must be all right. Hesitatingly, I surveyed the scene. Yes, we were safe. Breath rushed from my lungs like water from a tap. My heart resumed its rhythm, the trembling petered out. Drained, I fought tears.

'For Nessa,' Zahra's firm little voice rang out. I looked up to see her hugging a can of Coke to her chest. 'Here, Nessie.' She held the can out and as I took it I saw a worried smile flit across Annie's face.

'Thank you, baby,' I said, then in English, 'Sorry, Annie.'

'I'm *not* a baby,' Zahra reminded me firmly.

Annie smiled. Her arm, still around my shoulders, tightened. 'Are you okay?'

I nodded, and saw my brothers and Rashid approaching.

'Nessa, I'm sorry. I should have warned you. Everyone got a fright.' Rashid's voice echoed concern. 'That boom was an old cannon firing. It's not dangerous. It fires every day to signal one o'clock in the afternoon. The locals set their clocks by it.'

Back at home after we'd carried in the mountains of shopping, Mum said, 'I bought some cardamom so I'll make a cup of tea.' It would be the first time we'd had our favourite aromatic spice since leaving Afghanistan.

As Rashid had gone home, Hassan translated as best he could. Annie smiled, nodded, and said, 'Thank you.' But when she tasted the hot, fragrant liquid she grimaced, though quickly tried to cover it up. Then, smiling, pointing to the tea and shaking her head, she said, 'I can't drink.' There was something more, too, but I could only make out the words 'you' and 'yoghurt'.

'Yes,' I nodded, smiling at her, too. She'd been so kind to us all I couldn't think what we'd have done without her. Annie

216

went on talking and this time I made out the words, 'you', 'go' and 'school'. Was she asking if we'd been to school?

'Yes, thank you,' I repeated.

'Yes, thank you,' everyone chorused, smiling and nodding.

Annie looked pleased. She stood up and tapped her watch. 'Goodbye. See you tomorrow. At nine o'clock in the morning.'

Hassan, Zainullah, Zahra and I nodded. 'Nine o'clock,' we chanted. Annie picked up her bag and waved. 'Goodbye, thank you,' we chorused again. Mum, too, as the front door closed behind Annie.

'Can we watch TV now?' Zainullah asked.

'Me too. Me too.' Zahra was still wound up.

'I guess so.' Mum looked at Hassan. 'You too?'

'I'll see what's on,' he replied.

Mum turned to me. 'Gulnessa, let's go outside and sit in the sun to drink our tea. You can tell me about that ring.' As we picked up our mugs I noticed Annie's full one on the table.

Settling ourselves on the grass, Mum looked at me quizzically. 'Now, isn't that the family talisman ring Abdul showed us?'

'Yes, it is . . .' I began, as Hassan burst through the door.

'It's the kids' show,' he announced. 'What are you doing?'

'Gulnessa's about to tell my why she's wearing Abdul's ring.'

'Is she?' Interested now, Hassan sat himself down, too. 'So what are you doing with it, sis?'

'Well,' I began again, still not at all sure how I was going to explain it and keep hidden my secret feelings, 'Abdul handed it to me as I was getting on the bus.' That sounded pretty casual. My eyes glued on the ring, I continued, 'He said he'd been thinking about how we were his family here, and as he couldn't be with us to help find a house and settle in, he wanted me to take the ring to bring us luck – like it brings luck in the story. He felt he could help that way, and when he comes, I'll give it back.' I looked up. Mum and Hassan were both nodding. Phew!

'Well, you must take good care of it, Gulnessa. I'm not sure that you should wear it. What if you lost it? Perhaps you should give it to me.' Mum looked at me.

My face expressionless, I tried to ignore the double-time drum beats in my chest, and said nonchalantly, 'It's okay. Abdul said to wear it. It's the safest way to keep it.'

Mum's fixed stare said silently, Are you telling me everything? And my blank response returned, That's all there is for you to know. Then Mum said, 'It doesn't feel right being here without Abdul. I wonder what we can do to help him get his visa. I've been thinking a lot about that.'

'Me too,' Hassan and I said. I didn't dare to say more.

'I think we should ask Rashid's advice, and Annie's,' Mum continued.

Here was the break I needed. 'Could we phone and tell him we've arrived safely? I know I'd feel better if I was in his place and I knew what was happening to the rest of us.'

'Yes, you're right. We'll ask Annie tomorrow.'

CHAPTER 25

We were still getting dressed when Annie arrived the next morning, with Rashid. I'd been awake half the night after my recurring dream about the Terror killing Abdul's dad. Only this time it was Abdul. I'd been so upset that Mum got up with me and we made a cup of tea. I felt guilty that I'd upset her. She woke in the morning with a splitting headache, so I took a cup of tea and some Panadol to her in bed.

Annie looked at her watch and spoke to Rashid. He said, 'Annie made an appointment for us to be at the school at nine thirty.'

'We won't be long,' Mum replied, hurrying us along.

'Do we have to go?' I asked.

Putting my question to Annie, Rashid translated her answer, 'Annie thought you *wanted* to go to school. When she asked yesterday you all said, "Yes, thank you," so many times.'

'No way,' I answered. 'We didn't understand.'

Rashid laughed. 'Now Annie's made an appointment to see the school principal we'd better go. I'm sure you needn't start straight away.'

'Come on, everyone. Get dressed quickly.' Mum went off with

Zahra. She's taking over as 'Mum' again, I noted in relief. I hope it lasts.

By the time we were in the van it was nearly ten o'clock. Back in the house I'd watched with interest as Annie had used her mobile phone to talk to someone. Rashid explained she was calling the school, to change our appointment time. I thought, perhaps she'll lend it to us so we can talk to Abdul.

I was working out how to make this happen, when Hassan's shout sent my plans flying. 'Duck everyone!' he yelled. 'A man's pointing a gun at us!' I dropped as far as the seatbelt would let me, dragging down Zahra, too.

'Ow,' she squawked. 'You're squashing me, Nessie.' I peered out, anxiously. All of us in the back crouched below line of sight through the windows, except Rashid.

'Don't panic. There's no gun, you're safe.' His voice was calm. 'Yes, it's okay to sit up, Fatimeh. I should have warned you. But you never know where they'll be. Already I have forgotten things which alarmed me when I arrived here three years ago.' When we were upright again he explained about police and radar guns trapping speeders.

The school was close to our house and didn't look too scary. Rashid was a great interpreter. He gave us his spin on everything we saw as the principal showed us around the classrooms, which were much better than the one in the Camp. It turned out to be a school that had lots of kids like us who came from heaps of different countries and most didn't speak English. Here, we'd learn English before going into classes that Australians went to. As Rashid said, 'What use would it be going into a mainstream class if you couldn't understand what the teachers were teaching you?' Hassan was too old for this school and would have to go to 'high school'. Was it on a mountain? I wondered.

Our next stop was at some shops, different again. They seemed huge. In one, Annie bought us clothes, mainly to wear to school but also another outfit – jeans and a jumper – as the weather was growing cool, cooler than it had been since we arrived in Australia. She also bought us some things to sleep in. No one wore different things to sleep in at home and when we got back we weren't sure which clothes we'd bought were for bed – they all looked good to us.

In another shop we bought lunch boxes and drinking bottles. Annie said she'd find us backpacks. She thought she might be able to get them from somewhere they stored things people had donated to help refugees. She'd already brought us T-shirts from there. If people give away their things to help us, they can't mind us being here, I thought. I decided to tell Abdul about it so he could put the guards straight.

It was the first time we'd had any school things and although Zahra was too young, she had to have hers, too. The principal had said Zahra could go to pre-school in July, in the mid-year intake. It was still only May. I wasn't sure of how the months of the year worked here yet. It was one of the trillions of things I had to learn.

Rashid came home with us to help fill in our papers for school. In my whole life I'd not seen as many papers as had to be completed for us since we'd been in Australia. There had been papers for the Camp, papers for our visas, a paper from the hostel, papers from the bank, papers from Medicare and goodness knows where else. Now we needed to fill in more for school. How does anyone keep track of them? I wondered. We didn't even have papers to show we were born.

Rashid, Annie and Mum sat at the dinner table to work while we went to try on our new clothes. I'd just put on my jeans and top when Mum called, 'Come here, all of you, please.'

'Whoo-hoo!' Annie whistled as I came into the room. She held up her hand, forefinger and thumb joined to form a circle, beaming a smile at me. 'You look great.'

'O-o-oh, Gulnessa,' Mum sounded surprised. 'You look like an Australian teenager.' I gave them the thumbs up! And, as Hassan and the two Zs followed, exclamations of approval accompanied their arrival, too.

When we were all seated, Rashid began, 'Before we get to the registration papers for school, I should explain some details about the temporary protection visas – TPVs – that the government now issues to refugees in Australia. So you know what you're allowed to do, and what you can't. Firstly, you know they're temporary. After three years you have to apply for another visa?' We nodded. 'Well, the government did this so refugees wouldn't want to come here.'

'But there's so much here and so much space. Why don't they want to help us? We'll work hard, too.' I asked the question that had bugged me in the Camp, and now I saw how rich this country was it puzzled me even more.

'That is something we don't understand. But there are people like Annie who do want to help and they are working to let the rest of the community know about us, hoping it will make the government change its policy. Anyway, because the visas are temporary, we have few rights. For instance, you can't join Centrelink employment programs or most other services like teaching English to migrants or settlement support services. You have to do it all privately with people and organisations who want to help.'

But that's not fair, my mind screamed. If they won't help us learn English at least, it makes it so much harder. But I said nothing. Rashid's voice continued, 'It makes you second-class citizens.'

His face looked sad, but the full implications of what he'd said didn't sink in with me until later. 'But that's all you need to know for now. At least children are allowed to enrol in government schools. Fatimeh, do you want to do the birthday thing?'

Mum took over. 'Do you remember when they prepared our Immigration papers in the Camp?' We nodded. How could we forget? I watched her closely to see if talking about it was hard for her. 'I told the officials we had no birth certificates and I had to work out how old each one of you is using the Australian calendar.' We nodded. 'They said that January first of whatever year I thought each of you was born in would be our birth dates. Well, Annie says that Australians hold a celebration party on their birthdays, especially children. It'd be better to have our birthdays spread over the year. What do you think?'

'Sounds good to me,' I said. If parties were like the first night we'd arrived in the Camp, I could do with one every week.

'Hmm,' agreed Hassan. I don't think Zainullah heard – he was too busy examining his new drink bottle.

'What's birfday?' Zahra's little face wrinkled up as she tried to puzzle out what Mum was talking about. 'What's party?'

'It's a special time to be happy and have fun.' Mum wasn't going to explain the deeper meaning of 'birth'.

'And to get presents,' added Rashid.

'What's presents?' Zahra wanted to know – me too, and I'm certain the boys didn't know either.

'Something people give you, because they love you,' Rashid explained.

'Like Bahkhul sent things with Mum?' I asked.

'That's right,' Rashid agreed.

'We're going to work out a birthday for all of you,' Mum put in. 'I clearly remember the time of year when each of you was born and Annie will tell us what month that would be. Then, you can choose a day in your month for your birthday.' Mum had gone over all this with Annie through Rashid.

'Does that mean we each have a party, and get presents?' Hassan wanted to be sure he had this new concept crystal clear.

'Sure does,' Rashid answered.

'Yes!' Hassan punched the air, as he'd seen people on TV do.

'Yes!' mimicked Zainullah and Zahra.

'Okay, let's start with Hassan,' Mum said. 'You were born in late autumn when all the grains and beans were dried.'

Rashid translated for Annie, then reported to us what she'd said. 'November is the last month of autumn in the northern hemisphere where Afghanistan is. You were most likely born then, Hassan. November's your birth month. What number would you like to choose?'

'Seven-four-seven.' Hassan didn't miss a beat. 'That's the number of the plane we flew on.'

Rashid said something to Annie and they both smiled. 'Sorry, mate, but November has only thirty days in it, so you have to choose a number up to thirty.'

'Oh.' Hassan looked disappointed, then he said, 'Well, I'll have thirteen because Arjay called that a cook's dozen.' Rashid told Annie, and she wrote it down.

'Oh,' Zahra spoke up, as if to fill the silence. She'd picked up her old saying again, after being so quiet in the Camp. I felt sure that was a good sign.

'Hassan, Annie says you must remember your birthday is the thirteenth of November,' Rashid announced, 'and that you're fourteen years old now, fifteen in November.'

'Now, your turn, Gulnessa,' said Mum. 'You were born when it had been snowing for a long while. I was afraid that Arjay Aqila wouldn't get to our house in time, and my labour pains were very close together.' I knew the story of my birth well as I used to ask Mum to tell me, over and over again. How Arjay Aqila and Arjay helped Mum who was crouching on the floor, rocking backwards and forwards, praying. And how, when they put me in her arms, a tiny little mite with thick, black hair, the first thing she noticed was that my fourth toe was curled inwards, like hers.

'Annie says it's always coldest in late winter, so February is your month, Gulnessa. It usually has twenty-eight days,' Rashid told me.

'Well, I'll have the middle one, the fourteenth, please,' I replied, and he relayed it to Annie, who said something with a smile.

Rashid said, 'Annie said there's another celebration on that date, too. Valentine's day. A celebration for lovers.' I tried to look nonchalant as my heart began a race with butterflies in my stomach. Was it an omen that I'd chosen the day of lovers? 'It's now May.' Rashid appeared unaware of my turmoil. 'So you've passed your birthday this year. You're thirteen now, Gulnessa.' I nodded, unable to trust my voice not to betray me.

Mum was speaking again. 'Zainullah, you were born in spring after the snow had melted and when the fruit trees were in full blossom.' Annie said his month was probably May, the month it was now, and if he chose a number close to its last day, he'd be able to have his eighth birthday party soon. Zainullah chose May twenty-eighth.

'And, my baby Zahra. You were born in autumn like Hassan, but earlier, when we had lots of vegetables like carrots and turnips, and the beans and grains for winter were still drying.'

'Mummy, I not baby.'

'Darling, you'll always be my baby.'

'Well,' said Rashid, 'Annie says you're a September girl, and her Arjay was on the twenty-fourth so that should be your date, too. This year you'll be five.'

'Oh,' Zahra nodded, her beautiful eyes round as she solemnly gazed at Rashid.

'You have to have a birthday, Mum,' Hassan prompted. Hers was settled as October twenty-eighth. Then we chose Dad's as August seventeenth.

'I wonder if we should give a birthday to your little sister, who died as a baby,' Mum said to us, in a faraway kind of voice.

'What are you talking about?' I asked.

'When you were a toddler, I had a baby who was tiny when she was born. She never drank properly and was always sick. She died before she had been with us for all the seasons.'

'Mum.' Hassan sat up straight. 'I'd forgotten. But now I think I remember a baby crying a lot. I have a picture in my head of Nessa when she was little, standing by the baby's cradle and trying to see in. But that's all I remember.'

'That's right, Hassan. We had no doctors near us. Many families lost babies.'

'Like the baby on the boat in the storm.' I could never forget the sound that mother made. Had the loss of my baby sister affected Mum like that? 'Did our baby have a name?'

'Of course she did. It was Aqila, after your Arjay. If we give her a birthday, we can think of her on that date every year. She was born early in summer on a very hot day, and she died in the depths of winter when she would've been about the same age as Asad's baby.'

Rashid explained to Annie what we'd been discussing. She suggested June as Aqila's birth month. Mum chose the tenth.

'We should give Abdul a birthday, too.' I had an idea.

'Nah, he's gotta choose his day,' Hassan shook his head.

'Yeah, I guess you're right,' I agreed. 'But speaking of Abdul . . .' Was this too obvious? 'Why don't we ask Annie about phoning him?'

'Good idea,' Mum agreed. 'And about his visa.'

By the time Annie and Rashid were ready to leave, it had been settled that we'd visit Annie's house for lunch the next day, and phone the Camp from there. She and Rashid said they'd make enquiries about Abdul's visa, and see what they could do to try to speed things up.

That night I lay in bed imagining Abdul back with us and us all singing and dancing as we had on the first night we'd felt safe again. I especially remember two things. One, my vision of Abdul's handsome face with his smiling eyes, saying to me, 'Nessa, I love the way your soft dark eyes and long black hair shine in the glow of the light when you dance.' And two, me thinking that in Australia I don't have to wear a scarf.

CHAPTER 26

Annie's house was beautiful. Not as big as the one we were in but like her personality – sunny, welcoming and interesting. She had colourful pictures covering the walls and fascinating objects all around. But the thing that intrigued Mum and me the most was watching how she cooked. She'd gone to the halal butcher and asked for a special cut of meat, so she could give us a traditional Australian meal, roast lamb.

I watched her serve up carrots, peas and something I didn't recognise from little saucepans. 'Mum, you taught me how good cooks mix foods and spices in their pot to bring out flavours. If things aren't mixed, does it mean they have no flavour?' I asked.

'I don't know, Gulnessa. We'll soon see. It might just be a different way of doing things. Remember the food we had in Indonesia was different, and we liked it.'

'Yes, but it was still all cooked together.'

'Annie, what is called?' I asked in my halting English, pointing to a dark-green, mushy-looking vegetable Annie was putting on our plates.

'Spin-ach,' she said slowly and clearly.

'Spin-ach,' I repeated, and Hassan did, too.

'Good,' Annie encouraged. Rashid wasn't with us, so we couldn't really talk with her. We used signs to get across stuff like where to sit for lunch, how to get drinks and things like that. And we said lots of, 'yes thank yous'. I have to say that I didn't really like that Australian food. It tasted boring. I recognised 'spin-ach' when I tasted it but it wasn't nearly as good as when Mum prepared it with spices in a special dish she cooked. So when Annie put chilli sauce on the table I poured it over everything. Mum cut up Zahra's and mixed it together with the gravy. As usual she ate only a few mouthfuls. But we finished the meal with icecream cake and we all ate lots. That was delicious.

Annie stood to clear the table and I said, 'Mum, can I wash the dishes?' It was still a novelty to see how easily plates and glasses came out sparkling. Mum nodded, so I carried a pile to the sink. Annie shook her head and said something I couldn't work out. I nodded to her, miming washing up. She shrugged, smiled and took out a bottle of detergent, which she squeezed into the running water. I plugged the second, smaller sink and started to fill it with clean water, but Annie caught my hand, shaking her head.

'No, Nessa . . . no . . .' was all I could understand, so I stopped.

'Hassan, d'you know what Annie said?'

'No,' he answered, 'but can't you see she doesn't want you to fill that sink.' It hadn't taken him long to start teasing again.

'How am I going to rinse the dishes?' I asked Mum. Since we'd been washing up the Australian way, she had insisted we rinse everything as she said detergent could make us sick.

'I don't know. Just do what Annie wants,' Mum answered. We'd all learned to watch and copy.

'Hassan, there's the tea towel.' I'd seen men doing housework on TV and thought that after his job in the Camp my brother should help. After all, here he didn't have to work on the farm from dawn 'til dark so why should Mum and I wait on him and Zainullah? Even Zahra was learning. She loved to stand on a chair next to me and help.

'Get lost. That's women's work.' Knowing Annie couldn't understand Dari, he made it clear that he wanted to keep the Hazara approach to housework.

'Not in Australia.'

'I'll help you, Gulnessa,' Mum said.

'Why can't he?'

'It's not our way.'

'Mum, we're in Australia now.'

'Shhh. We can do this.' I could see she looked worried. A picture of her lying on her bunk in the Camp, tears running down her pale face, stopped me from saying more.

When the dishes were all done, without rinsing, I watched as Annie put them away, taking a mental note of how she organised her kitchen. Then, beckoning to us, she said, 'Come with me.' We followed her to the next room, which looked like one of the offices she'd taken us to in our first week. She touched a television set and said, 'Computer.'

'TV?' I asked.

'No. Com-pu-ter.' We obviously looked puzzled because she touched a flat board of buttons. The screen filled with a moving picture of an underwater scene. So, I thought, it is a TV. What's she saying this other word for? Then she pressed other buttons, and lists of words and writing came onto the screen, and then she made words come onto the screen, one letter at a time.

'Com-pu-ter,' she said again. We repeated it, whatever it was.

Then Annie picked up a something like a mobile phone. She pressed some buttons and spoke, then beckoned to Mum and passed her the handset. My heart started its Abdul-thumping and I sat on my hands to stop them shaking. This had seemed such a good idea until now. How was I going to talk to Abdul with everyone around? I wanted so much to hear his voice. Mum was talking. I forced myself to listen.

'. . . and now we're at Annie's house . . . Yes, we're all here, waiting to talk to you. Everyone's fine. We're staying in a house until we can get our own . . . Good . . . Any news about your visa? Annie's trying to help . . . Sure . . . Yes . . . Annie will give you her number. You can leave a message if you get news. But she only speaks English . . . Yes . . . Now we must be quick. Here's Hassan. Bye for now. Our love is with you.'

Hassan took the handset. 'How goes it, mate? . . . Yep, kitchen work? . . . You wouldn't believe . . . no, it was KAZ81, Mohammed, and . . .'

My turn next. Please make it my turn next . . . Mum poked my arm and pointed to the phone. I'd never hear over the thudding in my ears, but I had to try, 'Hello, Abdul . . .'

'It's good to hear your voice, Ness. I've missed you a lot.'

'Me too. Are you all right?' No one else was alive. Just me and him.

'I'm a lot better now I hear your voice. I know we can't talk privately but just your voice is happiness. Ness, I've been thinking "future" since you left. I have to say this. You're the one I see in my future. Just say *yahk* if you feel like that, too.'

'*Yahk*.' The 'one'. My heart beat faster and my hands shook.

'I think I've known you were the one since we were little kids. Watching you with your family, I knew. Watching you run towards the river chasing Zainullah, your beautiful hair streaming behind you, I knew.'

'I didn't know you saw me. You were Hassan's friend.'

'Yes, but I watched you. While I am locked up here I think of

231

all that. And our future. That gives me strength and the hope I need to get through it.'

I swallowed hard, aware of the eyes watching me. I said slowly, 'That is good. We all thank you for sharing the luck of your family's ring with us, and we hope it brings you to us very soon.'

'Wise Nessa. I wondered what you'd tell them. When we're together I want to hear everything. But tell me, now you're out of here, have your nightmares gone?'

'They don't come *every* night. We've been so busy. Seen such a lot . . .'

Mum poked my arm, 'Zainullah's turn.'

'Abdul, I have to go. The two Zs want to say hello. We'll talk soon. Our love is with you.'

'And mine is with you.'

I passed the phone over, and sat on Annie's big, soft chair, not hearing another word. My thoughts tumbled over each other. I am 'the one' for Abdul? He is for me, too. He has missed me? Me too. 'Just your voice is happiness'? Like I feel now. How long will it be before he's here? Over and over I replayed our conversation, wallowing in the rush it gave me. And the anticipation.

In bed that night I was too excited to sleep. At least I think it was excitement. My memory dredged up many snippets of times I thought had gone forever about when we were at home as I went over in my brain what Abdul had said. Playing football with our homemade rag ball; watching the sheep; in the rock playhouses my friends and I had so painstakingly built, and Hassan was trying to knock down when Abdul yelled to him . . . Perhaps he did that for me? Don't get carried away, my sensible mind warned me.

I began to mentally trace our flight from home, trying to

recall being so close to Abdul for so long, and how I'd felt. From the dawn we followed Bahkhul outside our house, my surprise at seeing Abdul waiting there, then creeping secretly to the outskirts of our village and waiting nervously, afraid. On the long journey across Afghanistan with fourteen people squashed in one car. When we had to lie still, covered with blankets, and keep silent. Scared stiff. At the crowded, dusty border camp so like a gigantic beehive, crawling with desperate, homeless humanity. Anxious and sad. On the plane trip to Indonesia and the endless bus ride at the other end, searching – for what we had no idea. That was where I really got to know Abdul.

Hassan, Abdul and I sit together on the rattling bus, talking. We decide the bus driver's trying to find somewhere that people will let us stay. Visualising our family in a house like those we see around us on stilts, we think it could be fun to sleep outside under the house on hot nights – and they all seem hot, here, and sticky. We decide, too, that we'll all help earn money to buy food and clothes. We'll grow vegetables and fruit. The soil looks rich, and there's clearly much more water here than there'd been at home. We'll sell produce we don't need at a roadside stall, like those we see in villages we drive through. Yes, we decide, we'll make a life here . . .

Yes, I thought, I always felt safer when Abdul was near. I went over our lighthouse night and how Abdul joined in our game. I *had* felt a flutter of something then, but dismissed it as excitement about the news of our coming boat trip. Abdul came from our village but he knew things I didn't know, reassuring things. He made me feel as though everything would be all right in the end, like Dad did. Even after we discovered we were to be put on a boat to sail over that enormous sea to a strange country . . .

233

The group from our bus crouches on the sand about two metres away from other people waiting there. My flash of excitement at the sight of the boat morphs into anxiety. Everyone looks worried. No one speaks. Mum's face is drawn. I see her jaws flexing as she grinds her teeth. All colour has drained from her normally glowing, dark complexion. That is, all but the fading, yellow-tinged, purplish bruising around the lingering remains of the lump near her eye – her last 'gift' from the Terror. She kneels on the grey beach sand, staring out to sea. One arm is around Zahra, the other clutching remnants of our old life. She's praying as she has continually since we left home.

'Mummy?' Zahra's plaintive voice quavers. There's no sign that Mum hears her. 'Mummy?' A little louder. Still no movement, except Mum's lips as they mime her prayers. Zahra twists around and, taking Mum's face firmly between her small hands, she says urgently, 'Mummy, where Daddy? We forgot him.'

A sword plunges into my guts. Pain worse than anything I know. Real pain. Dad! I miss him so much. He made my fears disappear. Made me believe that everything would be all right. But now, the fears have grown so I can hardly bear them. Where is he?

'My darling Zahra.' Mum cuddles Zahra to her chest so that Zahra can't see her tears. 'Daddy wants us to be safe. He'll come after us, and find us.'

Zahra wriggles free of Mum's arms and stands facing her. 'How?' she demands. 'I want my daddy. Now.'

'Soon, darling, I hope.' Her voice grows desperate. 'We have to believe that.' I slide my arm around Mum's shoulders. I hate seeing her like this. What will become of us if anything happens to her? I push the thought away . . . Abdul moves closer to us.

A shout makes me jerk around to face the dark water. Two men walk towards us, our agent following them. Another man wades out to a fishing boat moored about twenty metres from the beach where

234

a small dinghy waits near the water's edge. The two men, little older than Abdul, stop in front of the waiting crowd. One steps forward, gesturing for us to rise. He stands silent until everyone is on their feet.

'Show us papers. We take you boat.' The young voice sounds hesitant, the words clearly not in his language. 'Take women, children . . .' he waves towards the dinghy. 'Men walk, climb ladder.' He points towards the third man, expertly climbing a rope ladder on the side of the moored boat. Reaching the top, he leaps over the railing on to the deck.

A man in the crowd shouts, 'We won't all fit on that old tub!'

'Yes.' But the young face reflects uncertainty.

'No!' The questioner narrows his eyes. He shakes his head, speaking clearly, deliberately. 'That boat is too old, too small. We are many people. Maybe one hundred.' He gestures at all of us on the beach and holds up his hands, fingers outstretched, flexing them quickly, many times. 'We cannot all fit,' he repeats slowly and clearly.

'Yes can.' The fisherman nods.

'No. My family won't get on that boat. We need a bigger boat.' The man signals to his family, who sit down again. His wife cradles their baby in her arms. Their daughter, about Zahra's age, tries to sit on her knee. It's the first time we see Asad.

The fisherman turns to his companion and they talk rapidly in their language. Our agent stands to one side watching, face expressionless. The fisherman begins to nod. He turns to the sitting family. 'You get on fishing boat. We take you bi-i-i-ig boat.' He gestures to the distant mouth of the bay, and the open sea. As the man and his wife discuss this development, everyone begins to talk.

'What do you think?' Hassan asks Mum.

'We have to believe,' Mum says slowly. 'We can't go back.'

'Yes,' agrees Abdul. 'Remember, if anything happens to the boat, those men are on it, too.' This makes sense.

235

Abruptly the buzz of voices stops and I look up to see the family gathering up their few belongings. The fisherman nods to them, then gestures to include everyone. 'You listen. First, we see papers.'

People pull their papers from wherever they are hidden and we wait in silence. Satisfied at last, the fisherman hands over our groups' papers to our agent, who walks back to the bus. The fisherman speaks. 'We take women and children find place, deck. Stay there. After, men walk.'

Waiting silently for our turn, we watch the fisherman show people in front of us how to climb into the dinghy, and how to sit so the boat won't rock. Then the man punts the dinghy out to the rope ladder hanging from the boat and we watch the people climb on to the deck.

At last it's our turn. Clambering into the dinghy, Mum and I sit unsteadily on a narrow board and draw the two Zs onto our laps. Hassan and Abdul start to climb in but the fisherman shouts, 'You men. Wait.'

I can see Mum going to say something so I get in first. 'Mum, they'll be okay. They don't have to wade far.' Mum nods to the boys and they step back from the dinghy. Two women and two more children climb aboard and half smile at us as they settle themselves on the other sitting-board.

I look back at Hassan and see his worried frown. I understand his feelings. I don't want to let Mum out of my sight, either. Then I see Abdul put his hand on Hassan's shoulder, and say something to him as they watch us from the water's edge. Suddenly the boat moves and I hold tightly to Zahra with one hand and the side of the boat with the other as the fisherman pushes off.

'Sit still,' he warns as the boat slides smoothly off the sandy bottom.

The short ride in the quiet waters of the bay is exciting. It increases my confidence. It gives no hint of what's ahead of us.

Yes, Abdul was a rock throughout the whole ordeal. To us all. Someone there to support and help us. It gave me comfort to be near him but nothing like the rush I felt when I thought of our parting at the Camp. Or heard his voice. Or even planned to phone him again. When did I begin to feel so differently about him? Was it when I started to talk to him, really talk, in our sanctuary in the first compound at the Camp?

I don't remember it but at some time that night I must have dozed off.

I'm running as fast as I can. Straining to go faster. I look to the left. Dung-face is next to me. Laughing maliciously. Pulling the ground back under my feet towards a gaping pit in the red soil. I can't move past him no matter how I throw myself forward. He just pulls harder. I see human excrement bubbling in the pit, which is also packed with coiled razor wire. I struggle even more. There's Abdul in the distance, holding out his arms. I lunge . . .

I woke suddenly to find myself on the floor.

I'd started the night in a smaller bedroom alone, the first room I'd ever had to myself. I'd wanted to concentrate on my wonderful feeling – and Abdul. Now that had gone.

I crept down the passage and into the big bed Mum and Zahra shared. Only Zahra's little form was there in the middle of the bed. She was asleep cuddling her pillow, with Theermie wedged between it and her chest. I lay next to her with my eyes closed, listening. I didn't feel like talking to Mum just now. I hadn't talked to her about my anxiety or dreams, and I didn't want to. I still felt she was like a glass person who'd break if she were squeezed too hard. Although she joined in and was more like our mother of old, there was something forced about the way she was. Like she had to try hard to do things.

I sensed a movement and squinted through my almost closed

lids. Mum was getting back into bed. I pretended to be asleep. It was nothing new to find an extra one or two of us in bed with her, or each other. Even though we knew we were safe, for the time being anyway, the horrors of the past returned at unexpected moments, especially at night. We needed no words. The comfort of physical nearness was enough.

That night seemed to go on forever. Dream snippets woke me a million times. At last when I opened my eyes for the million and first time, the greyness of dawn was pushing away darkness.

CHAPTER 27

Annie had explained to the school principal that we needed time to organise our new life so we had two weeks grace before start-ing. We spent it exploring, and completing 'business', driving in Annie's van to visit more offices and see more people. Most often none of us could understand what was happening but some-times when there was an interpreter Mum had to tell our story again. She told these people about Abdul, too. I was worried this might send her back into her blackest depression, but she said she only had to give a short account of what happened.

Most people we saw seemed understanding and wanted to help, especially the doctor Annie took Mum to see. She pre-scribed different tablets, which she said would kick in in about two weeks. And Annie organised for us to see a counsellor who helped people who'd suffered traumas. Mum was to have the first appointment, then we'd go as a family. After that they'd organise individual appointments for us all.

We explored our suburban neighbourhood on foot, discov-ering a park with playground swings and slides, which the two Zs loved. There'd been no luxuries like that at home. And there was a separate construction at the side of the park, where we watched kids skateboarding. Hassan wanted a go and one of the kids let him try on a flat part. He actually managed to stay on it for a few metres. The kid gave him a thumbs up.

Near our house were some small shops we could easily walk to. The first time we went by ourselves was when Annie came over to talk to Mum. We'd run out of milk and even though it seemed weird to us, Annie liked milk in her tea. Giving me some money, Annie said, 'Nessa, put on your shoes to walk to the shops. You don't want doggie-do on your feet, do you?'

'Yes, thank you.' I nodded. Hassan fell about laughing.

We never grew tired of wandering the streets looking at different houses, mostly variations of our single-storey, brick and tile bungalow, and gardens with their strange plants. The only plants any one had grown at home were those you could eat. The flowers that came before their fruits were an added bonus, but no one ever picked those just for their beauty. Other things in the gardens, like bikes, and scooters, and cars, and big umbrellas with seats under them, fascinated us. We soaked it all up. How could families own so much? People doing things we didn't recognise, like washing cars and mowing grass, intrigued us. Mum warned us not to stare in case people thought we were rude and got angry, but it was hard not to. We wanted to know everything. All at once. Sometimes people stopped and spoke to us, but not understanding, we could only say, 'Thank you, yes'. Each time I saw something new I'd daydream about how I'd show it to Abdul when he arrived.

The only things we didn't like were the flies. Annie gave us some fly spray and showed us what to do with it. After the can ran out, Mum asked Hassan to buy another. She was sitting in the living room, sewing a tablecloth for Annie, and the flies were driving her nuts. Mum said that as she had nothing else to give Annie for her kindnesses, she wanted to make something for her.

When Hassan came back he sprayed the living room and kitchen. I started to sneeze. 'That's not like the one Annie gave us,' I complained. 'It smells revolting. It's choking me.'

'Well, go outside,' Hassan sneered, 'if you're so delicate.'

'Stop it,' Mum sounded tired. 'But it does smell awful. Please keep it away from me. I've got another headache. I didn't get much sleep last night.' She shook her head. 'I hope the counsellor will help us get rid of our nightmares.'

Just then, Annie's van pulled up. As she came inside Hassan was spraying a fly on the window, leaving a smudgy foam on the glass. Annie sniffed, and went over to him, holding out her hand. As Hassan offered her the can, she screwed up her face like she was in pain and beckoned us to follow her. Shaking the can, she walked out to the kitchen, opened the oven door and sprayed the brown marks there with white foam. Stepping back from the acrid smell, she took a sponge and wiped away the foam. The marks had disappeared!

This amazed me on two counts – one, that Hassan had been spraying flies with oven cleaner, and two, that a cleaner could remove dirt like that.

Every day we discovered new things, and we made plenty of mistakes. Rashid took us on the buses until we felt confident. That wasn't too hard. But the trains! I'll never forget the first one I saw rushing towards us along the rails. We were waiting on the station with Annie. She pointed out the name 'Fremantle' on a sign and said slowly, 'This is Fremantle Station, our station.'

The train looked like a line of buses linked together. It took us all the way into Perth Central and as we stepped onto the busy station platform, a snake inside me writhed uncomfortably. So many people. Everyone seemed to be rushing. But there was no sign of soldiers or people with guns. Still, a feeling of disquiet lingered.

Annie took us to the art gallery. There were so many amazing paintings and photographs in it. It was fantastic. Photos were new to us and it wasn't until later, when I asked Rashid about them, that I discovered how they were created. I wished we could send some to our family at home to show them the marvellous things we'd seen. And to Abdul. How good it'd be if I could see a real picture of him, and send him one of me.

Walking back to catch the train home we came face to face with a line of six stony-faced women marching towards us. We moved aside to let them pass, but there still wasn't enough room. One shoved me out of the way. I tripped, stumbling sideways. Regaining my balance I saw another woman pull hard at Mum's scarf. Mum had both hands on her head holding it, forearms together, covering her face.

Annie marched up to the woman and spoke through gritted teeth. The woman let go of Mum's scarf, side-stepped and yelled something at us. Then, hate distorting their faces, they stomped off. So that's what the guards meant, I thought, feeling strangely calm. I slid my arm around Mum's waist as she adjusted her scarf, and Annie on the other side had her arm around Mum's shoulders. Zahra began crying. Zainullah's face was pale. Hassan put his hand on Zainullah's shoulder, saying quietly, 'Don't worry. It's not as bad as guns.' As we started walking my knees began to shake – so hard I thought they'd buckle – but I went on, a step at a time.

Sitting on the train, I breathed more easily but could see Mum was still shaking. Annie sat on one side of her, comforting, reassuring, talking in a low voice. Even though Mum couldn't understand Annie's words, her gentle tone and the rhythm of her speech slowly soothed her – and me. Annie's distinctive accent made me think of other kind Australians we'd met. The old couple at the service station who'd taken us under their wing; friendly people in offices who'd given us drinks and biscuits; the doctor who arranged to have an interpreter present for Mum; shop assistants who smiled and mimed so we could understand. I knew there were more good people in Australia than those filled with hate.

But every time something bad happened, it brought back the old terrified feelings. Incidents occurred quite often and always it was someone we'd never seen before. A hand or shoulder would shove one of us. Mum was a target with her veil, or Hassan or me because we were bigger. Or they'd shout at us and although we didn't understand most words the hate was unmistakable. Like one day when Mum and I were walking home, Mum wearing her scarf as she always did outside. I heard a shout and looked up. A man, leaning out the window of a passing truck, was yelling and shaking his fist at us. I made out the words, '. . . get out ya bloody . . .'

Why do these people hate us? What do they know about us? We've done nothing to them. They have a wonderful place to live – paradise. How can we show them we only want to live safely like they do?

Now on the train, sitting on the other side of Mum, I held her hand while Zahra sat on my lap, head resting on my shoulder. Suddenly Annie leant forward and spoke slowly, 'Tomorrow. May twenty-eighth. Zainullah's birthday. We have party. Then school in two days.' She held up two fingers.

Understanding, I brightened, and ignoring the school part, said, 'Yes, thankyou party. Where?' Hassan and Zainullah leant forward, too.

'I come to your house. Rashid too.' We all beamed. 'We bring birthday presents for Zainullah.' His face lit up.

243

'What time?' Hassan asked. We'd begun to understand that, to Annie at least, time was important.

'Twelve o'clock,' Annie answered, tapping her watch. 'Twelve o'clock.'

Zahra piped up with a bit of information for Mum that I'd missed. 'Annie bring presents.' I hadn't realised how much she understood already.

CHAPTER 28

When I woke next morning I heard a gentle pattering sound so I decided to get up and investigate. I wanted to be ready early for Zainullah's birthday party. I'll wear my new jeans and top, I decided. Peering out my bedroom window, I discovered it was raining. Really raining, not just short showers like we'd had a couple of times since we'd been in Perth. The sound had developed into a dull drumming as rain beat down. My room looked out on the road and I pressed my face against the cool glass, watching the cars struggle past in the downpour. Movement on their windscreens caught my eye. Something was wiping away the rain so the driver could see!

I felt a tug at my sleeve and looked down. Zahra's upturned face, eyes shining, watched me. Zainullah danced around behind her.

'Let's go outside,' he shouted. 'Can we, can we, Nessie?'

'Canwe canwe canwe . . .' echoed Zahra.

I ran towards the back door, little feet scurrying behind me. Unlocking the door – another thing we'd not done at home – we burst out onto the back lawn. Faces to the heavens, arms stretched wide, we spun round and round until, too giddy to stand, we dropped onto the grass, giggling and stretching out on our backs, drinking in the rain. Soon I realised Hassan had joined us, but was standing with his hands on his hips, laughing his head off. When finally I sat up and looked towards the house, Mum's smiling face was at the window. And I felt happy. Until I thought of Abdul.

❧ ❧ ❧

Annie arrived for Zainullah's party carrying a big, blue plastic box with round holes punched in its sides. On top was a handle and a huge red bow. A lady carrying plastic carry-bags followed her inside. Annie introduced her friend, Trish, and we'd just finished each saying our names for her to repeat when Rashid pulled up in our driveway. The rain had stopped but looked like it would start again at any moment.

'What a great car!' Hassan raced outside. I followed. 'When did you get it?'

'About three months ago,' Rashid answered.

'What is it?' Hassan walked around it, inspecting it closely.

'A Commodore. I work at night in a restaurant, washing dishes,' Rashid explained, 'and I saved up. It's a used car, you know.'

'I'm going to get one, too. Soon as I can get a job.' Hassan couldn't take his eyes off it. The car looked okay to me, but buying one certainly wasn't my top priority.

'Give me a hand with the birthday lunch,' Rashid said, passing delicious-smelling chicken and chips. Big drops of rain began to fall again and we ran for the front door.

When we were all inside, Annie spoke to Rashid, who translated for us, 'Annie asked me to get chicken and chips for the party, and she's brought the birthday cake. That's a surprise. She says to eat the chicken now before it gets cold. Then we can have the cake and presents.' We didn't need a second invitation.

When we were all sitting cross-legged around the food, with Annie and Trish in chairs. Annie held up her glass of Coke and said, 'Happy birthday, Zainullah.'

'Happy birthday,' Trish repeated, also holding up her glass.

'Happy birthday, mate,' Rashid added, holding up his glass, too. 'Let's toast the birthday boy,' Rashid translated for Annie. 'That's when you drink to wish someone good luck.'

We all held up our glasses, 'Happy birthday, Zainullah!' We drank our first toast. Zainullah for once looked down shyly.

Zahra sat quietly, close to me. There was a new person with us so she'd withdrawn again – at least for now. Trish must have sensed this for she leant over and took my hand, holding the glass in her free one. Then she moved our glasses towards each other until they touched, making a 'chinking' sound. 'Cheers,' she said clearly, and lifted her glass to take a sip.

'Another way to toast each other,' explained Rashid. I wondered how he'd learned all the new customs. But I liked these.

Trish turned to toast Zainullah, so I turned to Zahra, helping her chink glasses. Without any prompting from me she immediately said, 'Chiz!' and took a sip. Trish, who'd been watching her, clapped, and Zahra smiled.

By the time the rest of us had finished our chicken and chips Zahra had been around the whole circle, chinking glasses with everyone. I'd managed to pop chips in her mouth, one at a time, and so had Mum, but she wasn't interested in eating.

Then Annie said something to Rashid, got up and left the room. 'Annie wants us all to wait here,' he said. 'She'll be back in a minute.'

'Chiz, Rashid!' Zahra sang, coyly smiling up at him through her lashes. He tousled her hair. She's flirting! I suddenly thought, watching her. I wonder if it's instinctive with little girls.

247

Trish burst out singing, 'Happy birthday to you . . .' Annie appeared in the doorway singing, too. 'Happy birthday, Zainullah, happy birthday to you.' That was the first time we'd heard the birthday song and the first time we'd seen a cake with lit candles on top. Rashid reached up, took the cake from Annie and carefully lowered it to the floor. Eight candles flickered, then burned brightly.

'These birthday candles show how old you are. Now you must blow them out, Zainullah, and make a wish,' he directed, demonstrating and explaining about wishes. Zainullah blew the rest out with one huge blow, sitting back on his heels and looking proud of himself. Zahra was beside herself, dancing around, clapping her hands and giggling until Mum caught her, drawing her down onto her lap.

'Shhh, darling,' she whispered, but not very forcefully. I could see she was as delighted as Zahra – for different reasons, I suspected. But Zahra was not to be held. She sprang to her feet, nearly toppling over again, so I reached out and grabbed her.

'My turn. Pfffffffff . . .' she blew, spitting at the same time.

'Wait a minute and watch Annie,' I whispered, trying to quieten her. Annie was busy cutting the dark cake into wedges.

'Chocolate – mud – cake,' she said clearly. 'My favourite.' After my first taste I decided it was my favourite, too.

'Shoc – lit – mut – cae – shoc – lit – mut – cae . . .' Zahra squirmed out of my arms and was off chanting and dancing again.

'Will you ask Annie if Zahra can blow out the candles, please?' I asked Rashid. Annie nodded. Then she set the candles in the piece of cake that remained on the plate. Zahra's eyes lit up as brightly as the candles as she watched Rashid light them. Then he sat back.

'Pff,' she blew. The candles didn't so much as flicker.

'Pffff.' Still nothing.

'Pffffff.' She was going red in the face.

'Darling, lean closer,' I whispered.

Zahra grabbed my shoulder and leaned as far as she could, 'Pffffffffff.' With a little help from me the candles flickered wildly, then snuffed out. Zahra jigged up and down, clapping and giggling.

As the noise died away, Annie stood up and said clearly, 'Present time.' She and Trish went out of the room.

Zainullah beamed. He turned to Rashid. 'Is this when everyone gives me things 'cos they love me?' He'd memorised that brilliantly.

'It is,' Rashid assured him. Mum looked up. We had nothing to give. Rashid smiled, holding a finger to his lips as Annie and Trish returned, carrying the plastic bags and the big, blue plastic box, which she put behind her chair. Trish held open a plastic bag and Annie pulled out of it a brightly wrapped small, flat parcel, passing it to Mum, and indicating with her eyes that it was for her to give to Zainullah. Zainullah frowned and opened his mouth to speak, but Rashid got in first. 'Fatimeh, say "Happy birthday" and give him a kiss.' Annie had thought of everything.

Mum did as Rashid said. Zainullah ripped open the paper, pulling out an orange T-shirt with a picture on the back of a kid riding a surfboard on a huge wave. He immediately pulled it over the one he was wearing. Then he proudly puffed out his chest, flexed his biceps and said in English, 'I'm good Australian.' We all clapped.

Annie had brought something for each of us to give: a fluorescent purple and orange pencil case; a pack of coloured pencils; a cap with a picture like the T-shirt; and a big money box of Smarties. We'd all fallen in love with chocolate – but we had yet to discover what a money box was for.

Then it was Rashid's turn. Zainullah, almost drunk with excitement, pulled off the bright paper decorated with toy cars and trucks and threw it over his shoulder. He stood spellbound gazing at the toy truck he held. Raising his eyes to Rashid, Zainullah gave him the most brilliant smile. It made me want to laugh – for joy. The truck was a replica of the trucks that hauled shipping containers around the country, and best of all it had two sections to it that could be hitched and unhitched to the cab section. Zainullah had plied Rashid with questions about trucks we passed whenever he'd been in Annie's van with us, and he'd obviously remembered.

After giving Zainullah time to try out his toy truck, Annie stood up and pulled from behind her chair the big box. Putting it down carefully in front of the birthday boy, she said, 'Happy birthday, Zainullah.' And she kissed his cheek. He looked at her, overawed.

Then Annie said, 'Open it.'

He took the lid off the box and you ought to have seen the expression on his face. He couldn't speak. I leant forward but he pushed me back firmly. Then he reached in and lifted up the cutest black kitten. Around its neck was a blue ribbon.

'Thank you, Annie,' whispered Zainullah, cuddling it. Then grudgingly he let us all have a turn.

Finally Annie said, 'I think it might like a drink of milk.'

Rashid translated. Zainullah quickly disappeared through the kitchen door, closely followed by Hassan.

'I must go. I start work soon. At the restaurant,' Rashid said.

'Thank you, Rashid. You have been so good to us.' I could see tears glistening in Mum's eyes.

'No. Thank *you*, Fatimeh, for sharing this with me. My family are in Iran. I have not seen them for more than three years. When I escaped, my daughter was a baby, only a few months old, and my son was two. I try to reach them often, even the Red Cross try for me, but I can't get news. My parents and brother were killed by Government Intelligence. They searched for me. I had to escape. My wife and children stayed with her parents so I could find somewhere we could all live safely. I apply many times for them to join me but the Australian Government won't let them come. I am lonely for my family. For me it is a special privilege to share a child's birthday.'

'Please join us at any time, we'd be honoured,' Mum said.

Later, when everyone had gone home and Mum and I had cleared up, we were sitting around the living room, too full of birthday food to move, and Zainullah announced, 'That was the best day in my whole life. Ever.' He stopped and looked at Mum, adding, 'But I wish Dad was here. He'd like birthdays.'

'I'm sure he knows what a wonderful time we had,' Mum said quietly. I looked at her closely and decided with relief that she was sad, but okay.

'The best bit,' Zainullah went on, 'was when I gave Midnight his bath. Midnight's his name.'

'A bath?' Mum said.

'You don't bath kittens! Haven't you watched them clean themselves?' I exclaimed.

'He liked it,' Zainullah said smugly, 'so I gave him two.'

'Well, if you're not scratched to bits, he can't have minded too much,' Mum said. 'Anyway, where's he now?'

'Asleep. Behind there.' Zainullah pointed to the lounge chair I was sitting on, so I kneeled up to look over its back. There was a ball of black fluff almost hidden by a huge red bow. I wish Abdul could see him, I thought. He should be here to share all this.

But Midnight wasn't part of the family for long. After the first week, Zainullah would forget to feed it and change its tray. Mum got cross with Zainullah and said she had enough to do without having to look after a kitten, too. One day when we got home from school the kitten was missing. We searched everywhere and went around the streets calling its name. No luck. We never saw him again.

CHAPTER 29

A few days later we set out for our first day of school. Annie had said she'd meet us there, as it took only minutes for us to walk. Hassan, Zainullah and I each wore our favourite T-shirt and a jumper with jeans, but Zahra, who loved an outfit of pants and top with little teddy bears all over them, insisted on wearing that. Of course she came with us even though she couldn't stay there yet.

By the time we arrived at the school gate, I felt really anxious. Remembering my first day at the Camp school when Tara was with me, I wished she was here. I missed her. Annie and Rashid were waiting but there was no sign of any boys and girls. 'You're late,' Rashid said. 'The other kids have gone into class.'

'Eight thirty,' Annie said clearly. 'I said eight thirty. Now, it's nine o'clock.' I think she'd grown impatient with us. Being somewhere at a certain time was something else we'd never had to do before. Our days in Afghanistan had flowed from one task to the next, from the time we got up in the morning until bedtime. Things took as long as they did to finish, then we got on with the next job. When it was too dark outside, we stopped to eat and went inside, or sat beside the fire at the back of the house when the weather was good enough.

Rashid, smiling slightly, passed on a message from Annie. 'In Australia when someone tells you a time it means *exactly* that time. Or five minutes earlier, never later. Most things won't wait for you, like school starting time, and buses and trains. Anyway, we'll go in and see if you can still start school today.' Secretly, I hoped we were too late.

When we got to the school's reception a smiling lady greeted us and waved us to some seats. Then Annie spoke to her and handed over our papers. The door to the principal's office opened and she walked out, greeting us each in turn. When she got to Zahra, she said, 'What pretty pyjamas, dear.' Zahra slid behind Mum. Rashid just smiled.

Annie and the principal talked for a while, then moved towards the door while Rashid explained, 'The principal will take Zainullah and Nessa to their classes now. The teachers are expecting you. She said that as you've never been to school, Nessa, you can stay here for the rest of this year to learn English, even though you're old enough to go to high school with Hassan. You'll start there next year. Zahra will start preschool here after the school holidays in a few weeks. Hassan, your mum and Annie and I will take you to your school when we leave here.'

Gritting my teeth and clenching my fists, I felt my fingers close over Abdul's ring. The vision of his face helped calm me as we followed Annie and the principal out of the building and across the playground. We stopped at a classroom door on the opposite side of the wide paved area. The principal knocked, opened the door, and walked in, gesturing for us to follow. The murmur of voices stopped and as we entered around twenty-five pairs of eyes looked towards us. Instantly I noticed that nearly half of the faces were varying shades of dark skin. Good, I thought. We won't be so different here.

'Miss Walker, this is Zainullah,' the principal said. I felt confused. The first word meant nothing to me but I knew what 'walk' meant and 'this is Zainullah'. Perhaps she meant him to walk – or did she mean me? While I was puzzling about this the teacher spoke. 'Good morning, Zainullah.' He nodded and smiled hesitantly. 'Come. You can sit here.' She pulled out a chair at a group of desks in the front of the room and spoke to a pale-skinned boy sitting in the next chair.

'Hello. I'm Leigh,' the boy said to Zainullah.

'Zainullah.' Pointing to himself, Zainullah's answer came out automatically, we'd done it so often. He sat down and I saw Leigh say something to him.

I waited for the teacher to come back for my turn but she said something to the principal, who smiled and moved towards the door. Annie followed her and I stood uncertainly, looking from them to Zainullah, anxiety welling up again.

The teacher, smiling gently at me, said clearly, 'Zainullah's in this class. You're . . .' and she pointed to the door. It hit me – we were going to be in different rooms. That was something I hadn't even considered.

I moved to follow Annie and the principal, suddenly feeling really scared. I was used to having at least one of my brothers or my sister with me. Come on, Gulnessa – I only used that name to give myself a pep-talk. Look at Zainullah. He's made a friend already. You'll be fine.

❧ ❧ ❧

At home that afternoon after school, we compared notes. 'Zainullah and I weren't in the same class,' I told Mum and Hassan. 'At first it freaked me out. I wouldn't move from my desk. But these two girls sat with me. We couldn't talk each other's language, just a bit of English. But they were friendly. They took me around the whole school. One comes from Bosnia, the other from Somalia. The teacher showed us each other's country on a map of the world. That's a big picture.' I demonstrated, feeling proud to be able to explain things to Mum.

'Sounds good,' Mum said. 'And how did you go, Zainullah?'

'Leigh talked to me a bit – only English though. But when he went away I was scared. I hid my head – on the desk. But then I heard kids playing. Truck noises. I peeped and these kids had a "Mack" truck. In the classroom. I played with them *all* day. The teacher let us. I can say "Mack" in English. The teacher went . . .' Zainullah gave a thumbs up and his eyes shone as he talked. Mum hugged him. Hassan said his school was okay, but he didn't talk to anyone until he met another boy from Afghanistan. After that they hung out together.

❧ ❧ ❧

We'd only been at school a week when Annie said it was time to look for a new house because ours was needed to help another family get started. Our money was now coming through from the Centrelink Special Benefit, so we could pay for rent and food. We wanted somewhere in the same neighbourhood, so we wouldn't have to move schools, and because we knew our way around. I'd been relieved that after the first day I felt really comfortable going to this school. I think it was because there were lots of other kids from different countries and the Australian kids were used to having different kids around.

The next Saturday morning Annie came to pick us up, bringing Rashid with her. As we drove to see a house she'd found for rent, I thought: this will be our first real home in Australia. The conversation about our dream home that Mum and I had had in the bus on the way to the Camp – before we were stuck in prison for two long years – popped into my mind.

'Mu-um,' I said, 'd'you remember what you wanted in your dream house?'

'Why do you ask that, Gulnessa?'

'Oh, forget it.' Why can't she just answer my question?

'No, tell me why you asked about it,' she persisted.

'It doesn't matter. Forget it.' I didn't want to blast off in front of Annie and Rashid, but she was getting under my skin.

She must have recognised the warning signs because she dropped it, and said, 'The house we've been living in has more than I ever imagined we could have. In the Camp I used to dream about having my own kitchen, to cook our meals and store our food and water running from a tap.'

'Practically all houses in Australia have those,' Rashid said.

The van stopped in front of a house with an orangey tiled roof and white walls, which Rashid explained were made from bricks – not mud bricks – and covered with a sort of white cement coating. Zahra immediately fell in love with two black cement swans sitting either side of the front steps, which led to a verandah with fancy white-painted wrought-iron railings around it.

I listened to the man who owned our new house, trying to understand some of his words as he talked to Annie and Rashid in strangely accented English, and used both his hands as well, to explain himself. Rashid told us that he'd come to Australia from Italy with his parents when he was about Zainullah's age and when he arrived he couldn't speak a word of English, either. Zainullah looked proud when the man put his hand on his shoulder. He said his name was Primo Farinelli and he understood how we felt in a new country. His English still sounded

like Italian for all I could make of it. That made me more determined than ever to learn English as fast as I could, and to sound
like an Australian when I spoke.

The house was freshly painted in the colours of the sun and
the sea, Mr Farinelli told us, miming his meaning extravagantly
so that we could all understand. I loved it as soon as I stepped
inside. The colours made me feel happy. There were three sunny
yellow bedrooms and the lounge and kitchen/dining room had
Mediterranean blue walls. Annie said that laughing, but I'm
not sure why. The ceilings and woodwork were white, and the
kitchen had brilliant-orange benchtops. The floors were all
covered in a hard brown material that looked like tiles.

When we got to the bathroom I could hear Mr Farinelli saying 'old' lots of times. It looked fine to me, not as new as the
first house, but it had taps with running water, a shower, and a
blue bath and hand basin. Rashid said Mr Farinelli repeated that
although they were old, they didn't leak and worked well.

Suddenly realising we hadn't seen a toilet and not wanting to
mention such a thing in front of a strange man, I pulled Annie's
sleeve and whispered, 'Toilet?'

I'm not sure if Mr Farinelli heard or it was the next place he
would have taken us anyway, but he walked towards the door,
saying, 'Come.' We followed him through the kitchen and out a
door to the 'back verandah'. The floor was shiny red concrete and
to the left two doors led off it into two small rooms. Thankfully,
one was a clean toilet! The other had in it only two big cement
tubs fastened to the walls, with a tap over each. There were also
two taps on the wall next to the tubs, with nothing under them.

'Why are these taps here?' Mum asked Rashid.

'It's the laundry,' he explained. The verandah opened onto
a back garden of mainly flat, neatly mowed grass. Low bushes

lined the fence on the right, and there was a long dirt bed with nothing planted in it against the back fence. In the far right-hand corner was a small, old, run-down brick building, with a door that looked as if it hadn't been opened for ages. Between that and the house, springing out of the lawn, was a steel thing that looked like an enormous umbrella with no cover.

'What's that?' I asked Rashid.

'It's a clothes line to hang out your washing,' he said.

'What about the little house further back?' asked Hassan.

Rashid laughed. 'That's an old toilet. Hasn't been used for years.'

On the left side of the yard stood a wooden frame with a vine growing over it. Next to this was a big lemon tree with both green and yellow fruit peeping between the glossy dark-green leaves.

'Cool! A grapevine,' Rashid said. 'It grows bunches of juicy fruit, the size of big berries,' he went on before we could ask.

'Very old,' put in Mr Farinelli, seeing what we were discussing. 'Muscatel grapes. Very sweet. Good.' He grouped the fingers of his right hand together, and touched the tips to his lips with an extravagant gesture.

We were sold. Everything we wanted in a home. And even though the toilet wasn't quite inside, it was undercover and had its own light. I was more than satisfied.

Zainullah was zooming around the back lawn and I realised I hadn't seen Zahra for quite a while. 'Zahra, where are you?' I called. No answer. Everyone started to call. I began to feel panicky.

'Hassan, you and Zainullah look in the garden, Gulnessa and I'll look in the house.' Mum was worried, too, and we moved quickly towards the back door.

Annie came with us, saying, 'Don't worry. She won't be far.'

'Zahra, Zahra,' I called, 'where are you?' Mum was almost running as she checked the bathroom and bedrooms. Annie followed.

I went to the lounge. Looking through the front window, I stopped. Relief flooded through me. 'Mum, it's okay. Come here. Quickly.'

There was Zahra riding on the back of one of the black swans, one arm holding its neck, like reins. Now we were quiet we could hear her clear voice singing, 'Lalay lalay, ate-aya . . .'

We got to the steps at the same time as Hassan, Rashid and Mr Farinelli. I could see Zahra's doll on her knee, wrapped in Theerma's scarf.

'Look at my pony,' she grinned. 'I take Theermie for ride.'

'You must tell us if you go away,' Mum said, not crossly but her voice was sharp with worry.

It didn't take long for Mum, with Annie and Rashid's help, to sort out the business details. We were to move in next weekend.

During the following week, Annie organised lots of things we needed, like beds, bedding, towels, mattresses, crockery and cutlery, saucepans and a table and chairs. Rashid told us lots of people donated household goods they didn't need to help refugees start their own homes. These items were stored in the big CARAD warehouse. CARAD, we'd found out, was the Coalition for Asylum-seekers, Refugees and Detainees. Annie also took us to secondhand shops to buy a fridge and washing machine. We'd wait and save up to buy other appliances, clothes and things.

Rashid helped us to move and Annie helped us to settle in. Mum said Zainullah and I had to share a bedroom, as Hassan needed his own. He had lots more homework than we did. Typical. Annie got him a desk from the warehouse, so two beds wouldn't fit in his room anyway. Zahra and Mum shared the other room. I worried about where Abdul would sleep when he joined us.

The landlord was good to us, but I tried to duck out of his way every time he tried to pinch my cheeks, rattling away in his Italian-English. He found us some old bikes and often brought us vegetables he'd grown in his own garden, not far away. When Mum said she'd like to start a vegie garden, too, he dug the bed along the back fence, and came around regularly to cut our lawn. Mum said she couldn't bring herself to put precious water on plants that were not useful, so we didn't add any flowers to the shrubs that were already in the garden.

Before long we met the neighbours, who were all friendly. The man across the road gave us a trampoline his kids didn't use any more and we learned to use it in record time. Soon we could bounce higher than the house, and we invented all sorts of different ways to jump and somersault.

Our learning curve during the next few months was like climbing a mountain. English was top of the list but we learned lots of other things, too. Even a basic thing like locking the house was new to us. To begin with, remembering a key caused so many arguments.

'Who locked up when we left?'

'I did.'

'Well, where's the key?'

'Haven't got it.'

'Did you lock up with it?'

'No, I pressed the button.'

'How many times have I told you only to lock up with a key, so you won't forget it?' No response. 'Well, go and ask our neighbour, Mrs McAllister, if she'd phone Annie and ask her to come over with her key . . .'

One of the lessons we took longest to learn was being on time for things. I don't know how many trains to school Hassan missed and then had to sit at the station waiting for the next – and also how many jumpers, lunch boxes and other things he left on them, because he was so vague. When we were forty-five minutes late for our first appointment ever with a dentist, he couldn't see us. We had to go back at another time. Though when he filled one of my back teeth, I thought missing his appointment wasn't such a bad idea. We all needed dental treatment, as we hadn't heard of it at home.

In Afghanistan all our days had been the same. It didn't matter too much at what hour we did our chores. Even praying was flexible. Most people did that before meals, and three times a day.

Mum was learning English, but as she can't read or write in our language she had to learn that as well. She said she knows it'll take her much longer than it'll take us at school, but she won't give up. She went to English lessons with a lady at a church, not ours, where she met and made friends with women from many different countries, including three women from Afghanistan. Sometimes we visited their houses but they all lived a long way from where we did. Another lady began to come to our house once a week to teach Mum, too. And Mum had her first appointment with the counsellor. Annie took her. After Mum came home she went to bed for the rest of the day.

At school in my third week, just after we'd moved house, I got a huge fright. One afternoon my teacher said, 'Gulnessa, you're lucky you came when you did. We're going on camp next week, the last week of term.'

I recognised my name and the words 'camp' and 'next week'. That was enough! The 'Camp'? It couldn't be true! Why would they send me back next week? Weren't our visas for three years? My face must have shown my fear because Mrs Pea said in a worried voice, 'What's wrong?'

Panicking, I gasped, 'The Camp? Why?' Shaking my head I pushed myself to my feet, sending my chair flying and shouting, 'No. I won't go. Even to be with Abdul I can't.'

Mrs Pea's face was a mixture of puzzlement and concern. 'But camp's fun.' How would *she* know? Living in this wonderful place she couldn't begin to imagine.

'No! No! No!' I was almost hysterical. I lunged towards the door, my heart thumping wildly – but not the Abdul kind of thumping.

Mrs Pea's arm encircled my shoulders, and she said, 'Gulnessa, I'm so sorry. I . . .' I could understand no more, but I looked up. Was it possible this was a mistake? That I didn't have to go?

Everyone gathered around me and started to talk. They looked worried, but sounded encouraging at the same time. It took a while but before we went home that afternoon I'd worked out that it wasn't the detention camp they were talking about, but somewhere else the class was going the following week. I took home a note that explained it. Rashid translated it for us.

Dear Parents,

It's time for the annual Year Seven camp. This note is to remind you about details I explained in previous letters.

*We will be staying in huts on the Dwellingup Camping Reserve. We **leave school next Wednesday, June 22nd at 9.30 a.m. sharp**, and **return on Friday, 24th June at 3.00 p.m.** Two teachers and six parents will accompany our 28 students.*

Meals are provided. Students will be rostered to assist parents with each meal, as part of their teamwork training.

A full timetable of activities has been planned for the three days.

Details of these followed and a list of things we would need to take, then some rules and a place for Mum to sign.

'Your school sounds different from the ones I went to in Iran. They were very strict and we didn't go outside the classroom to learn,' Rashid said.

'How long did you go to school for?' Hassan wanted to know.

'Many years. It's how I first learned English. Then it was much easier for me after I arrived here. I went to school and university in Iran. Then I worked as an engineer. For the government. But then I couldn't do it. I didn't want to help them commit more crimes. It made me feel like a traitor to humanity to work for them. It's ironic, they called me a traitor because I demonstrated against them.'

That last stuff sounded too hard so I asked, 'Why do you wash dishes here?' I felt in awe of Rashid. He'd been so well educated, while I knew so little.

'Because this country doesn't recognise my qualifications. I'd have to study more to be allowed to work as an engineer here.'

'Why don't you, then?' I asked.

'It's not that easy. I would have to pay a lot to be allowed into that kind of course of study. I can't afford that yet.'

'Would you go back?' I wanted to know.

'I'm dying to see my family, but if I went back, the people who wanted to kill me would find me. I'm still on their list. One day perhaps my family will be allowed to join me.' He looked so sad as he said this I wanted to throw my arms around him and comfort him, but I couldn't. Mum would have had a fit.

'Oh.' I couldn't handle this yet. I didn't want to have to think about life and death issues, or visas. That made me feel guilty. I couldn't help Abdul. And I didn't want to think about returning to Afghanistan. I tried to push away the anxiety crawling up through my body . . . 'Rashid, would you help me fill in the form I have to take to school, please?'

'Sure, Nessa.' He turned to Mum, who was silent, working on the tablecloth for Annie. 'Fatimeh, can you sign the form?'

'Yes,' Mum put down her sewing, and proudly wrote her name on my school camp permission slip.

CHAPTER 30

As it turned out, camp was cool, like a holiday. No one at home ever took holidays. There'd been neither opportunities nor money. We spent the two nights in huts in the bush. I called it 'forest' but the other kids said it was 'bush'. This confused me, as I thought a 'bush' was like a shrub. We slept in bunks – but I still wouldn't try the top ones – in sleeping bags. Rashid had borrowed one for me. During the days we were kept busy but it didn't seem like school activities. We explored, played games, drew pictures and even paddled in a dammed-up river.

The teachers said if we really wanted to swim we could, even though it was winter. Only two kids who tried to be heroes went in, but they didn't stay in long. I was glad we didn't *have* to swim, as I couldn't, and the hand-me-down swimmers I had I wouldn't wear in public. Some of the kids' bikinis were great, and I'd love those. Orange ones. As if Mum would let me, even though I do a lot now I could never do in Afghanistan. Annie keeps telling us, 'in Australia you can do whatever you want', but that won't change Mum's mind about me wearing bikinis.

In many Muslim countries women mustn't show any skin other than their faces outside their homes or even inside, except to their families. Although we don't cover up that much in Australia and Mum wears other Australian clothes, she always wears her scarf. I'm torn about what I should do, as I love trendy clothes. But I'm a Muslim, too.

The other things that tear me apart are dreams that haunt my sleep. They're as vivid as they ever were. I was scared I'd have nightmares on camp, but I didn't. Perhaps I was too tired because we were full-on until nine o'clock at night when we had to go to bed. Then, the six of us in our hut talked until we fell asleep. I learned more English that way than in all my school classes.

When I got home from camp our *own* phone had been connected in our new house. Another first. We phoned Abdul the night after I returned but everyone was listening in again. When I heard his voice I got jittery and couldn't say much. I was furious with myself later.

Abdul told us he'd been able to get no further word on his visa, but was 'holding up okay'. He also said thinking of me was the only good thing about most days. That got me worrying again about what he'd do if nothing happened soon. I had to talk to him by myself.

That night I dreamed Abdul was standing behind a barbed-wire fence. A sheet was on the ground under his feet, his arms sticking through the wire. He was calling, 'Help me! Don't leave me!' But I couldn't make my feet move in the right direction. Something dragged me the other way. The more I tried to get to him, the more it dragged me away . . . I woke shaking, wet with sweat, sick in the stomach and heart hammering like it was trying to escape from my chest.

The Abdul hammering didn't happen any more. I missed Abdul, and held the puzzle ring to my heart whenever I was in bed, trying to bring him closer. But thinking of him made me worry he was becoming depressed and giving up hope. Then I panicked, so I tried not to think about him too much. But that was hard because I wanted not just to think about him but to have him here. Like I wanted my dad here.

Judy, the counsellor who Mum had seen, visited our home during the school holidays. The first time she came she brought an interpreter, even though she could speak Dari quite well. She told us she'd spent two years in Pakistan working in the border camps with refugees from Afghanistan. I wondered if she'd been there the night we'd passed through. That all seemed so long ago.

Judy told us our dreams were part of what she called Post-traumatic Stress Syndrome. She explained that many people suffer this after something terrible has happened to them. And that meant nearly every refugee.

Judy *did* try to help. I liked her from the beginning. She really listened when we talked and if she didn't understand she asked until she did, but she never pushed us. That first family session was more like a talk between friends. Even the two Zs chatted but said they couldn't remember much about their dreams.

At that first session I just said general things, but later I talked to her a lot about my dreams. And just a little about Abdul. She promised to make enquiries about his visa. Hassan, on the other hand, wouldn't talk about his dreams at all. He seemed to have decided he was the man of the family. I think he thought he had to be 'tough', and that meant silent. Mum wouldn't talk in front of us either.

Judy came to school, too, to see some of the kids there, as well as Zainullah and me. I felt important when I went to talk to her because it was in the teachers' room where kids weren't usually allowed to go. In a session with Judy a month or so after term three started, I told her about how the Terror took Dad, trying to talk calmly like I had in the Camp interviews.

266

'Do you dream it just like that, Gulnessa?' she asked as I finished.

'Sometimes I don't know if it's a dream, or if I'm awake and my brain's rerunning what happened. When it's over I feel as scared as I was then. And I wake up shaking and sweating. It takes ages before I'm normal again,' I replied. Then added, 'Please call me Nessa? I don't like my full name.'

'I'd love to, Nessa.' She smiled at me. 'One day I'll tell you my real first name. I don't like it, either. But now I want to know about you. Do you have other dreams about your dad?'

'Sort of. I dream bits of what happened then and bits of other things all mixed up with things that couldn't happen at all.'

'Can you tell me about one of those dreams?'

'There's one that comes quite often. We're all in bed, sleeping together on our rugs – Dad's never there though. A huge bang wakes us. I jump up and look out the window. The Terror – gunmen – race towards our house. I yell to the others that we have to get out – to climb out the window. I push Mum and the two Zs out of the back window onto the roof of the summer kitchen. But we didn't have one at our house. Only Arjay Aqila did.' I stopped and looked up from my hands to see if Judy was listening. She was, and was watching me closely.

She nodded, and when I didn't continue, she asked, 'Is there more? Can you go on?'

'Yes. Hassan pushes me out the window and as he climbs out after me I hear the Terror at the top of the steps, near where we sleep. We slither off the roof. The gunmen see us and start climbing out the window. We run, so fast. I see pools of light ahead, which flash past before I can make sense of them. My heart beats in my ears. Or is it footsteps behind me? I'm not sure, but I can't look. I can hear nothing but *thump, thump, thump* . . . Through

267

the darkness I race on, towards where the village well should be. But I know it shouldn't be this far. Why isn't it here? Why do safe things vanish? I push on. Panicking. Frantic. I realise I'm by myself. Still running, straining to go faster. I have to. I must reach safety and find the others. But where? I jump at every shadow. I still only hear *thump, thump, thump*. Then I see it. But the well's surrounded by razor wire. Circles and circles of razor wire. There's a dark shadow near the top. I race up to it. It's Abdul. Hanging from the coils, cutting at his wrists with a blade. His blood drips in huge drops down into the well. I scream. He doesn't hear me. *Thump, thump, thump*. It's deafening, masking everything. Screaming soundlessly, I start to climb the wire. The blades cut my flesh and I drop down into the dark well. I grab at the rim and my fingers catch it. I hang there by my finger-tips. Abdul's blood drips on them. It's so dark down there. The well goes down forever. I try to curl my feet under me. Formless monsters snap at my toes.

'"I'm slipping," Zainullah screams. I realise the others are hanging from the rim, too.

'"Hold tighter," Mum screams back. I see one of Zahra's hands slip off the edge and I grab her, tucking her under my arm. My other hand supports us both. My arm's like steel. I must protect my little sister.

'I hear the Terror shouting, over and over, "Come out, we know you're there. Come out or we'll shoot." A face appears at the top of the well, then a ring of faces. Gun butts hammer at our fingers. Hassan moves his hands fast one after the other, attracting their attention. His fingers dance like drunken, giant spiders. They all try to hit his fingers. They do. He lets go, yelling, falling – into the darkness. Screaming, I turn to look. My hand slips. Zahra and I fall after him . . .'

I was suddenly aware my voice had stopped. It was as though it had been someone else talking. I stared into my lap and my hands held each other tightly. Then another pair of hands gently separated mine. My head jerked up, and Judy's grey-blue eyes caught mine, holding my gaze, reassuring me. I felt calmness flow from her hands through mine, up my arms, into my chest and then through my body, washing away the panic. Finally, when my body stopped shaking and I breathed regularly again, I felt calmness rise through my neck, relax my jaw and forehead, and enter my brain.

As Judy's eyes held mine I became aware of her pale, heart-shaped face framed by greying but mostly honey-coloured curls. It was a face etched with fine lines that drew a picture of kindness and compassion. I knew she understood.

When she saw I was ready, Judy dropped my hands, sat back and said quietly, 'Nessa, do you know all that's over now?'

I nodded.

'Then, when you come out of a dream like that, you need to tell yourself it's in the past. The Terror cannot get to you now. And you're out of the Camp. You won't ever go back. Abdul hasn't cut his wrists.' She paused as if to let that sink in, before continuing. 'That name, "the Terror". Where did it come from?'

'I – I don't know.' I cleared my throat. My voice sounded strange. Judy waited, so I went on. 'We called them that. They made us feel terror. Every time I even thought of them I felt it. I still do. They did terrible things.' The shaking started again. Judy took my hands in hers and we sat like that, waiting until I was still again.

Then she said, very gently, 'It is over, Nessa. They cannot get to you now. You're safe here. You know that, don't you?'

I nodded.

'*Tell* me that you know it's over.' She waited, but no words would come. Then she went on, 'Your mind knows it's over. But somewhere deep inside you don't believe it. It's buried there. You still feel the fear. You need to tell yourself, out loud, and in your head, as often as you can, that you *are safe*. That way you can re-train your thoughts to believe, and your emotions to feel safe again.'

I nodded once more.

'Try saying something like, "I am safe. My family is safe. We live in a safe and happy home." It doesn't have to be exactly that. Whatever you feel comfortable saying.' She looked at me, nodding encouragement. 'Now, you say it.'

'I am safe. My family is safe. We live in a safe and happy home,' I repeated.

'Once more.'

I repeated it again.

'Do you feel comfortable saying that?' Judy asked. I nodded, but truthfully I felt a bit stupid. 'Try it or something like it whenever you feel fearful or anxious. It's a good idea to write it out, too, and keep it where you can read it. At the very least it will take your mind off bad thoughts.'

'Thank you,' I nodded, thinking, I'll write it when I know how to.

'You know you don't ever have to go back to the Camp, don't you?'

'What about our TPV?' I asked. 'What if they send us back after three years?'

'You must believe that won't happen. Things might change before your visa expires. I know it's hard when you have to live with uncertainty, but for you to get better you have to learn to believe in yourself, and in others, too. And *really* understand

and believe that although bad things, *terrible* things, have happened to you, they are over now. And there *are* good things to look forward to and to work towards. Do you understand?'

I nodded.

'Can you think of something that made you feel really good?'

I nodded, but didn't speak.

'You don't have to, but I'd really like to hear about it.'

I launched into the story of our lighthouse night and how I'd often tried to relive it when I felt down. When I stopped talking Judy said, laughing, 'You are wise for one so young, Nessa. You worked out for yourself what I was going to suggest. Well done, you. Does it help?'

'Sometimes yes. But sometimes no.'

'Keep trying. You've begun to heal yourself without knowing it. It will take time. You can never get rid of your experiences, Nessa, but with some work you will be able to remember them without feeling fearful. Can you believe that?'

'I thi-i-ink so.'

'Great. You know that everything that happens to us makes us into the person we are? And you're a *very* special young woman. You already understand things that some people *never* learn. If you let them, these things will help you in your life.' My face must have shown my lack of comprehension, or disbelief, because Judy said, 'That's more than enough for now. Until I see you again I want you to tell yourself that you are safe. As many times a day as you can manage. Will you do that?'

'Yes. Thank you, Judy.'

'And think of things to make you happy. I'll look forward to hearing about those. And perhaps you'll tell me about Abdul?'

I waved as I went out the door. I didn't know if I was ready to talk about Abdul to anyone. I didn't even know what I thought any more. The longer we were apart, the more I worried about him, and the less I could feel of that wonderful, warm optimism. Perhaps I could focus on bringing that back, I thought. It's the best feeling I could remember. And those first few weeks here when it was so strong, even though he wasn't with me, I was happier than I'd been at any time in my life.

CHAPTER 31

I don't know if Mum talked much about her dreams, but Judy visited her once a week while we were at school. Zahra had settled happily into preschool, so Mum had four days a week to herself during school hours. Zahra didn't go on Fridays. Mum's English lessons continued twice a week and she enjoyed talking to her women friends from Afghanistan on those days, but wished we lived closer to them. Annie visited us often, and Rashid, helping sort out any household or school problems.

Dad's birthday on August seventeenth was a strange day. Mum didn't want a party without him. It was a very cold night so we sat in the lounge together, in front of the gas heater, and talked about good times we'd had with Dad. Although he'd never had a chance to live in a safe country like Australia, we had warm memories of his love for us. Mum was very quiet just sitting and sewing while we talked.

Zahra found Theermie's scarf and wrapped it around her doll. Then she put her into her 'cot' – an old shoe box of Annie's – and sat close to me on the floor near the warmth from the heater. She rocked her doll, singing softly. Suddenly she stopped and looked up. 'Nessie, is Aqila lonely? Does she want to sleep with

Theermie?' The mention of Aqila gave me a start and instantly I pictured my grandmother, standing at the fire, stirring the big cooking pot.

'She might. Go and get her if you like.' Off ran Zahra and a few minutes later reappeared with my doll and a change of her clothes.

'I have to put her in her 'jamas,' she told me seriously. Now she knew about special clothes to sleep in she'd asked Mum to make pyjamas for our dolls and she dressed and undressed her Theermie every morning and night.

'She wants to sleep with Theermie every night,' she told me, tucking in the dolls side by side.

'What a good idea,' I agreed.

The next morning I heard horrible retching sounds coming from the toilet. I saw the time – eight o'clock. Mum hadn't woken me. Jumping out of bed, I raced to see who was there. Mum was sitting on the floor next to the toilet bowl, her forehead resting on its rim.

'What is it, Mum?' I felt both irritated and worried at once.

'I don't know,' she answered faintly. 'I feel terrible. And my head aches so much I can't think.'

'I'll get you some Panadol. Can you walk back to bed?'

'I think I need you to help me.' I put my hands under her arms and supported her as she pushed herself up, still leaning on the toilet bowl. Then we struggled back to her bed.

She lay down. 'I can't sit, I feel so dizzy. I took two Panadol not long ago.'

'Well, you must've brought them back up,' I told her, going to get the packet. I felt scared to see her like this but couldn't shake my irritation.

'Please leave the blinds closed,' Mum said after she'd swallowed the tablets. 'The light hurts my eyes. I have to stay here for a while.'

'I'll stay home today, and Zahra can, too,' I said. 'You might need something.' She'd got sick like this a few times before, and although I never said it to her, I was scared she'd die. I didn't want to let her out of my sight.

The boys wanted to stay at home, too. I wasn't going to argue. They probably felt like I did. I went to ask Mum if she could eat anything.

'No, thank you. My head is still so bad.'

'I think I should phone Annie and ask her to get the doctor to come.' I'd done this when Mum was sick before, but not until the second day, and the doctor had told me to call her straight away if it happened again. Mum didn't answer, so I took it as a yes and went off to make the call.

The doctor arrived just after lunchtime. She gave Mum an injection and said to me, slowly and clearly, 'She – will – sleep – now.   Don't – wake – her.   When – she – wakes – give – her – one – of – these.' She held out a packet of tablets 'With – food.' I took them and nodded. 'Do – you – understand?'

I wanted to scream, I'm not a moron. I mightn't speak English fluently, but my English is better than your Dari. But I knew she was trying to be helpful, so I said, 'Yes, thank you.'

'Good. Phone me if the pain is still there tonight.'

'Yes, thank you.' I grinned inside. I had understood.

Mum slept soundly through the afternoon and the night, but I only dozed as I felt I needed to check on her, regularly. Zahra and I shared Mum's bed so I'd know if she moved a muscle. When I opened my eyes and it was light, Mum wasn't there. I sat upright, panicking, but then heard the sound of running water. I found her soaking in a hot bath. She smiled at me.

'Are you okay?' I asked, relieved and puzzlingly annoyed.

'Much better,' she answered. 'My head still aches but I had to have a bath.'

'Can I get in, too, Mummy?' Zahra had slipped under my arm and out of her teddy 'jamas before Mum could answer.

I went to the kitchen and made some toast and cardamom tea and carried it to Mum's bedroom, arriving as she and Zahra came in. 'Here's your tablet. You have to eat with it.' I still couldn't work out why but I felt irritated with Mum.

'Thank you,' Mum said. 'I might have it in bed. I feel giddy, and my head hurts, but not nearly as much as before. Look at this bruise.'

'I'm staying home again,' I told her, studying the bruise on the back of her hand where the doctor had injected her. Somehow her thanks annoyed me more, but as she didn't argue I went to tell Hassan.

Seeing how much improved Mum was, Hassan decided to go to school, but Zainullah wasn't keen.

'Come on,' Hassan said, 'it's just us men. I can walk you to school before I catch my train.' Just when I least expected it, he'd come out with something sensible like that.

❦ ❦ ❦

Mum was sick for a whole week after Dad's birthday. I asked her if we should stop talking about Dad, but she said we must remember him. As if I'd forget. Mum's sickness worried me. I was scared the depression would get her again and she'd do something bad to herself, so I'd stay home from school to be with her. It seemed to happen every few weeks. I'd feel scared, and at the same time annoyed that I had to do so much for her and couldn't go out and do the things my friends at school talked about, like going to the movies, or shopping, or to each others' houses.

Even though I loved Mum, something had happened to us. We always seemed to be arguing. It started in the Camp when she was so sick and I had to look after everyone. Then I didn't want to tell her about Abdul because I knew she'd say I was too young to be thinking or feeling things like that. But I *was* feeling them, wasn't I? I started to answer her questions as briefly as I could. I figured the less I said, the less she'd have to complain about. She was always saying, 'Why don't you talk to me any more?' Can't she see that I've grown up a lot? That I need my space? That I've got my life? It's two and a half years since we left Afghanistan. Next birthday I'll be fourteen. In Afghanistan I could have been married off then.

One day when Mum kept at me to talk to her I let her have it. 'Why can't you call me "Nessa" like everyone else does? "Gulnessa" is such a *dumb* name.'

'How can you say that? It's a beautiful name and I gave it to you.' I even tried not answering when she called me that. And it got worse . . .

'How can you expect me to talk to you if you say "no" to everything I ask?'

'What have I said "no" to?'

'Well, you let your pet, Hassan, have a room by himself, but I have to share with Zainullah. His half of *my* room's like a tip. And when I asked you if the boys could share, what did you say?'

'Gulnessa, you know why I said no.'

'Of *course* you always find an excuse for him to get what *he* wants . . .'

'Gulnessa, I'm surprised at you. Have you forgotten already that back in Afghanistan, and in the Camp, we *all* shared a room? You have so much more here and you still argue.' She always brings up what we didn't have. As if I don't know. And so it went on . . .

I really tried to put into practice the strategies Judy suggested – most of the time. I'd been seeing her at school once a month for more than a term. Still, sometimes bad things grabbed me when I wasn't expecting it, and sometimes it was just too hard trying to work against the fear and the anxiety which tried to over-whelm me.

Although we liked our house and school and neighbourhood, Mum wanted to live closer to her Afghan friends. Since Zahra had started at preschool there were days when Mum stayed in bed all day. That irritated me, too. I'm not sure why. Mum thought if she could see her friends while we were at school, they'd be able to help each other and she'd get better quicker. It was after Zahra's fifth birthday that Mum made the decision to move, even though the rest of us didn't want to.

Annie, Trish and Rashid, and Mum's Afghan friends had taken us to the zoo for a birthday picnic, complete with choco-late mud cake and candles. We'd invited our teachers, too, but it was in the school holidays and they couldn't come. It was a magic spring day, so still that the candle flames burned straight up and I had to 'help' Zahra blow them out. Mum said it was good to have women with us who she could talk to in our lan-guage. She'd missed that.

Mum was planning for us to move during the Christmas holi-days, when our six-month lease would end. I did *not* want to go. The only thing that made me not argue too hard was the thought that if Abdul's visa came through we didn't have enough room.

278

Christmas was something else we'd never even heard of 'til we came to Australia, and our only experience of it in Camp was icecream for dinner. We had no idea how it was really celebrated. There's no Christmas in our religion but after our Ramadan we celebrate with Eid. Every ten months, Ramadan comes around. It lasts a month and for that month adults aren't allowed to eat or drink – not even water – during the daylight hours. They eat breakfast before the sun rises and dinner after it sets, and they don't eat lunch at all. This year for the first time I kept Ramadan with Mum. It was especially hard at school when everyone else was eating lunch.

After Ramadan, at Eid, Muslim families and friends get together like Australians do at Christmas, and eat and eat until you can't fit in another crumb! Because we didn't have many family members here to share Eid with, Mum saved up to buy us new clothes, and herself a new scarf to wear for it. But it turned out that we did have someone special to celebrate with, after all.

CHAPTER 32

When we returned to school after the holidays, Mrs Pea said to me, 'You'll have a surprise when you get to school tomorrow.' Zainullah's teacher told him he'd get a surprise, too. We could hardly wait to see if Mum and Hassan knew anything about it. They didn't, so we spent all night trying to guess what it was.

'Dad's coming!' Zahra said what we all still hoped. I daydreamed that one day he'd miraculously appear, but I knew deep down it wasn't likely to happen.

'It could be Abdul,' Zainullah shouted. How I hoped he was right. But it didn't make sense that he'd come without saying anything. We'd kept up our weekly phone calls, which hardly varied from his end, and he didn't tell us last weekend. Anyway he wouldn't go to school, instead of home – unless he wanted to surprise us.

'Perhaps you're going to get a good work certificate tomorrow,' Mum suggested.

'Der! It's not even assembly day,' I scoffed. 'Anyway, that wouldn't be a surprise.' Both Zainullah and I had already received a merit certificate for 'good progress in English'.

Still mystified, we arrived at school the next day as the bell went. We'd just filed into the classroom when in walked Tara with her mum! Forgetting everything else, I raced over and we threw our arms around each other, dancing round in circles.

'It's so-o-o good to see you,' I finally managed, then blurted, 'What are you doing here? My English is better, isn't it?'

'Yes! It's great. And great to see you, too!' Tara sounded as excited as I did. 'We got our TPVs.'

'Is Ali here?'

'He's in Zainullah's class.'

'Where are you living?'

'We're staying with friends near here.'

'Cool! We can show you round . . .'

It was fantastic to have Tara's family here at last. We'd kept in touch through Abdul. I introduced Tara to my friends at school, and after school hours and on the weekends we took them to all the places we'd been. It was fun watching their reactions at many of the things that had amazed us. And they'd grown up in a town in Iraq where they had electricity.

I loved being able to give Tara some of the clothes that had been given to me. Zainullah did the same for Ali. Tara was as fascinated as I was about the way Australian girls dressed and said she didn't think her mum would ever let her show that much skin. Explaining things to Tara's family made me realise how much we'd learned since we'd been here. And their arrival lifted my hopes for Abdul to follow soon. They told me he'd been very quiet recently, as RSW19's visa had come through and Abdul hadn't heard from him since he left the Camp. So I worried about that, and resolved to phone him more often. At night to keep my mind on good things, I'd try to imagine what it'd be like when he came. We'd race to each other and embrace.

Having our friends here lifted Mum's spirits, so one day I gathered up my courage and asked in my most persuasive tone,

'Mum, now that Tara's family's here, couldn't we please stay in this house, instead of moving?'

'No. They're only here 'til the Christmas holidays, then they're moving, too. They've found a house in a suburb near the sea.'

'I should have known you wouldn't listen,' I exploded. Even as I said it I knew I wasn't being fair, but I couldn't help it. I didn't *want* to move. This house was great, and it was our first real Australian home. And, I was scared of starting again. It seemed we'd only just settled into this neighbourhood. People didn't stare at us any more and were kind, giving us things for our house, and clothes they didn't need any more. The people in our street all said 'hello' and our kind neighbour, Mrs McAllister, looked after a spare key now, for when we locked ourselves out.

I had to admit that sometimes Mum tried to let me have what I wanted. Even though she said it was too short and the neck was too low, she *had* let me have the T-shirt I really wanted for Eid. She didn't like it – neither did Hassan. He was taking himself so seriously in his self-appointed role as 'man of the house'.

When we celebrated Eid, Tara's family came to our house and we each had a friend from school over to share the feast. Then it was Mum's birthday. Zahra and I cooked her birthday dinner and Annie brought the now traditional (for our family's new custom) scrumptious chocolate mud cake. Tara's family came, too, bringing halal spicy chicken to go with our adaptation of an Afghan dish: all-in-together minced lamb, vegetables and lentils. We'd bought candles for the cake and as Mum wouldn't tell us how old she was we put on the whole packet. What a bonfire!

For Hassan's birthday a couple of weeks later in November, the weather was even warmer and he wanted a beach party. We met Mum's Afghan friends, who were refugee families, too; Hassan's schoolfriends, Saeed and an Australian called Pete; and

Annie, Trish, and Tara's family. We picnicked on the lawn under some trees next to the sand. After cooking sausages on the barbecue, the men played football, the kids swam, and the women sat watching. In all our life we'd not had as many celebrations as in the six months since we'd arrived in Perth. I imagined watching Abdul playing football, his strong arms catching the ball . . .

Mum told us later that some Afghan people weren't sure if Muslims should have birthday parties because it wasn't clear in the Koran. But I feel sure Khuda knows that birthday parties are fun, and fun is good. It's also a way to show others that we care for them, and that is important for everyone. Khuda, or God, is in lots of Dari expressions, like *Khuda hasec*, meaning 'goodbye', or 'go with God'.

❦ ❦ ❦

It didn't seem long before the end of the school year, which we celebrated with parties in our classrooms and lots of goodbyes and promises to keep in touch. I knew I'd have to start at high school the following year so it made it easier to leave.

On Christmas Eve we were going to an Australian 'barbie', but when Mum said that we had to take our own halal meat, I was so embarrassed I didn't want to go. I hate it when we seem different. The barbecue was at Hassan's friend Pete's house. Saeed and his family were going, too, but we didn't know their families or anyone else. I was nervous about meeting new people but Mum was keen to meet this other Afghan family, as she still found it hard to talk much English. I was more worried about what to wear so that we didn't look out of place. Hassan was no help – he just kept saying Muslim women should dress traditionally and wear a scarf, even though he always wore western gear. In the end I decided to wear my jeans and T-shirt.

I was so relieved when we got there to discover most people had on jeans, and everyone had brought meat and things to drink. But I noticed the others' meat went on a tray all together and we had to keep ours separate. I wondered if it seemed rude to Australians, and I wanted to explain it but didn't know how. Still, no one seemed to notice.

It was a warm night and we were out in the back garden. Pete's parents and sister came over to where our family group stood to talk to us. Hassan of course had gone off with his mates as soon as he saw them. Pete's sister Caiti, who was quite a bit older than me, looked like a model. She was so gorgeous. I loved her brief, strappy top, and thought Mum's eyes would pop out when she noticed Caiti's ring in her navel. She wore beaded earrings that touched her shoulders, and I examined them surreptitiously to work out how they were made. I wondered how Abdul would react. I knew he'd be horrified if I ever wore such a brief top. It turned out to be a good night, and when we got home I fell into a dreamless sleep as soon as my head hit the pillow.

The next day for Christmas dinner Annie had asked us to her house. Rashid came to collect us. He'd told us earlier that Annie was visiting her family for lunch, and wanted to give us a traditional Aussie Christmas dinner for our first one ever, so she wouldn't let us bring part of the meal. We took a box of fruit, some chocolates, and Mum's embroidered tablecloth wrapped in Christmas paper for Annie. We had a small parcel for Rashid, too.

We rang her doorbell, and waited. When the door opened, wonderful cooking smells poured out. Annie ushered us straight through the house towards her back courtyard. 'This is your first Christmas,' she said clearly. 'I want to make it special.'

When we stepped outside the sight took my breath away. It looked like a movie set. The courtyard with its creeper-covered pergola and exotic plants was usually a leafy green oasis, lit at night by a single powerful light over the table. Now, Annie had strung tiny, white lights through the leaves of all the plants and they twinkled magically. At the end she'd transformed a small bush into a Christmas tree covered in tiny, coloured lights, blinking irregularly. A small spotlight also highlighted the tree and its decorations, which sparkled and bobbed in the slight breeze. To one side of it sat a cane basket filled with packages in festive wrapping, with straining balloons tied to a handle on each side.

The circular table was a work of art. Its centrepiece was a shimmering silver mini Christmas tree and flowers. Nuts and dried fruits lay scattered around it. A place was set for each of us. A sparkling glass sat on one side of each setting, with a folded red or green paper napkin in it, and on the other side lay a brightly coloured paper roll. Between the knives and forks stood a cone-shaped, shiny, golden, cardboard hat that trailed multi-coloured streamers from its point.

We must have looked like a row of goldfish with our gaping mouths shutting and opening soundlessly. Earlier that week, Annie had taken us for a drive at night through the city to see the Christmas decorations. We'd gasped and exclaimed over those, and the Christmas trees we'd seen in many shops, but none of that made the impact this did. Perhaps it was because it was personal, or because we knew the unadorned courtyard so well. Whatever it was overwhelmed me – all of us, in fact.

'Do you like it?' Annie asked, and as I glanced at Mum I could see tears glistening in her eyes – like mine.

'Oooh, ye-e-e-es!' It was like someone had pressed the same button in us all. That is all of us but Zahra. Her little face shone. Her eyes and mouth stretched into the biggest circles possible and she stood absolutely still, transfixed.

After eating most of Annie's Christmas dinner of halal turkey and vegetables, we pulled the crackers and each found a treasure inside. Zahra's delight erupted in squeals and Zainullah couldn't keep still. Then came our first plum pudding, but that wasn't such a success.

'Lucky I got an icecream cake, too,' Annie laughed. Was there no end to the treats?

Finally it was present time. Rashid disappeared inside. After a few minutes he came back dressed as Father Christmas. 'Ho, ho, ho,' he boomed, 'Happy Christmas, everyone.'

Zahra's expression instantly changed to one of terror. She spun around to Mum, screaming, 'I don't want him!'

'It's just Rashid playing,' Mum soothed.

'I don't want him! Go away!' She was sobbing now.

'Shhh, shhh. Look, Zahra, it's okay. He's gone.'

Rashid had pulled off the beard and hat, and said in his own voice, 'Look, Zahra, it's me.' She peeped out cautiously, and seeing Rashid's familiar face bending close to hers, she slowly sat up, staring at him intently through eyes wet from her tears.

'Do you want to try on the hat?' he asked brightly.

'No!' She buried her face in Mum's lap.

'Sorry. I'll put it away.' Then, turning to us all, he said, 'We'll do without Father Christmas. I should have realised it could frighten her.'

'I like Father Christmas,' Zainullah said rather uncertainly as he slid behind Hassan's chair. 'But he's not like my dad.'

I lifted Zahra onto my knee and she cuddled close, pulling Theermie out of her top. Rashid came out again, costume gone, and said, 'Zahra, here's your present? It's like a birthday.'

That made her sit up, but she looked around carefully, 'Yes, please,' she said. 'I stay with Nessie.'

Rashid passed out parcels to everyone and Hassan gave him and Annie theirs. Annie looked delighted with her tablecloth. She shook it right out and admired Mum's fine stitching. In one corner Mum had embroidered 'Annie'. She hugged Mum, hard. Then she said slowly, making certain Mum understood each bit, 'It's a beautiful treasure. You are very good. I love it. Thank you, Fatimeh.' And Rashid said he loved the Turkish delight Mum and I'd made for him, offering it around, but we were all full.

When Mum opened her present she smiled her thanks, putting it on her head: a new scarf, dark green with gold edging. Hassan got a wallet into which he immediately transferred his student card and the bit of money he had in his pocket. Zainullah's present was a wind-up car, which he proceeded to send all over the brick paving and it rattled around bumping into people's feet. I thought he'd explode with laughter. Zahra was delighted with her new doll – tears forgotten. It was about the size of Theermie, but had a proper body and limbs, long golden hair and came with two outfits. I noticed Zahra tucked Theermie inside her dress before she examined her new toy. Theermie had a safe place in Zahra's heart.

My present was a big, red envelope tied in tinsel. I opened it carefully to find a card the size of an exercise book, dotted with dozens of small, greenish balls that looked like they were spinning fast. The background was a vivid purpley-blue, star-studded sky. Wow, I thought, what a fantastic painting. I'll hang it over my bed. I looked over at Annie, who was watching me and half smiling. Two words were printed in the middle of the card in large silver letters: 'WHIRLED PEAS'.

I studied them carefully before proudly reading aloud, 'Whirled peas.' I knew what 'peas' meant, but 'whirled' had me flummoxed.

Rashid, who hadn't seen the picture, repeated, 'World peace?' And then in Dari he went on, 'World peace. That's a good Christmas message. May I see your card, Ness?'

I handed him the card, wondering why he had suddenly started on about world peace. Suddenly he burst out laughing. 'Good one!' he said in English to Annie.

'I liked it so much I had to get it,' she answered, 'but I wondered about getting its message across.'

Rashid explained the English play on words. That really tickled my fancy so I repeated, 'Whirled peas, world peace . . .' until Zahra took up the chant.

Softly she talked to herself, trying out these new sounds, 'Wird peas, wird peas . . .'

Annie spoke over the little voice, 'Nessa, open the card. Something's inside.'

I pulled out a folded slip of paper, smoothed it open and read slowly, 'Dear Nessa, Happy Christmas. Love from Annie. PS IOU new school books.' Looking up at her I tried to work out what it meant. I knew I needed to buy books for high school, but why would Annie write that down? I'd been talking to Mum about how we could pay for them, but when I suggested getting a job Mum was horrified.

'What is PS IOU?' I asked in my best English.

'Say this much,' Annie pointed at the last three letters.

'I-O-U,' I repeated. Annie nodded expectantly.

It was too hard so I retreated behind, 'Yes, thank you.'

'I'll go through it.' Rashid turned to me, explaining that Annie was promising to buy me my school books.

'Great! Thank you, Annie. You're very good.' I threw my arms around her neck, hugging her tight.

Driving home I thought of Abdul in the Camp, having no idea

of what Christmas was really like. If they even bothered to give people icecream, it wouldn't have been an icecream cake like we had, I thought. I felt guilty at enjoying all the food and presents we'd been given, when Abdul was still shut away.

'Mum, please can we phone Abdul, to tell him about Christmas?' I asked.

'Yes, of course. Tomorrow,' Mum replied.

'I wish we could phone Dad, too,' Zainullah added. I wished fervently that Dad would miraculously find us. He would so love it here.

CHAPTER 33

We moved house a few days after Christmas, when Tara's family went to their new home near the sea. One of Mum's friends had found the house in the street next to where she lived, and arranged the lease. Rashid had driven Mum over to see the place and sign the lease in our last week of school, so none of us had seen it. All Mum told us was that it was bigger than Mr Farinelli's house. Well, I thought, I suppose that's one good thing. We'll have room when Abdul gets here.

When everything was out of the house, Mum and I scoured it thoroughly. For once Zahra didn't insist on 'helping' but instead sat singing, in her favourite place – on the swan's back.

After inspecting the house, Mr Farinelli said, 'It is beautiful,' kissing his fingertips dramatically, 'like the young lady.' I could see Mum hadn't understood the last bit, and I tried to look as though I didn't either.

Rashid took us to our new home. As we waved our goodbyes, Rashid said, 'Mr Farinelli says he'd be happy to have you back any time. You were the best tenants he's ever had.'

As soon as we pulled up in front of our 'new' house I could tell I wouldn't like it as much. It looked like a bigger but neglected version of the last one, with its orangey tiled roof and whitish-grey walls with render chipping off all over the place. The grass at the front looked wild, and it had no verandah and certainly no swans. There was only a square of cracked red cement at the end of the worn path leading to the front door. There were no fences, and just one straggling gum tree out the front.

Inside it was much the same, neglected. All the walls were the same grubby white. The rooms were bigger than in our last house and carpeted with different bits of multicoloured carpets that all smelt musty. There were three bedrooms, a lounge and a kitchen, with a dining area in a room next to it. Out the back, through the kitchen, was a section a bit like the back verandah of Mr Farinelli's, but it was all closed in. There was the bathroom, toilet and laundry and another bedroom that you had to walk through to get to the toilet and bathroom. It seemed to me that nothing had been planned but rooms just added on, willy-nilly. Annie had used that expression to describe how she'd planted her courtyard plants and I thought her willy-nilly worked much better than in this house.

At least Mum agreed to my pleas for a bedroom to myself, and Annie arranged to get me a desk to go in it. Hassan and Zainullah shared one big bedroom, but Hassan put his desk in the back room. 'So you kids won't disturb my study,' he said loftily. Mum and Zahra shared the other front bedroom. To tell the truth, I wasn't happy about the idea of sleeping alone in a room, and thought I'd probably slip into Zahra's bed after she was asleep. Darkness still scared me and made me feel panicky and anxious if I found myself alone.

'Hope you're happy now, Mum,' I grumbled as we washed the dishes the day after we moved in, at the end of a hard day's unpacking and cleaning. 'You've got your friends nearby, but we've got no one. And this house isn't nearly as friendly as Mr Farinelli's. It looks like it's never been loved.'

'As soon as you start your new school, you'll have more friends than I've got,' she replied calmly. 'In the meantime you can play with each other and explore the neighbourhood.'

'As if I can *play* with Hassan. Or the little ones . . . You don't *realise* I've grown up, do you?' With that I threw down the tea towel and stomped out of the kitchen.

'Gulnessa, come back here this instant, or . . .'

The rest was blocked out by the slamming of my bedroom door. I felt a bit sheepish about bringing Zahra into it. She was a great kid and always wanted to do everything with me, but that wasn't the same as having friends my own age I could really talk to. One thing was certain, I wasn't about to spend any more time with Hassan than I had to. Whatever I did he seemed to disapprove. He was worse than Mum. As for Zainullah, he was a waste of space. Only interested in cars, trucks and football.

❧ ❧ ❧

This time, getting to know our neighbourhood wasn't nearly as hard. I guess we knew what to look for. There was a primary school in the next street, a deli at the corner of our street with a postbox next to it, a park two blocks away, with a big space for kicking a football and basketball rings at each end of a bitumen area. But there was no skateboard zone and no playground equipment for the two Zs. The whole area somehow seemed not as well cared for. Even the neighbours weren't so friendly, except of course Mum's friends and their families. No one came to introduce themselves or to ask if we needed anything. They weren't horrible either, just didn't seem to notice us.

Annie came with us on our first visit to our new shopping

centre. As well as a supermarket, chemist and other small shops, it had the most amazing shop I'd ever seen. When Zahra saw it she stood, nose pressed to the glass, entranced by little dolls with wings 'flying' in the window. It was decorated to look like a clearing in a forest with flowers, butterflies, little animals and tiny mushroom houses with white dots on their red roofs.

'Why are dolls flying?' Zahra asked Annie. Her English was as good as anyone's in the family, when she chose to talk. From the time she made friends at preschool she seemed to have soaked it up.

'They're fairies, Zahra.'

'What are fairies?' Zahra's eyes shone and her smile made me smile. The fairies were cute, too. I hadn't liked to ask Annie about them because I thought I should've grown out of dolls.

'They're magic. They live in gardens and in the bush.'

Zahra looked up at Annie, serious now, and said, 'They weren't in Afghanistan. The Terror must have killed them.'

'Oh, Zahra, how awful! I'll buy you a book about fairies. They're magic and they do all sorts of wonderful things.'

'What's magic?' Zahra was intrigued – so was I.

'Magic is doing something that people can't do.' I could see Annie was having difficulty explaining but I was no help. It was new to me, too.

'Oh,' Zahra nodded gravely.

We went into the shop. That is, all of us but 'the man of the family', who hung outside trying to look cool. Zainullah stayed with Hassan at first, imitating big brother's bored-looking kicks at imaginary flaws on the tiled floor. Before long, however, his curiosity got the better of him and he sidled in the door.

Zahra's head moved like a mobile in the wind as she tried to take in the sparkling wonders of this fantasy world. And I was pretty interested. The shop lady came out from behind the counter as Annie finished explaining to her, 'They haven't heard of fairies.'

The lady, watching Zahra's face, reached for one of the fairy dolls and said, 'Would you like to hold her? The rose fairy?' Zahra's eyes rounded, and unable to get out any words she nodded. She held that doll like it was made of the finest glass, gazing at it until the lady gently prised it from her fingers. Then the shop lady balanced the fairy on a hook so she looked like she was flying. Zahra stood motionless, bewitched.

Mum whispered in Dari, 'Say "thank you" to the kind lady.'

'*Tasha kur*,' whispered Zahra, still in a trance.

'No, darling. In English.'

'Thank you,' Zahra whispered again.

The lady smiled and said to Annie, 'It's thanks enough to see her face. Here's a good book to start with. It's about a delightful fairy and other fairyland folk, like pixies and elves. They live in a magic garden. Fairy Queen Caroline reads the four stories on the read-along CD in the back.' I could work out most of what she said, but what were 'pixies' and 'elves'?

'Thank you. It sounds perfect. And the family's learning to read in English so the CD'll be a great help.'

That night we sat listening to the read-along CD – at least Mum, Zahra, Zainullah and I did. Hassan pretended to be watching a current affairs program, but I noticed he had the volume down and an ear open to keep track of what we were doing. Zainullah didn't mind doing anything that interested him with just the family at home, but out in public it was a different matter.

I read the story silently, along with Fairy Queen Caroline's voice, and understood most of the words. Soon I'll be able to read this to the two Zs as a bedtime story, I thought proudly. Zahra insisted on turning the pages when she heard the wand's sound, and Zainullah didn't argue, as he was so engrossed with the pictures.

Suddenly Hassan interrupted. 'There's a hunger strike at the Camp. Apparently lots of people have refused to eat for days to protest about how long they've been kept there. I hope Abdul's okay.'

'But they have to go to the mess,' I said, heart leaping into my throat.'

'Well, I guess there's not enough guards to get them all.'

'What's protest?' asked Zainullah.

'Did it say anything else?' I pictured Abdul, lying on his bunk, not talking to anyone and getting thinner and thinner.

'A protest is like what you did when you climbed the fence to try to help people get their visas. They showed people sitting on the ground in the exercise yard.' Hassan tried to answer us both at once.

'Did you see Abdul?' I held my breath.

'No, but I think we should phone him tomorrow – that's if they'll let us speak to him with all this going on.'

'Good idea,' Mum agreed. 'I think about him a lot.' Not as much as me, I thought.

'Hey, you Zs. Did you enjoy the stories?' Hassan asked and I wondered why he changed the subject so quickly. Could my strong brother who wouldn't talk about his dreams or the Camp still have the same demons as the rest of us?

Zahra didn't answer. She had turned back to the beginning of the book, and although her voice was low I could hear it rise and fall as if she were reading the story.

'Mum, do you think we should be letting them hear stories like this?' Hassan asked, his tone becoming serious.

'Why not?' Mum replied. Good on her for a change, I thought. What's eating Hassan?

'Well, we should be telling them more Afghan folk stories.'

'Der! What do you think Mum and I do every bedtime?' I was outraged. '*You* never bother to tell the Zs stories.'

Ignoring that, he said, 'You only tell them family stories, not traditional ones.'

Mum opened her mouth to speak, but I beat her to it. 'Shows how much you know. What do you call the Mulla Nasrudin stories, then?'

Hassan's face registered his surprise, but he went on in the same annoying tone. 'Which ones?'

'Well, the one about the twelve marbles, for starters.' I could tell he didn't know it.

'You'd better tell it to us now, Gulnessa.'

'You tell it.' I couldn't believe his arrogance.

'Go on, Nessa. You tell it good,' Zainullah said. 'Please.'

I felt caught. I didn't want to drag Zainullah into this so I said, 'Okay, I'll tell you the short version and then it's Hassan's turn to tell another story.' If I couldn't catch him out with this story, I'd test him with another. Zainullah nodded, wriggling closer as I started. 'One day, two boys found a bag of twelve marbles. They couldn't agree on how to share them, so they decided to ask the Mulla for advice. Their spiritual leader asked them, "Do you want to divide the marbles as a man would, or as God would?"

'"Of course, as God would," they replied.

'"Very well." The Mulla pushed nine marbles to one boy, and three to the other.'

Hassan watched me intently and when I stopped talking a strange look crossed his face, then he asked Zainullah, 'Do you know what the lesson in that story is, mate?'

'Yes, it means that God gives some people more than others.'

'A bit like Australians and Hazaras,' I added wryly, 'but some Australians have chosen to share with us. And now it's your turn, big bro.'

'You see, Hassan,' Mum interrupted, 'women do educate their children.' Good on you, Mum, I thought begrudgingly, but couldn't bring myself to say anything except repeat to Hassan, 'Now it's your turn.'

'Okay, I'll tell you the one about Mulla Nasrudin and the rocks, gravel and so on. Do you know it?' Zainullah shook his head and moved closer to Hassan for this historic event – his first storytelling session. 'Zahra, do you want to listen too?'

'Come off it, Hassan,' I put in. 'That story's way over her head – Zainullah's, too, I think you'll find.' I was too late. Zahra had heard the magic word. Holding the new book carefully, she moved over to sit next to me. 'Hassan's telling this story,' I explained to her and her eyes widened, but wise little Zahra said nothing.

'Are you ready?' Hassan enquired.

'It's not a race.' I got a withering look.

'One day, Mulla Nasrudin was asked to talk to a group of students about how to fit their spiritual practices into their busy schedule,' Hassan started in his schoolteacher voice. 'The Mulla stood in front of the crowd of students with a wide, tall jar on a table in front of him. He picked up a bucket of fist-sized rocks and packed them into the jar until it was full. Then he asked, "Is the jar full?"

'"Yes!" the students shouted.

'"Really?" said the Mulla, and he picked up a bucket which contained gravel. He poured this into the jar over the rocks, shaking the jar until the gravel settled in the cracks between the rocks. "Now is the jar full?"

'"Probably not," the students shouted.

'"Good!" replied the Mulla. This time he picked up a bucket of sand and poured it into the jar and the students watched as it trickled down, filling up all the remaining small cracks. "Now, is it full?" he asked again.

'"No!" shouted the students.

'"Good," responded the Mulla.'

A rustle made me glance at Zahra, who was quietly turning a page of her book. But I was impressed by Hassan's effort, and Zainullah still seemed to be listening.

'Now the Mulla picked up a pitcher of water and slowly poured it over the jar until the wet sand had settled, and the jar was full to the brim. Then he asked, "What is the point of this demonstration?"

'One eager beaver student called out, "All things, even though they seem to be full, are empty of self."

'"No!" snarled the Mulla. "This is a Nasrudin story, not a Zen one."

'Another eager beaver tried, "Does it mean that no matter how full your schedule is you can always fit in more?"

'"No. It means that if we don't get our values straight and fit in the most important things first, we'll never fit them in."' Hassan stopped, looking around at us all. Like he wants applause, I thought, knowing that was ungenerous of me.

Mum said what I was thinking, and I had to admit she did it better than I could have. 'Hassan, you told that story well, but the concept is too hard for the Zs just yet. They have to practise it before they can understand it. Do you understand me?' Hassan, looking surprised, nodded, and Mum went on, 'That is why women tell simple stories first, and wait until we can see the children are ready for harder ones. How do you think you learned that story?'

298

'From you, I guess,' Hassan agreed. 'I'd forgotten.'

'Well, if we want to make Australia our home, it is important that the young ones learn stories from our new country as well as the old. Don't you agree?' Hassan nodded. Mum continued, 'If we do that, when our visas run out and we have to apply again to stay here, that will help us show how much we want to be part of this country.' This was the confident, wise mother I'd known in Afghanistan.

Then she blew it. 'Gulnessa, pick up the boys' shoes on the floor there, and put them away. Zainullah can stay up until you've put Zahra to bed.'

'Mum, we're in Australia now. You were just saying we have to learn their stories. We have to learn Australian customs, too. Here, everyone is responsible for their own things.'

'Do as I say, Gulnessa.'

'What did your last servant die of?' I muttered as I took Zahra's hand, collecting the shoes in my other.

'What did you say?' Mum called, but we'd left the room.

CHAPTER 34

Each day for the next three weeks, we tried to speak to Abdul on the phone. Each time, the Camp guards refused us. We watched the news every day to see if Abdul was on it. As time wore on and the scenes became more frightening, I asked Annie to help. As she lived much further away now we didn't see her as often and I had to phone. She said she'd make enquiries and at least see if he was safe and well.

When there was a report about people sewing up their lips, we couldn't work out what it meant. It wasn't until Rashid visited us that we really understood the horror of what those poor people did to themselves. Annie told us she'd had the same response from the Camp when she phoned, as we did, but they did tell her that no one had died, although some men had been taken to hospital. Annie had also asked her Member of Parliament to help and had just heard back from her.

'But the government don't want us here,' I said to her in English. 'Why would they help us?'

'The government is different from individual politicians. Some people think the policies are wrong and they do want to help,' Annie explained. 'So my MP asked a question in the

House, about friends and relatives being refused permission to talk to detainees.' I looked at her blankly. She'd lost me after the first few words. Hassan looked as confused as me, and Mum wasn't even trying to follow. Thankfully, Rashid came to the rescue.

'I think I understand,' I told him in Dari when he finished explaining. 'What happened after that?' I asked Annie.

'She didn't get a straight answer and the papers printed the story as well as an interview with her. That was two days ago. In the interview the MP said she disagreed strongly with what was happening to people who were coming to Australia for protection. She said this government was breaking international law by keeping people imprisoned when they were seeking asylum. And she said that as soon as all refugees were processed, they should be released to live in the community while they waited until their cases were heard. She finished by asking why people who were asking us for help, women and children especially, were kept behind bars, as they were no threat to anyone.' I looked to Rashid, and he translated.

'She said that? We ask that, too.' I told Annie. 'What else happened?'

'I don't know if I should tell you the next bit.' She turned to Rashid, talking too quickly for me to follow.

He kept nodding and then said to her, 'I will tell them. They should understand what it's like.' Turning to us he went on in Dari, 'The day after the article was in the newspaper the MP received a lot of letters. Many agreed with her and offered their support, but some didn't and said awful things.'

We stared at him in silence. Mum stood up and walked out of the room. I guessed she was going to check on the two Zs, who had got bored and wandered off to play. Every time something like this happened I thought, what if these people become violent? What if they get guns?

My dreams erupted again and every night I woke in a sweat. It took ages to go back to sleep – if I was able to at all. Every day as soon as I got up I went to phone Abdul. No luck. We were all worried.

Finally when Hassan made a call the Good Guy answered. I heard him say, 'Please may I speak to AXZ26?' It was even more shocking to use numbers now than when we were in the Camp.

'It's Hassan. Abdul's like my brother. I was AXZ22.' Hassan grimaced as he said it. Silence.

'Thank you. Yes. We called you "the Good Guy".' A longer silence.

'That's great. Thanks, mate.' Hassan turned to Mum who'd joined us, and me. 'It's the Good Guy. Remember him?' I nodded. Mum looked puzzled. 'He said he shouldn't do it but he'd let us have a quick talk.'

'Fantastic!' Relief and excitement fought inside me.

'That's good,' Mum agreed. 'You two can talk, then, and tell me the news.' I searched her face but it gave nothing away.

Turning to Hassan, I asked, 'What else did the Good Guy say?'

He sounded pleased when I told him what we called him. "Troo-oo? I like that. Lis'n, mate. I'm not supposed to do this but I reckon AXZ26 could do with some cheerin' up. Y'll have ta make it quick."'

Suddenly Hassan's voice returned to normal. 'Abdul, are you okay? We've been worried. The TV reports.' Silence.

'Really. Okay, then. As long as you're right.' Silence.

'Phew! That's a relief. Yes, she's here. I'll put her on.'

I grabbed the phone and gasped, 'Abdul, I've been worried sick. Are you okay?'

'I'm fine, dear Yahk. So sick of this place. But what about you? I miss you. I want to be with you. All the time.'

'Dear Yahk,' I was past caring that Hassan was next to me, and Mum, 'I'm better now I can hear you. What's been going on?'

'Good Guy said I wasn't to talk about it. He's sticking his neck out for me. We can only have a minute or so more.'

'Okay. There's something I want to ask you. Tara said . . . Oh, remember BTY16? Her family's here now, and they said RSW19 got his visa.'

'Yes, I heard from him just before the strike. He should almost be in Perth. They took him to Melbourne from here. He asked to go to Perth but they told him, "You go where we take you. You're lucky to get out." He had to get registered in Melbourne and then earn enough money for a bus ticket to Perth. When he phoned he said he'd be leaving Melbourne soon. He said he'd contact Hassan when he arrived. Say hello from me. He's a good friend.'

'Have you other friends to talk to now?'

'All the card group, though you're the only one I really talked to. Oh, have to go. The Good Guy's waving. Take care, Yahk. I love you.'

'Me too. We all send our love. Bye.' As I put the phone down I could feel Mum's gaze. Swallowing, I turned and said as casually as I could, 'Abdul sends his love. He says RSW19 will be in Perth soon.'

'Cool,' Hassan sounded pleased. 'Where is he now?'

Mum asked, 'Who's RSW19?' I'd forgotten she knew nothing about him. Hassan explained. When he finished, Mum was still looking at me in a funny way but she said nothing more.

❦ ❦ ❦

The following week we had to get ready for school. When Annie took us to enrol and to buy our books, she said to me, 'Tell your mum I'd like to buy school books for you all this year. And so for you, Ness, as a Christmas present, I'll give you a new backpack. Yours is nearly in pieces.'

'Thank you. That's fantastic!' At my last school I hadn't wanted to seem ungrateful, but I'd always tried to hide my daggy old bag. Facing an unknown school and kids who spoke a language I wasn't yet fluent in was daunting enough, and I wanted as much as possible to look the same as the others.

On our first day we all felt nervous. No one wanted to sit down for breakfast. Zainullah put on his backpack as soon as he got dressed and refused to take it off again. Zahra insisted on taking our fairy book with her. By now she almost knew the stories off by heart. My reading had improved hugely, as the Zs had wanted me to read a story from the book most nights. Hassan kept at me to hurry up.

'That's a turn-up,' I snapped at him. 'You're the one who's always late. I'll be ready on time. Get off my back, will you?'

At last Mum finished fussing about our lunches and I had Zahra dressed and was sure I'd packed everything I needed in my smart backpack. As Zahra was starting 'proper' school, Mum said she'd walk with her and Zainullah, but Zainullah, who'd met a couple of boys in our street who went to the school, wanted to run along first. Hassan and I stood impatiently waiting to say goodbye as she lectured him.

'Listen to me, Zainullah,' Mum bent low and looked him in the eye. 'You must look after your sister now. You're the only two from our family at your school and you're the biggest, so you're in charge. It's your responsibility.' That seemed to ring a bell with him.

'Zahra, you must walk next to me on this side.' He banged his right side with his hand.

'Okay.' She nodded and moved to his side.

Mum went on, 'And I want you to go to Zahra's class after school and walk home with her.'

'But, Mum, I want to walk with my friends.' An extra burst of anxiety about my little sister boosted my already uncontrollable butterflies.

'Zainullah, didn't you understand me? You're the man of our family at your school. It is your duty to care for your sister.' I always marvelled at the way this tone of voice impressed on us the importance of whatever Mum said.

Zainullah glanced up sharply, and with a quick nod said hurriedly. 'Yes, Mum.'

'Mu-u-um,' Hassan cut in, 'we have to go.'

'Oh, all right. Let me look at you.' She nodded as she inspected us, and kissed our cheeks. 'I hope you enjoy your new school. Be careful on the train and if there are any unpleasant people, move away from them.' We were almost out the door as she finished speaking. Does she think we're Zahra's age?

Our new school didn't have special English classes, but as my English was much better now I wasn't too worried about being in with the other kids. As it turned out I met Yanthe, Sasha and Miranda that day and we're still best friends. Sasha was new to Australia, too. Her family had just migrated from Ireland.

That afternoon I met Hassan at the station. He seemed in an okay mood. We compared notes about who we'd met, and where we had to go for different classes. He actually admitted that he felt better at this school because his English had improved so much. In his homeroom he'd sat next to an Aussie boy named John who'd told him a lot about the school.

The two Zs were bouncing around brightly when we arrived home and they greeted us with, 'School's cool!' They were full of what they'd done and their new 'best' friends. Zahra's friend Merry had long blonde pigtails, and her other friend Suki had light-brown curly hair that she wore in a ponytail with a bright-blue scrunchie. Zahra had developed a fascination with people's different skin and hair colouring. Zainullah's friend was Zac, the son of Mum's friend who he already knew. He did say that at lunchtime some of the bigger boys had yelled at them to get away from where they were kicking a football, but he didn't seem too worried about it. That could have happened to anybody.

We'd only been at school for about three weeks when it was my birthday. I'd had to wait longer than anyone so I wanted to make the most of it. We planned a dinner and of course Annie was coming, and Rashid, who was bringing Zahid – who we'd known as RSW19 in the Camp. Strangely enough, the first person Zahid had looked up when he arrived in Perth from Melbourne was Rashid. A friend he'd made in Melbourne had given Zahid his name as someone who'd help him, so it had been easy then to find us. Zahid was living in Rashid's house until he found work. I was dying to talk to him and get news of Abdul.

I invited Judy and Mrs Pea from my old school and was delighted they could come. Tara's family would be there, too, and my new friends Yanthe, Sasha and Miranda. Mum's Afghan friends were also coming for dinner, as it was the first party in our 'new' house. When Sasha's mum found out that Mum hadn't baked cakes before, she came over and cooked my birthday cake with Mum, to show her how.

We had dinner, then chocolate cake with candles. Next came the presents. I was so excited I had trouble unwrapping them. I got some fantastic things: a T-shirt, handbag, earrings, soap and talc, perfume, new jeans and a groovy belt. Mum gave me a box of nail polishes she'd saved for. That meant a lot. I felt embarrassed to be the only one opening presents. I like giving presents, too.

After that most of the adults went home. As I said goodbye to Zahid, I whispered, 'How was Abdul when you left the Camp?'

'Holding up – but only just. He lives for your phone calls.'

Mum was standing next to me so I said no more but resolved to phone the next day and tell Abdul about my party.

Tara's parents took Hassan and Zainullah to spend the night with Ali. I was having my first girl's sleepover. Yanthe, Sasha, Miranda, Tara and me – and of course Zahra, who as a special treat was allowed to stay up with us. Mum stayed in the kitchen with her friends and did the washing up while we spread out mattresses Afghan-style, wall to wall in the lounge. Then Mum's friends went home and she went to bed, telling Zahra she could join her any time. As if – Zahra was already one of the girls!

First we put on the nail polish. There were so many colours that we painted each other's toenails and fingernails with each nail a different colour. Then started the video-fest. We'd chosen enough to watch them all night if we wanted to, and we nearly did, keeping ourselves alive with potato crisps, chockies and Coke, as well as party leftovers.

At about five a.m. when we decided to try to sleep at last, I lay there remembering how I'd felt back in Afghanistan when we never had enough to fill us up. And during all those days on the boat when we'd run out of food and had to exist on one small bowl of rice per day. And at the Camp when I'd eaten only enough to stop the hunger pangs, the food was so boring. This place is paradise, I thought. Except where's Abdul? And Dad?

If I miss Dad so much, imagine what it's like for Mum. I'll try to be more understanding. If only she'd trust me to make decisions for myself. She was so amazing to bring us four kids to Australia by herself – and Abdul, too, though he helped us a lot. I did love Mum but when we started talking she irritated me so much that I forgot it and was angry with her, until I got away and cooled down.

I pushed from my mind the adults' conversation I'd overheard earlier about temporary protection visas that would expire. And how six months before the visas expired we'd get letters which would mean we'd have to start all over again with the interviews. I didn't want to know. Anyway, it was nearly two years before we'd have to face that, and that seemed a lifetime away.

CHAPTER 35

Life had its usual ups and downs over the next few months. Mainly we enjoyed school but we all met some kind of teasing or bullying. Yanthe, Sasha, Miranda and I were walking across the assembly area one lunchtime when we stopped to speak to Hassan and John. A loser yelled out, 'Whadda youse kids wanna hang out with towel-heads for? They don't belong here.'

And his loser mates started chanting, 'Auss-ie. Auss-ie . . .' A teacher loomed up and said, pointing, 'Get down to my office, now. You. You. You. And you. *Racists* don't belong here.'

One day in term three, something amazing happened in my Society and Environment class. The teacher, Tracy, who reminded me of Gum Tree because she really listened to us, was talking about different values and what they are. She wanted us to call her by her first name, as she called us by our first names.

She said it was crucial (I like words that sound powerful, and Tracy doesn't talk down to us) to recognise the most important values and people in our own lives. Then she said, 'I'm going to demonstrate what I mean. Before I do I want each of you to write down the values and people most important to *you*, in order of their importance to *you*. It's hard, and you might want to change them later if you realise that you missed something. That's okay. We should all do that. Reassess our beliefs to see that we feel they are right for us. But for now, do your own lists. Your beliefs may be different from other students'.'

When we'd done that, Tracy stood at the front and produced a huge glass jar which she filled with golf balls. Then she asked the class, 'Is the jar full?'

'Yes,' everyone called out.

She took out a bag of small, glass marbles and put some in the jar, rattling it until they rolled down to fill the gaps between the balls. 'Is it full now?' she asked again.

'Must be,' someone called out and everyone nodded.

This time Tracy picked up a bucket of sand and poured it into the jar, shaking it until the sand settled into all the spaces you could see. 'Well, do you think it is full now?' she asked.

'Has to be!'

I was hypnotised. What did this mean, here in Australia?

She pulled out two cans of beer, popped their tops and poured it into the jar. I just gaped – here was a turnaround. 'That demonstrates an important Aussie custom,' she announced. 'No matter how full you think your life is, there's always room for a beer.' Everyone laughed and cheered.

When they'd all settled down, she said to the students, 'That last part was just some fun, but this demonstration has a really serious side. The golf balls represent the most important values and people in your lives, the things that you wrote at the top of your lists. Whatever and whoever you believe are most important to you and will help you live a full and happy life is what the golf balls represent. Is anyone willing to share some of the things they've written.'

Someone called out, 'My family.' The teacher wrote it at the top of the board, and added 'loved ones'.

'I've included those we love with family. Any objections?' No reply, just a shaking of heads. 'Any more ideas?'

Another kid said, 'God.' There was a groan from the back of the room.

The teacher said, 'I'll write down "my god and religion" so it can mean whatever you believe. We've got students from many countries and cultures in the class. And another thing, I didn't ask for personal comments about anyone else's suggestions. That's not valuing "consideration of others' feelings". Now, more suggestions?'

'Treating others how you want to be treated,' a voice called. I thought, if someone said that in Miss Mo's Maths class everyone would have yelled out 'crawler' or 'teacher's pet', but everyone was fine about it here. Miss Mo thought she was better than us kids. She yelled, bossed us about, and put down kids who got things wrong – *and* she bleached her moustache with peroxide.

Answers came thick and fast.

'Being sincere, telling the truth and trusting others.'

'Working for peace.'

'Being honest with all people.'

'Getting a good job.'

'Money.'

'Good manners.'

Tracy wrote them without comment until the list reached the bottom of the board. Then she said, 'Enough, enough. We could go on for ages but this will do to understand the concept. Now, what we have here is a composite list of different people's ideas. There may be some things on it which you didn't even consider. I'll give you a few minutes to check your lists to add anything or reorder it. Just number them from one for the most important value.'

After a few minutes she said, 'Now, back to the jar. Your number ones, twos and threes are the golf balls, and the jar is your life. Can anyone suggest what I'm getting at with the other things?'

'That the jar is not really full when you put in the golf balls?' a kid called Ted suggested.

'Okay, that's what happened, but can you take it further? What does that show us?'

'That other things will fit around the golf balls?' Someone else answered.

'That's a good point. Now, can anyone substitute exactly what Ted might have meant instead of the words "golf balls"? And what are the "other things"?'

'Um. Well, that the values lower on the list will fit around the most important ones at the top of the list.'

'Impressive, Jenny. That's certainly one way of putting it. Another way is this. If you don't fit in the most important things first, you'll never fit them in.' At that moment the siren blasted. Tracy waited until it died away, and added, 'Next time I'll ask someone to explain this, so talk about it amongst yourselves.' Everyone started to move out.

As he walked past her, Ted said good-naturedly, 'That's gunna be the hot topic every lunchtime, Tracy.'

Tracy laughed, 'I didn't realise you were a philosopher, Ted. I'm impressed.'

The rest of our 'gang of four' were at Art, so I was slow packing up my gear. As Tracy started towards the door, I caught up with her and said hesitantly, 'Excuse me, Tracy.'

She stopped and smiled. 'Hi, Ness. How's things?'

'Good,' I grinned, relaxing. 'You know we've a story in Afghanistan like that.'

'Have you?' she sounded surprised.

'Yes, but it's got rocks and gravel in it. And no beer.'

Tracy laughed and said, 'I'd love to hear it, but better than just telling it to me, would you tell the class next lesson?'

'I couldn't. My English –'

'. . . is fantastic,' Tracy took over. 'I'm so impressed that you've come so far after only being in Perth a bit more than a year.' How did she know that? I wondered. She's got so many classes she can't possibly know about all the students. 'But I understand. It's a bit daunting talking to a lot of people until you're used to it. I've got an idea. In my office I've got a small tape recorder. I'll show you how to use it and you can take it home and tell your story onto it. You can change it as many times as you like until you're happy with it.' I wasn't at all sure what she was talking about and she must have seen it in my face because she went on, 'Tell you what. Bring your friends to my office after you've had lunch and I'll show you all. You can have a bit of fun with it. Got to go to another class now. So do you.' I grinned and raced off.

I caught the second train home after school that afternoon as I stayed back to make plans with the girls to meet on the weekend for a recording session. Rushing into our house, I found Hassan already there, in the kitchen feeding his face. Mum was listening to Zahra rattle on about how she and Suki had been allowed to stay in the classroom now that the weather was cold, to listen to the fairy CD at lunchtime. Then the teacher had played a story to the whole class.

'Where's Zainullah?' I asked.

'At Zac's place,' Mum told me. 'Why?'

'I want to tell you all something.'

'Take it easy, sis.' Hassan and I were getting on a bit better now I was at high school – except when the issue of my clothes and makeup came up. 'What's up?'

'Oh well, I guess it's really for you and Mum.' I calmed down, a bit. 'Just listen to this, will you?' I filled in the background about Tracy and then told them the whole story.

As I finished, Hassan nodded, this amazed look on his face, 'I'm impressed. I might even rethink what I said about Australian stories.' Hassan was being so positive that I began to suspect something. Had he fallen in love?

'Perhaps I didn't need a school so much, after all,' Mum said smiling. 'My mother and grandmother and the other village women told me those stories and many, many more. Now you are learning them at school. It shows that some things in this country are not so different.'

'Ness, where's the tape recorder?' Hassan asked. 'I'll help you set it up if you like.' This was spooky.

'Do your homework first.' Mum's after-school mantra had started. 'Then I want you to hear Zahra's reading, and help me with dinner . . .' I tuned out and took my bag to my room. What a great way to talk to Abdul, I mused. I'll ask Tracy about how to get these machines.

Since the protest in Camp, contact with Abdul had been harder. Phone calls were limited. He tried to sound cheerful but I could hear strain in his voice. I felt helpless. Tape recorders might give us a way to really talk again. It was worth a try. Anything was, to make this interminable wait bearable.

CHAPTER 36

It was the week before the October school holidays when I returned from school one day to hear loud banging inside the house. Mum's voice pleaded, 'Please open the door, Zainullah. Please talk to me.' I rolled my eyes. What's he done this time? I took little notice and plonked my bag down and pulled open the fridge door to get a drink.

I heard Hassan's voice. 'What's the matter, Mum? What's he done?' It was weird that as soon as Mum and I had started fighting a lot, Hassan seemed to get on with her better – and me, to a certain extent.

Sticking my head into the passage to see what was going on, I could hear sobbing coming through the closed bedroom door. Mum looked upset so I listened as she explained to Hassan, 'Zainullah ran home from school at lunchtime. He threw his bag down and shouted, "I'm never going back to school!" Then he disappeared into his bedroom and locked the door. He won't talk to me and every time I try to get him to, he bursts into tears again. The school rang to see if he had come home. But I couldn't explain anything. I didn't know what had happened anyway.'

'He's been in there since lunchtime?' Hassan asked.

315

'Yes. I don't know what to do. I tried phoning Annie but there was no answer.'

'I'll try again,' Hassan offered. Mum nodded and slowly walked back towards the kitchen. I didn't speak. It was too hard. I did feel bad for her, but couldn't help thinking this wouldn't have happened if she hadn't made us move here.

Just then Zahra came in. She looked up at me, seriously. 'Zainullah's sad. Some big kids did something bad to him.'

'What did they do?' I crouched conspiratorially next to her.

'Well,' she swallowed and I could *see* her thinking. 'Well' had almost replaced 'oh' as her most repeated word. 'Well, I thi-i-ink they weren't nice to him.'

'But did you see what they did?'

'No. I was eating my lunch in our lunch place.' Little Miss Proper, in person.

I tried to ask patiently, 'Do you know what happened?'

'Well.' Frowning. 'My teacher came and asked if I'd seen Zainullah.'

'And what did you say?' Sometimes getting a story from Zahra was like creating the universe.

'We-e-ell, I said "no". 'Cos I hadn't.'

'Ri-i-ight. What happened next?'

'We-e-ell, she said to tell her if I did, 'cos someone saw him running across the playground.' She blurted out this last bit.

'Anything else?'

'I finished eating and Katy showed me her Barbie . . .'

'Thank you. Would you like a drink?' That was all I'd get.

When Annie arrived and had heard the story she went to Zainullah's door. The rest of us crowded behind her in the passage. 'Zainullah, it's Annie. I know about schools. I'll help you.' Pause. 'But I can't unless you open the door. If there's a problem,

I can help sort it out.' No answer. She went on talking like that for ages, until slowly the door opened.

Mum motioned for us to stay where we were and Annie disappeared into the bedroom. We crept a little closer so we could hear through the partly open door . . .

'Here's a box of tissues.' Nose blowing. 'Is that better? Now, tell me what happened?'

Zainullah blurted out a string of unconnected things in our language, like, 'my lunch . . . horrible names . . . they caught me . . . stamped on it . . . laughed . . .'

When he paused, Annie said gently, 'Zainullah, you'll have to tell me in English. Now, when did this happen?'

'Lunchtime . . .' sob '. . . I was going . . .' sob '. . . to sit . . .'

'Here, wipe your eyes and blow your nose again. Then try to tell me slowly . . .' The conversation went on like this for ages.

I couldn't listen any more, my stomach rumbled so much. Making a sandwich, I seethed. How dare *anyone* upset my little brother like that. Soon the others joined me in the kitchen and for once I helped Mum peel the vegetables for tea without being asked – no, without being hounded – to do them. Finally Annie appeared. 'Zainullah's in the bathroom. He'll be here in a minute.'

'What he tell you?' Mum looked so anxious that I wanted to hug her, but I couldn't.

Sitting down at the table, Annie began, 'I think I got the whole story. Hassan, you and Nessa will have to translate for your mum. Apparently, two big kids stopped him and grabbed his lunch box. Of course he was scared. And, they'd teased him before, he said. The big kids threatened him, yelling things like, "Get outta here, son of Osama bin Laden. We don't want you. Get out!" and more. Then they tipped out his lunch and jumped all over it, throwing his lunch box in the rubbish bin. No wonder the poor kid feels traumatised. As if he hasn't suffered enough – you all have.' She looked so sad I went over and put my arm around her while Hassan told Mum what she'd said.

I hurried home from school the following day to find out what had happened with Zainullah. That morning he had been refusing to leave the house. Now, Annie was sitting at the kitchen table with Mum and there was no sign of the Zs.

'Hi, everyone. What's new?' I greeted them in English.

'Hello, Gulnessa. Annie came round to tell us what happened when she went to the school this morning. She wants you to translate.' Mum smiled at me, speaking in Dari. Why couldn't she speak English? She'd been here as long as we had.

I didn't bother to respond, but asked Annie in English, 'What happened about Zainullah?' Just then Hassan arrived and sat down to listen.

'Zainullah stayed home with your mum. I took Zahra to school and went to see the principal. I explained to him and Zainullah's teacher what happened yesterday,' Annie began. 'They seemed horrified, and asked me to talk to all the teachers about it, and about what your family has gone through, which I did. The teachers offered to talk to their classes and try to help the kids understand that they must help the two Zs, not tease or bully them. After the meeting Zainullah's teacher and two boys from his class, who said they were Zainullah's best friends, came home with me. I don't know how they did it but they got Zainullah to go off to school with them.'

'Is he home yet?' I wanted to know as Hassan began to translate for Mum.

'Yes,' Annie told me. 'He's playing soccer in the backyard with Zac and two others. He said they stayed with him all day at school. He's wary of big kids, but at least he seems happy to go to school again.'

I went outside to see for myself and, sure enough, they were racing around yelling and kicking a black and white ball – the only thing he'd begged us to give him for his last birthday. Trucks had taken a back seat. The big backyard, covered in straggly grass, was as empty of plants as the front one. Near the house Mum had started a vegie garden and she had some cabbages and lettuces waiting to be picked, as well as mint and parsley growing thickly. There was one tree here, too, and the clothes hoist, and that's about all. On the back fence at each side the boys had drawn a wobbly black line to show the goals. Playing two-a-side, they were interested in nothing else. My little brother is a bit like that ball he loves, I thought. So good at bouncing back after dramas.

❧ ❧ ❧

When I played my taped Mulla Nasrudin story in class everyone was engrossed. Hassan and the girls and I had worked together on it all Sunday. Hassan was keen to operate the tape recorder. I agreed he could do it if he'd take the part of the Mulla. Yanthe and Sasha were the students, I was the storyteller and Miranda the director. She was a slave-driver with my pronunciation, but the result was impressive. In class when it finished playing everyone whistled and cheered and then talked about it for ages. Tracy too. So many kids had no idea about Afghanistan and they asked all sorts of things. They couldn't believe we had so many stories and were intrigued by things I told them. Especially about our people's long history. They all examined my bracelet that Bahkhul gave me and I told them the story of Abdul's puzzle ring and how he gave it to me to wear until he joins us. Nothing more of course. Some kids even said they were jealous of my ring and bracelet – not my experiences.

After that Tracy said that because we'd been so interested in finding out about different people and places, we could work with someone who came from a different background to find out about it. We didn't have to choose partners from different countries, though that would make it easier, but partners might come from different parts of the community. Like someone who only had one parent might work with someone from a two-parent family, or someone whose folks were on the dole might work with someone who was self-employed, and so on. We voted to do it, and we could choose to keep what we talked about between partners or, if both agreed to it, to present a talk to the class.

I held back from asking anyone, as my close friends weren't in this class, but I really wanted to find out more about Australian families. Some kids paired up quickly but lots were like me. Tracy helped us to sort out partners and I felt so good when nearly all of those kids said they'd like to work with me. Finally I got to work with Amber, who caught the same train to school as me. She came from an Australian one-parent family and she's got a younger brother and sister, too. No older brother, though, and I told her she should be glad of that. After some other kids started planning their talks we decided to give one, too. It was great, but the most impressive thing I learned was that there were more similarities between our families and the way we lived than there were differences. And that was counting the fact that I'm a Muslim and she's Catholic.

CHAPTER 37

I found schoolwork harder than at our previous school. So did the others. But there were good things, too, like sports. We'd never played sports in Afghanistan, unless you called boys kicking around a homemade ball sport. Now we discovered we were all well coordinated, fast runners, and good at sport in general. Annie told us it had a lot to do with our active life before we came here. We hadn't sat in front of a TV – we never had the chance. And it was funny to think that games helped to make friends, but they did.

We all loved the beach and learned to swim – except Mum, who said she wasn't going to, ever. She couldn't see herself wearing bathers in public. Hassan turned out to be a champion swimmer and even I had to admit he was a brilliant soccer player. His greatest ambition was to play for Perth Glory, and of course Zainullah planned to follow him. Zainullah was one of the best runners in his school and, as well as his first love, soccer, wanted to play tennis soon. I was a fast runner, and could shoot goals in netball better than any girl in our year. Zahra could swim strongly, and she was the fastest girl runner of her age.

It was funny when we went to the two Zs' first school sports day. Zahra pleaded with Mum for me to be allowed to watch her, so Mum let me take the day off school to go with them. Annie came, too. The four factions sat in their areas alongside the 100-metre running lanes marked on the school oval. Spectators sat opposite.

The first race was the five-year-old girls' 50-metre race. The kids lined up. Zahra waved to us. She looked so cute in her red T-shirt and white shorts. They got off to a good start. We clapped and cheered Zahra, who'd raced away and was about three metres ahead. Then, just as we expected her to break the tape a clear winner, she slowed, touched the ground beneath it with one foot and, turning 180 degrees, raced back to the start. The others followed her – just as they'd done at practice sessions in the playground!

What a riot! The bigger kids and spectators cheered and clapped and laughed. Me too. I felt both proud of my little sister and embarrassed for her. But the mini-athletes didn't have a clue they'd done anything wrong, and skipped around excited by the applause. Their teacher eventually got them together and sat them down to watch the bigger kids' race. Then they ran again. Zahra still won by a mile.

Some people from Afghanistan kept telling Mum they weren't sure girls should play sports because the uniforms are so short. Mum wasn't happy that I was doing it – so what's new? – but she let me. Annie told her again, 'Girls can have a go at anything they want to, in Australia.' We want to make good Australians so I say we should do as Aussies do.

Something else that annoyed me and *really* surprised me was that during a phone call to Abdul I told him about being goal-shooter for the school netball team and he sounded as though *he* didn't approve of me playing sports, either. I'd assumed he'd be proud of me like the kids – boys and girls – at school were. I needed to talk to Abdul without others listening to find out what was the matter. I was trying to save up for a tape recorder to send him with a message, but as I had to rely on odd jobs like washing Annie's and Tracy's cars, it was taking forever.

I loved Australian clothes and shoes but I couldn't have many. We'd no money for things like that – 'luxuries', Mum called them when I tried to talk her into some new slides. To help out, Hassan managed to get a job during the Christmas holidays picking strawberries as well as doing some shifts at a fast-food place. He wanted to save up to get his driver's licence and buy a car as soon as he turned seventeen, but employers would only give us menial jobs. I wanted to get a job, too, and had an offer to work in a cafe, with Miranda, but that was another thing Mum wouldn't agree to. 'No. Good Muslim girls don't do that sort of thing. Anyway, it's not halal food.'

'I'm an Australian first and a Muslim second,' I yelled at her, but I couldn't budge her on that one.

Throughout the year while we went to school Mum kept up with her English classes. When we visited Annie's friend Trish, who we hadn't seen for a while, she said, 'Fatimeh, I can't believe how good your English is!' Trish gave Mum a second-hand sewing machine. Threading it was the trickiest part, but she mastered that and quickly got the hang of making us clothes with it, much faster than by hand. In Afghanistan, men used machines to sew with and now some of them came to borrow Mum's which pleased her. So there *was* a hint of Australian attitude. Our Australian friends couldn't believe her beautiful hand stitching and for Christmas she gave them cloths and doilies she'd stitched herself.

I still felt guilty doing things that Abdul couldn't while he was shut away, but I had to or I'd explode. Sometimes when I was down, I had to *make* myself do stuff or I'd have stayed in my room all day. I grew afraid of getting sick with depression, like Mum had. I'd give myself pep talks, like, 'Stop thinking of bad things. You'll be no good to anyone if you get sick. Abdul *will* get his visa and we'll be together again.' We still phoned him every week and I managed occasionally to talk to him when no one else could hear. But it was getting more and more difficult to remember how that rush felt. It was so long since I'd seen him. Over two years.

Sometimes he asked if I'd wait for him – *he* hadn't forgotten I was a woman now. I told him I wore his ring all the time, except when I was swimming. He said he didn't think I should go swimming! I don't remember disagreeing with him about anything before I played sport. He did add that it made him happy to know I was wearing the ring, but I didn't think he sounded like he had on the day we left the Camp.

What's happening to us? I wondered over and over on the long nights when I had trouble sleeping. As soon as we saw each other, would it be the same as it had been, like in the movies? Or was I building a new life without him, and changing? Had Abdul given up hope of ever getting his visa? When I let myself think deeply about how he might be feeling and visualise him in that Camp, it made me vomit – literally. Six months short of four years was such a long time to be locked up, with half of that time by yourself. How did he stand it? I'd be desperate and do anything to get out. He must have felt like that, too.

A few months before after a phone call when I could hear tears in his voice, I'd tried everything to see if I could get someone to answer my questions – about Abdul's future, and ours. I asked Rashid to try to find out, and Zahid, and Annie, and the priest at the two Zs' school. It was a Catholic one and they helped whenever they could. But everyone came up against a big fat nothing. I was so upset I couldn't stop shaking and vomiting so Mum took me to see the doctor. She said I should talk to a counsellor again but I only wanted to see Judy. The doctor phoned Judy while I was still in her surgery and Judy said she'd come to see me.

She visited our house that afternoon when she finished work at our old school. I told her I worried all the time about Abdul. And about what was going to happen. She said she'd visit weekly for a while – but I don't want to go into all that again.

On television we saw news broadcasts about Camps, where there'd been ongoing protests. They showed detainees on hunger strikes, fighting with the guards, and on one occasion where they'd set fire to part of the Camp. Politicians said that Australia didn't want people who did things like that. It was so unfair. There was never anyone to speak for the detainees, to tell people why they did these things. One story was spread around that refugees in a sinking fishing boat threw their kids overboard to save themselves. Government ministers said they didn't want people like that here.

We watched programs about Afghanistan to try to find out what was happening, and others showing what the government and people in Australia thought of refugees. I was excited to see an interview with the kind nurse from the Camp, who helped the Kurdish boys. She talked about what it was really like where she'd worked, where we met her. She explained how hard it is on people who are kept there for a long time and don't know what will happen to them. And she told of how she'd suddenly been asked to leave her job there when officers found out she'd made friends with detainees, and wanted to help them. That had happened to others, too, she said. At last I understood why

Gum Tree left with no goodbyes. I guessed it was the same with Joanne from the first compound.

The nurse said it put people who escaped from horrors through another kind of horror to keep them in Camps here. She explained how everyone she met in the Camp wanted only to start a new life away from danger. And that they all said they'd gladly give to the country that let them live in it by being good workers and good citizens. Now people hear the truth, perhaps they'll do something to help, I thought.

It worried me out of my mind to hear television reports that single men from our country, as well as some others, were finding it harder and harder to get visas because the government said they could be terrorists. I felt sick, panicky. Was *this* the reason that Abdul's visa hadn't come through? How could *anyone* think he was a terrorist? He's so gentle and kind and brave.

Even Annie could get no answers, although she kept trying and so did her MP friend. She did an interview on a radio current affairs program where she said it was ridiculous to think that any terrorist came into this country the way refugees were forced to. Terrorists were backed by organisations that could afford to pay fares and arrange visas. Annie pointed out that not one person of more than eight thousand refugees who had come to Australia over the peast five years for asylum had been found to be a terrorist. That didn't help Abdul, though.

❧ ❧ ❧

Our second year in this house was much the same as the first. We'd made good friends, both with Australians and with other refugees. We'd begun to feel like we belonged, even Mum. Us kids had Oz friends, Oz nicknames, and Oz accents. The house didn't improve, though. We offered to paint it if the landlord bought the paint, but he said no. When the winter rains started again the back part leaked in the toilet and the extra bedroom, but we couldn't get the landlord to fix it. He only cared about getting his rent on time, and we always paid that. Mum started to say that although she liked seeing her friends every day, she was sorry we left the first house because Mr Farinelli had looked after us so well. I wanted to say 'told you so' but didn't want to encourage her to move back. To be truthful, now all my friends were near this house, and I liked my school.

As the year drew to a close, Mum, who still had many ups and downs in her fight against depression – and me – began to get worse. So did Hassan. So did I, worrying about what would happen to us. Mum missed her brothers and sisters and parents a lot, and we missed our grandparents and cousins. But nothing had changed in Afghanistan. Even though the Terror was no longer in power, those who took over still fought and victimised Hazaras. And we were into the third year of our TPVs, which meant they would soon be up for renewal. Not temporary, but permanent visas, we hoped and prayed. I tried not to think about what would happen when they ran out.

BACK TO WHERE I STARTED . . .

Perth: 21st December

I began writing my story six months ago after our visit to the zoo for Zainullah's tenth birthday, on May twenty-eighth, and now it's caught up with real time. I've worked at it in every spare moment since then. I wanted to finish this year before our visas expired. This deadline was important to me because after we have our permanent visas – the new, positive me talking – I'll have Years 11 and 12 to face at school. Then I'll need all the time I can get to study. I have a total of five and a half years to learn what most kids here learn in twelve.

Hassan was seventeen on November thirteenth. He'd got his learner's permit three months before and had had driving lessons. He passed his licence test after one knock back. Yesterday he bought the car he's secretly saved a deposit for all year. A second-hand Commodore. And I have to say his driving's not bad. Last night he took us all over to Annie's place to surprise her. We sure did that because she'd gone to bed early and we woke her up. She admired the car, saying, 'I suppose you're the family chauffeur, now, Hassan?' I think that was her way of saying 'thank goodness you won't need me to drive you any more.' I don't blame her – she's been wonderful to us.

This morning I'm lying in bed wondering: Abdul, what's happening to you? Will I ever see you again? Why don't they let you come here? You'll be so impressed when you see Hassan's car. Abdul, I think of you every day. You've been shut away for so long. I don't know how you stay alive. You are amazing. I feel you so close. Almost next to me. I don't know what's the matter with me today. A giant hand is pummelling my insides. My heart thumps like crazy.

There's the phone. I hear Mum pick it up. I race out. Mum looks at me, closes her eyes, shakes her head. She talks into the mouthpiece. She nods, then shakes her head again. Tears run down her face. But she's smiling? I'm going to burst. There's a knife in my chest. Abdul, is it you? Mum beckons me over, holds out the handset. I take it. Hold it to my ear. I can't breathe . . .

'Is that you, Ness? Please speak to me.'

It *is* him. He sounds like he did the day we left the Camp.

'Are you all right?' I blurt out.

'Better than I've been since you left.' His voice is so full of life.

'Thank goodness. I thought something had happened. Today I feel so close. I worried you were hurt. Or worse . . .'

'Dear one, you felt close because I *will* be close, very soon. My TPV's come through at last! They're putting me on a plane tomorrow. I arrive in Perth at 11.30 a.m. Your mum said Hassan can drive you to the airport to meet me.'

'Oooohhhhh!' Nothing more comes out. I sit down suddenly.

'Nessa-a-a?'

'Abdul. I can't believe it . . .'

'Well, you'd better believe it. Don't be late! I've waited long enough. See you tomorrow, dear Yahk.'

'See you tomorrow.' I let the handset fall as I say the words, not able to believe them.

I see Mum on the other side of the room, smiling and crying at the same time. 'Crazy.' She calls to me. 'We've had two and a half of our three years, Abdul's just starting his. Such a waste! He should've been with us all that time.'

'But, Mum, he'll be here! Tomorrow. Stop being negative.' Today the whole world is positive!

❧ ❧ ❧

Time flies. I'm energy charged. I skip through the chores. It's already school holidays – only four days to Christmas. Everyone helps. We're all happy, all sunny to each other.

'Where's Abdul going to sleep?' I ask, wishing the impossible – that Abdul could share my room. But today I recognise that it's impossible, and that Mum's not to blame.

'Well, Zainullah could share with you, Gulnessa, and Hassan and Abdul could share,' Mum says. 'Or, Abdul could have the back room to himself if he wants to. What do you all think?'

'I think he should be in with me, at least to start with,' Hassan answers. 'He's straight out of Camp, sharing a room with six people. Being by himself might spook him.' I'm impressed he remembers.

'Yes, I think he'd prefer that, too,' I agree. 'And the back room still leaks.' Hassan looks amazed, so does Mum.

I don't want to have my messy little brother sharing my room again, so I suggest, 'What about Zahra sharing with me, and Zainullah with you, Mum? Girls should be together.'

'I don't mind which way we do it.' Mum hasn't knocked me back! 'Let the two Zs decide.'

'I'm with you, Mum, with yo-ou . . .' Zainullah yells, dancing

330

around. I wonder if his high spirits will ever calm down. 'Nessa always picks on me.' He darts behind Mum, peeping back to poke out his tongue at me. I ignore him. Nothing can spoil this day. I've imagined it so often and now it's here I might just fly!

'I'm sleeping with Nessie,' Zahra sings, 'I'm sleeping with Nessie . . .'

'That's settled. Hassan, will you and Gulnessa move the clik-clak from the lounge room to Gulnessa's room. That can be Zahra's bed.' We got the clik-clak from the warehouse when we moved into our first house, and it converts from a chair to a bed.

Sasha arrives as we're sorting out beds and working out what to do about sheets. We only have enough for the beds we use. 'What's going on here?' she demands. 'It's worse than the monkey house in the zoo at feeding time.'

'Come to my room,' I say quickly. The gang knows about Abdul – the *real* story. I've sworn them to secrecy, of course. I had to tell them when they drove me mad, giving me a hard time for not dating boys from school. It was the only way to get them off my back. They understood immediately about true love. Actually it gave me a new status in the group. We discussed endlessly how to keep the fire burning when fate kept two lovers apart. And what it meant when my feelings seemed to wane.

Studying *Romeo and Juliet* in English had become a personal journey. Sasha's and Yanthe's boyfriends changed often, while Miranda said she didn't have time for the 'children' at school. Whenever one of the others had a new boyfriend, I'd spend hours discussing problems, possible problems, and hoped-for futures.

'He's coming tomorrow. Abdul's coming!' I slam my bedroom door. Luckily Zahra's in Mum's room collecting her dolls.

Sasha's eyes and mouth fly open. 'What?' she screeches.

'Shhh!' I hiss. 'Abdul. He's really coming.'

331

'Ohmigod, I can't believe this.' Sasha sinks dramatically on Zahra's bed-to-be. She's our drama and fashion queen. She pulls me down so she can look into my eyes. 'Are you okay, Stevie?' The girls started calling me Stevie when we first met. They couldn't understand me when I told them my name.

'Let's call her something ordinary, something we can all at least say,' the practical one, Yanthe, had suggested, though with a name like hers that was some cheek.

'Stevie,' Miranda, the decision-maker, had said quickly. 'I used to want to be a boy and be called Stevie. If I couldn't be called that, at least you can.' So the name had stuck.

'Sit down and tell me everything,' Sasha orders, and I do, talking non-stop until a loud thumping on the door stops me.

As I open the door I remember . . . 'And, Sash, about borrowing those sheets?' I say loudly, as Mum walks in with Zahra, their arms full of clothes and dolls.

'Mum's got zillions.' Sasha grins at me. 'I'll go straight home and get them.'

That night I can't sleep. Life spins through my brain. I can't stop thinking about Abdul, especially our talks in the Camp, and on the day I left. Over and over. Plans for our future clog my head. Then doubts batter me. What if I see him and nothing's there?

As soon as she left our place Sasha got on the phone to the other girls. Yanthe then rang me with her advice. 'If the spark's gone when you see him, call him "big brother" right from that moment. It's not fair to keep him on a string if you don't return his feelings.'

I laughed and said, 'as if', in my most sarcastic tone. Now in the dark it seems a possibility. But worse, what if the spark's gone for him? How would *I* cope? I didn't want to think about it.

At last the sky begins to lighten and I get up and go out into the backyard to see the sunrise. It's nothing like my golden peach moment, but it *is* magnificent, and it calms me. I go to the bathroom, run myself a bath, adding lots of rose geranium oil, and soak leisurely in the steaming water. Yanthe gave me this oil last birthday with the whispered message that I must keep it for this very day. And I had. I choose my favourite jeans to wear with a pink top that has a deeper pink transparent overlay. And I put on the slides I'd wanted so much, which Annie gave me last birthday.

We set off in Hassan's car, early, which in itself is something special. The airport isn't busy, as only a small intrastate plane is arriving. Small it may be but to me it's the most important plane ever. We seem to wait for hours.

'I wonder if Abdul has changed much,' Mum says.

'Not as much as we have,' Hassan says. 'He'll be nineteen now.'

'I guess Zahra will have changed most,' Mum goes on. 'She was still a baby when we left and now she's an eight-year-old schoolgirl. And, of course, Gulnessa.' She turns to me. 'You're a young woman now.' She has noticed! I'm amazed. But I say nothing. Instead, moving away, I try to see which runway the plane might land on.

Suddenly we're caught by surprise. Door Two opens. A group of four dark-haired, dark-complexioned young men walk through it, followed by more people. One young man continues walking towards us. He's a bit taller than when we left, and very thin, but it's unmistakably Abdul.

My heart hammers. The rush nearly knocks me out. I stare like those Maori statues with huge eyes. I can't move. And I can hear nothing over the thrumming in my head. Mum walks towards him, holding out her arms. Hassan moves with her.

Hypnotised, I watch the pantomime unfold. Arms stretch around bodies, faces touch, tears fall. *He* steps back, picks up Zahra, hugs her to his chest. She looks shy, but delighted with this man, both familiar and strange. Zainullah dances around them all and as *he* places Zahra back on the ground *he* whirls to shape up to Zainullah, and they shadow-box closer and closer to where I'm frozen. Then they embrace.

It's my turn. Almost in slow motion Abdul takes one more step. He's facing me. A heartbeat away. I feel his breath. Arms stretch out – my arms, and his. We hold each other close. I feel his warmth, his ribs. He's so thin! I'd forgotten the Camp does that to you. Now we have so much food. I cannot see his face and mine's buried in his chest. I feel his T-shirt is wet, getting wetter. Tears are pouring from my eyes. I'm not crying, I think irrationally. They're happy tears.

'Ness,' he murmurs, 'my beautiful Nessa.' I feel him take my forearms in his hands and move back a step. 'I want to see you,' he says. 'You are a beautiful woman, Nessa.' And I see his face is wet, too. The wet patch on his chest makes me laugh, and everyone laughs, too.

When we get to the car everyone wants to sit next to Abdul. 'You should sit in the front. You can see everything better.' Hassan tells him.

'You're all I want to see just now,' Abdul replies, gesturing to include everyone, but looking at me.

'Yes,' says Mum, and I see she's seen Abdul's look. 'You sit in the front with Hassan and you too, Zainullah. The women will sit in the back.' How Afghan, I think. It's the most sensible solution but I don't want *sense*. I want Abdul.

Hassan drives us through the city centre and around the Swan River foreshore, which made such an impression on me when we first arrived. Everyone talks over each other. Everyone points out things. Abdul laughs a lot, his head swivelling to take in as much as possible.

'This is so amazing!' Abdul exclaims over and over. 'I thought I'd seen it all on TV, but the real thing is *so* much better.'

We head for home. It's almost midday when we arrive, and Zainullah drags Abdul inside to show him where he'll sleep. 'And it was my bed, but you can have it,' he says importantly. Abdul puts down his pathetically small bag of belongings.

'Thank you, Zainullah. I appreciate that.'

When we're eating the welcome meal Mum and I prepared last night, Hassan asks, 'What would you like to do today? Go out in the car and look around? Our friends we told you about, Annie and Rashid, Zahid, too, are coming for dinner. To meet you and talk about official things you need to do. They'll help with that.'

'Today I just want to be here. Tomorrow we can look around. I've already seen what RSW19 – sorry, no more numbers *ever* – what Zahid meant when he said "it's like paradise". But now, I want to see and talk to you.'

The rest of the day is amazing and frustrating. Most of the time we all sit on the lounge floor, talking. Really, *we* talk to Abdul.

'It's my turn to sit next to Abdul, now.' Zainullah edges out Zahra. This game of musical chairs continues all day. Abdul just smiles and goes along with everyone. He wants to know everything about our life here. About what we do each day. About our school. About where we shop. Who we know. Our friends. Everything. But he doesn't want to talk about the Camp. I understand that.

'I'll be in Year 3 after Christmas,' Zahra informs Abdul when Hassan pauses in his description of his licence test.

'Christmas?' Abdul asks, raising his eyebrows.

'Yes, our Australian friends don't have Ramadan, or Eid, but they celebrate Christmas. We join with them at Christmas, and they join us for Eid,' I explain.

'I see.' Abdul frowns slightly.

'It's only four days to Christmas.' Zahra can't contain her joy. She jumps around the living room, singing, 'Six white boomers, snow white boomers, on their Australian run . . .' at the top of her voice. Her class performed that song for the end of year concert. Abdul's frown vanishes and he laughs out loud. Phew, for a moment I thought he mightn't understand about joining a Christian celebration. But that can wait.

I love being in the same room with Abdul, watching him, listening to his voice, locking eyes sometimes, sending wordless messages. Every time he doesn't understand something, he looks at me. I want to be alone with him. I know that's impossible. But it doesn't stop me wanting it.

During the afternoon the girls just 'happen' to walk past our house. They pop in and I introduce them.

'Hi, Abdul. We've heard *all* about *you*,' Miranda says, giving him the eye. I see she fancies him.

'Welcome to Perth,' greets Yanthe, examining him minutely.

'It's sooo good to meet you at last,' gushes Sasha coyly.

Abdul is the perfect gentleman, placing his hand on his heart at each introduction, nodding as he says, 'Great to meet you.'

I usher them out the front door as soon as I can. 'You guys are so not patient,' I say, grinning.

'He's such a spunk,' raves Miranda.

'A bit skinny for my taste, but he'll do for you, Stevie. I approve,' says Yanthe.

'Go-o-orgeous.' Sasha is at her dramatic best. 'Did you see those eyes and lashes? I'd kill for them. You're so lucky, Stevie.'

'Well, right now I'd kill to have him to myself for ten minutes,' I say pointedly. The girls nod.

'All lovers say there's never enough time alone,' the drama queen pronounces, shooting me a knowing look.

'We'd better get moving.' Miranda, at least, understands.

'Remember, we share *everything*,' Yanthe reminds me, backing down the path.

❧ ❧ ❧

I spend the next week in a dream. Abdul and I are never alone but after the long wait it's enough to be near him. We touch fingers when I offer him bread. The electricity that runs through me almost makes me drop it. We try to sit or stand next to each other whenever possible, and touch each other.

We make Abdul's first Christmas as memorable as ours was, but at our house this time, with our friends joining us for an evening party. Everything and everyone in the world is beautiful. Mum and I even fight less.

Then reality bites.

Abdul's been here for a month now and it's even more than I dared hope for. He moved to share Zahid's house at the end of the first week. Mum says 'it's not proper for me to share a house with the man I want to marry'. Yes! She challenged me the day after Abdul arrived when he went out with Rashid to register for Centrelink Special Benefit. She was okay about it. I was blown away. She said that in Afghanistan I was the right age to marry – she married Dad when she was sixteen and he was nineteen. How's that for serendipity? She said if I wanted to be Australian I should wait and finish my education first. You know what? I agree. We try not to think about how near our visas are to their use-by date.

✤ ✤ ✤

Panic in our house today. Phone rings non-stop. People come and go constantly. Annie's here, comforting Mum. A letter from the Immigration people arrived this morning. I know what it says. I read it to Mum. When I say I know what it says, I mean some of it. The way it's written doesn't make sense. It sounds so cold. Annie calls it 'official mumbo-jumbo'. But we get its message. The government is offering us money and plane tickets if we go back to Afghanistan within six months. If we don't go, we get nothing.

If we stay and apply for permanent visas and the government refuses them – which we won't know until after the six months are up – they'll send us back, making us pay for ourselves, even though we don't want to go and we have no money. We're scared to return. We *really* want to stay in Australia. Good things happen here. There's a rumour that if the government won't give us visas, they'll send us back to the Camp if we can't pay.

Rashid's come over, too. He tells us news of a family who took the government money and returned to Afghanistan last month. They only just left the airport when gunmen held them up and robbed them. The gunmen took all the money the Australian government gave the family. Now they've no money even for food, and no home and no jobs. There are no jobs. No way to earn money, nowhere to live. No houses. So much has been destroyed. These people are Hazaras like us, so they're being persecuted. That family could be us. Apparently bandits lie in wait for people who've been paid to return and steal everything they've got.

Mum's hysterical. 'What will happen to us? We *can't* go back. They'll find and kill us. What *can* we do?'

Annie says, 'Do nothing now. I'll take you to a lawyer so you can apply to Immigration for permanent visas.'

Another man says, 'But it's only luck whether or not they believe you. There are no guidelines. If they say they don't believe us, how can we prove what we say's true?'

If they could see my nightmares, they'd know. Surely they don't believe we'd have left our grandparents and families, and our homes, unless we were scared for our lives? The trip here was hardly a luxury holiday to a chosen destination. Why are they doing this to us? Haven't we been good Australians? We don't want to leave our new country. Before we came we couldn't imagine a life like Australians live. Now we're Australians, how can we go back? And how could I say goodbye to Abdul again?

❧ ❧ ❧

I've cried and cried. And thought and thought. I've talked and talked. To Abdul. To Mum. To my friends. And I've made a decision. My friends all support me – us. They've sworn to help.

One important, life-changing lesson I've learned from living in Australia is that life keeps throwing things at you. Some good, some bad. To survive, you've got to learn to catch the good opportunities and dodge the bad ones – or throw them back.

And another thing I now know is that you always have choices. In everything. It's just a matter of finding one that allows you to get where you want to go. And to go for it.

I think the money we are offered to return to Afghanistan is a bribe. It can't buy us a home or job when there are none to buy, and it certainly won't provide safety. The only thing it can do is take us away from the place we want to be. That's not an option as far as I'm concerned.

I choose to fight for our rights as human beings to live in a safe place. To fight to become a permanent Australian. For us all. To fight for the right to an education that allows me to help others have their rights, too. To fight for a life. A positive life.

STRIDING ONWARDS...

Five Years Later

I've just re-read my life story – up to that awful day. I felt so confused then. I was on such a high after Abdul's arrival but I crashed after that letter arrived. Big time. Even though I'd decided to fight. I couldn't do anything. Couldn't even write – though hindsight shows me that was the right place to stop that part of my story. The following years are really the beginning of my Australian story – and I will write that, but not for a while. I'm keeping a diary again, but I'm going to add a few things here.

The most important event for us all was when, after a fight to stay here that lasted three years and nine months, we got our permanent visas! That was a year ago. Abdul got his last month. What a relief! The end of an eight-and-a-bit-year struggle for a new life in safety. We know we're among the lucky few. And we'll never forget the help and support our Australian friends gave us, particularly Annie.

Zahid chose to take the government's offer and go back to help rebuild his country, Iraq. Some of our friends from Iraq and Afghanistan have had to return to their countries. They lost their fights and we constantly worry about their safety, while being enormously relieved we have ours. Afghanistan is still the same – wracked with violence. We received some family news last year via a man who was sent back. He made enquiries for us. Our remaining three grandparents burned to death when the Terror raided our village and set fire to the houses. Once we'd recovered enough from our mourning period, we each resolved to dedicate our life's work to them. Without their sacrifice, we knew our lives would have also finished.

Our initial application for permanent visas was knocked back by Immigration, and that nearly killed Mum. Then a wonderful human rights lawyer, Malcolm, who has since become a friend, helped us to take our claim to the Refugee Review Tribunal. It resulted in our permanent status. At last we had a safe home!

But before that, after the letter arrived, I hid. From everything and everyone. The gang. Abdul. I was pathetic. I even doubted me and Abdul. I thought that now that he was out of the Camp he wouldn't want me. Thought that if I loved and trusted him, he'd disappear. Like Dad had. Like everything did.

Judy was fantastic. She helped so much during those school holidays and long after. She helped me see that my crash was the way my body handled the emotional rollercoaster I was riding. And the trauma of another disaster, as it seemed to me then. She helped me face Dad's death. I can accept now that the Terror must have killed him and he was more than likely buried in one of the mass graves that have since been discovered. His disappearance had nothing to do with his love for us. Or my love for him. And I accepted it *wouldn't* happen again if I trusted and loved someone. Without Judy I'd have wrecked Abdul and me. And I'd never have gone back to school.

The gang was great, too. We're still good friends, though

we've scattered in different directions. When we left high school we all did part-time waitressing jobs to help fund our studies. All except Yanthe, who worked in a posh pub.

Sasha's finished a Theatre Arts course and has just been accepted into NIDA in Sydney. She leaves in about a month. I tell her she's Australia's next Nicole Kidman. She's going to flat with Miranda, who's living in Sydney already. Miranda started an Arts degree here but after first year dropped out. She waitressed fulltime for a while and then took off for Sydney saying she wanted to work in the film industry. She worked her butt off in editing and administration and now she works for a big-time movie director.

Writing is my goal. Great writing. We studied *Cloudstreet* in Year 12 and I was hooked. When I read *Dirt Music* I cried – a lot. For different reasons. One was the landscape Tim Winton evoked. It was so vivid. It brought back how I'd felt when I first arrived and saw the red dirt and blue sky.

Annie's friend Trish – they're both still our friends and supporters – helped me so much. She was a teacher, then an editor and now she's a writer. She gave me confidence to do a Bachelor of Arts in Creative Writing and I finished last year. Now I'm enrolled in a course which will make me a Bachelor of Education as well. I know it'll be a while before I can make a living from writing but I will do it, with Trish as my mentor. Books have given me so much. I want above all to tell stories that may otherwise never be told. I love kids, too, so I'm starting out by teaching, and I hope to teach kids who've come from non-English-speaking countries.

Yanthe's going to be another Judy, I think. She's finished her psychology degree and is enrolled for honours this year. She wants to work as a school psych, too. The help Judy gave me made a huge mark on Yanthe. She admitted to me once I was well on the way to recovery, that when I was at my worst she couldn't believe I'd ever get my shit together again.

As a matter of fact I'm off to meet the girls tonight for a dinner to celebrate as this is the year we turn 21 and it's a 'good luck' dinner for Sasha before she takes off! Miranda's over for a holiday.

My birthday's in two weeks' time – and we're having a huge party at our house. The family's become real party animals. We celebrate everything we can – every day's a bonus. I'm a Muslim and I believe totally that God means us to celebrate life. And there's another celebration I'm hoping to have with my twenty-first – Abdul's and my engagement.

He was being pretty impatient and wanted to get engaged at New Year, a year ago, but I told him that while I *did* want to marry him, there were other things I wanted to do first. Like finish my degree. And travel. And that he wasn't to ask me again until he could see it was the right time. Now *I* feel it's the right time and I hope he can read my signals. I've been really subtle telling him that I want to travel together after we're married and qualified. He's 'waiting' (as opposed to waitressing) and putting himself through an environmental science course. He caught that bug from Zahid and a friend he made called Howie, an environmental scientist who's his best Australian mate. When Abdul and I are out together, I loiter at jewellers' shop-windows, pointing out engagement rings. But Abdul's not reacting, just smiling. I've a sneaky feeling he's paying me back.

Mum's loosened up a lot and we're good mates now. Amongst other things, Judy told her the way to 'keep' your kids was to let them go rather than tighten the reins. Of course there are still strict boundaries, like I'm not allowed to stay over at Abdul's, but most of them are reasonable. Mum kept on with her English and learning to read and write, and she's done really well. She goes to Judy's school, where we first started, and works as a teacher's aide with migrant children from ESL backgrounds.

You wouldn't believe it but we're back living in Mr Farinelli's house. We moved there the year Zainullah started high school. He's just finished Year 10. He's a great kid, full of energy and the life of any party, but Mum worries that he's not settling down or thinking of his future yet. I say to her, let him be a kid first. Hassan and I never had the chance. That stops her in her tracks. Hassan's studying to be a human rights lawyer like Malcolm, and he's Malcolm's protégé. He works for him like an apprentice. Unlike his studious brother, Zainullah, with his long-time mate Zac, heads for the beach at every opportunity. All they want to do is to be beach bums, and follow the surf.

Mum contacted Mr Farinelli about the house after we put in our permanent visa application. She was at her pessimistic worst then, saying we might as well spend our last months in Australia where we'd been so happy when we first arrived. Mr Farinelli was delighted to hear. He said he'd let us know when the current tenants moved out and said he'd paint the house for us again before we moved in. We could choose the colours. Guess what they were? Sunset colours, of course. And we're still there. We've more room now, as Hassan moved out to live with Abdul, and Mr F enclosed the back verandah for us to use as a study.

Zahra is still a delight and starts high school next year. Everyone loves our Zahra. It was serendipitous that her bosom buddy Suki and her family moved to live near us at Mr F's, when her dad changed jobs only a few months after we moved. Zahra is still maternal and says she wants nothing more than to have a family – and possibly be a nurse, mothercraft of course.

And a thought to tuck in your memory banks as a special treasure: KARMA. In the weekend papers a headline caught my eye: *Jailer becomes jail-bird.* Guess who? The guard we used to call Dung-face has been jailed for inflicting grievous bodily harm on some poor unfortunate detainee. Couldn't happen to a more deserving bloke.

PS Just for the record, I took my story to show Trish and she's encouraging me to submit it to a publisher. She says I've got a real talent. And like my English teacher when I was sweet sixteen, she says reading my story made her feel she was not just with me, but walking in my shoes.

So here goes.

Fingers crossed.

AUTHOR'S NOTE

In early 2001 I met my friend Dr Judyth Watson, a retired West Australian politician, who now spends most of her time as an advocate for asylum seekers and assisting refugees who hold temporary protection visas. She is co-founder of CARAD (Coalition for Asylum-seekers, Refugees and Detainees) in WA, and a Board member of A Just Australia. Since January 2000 CARAD has welcomed 2500 individuals from detention. It sets up households and provides ongoing support.

Judyth had drafted a picture book manuscript about her work with refugees, describing an incident with children who'd just arrived here, and how she'd been moved by it. The children had been clothed from a CARAD warehouse filled with donated items, yet when they met others who arrived after them, they insisted on sharing the T-shirts they'd so recently received. I, too, was overwhelmed at the generosity of those who have so little, and squirmed to think that most Australians have so much by comparison, but many are unwilling to share it with fellow human beings who've had to flee from all they'd known and loved.

It struck me that the public had never seen the human face of these refugees, and reports in the media were never from the point of view of those who sought asylum. I put a proposition to Judyth: if she'd help me by providing information, and introductions to some of the people she'd talked about, I'd undertake further research and write a novel from this hidden point of view. It would be a story derived from composite true experiences and told by a fictitious sixteen-year-old girl.

Throughout the long and difficult two years of researching and writing this book, Judyth gave me generous support and introductions to people who, after arriving in this country seeking refuge, were held in detention for months or years. She also helped by reading the manuscript and giving valuable advice.

In appreciation of her work, and my esteem for the refugees I've met who are now my friends, half of the royalties from the book will go to CARAD to assist their continuing work.

If anyone reading this book would like to offer donations, the contact address is:

Coalition for Asylum-seekers, Refugees and Detainees
PO Box Z5420
St Georges Terrace
Perth 6831
08 9321 2900
www.carad-wa.org

A special mention should be made of schools and teachers throughout Australia who welcomed children in the early days when asylum-seekers were not given right of access to schools. They put professional (and personal) values first, acknowledging the right of every child to an education.

Other people also offered unstinting support, information and assistance during the writing of this book. Some, particularly the patient, generous refugees I've come to know and love, must remain anonymous so their position regarding visas and status in the community will not be jeopardised. They know who they are. This book is a tribute to them and to all asylum-seekers. I thank them and express my admiration for their resourcefulness, courage, tolerance and commitment to the country in which they have arrived – in spite of inhuman treatment they have suffered.

Others I can acknowledge publicly, and thank whole-heartedly, include:

The Peter Cowan Writers' Centre, on the Edith Cowan University Campus at Joondalup, WA, who gave me much needed, uninterrupted writing time when they appointed me Writer-In-Residence for two weeks, late in 2002.

Glenda Koutroulis, who worked as a nurse at the Woomera Detention Centre, spent hours answering my questions and describing her experiences.

Dear friends, teacher/writer Anne Davis and artist/writer Denise McAllister, read versions of the manuscript and provided me with constructive criticism and generous support.

Good friend and Senior Counsel, Greg McIntyre, who checked the manuscript for legal implications.

Julie Watts, Penguin's Executive Publisher par excellence, for her perceptive advice – even though it meant another rewrite! Suzanne Wilson and Ali Watts, the wonderful editors I've been lucky enough to work with who gave me such positive feedback as well as their constructive criticism.

And my family, friends and the love of my life, my muse, Bela, a brilliant artist with an unbridled imagination, who encouraged me, talked me through many dilemmas I confronted, and understood me when the depression I battle constantly descended as I became Gulnessa and suffered with her as I wrote.

Also from Penguin

Mao's Last Dancer

LI CUNXIN

**From bitter poverty to the stardom of the West –
this is the extraordinary true story of one boy's great
courage and determination.**

'An honest and refreshing account.'

Adeline Yen Mah, author of *Falling Leaves*

'This moving and extraordinary tale combines tender-
ness with strength, just as Li Cunxin's dancing still lives
in the mind's eye, unique in its blend of softness and
moral power.'

Australian Book Review

Also from Penguin
for Young Adults

Boys of Blood and Bone

DAVID METZENTHEN

Two parallel stories about two young men, separated by nearly nine decades, in two very different eras. As Andy and his mates head inexorably towards the bloody, torturous Great War, Henry faces challenges, dangerous situations and tragedies of his own.

Winner, 2003 Qld Premier's Literary Award (Young Adults); Winner, 2004 NSW State Literary Award (Young Adults); Winner, 2004 NSW Premier's Literary Award (Ethel Turner Prize).

Also from Penguin
for Younger Readers

Little Brother

ALLAN BAILLIE

Set in war-torn Kampuchea, this is the powerful story of Vithy's search for his brother, lost in their flight from the Khmer Rouge.

Honour Book, 1986 Children's Book Council of Australia Book of the Year Award;

Notable Book, 1992 US Children's Book Council; Shortlisted, 1986 Guardian Children's Fiction Award.